SHERLOCK HOLMES

FROM A TO Z

C.V.SHEA III

<u>DEDICATION</u>

This book is dedicated to Leann, Chester,
and Jennifer Lee,
without whose support it would never have materialized.

Thankyou.

INTRODUCTION

Dr. John Watson introduced the world to the amazing abilities of his friend and colleague, Sherlock Holmes. Throughout his recording of their adventures, many individuals, good, bad, and otherwise entered their domain. Places, jewels, weapons, and other strange objects, of curiosity and in many cases of extreme importance, crossed their paths. This book is a compilation of all those people, places and things. Each individual person, item, curiosity, and place is listed, providing information obtained from the writings of Dr. Watson, Sherlock Holmes, and from an anonymous individual.

This work consists of two parts: Book One is an alphabetic compilation of all the people, places, and other things that made up the world of Sherlock Holmes. Each listing contains information consisting of: the adventure or adventures in which it appeared, a description, and, in some cases, a summary of the part it played in the adventure. Much of the information provided is from Dr. Watson himself, and in some cases the actual words of Dr. Watson appear, in other cases the material is derived from interpretation of the entire adventure. Quotes appear often, but are not meant to connote an actual quote from any individual, rather they are used to emphasize the material. In some cases they are exact quotes but not always.

Book Two is the Chronological listing of the events in the life of Sherlock Holmes and Dr. Watson. Some dates are not exact since Watson at times concealed the actual dates from the reader, but an attempt has been made to date each and every adventure and important occurrence as accurately as possible.

As a reader who has spent many enjoyable hours with the words of Dr. Watson et al, this work is especially dedicated to him. It was a true joy putting it together and I sincerely hope it can be enjoyed not only as a supplement to his works but by itself.

CV Shea III

CHAPTER A

A CASE OF IDENTITY:
Published in "The Strand": September 1891
Published as part of: "The Adventures of Sherlock Holmes"
>Involves the disappearance of Miss Mary Sutherland's fiancée, Hosmer Angel, a matter that Holmes is able to accomplish without much difficulty. Mr. Angel is actually Miss Sutherland's stepfather in disguise who whites to keep his stepdaughter unmarried, he being dependent upon her inherited wealth. Holmes tells the villain that 'no man deserves punishment more than he.'

A GRUESOME PACKET:
"The Adventure of the Cardboard Box"
>Title of article appearing in the "Daily Chronicle" detailing the receipt by Miss Susan Cushing of a package containing two freshly severed human ears.

A SCANDAL IN BOHEMIA:
Published in the 'Strand' July 1891.
Published as part of: "The Adventures of Sherlock Holmes"
>Holmes attempts to recover a photograph for the King of Bohemia from "the woman", Irene Adler. The King is planning to marry and believes the photograph in the possession of Miss Adler would interfere with his plans for marriage. Holmes prepares an elaborate scheme to force Miss Adler into unknowingly revealing the hiding place of the photograph to him. She immediately realizes her blunder and sets out, in disguise, to see Holmes. As Holmes and Watson approach 221B Baker Street, Miss Adler, in disguise, passes by them and says:

"Good-night Mr. Holmes." She leaves a note for
Holmes, when he returns the next day to her lodgings
with the King of Bohemia to retrieve the photograph,
revealing her knowledge of his quest. Holmes is so
taken with Miss Adler that he takes her photograph
as his "fee" from the King of Bohemia.

"A Case of Identity"
Holmes mentions the King of Bohemia and Irene Adler
in conversation with Watson.

A STUDY IN SCARLET:
Published November 1887, 'Beeton's Christmas Annual'
The First of the four novels.
The first of Watson's stories.
Part 1 - "Being a Reprint from the Reminiscences of John H.
Watson, M.D., Late of the Army Medical Department."

Part 2 - "The Country of the Saints."
It is in "A Study in Scarlet" that Watson tells
Holmes: "Your merits should be publicly recognized.
You should publish an account of the case. If you
won't, I will for you." This case concerns itself with
the tangled web of the Mormons and revenge.
Murders in London are the revenge for the killings
of a father and stepdaughter trying to escape the
Mormons of Salt Lake City, Utah, U.S.A.

Part 1 involves the London murders and subsequent
investigation by Holmes.

Part 2 concerns itself with the story of John and Lucy
Ferrier and their Mormon connection.

"The Sign of Four"
Watson mentions this case as a "small brochure, with

the somewhat fantastic title of "A Study in Scarlet."

"A Case of Identity"
>   Mentioned in conversation.

"The Boscombe Valley Mystery"
>   Reference regarding Lestrade.

"The Resident Patient"
>   Mentioned in passing.

"The Final Problem"
>   When Watson points out that he began his writings of
>   Holmes with "A Study in Scarlet" and he intended to
>   end with "The Naval Treaty" but he is forced to write
>   "The Final Problem."

"The Adventure of the Cardboard Box"
>   Holmes compares "A Study in Scarlet" and "The
>   Sign of Four" to the present case in that each case
>   must be reasoned backward from effects to causes.

ABBAS PARVA:
"The Adventure of the Retired Colourman"
>   A small village in Berkshire, the show caravan of
>   Ronder had camped there for the night when a lion
>   escaped and killed Ronder and maimed his wife.

ABBAS PARVA TRAGEDY:
"The Adventure of the Retired Colourman"
>   Name given to tragedy, which occurred at Abbas
>   Parva, which resulted in the death of Ronder, the
>   showman, and the maiming of his wife, by a very
>   fine lion named Sahara King. The tragedy occurred
>   in late 1889.

ABBEY GRANGE:

"The Adventure of the Abbey Grange"
Located in Marsham, Kent. A low, widespread house, pillared in front after the fashion of Palladio.

ABBEY SCHOOL:

"The Adventure of the Blanched Soldier"
An unrecorded case.
Holmes was clearing this case up when James Dodd requested he look into the strange disappearance of Godfrey Emsworth. Holmes notes that Watson wrote of this case in which the Duke of Greyminster was so deeply involved.

ABERDEEN:

"The Valley of Fear" Part 1: "The Tragedy of Birlstone"
Area in northern Great Britain, Scotland.

ABERDEEN SHIPPING COMPANY:

"The Man With The Twisted Lip"
Offices located on Fresno Street which branches out of Upper Swandam Lane. Mrs. St. Clair travels to this company to pick up a small, valuable package, which she has been expecting. It is after retrieving her package and while looking for a cab that she believes she has seen her husband calling to her from the room above the Bar of Gold opium den. It is from this encounter that she consults with Holmes.

ABERGAVENNY MURDER:

"The Adventure of the Priory School"
An unrecorded case.
Holmes sends Watson to investigate "The Adventure of the Priory School" since he must remain in London due to the upcoming Abergavenny murder case.

ABRAHAMS:
> "The Disappearance of Lady Frances Carfax"
>> He fears for his life and since Holmes is working on his case at this time, it is one of the reasons Holmes cannot go to Luasanne himself, and instead sends Watson to investigate the disappearance of Lady Carfax.

ACTON, OLD:
> "The Reigate Puzzle"
>> One of the county magnates of Surrey, had his house broken into prior to Holmes arriving in Reigate. Involved in a lawsuit against Mr. Cunningham.

ADAIR, HILDA:
> "The Adventure of the Empty House"
>> Daughter of the Earl of Maynooth and sister to 'The Honourable Ronald Adair'

ADAIR, THE HONOURABLE RONALD:
> "The Adventure of the Empty House"
>> Second son of the Earl of Maynooth, he resided with his mother and sister at 427 Park Lane. He moved in the best of circles, having been engaged to Miss Edith Woodley, of Carstairs, the engagement having been broken off by mutual consent some months ago. He was fond of cards, being a member of the Baldwin, the Cavendish, and the Bagatelle card clubs. His usual partner was one Colonel Moran. He was killed on the night of March 30, 1894 between ten and eleven-thirty by an expanding revolver bullet.

ADAMS:
> "The Greek Interpreter"
>> The guilty party in the Manor House case. Holmes

and Watson visit with Holmes' brother Mycroft at the Diogenes Club, where Mycroft states that he expected Sherlock to consult him over the Manor House case, believing Sherlock to be "a little out of your depth." Holmes responds that he has solved the case whereupon Mycroft says "It was Adams, of course," and Sherlock, "Yes, it was Adams."

ADDLETON TRAGEDY:
"The Adventure of the Golden Pince-Nez"
An unrecorded case.

ADELAIDE:
"The Disappearance of Lady Frances Carfax"
Town in Australia where Holy Peters received a severe bite on his ear during a saloon fight.

ADELAIDE-SOUTHAMPTON LINE:
"The Adventure of the Abbey Grange"
Shipping line with offices at the end of Pall Mall. Runs steamers between England and South Australia. One of its largest and best ships was the 'Rock of Gibraltar', which had reached port during June of 1895. Another of its ships was the 'Bass Rock.'

ADLER, IRENE:
"A Scandal in Bohemia"
Adversary in "A Scandal in Bohemia"
"The woman": to Sherlock Holmes she will always be "the woman"; "the best plans of Mr. Sherlock Holmes were beaten by a woman's wit"; "well known adventuress" Born in New Jersey in the year 1858. Retired from operatic stage, having been associated with Contralto, La Scala, and Prima donna Imperial Opera of Warsaw.

Was involved with Wilhelm Gottsreich Sigsmond
Von Ormstein, who wrote her some compromising
letters and with whom she was photographed. The
retrieval of that photograph is the basis for the
adventure "A Scandal in Bohemia."

Lived at Briony Lodge, Serpentine Avenue, St.
John's Wood. Married Mr. Godfrey Norton, a lawyer,
Holmes served as a witness to their marriage while in
disguise. Ceremony took place at the Church of St.
Monica in the Edgeware Road. Holmes kept her
photograph as his fee for the case and always refers
to her as "the woman."

"A Case of Identity"
Mentioned in passing.

"The Adventure of The Blue Carbuncle"
Mentioned in passing.

"His Last Bow" "An Epilogue of Sherlock Holmes"
Holmes informs the German spy, Von Bork, that his
capture is not Holmes's first involvement with Von
Bork's family. It was Holmes who handled the matter
with Miss Adler and the King of Bohemia while Von

Bork's cousin Heinrich was Imperial Envoy.

THE ADVENTURE OF THE ABBEY GRANGE:
Published in "The Strand": September 1904
Published as part of: "The Return of Sherlock Holmes"
Takes place at the end of the winter of 1897 when
Holmes awakens Watson with: "Come, Watson,
come! The game is afoot."

The matter involves the violent death of Sir Eustace

Brackenstall and the apparent burglary of the Abbey Grange. Holmes is able to discover that the burglary was a ruse, that Sir Eustace was an evil man and in the end, Holmes takes the law into his own hands, he being the judge and Watson the jury, as Holmes allows the 'criminal' to escape.

THE ADVENTURE OF THE BERYL CORONET:
Published in the 'Strand' May 1892
Published as part of "The Adventures of Sherlock Holmes"
Holmes is called upon to recover jewels used as collateral for a bank loan. The banker catches his son, who is in debt, in possession of part of the Coronet and accuses him of the theft. Holmes's study of the evidence and facts reveals the son to be protecting his father's niece who in concert with the actual thief, Sir George Burnwell, was planning to steal the coronet, and the son, having become aware of the plan and knowing of his father's deep love for his niece wished to protect her. Holmes deals with criminals in order to retrieve the valuable jewels but informs Mr. Holder that his niece has run away with the thief, Sir George Burnwell.

THE ADVENTURE OF BLACK PETER:
Published in "Collier's": February 27, 1904
Published in "The Strand": March 1904
Published as part of: "The Return of Sherlock Holmes"
Here Holmes looks into the murder of a retired whaler, Black Peter. It begins during the first week of July 1895. And concludes when he is able to lure the murderer to 221B Baker Street where he clamps the handcuffs on him.

The case involves Black Peter's coming into possession of money and securities, which were taken from a brokerage firm, which went under due

to the scandal. One of the principals in the brokerage
house, Neligan by name, was found at sea by Captain
Peter Carey. Captain Carey later killed him for the
securities Neligan possessed. Black Peter Carey is
killed in turn for refusing to share his ill-gotten booty
with Patrick Cairns. Holmes's client is John Hopley
Neligan, son of Neligan of Cornwall & Neligan, the West
Country bankers.

Watson tells us at the beginning of the story that
Holmes has never been in better form, both physically
and mentally as he was in 1895.

THE ADVENTURE OF THE BLANCHED SOLDIER:
Published in "Liberty": October 16, 1926
Published in "The Strand": November 1926
Published as part of: "The Case Book of Sherlock Holmes"
Holmes writes this adventure himself noting that
Watson has continually prodded him to do so since
Holmes feels Watson's work to be superficial and
pandering to popular taste instead of confining
himself to the facts.

Holmes takes a moment to acknowledge that his
companion, Watson, "has some remarkable
characteristics of his own which in his modesty he has
given small attention amid his exaggerated estimates of
my own performances." Holmes also notes that "it is
among the strangest happenings in my collection."

This story involves the inquiries being made by one
James Dodd into the strange disappearance of his
friend Godfrey Emsworth. Holmes is willing to look
into the matter and in the end not only locates the

missing Godfrey, who is in voluntary hiding, but is

able to help him as well. Holmes deduces the
problem affecting Godfrey and is able to overcome

Godfrey's father's objections by writing a word on a
slip of paper. It begins in January 1903.

THE ADVENTURE OF THE BLUE CARBUNCLE:
Published in the 'Strand' January 1892
Published as part of: "The Adventures of Sherlock Holmes"
The missing "Blue Carbuncle" is discovered inside a
Christmas goose. The gem has been stolen from a
hotel and an innocent man is jailed as the culprit.
Holmes becomes involved when a policeman
presents him with a Christmas goose, which was dropped
by a man being attacked in an alley. Holmes's search of
the origins of the bird reveals the true criminal.

"The Adventure of the Copper Beeches"
Mentioned in passing.

THE ADVENTURE OF THE BRUCE-PARTINGTON PLANS:
Published in "The Strand": December 1908
Published as part of: "His Last Bow"
The adventure begins during the third week of
November 1895. Holmes, at the request of his brother,
Mycroft, recovers some submarine plans, which have
been stolen from a government office. Holmes himself
becomes a burglar in order to eventually retrieve the
missing plans. The investigation centers on a young man
planning to be married, the discovery of his death and
possession of some of the submarine plans. Holmes is
later rewarded by Queen Victoria for his success in
recovering the missing documents.

THE ADVENTURE OF THE CARDBOARD BOX:
Published in "The Strand": January 1893
Published as part of: "His Last Bow"

Takes place in August when everyone was out of town and Watson wished to be likewise, either at New Forest or Southsea. Holmes is called upon to investigate the sending of a gruesome package to one Susan Cushing containing the two severed human ears. The case concerns itself with a husband's revenge against a sister- in-law for her interference in his marriage to her sister.

THE ADVENTURE OF CHARLES AUGUSTUS MILVERTON:
Published in "Collier's": March 26, 1904
Published in "The Strand": April 1904
Published as part of: "The Return of Sherlock Holmes"

Here Holmes is called upon to retrieve some embarrassing letters from a blackmailer. Milverton purchases information from discharged and or dissatisfied maids' etc. and uses it to blackmail individuals at opportunistic times. Holmes and Watson witness his murder and later decline to assist

Lestrade in locating the murderers, who they know to be a woman previously blackmailed by Milverton. This story provides the only description of Watson, which is detailed by Lestrade from the description of the individuals seen running from the scene of the crime.

THE ADVENTURE OF THE COPPER BEECHES:
Published in the "Strand" June 1892
Published as part of: "The Adventures of Sherlock Holmes"

Miss Violet Hunter consults Holmes about a position as governess at an unusually high rate of pay

and other strange requirements, one, which is to cut
her beautiful hair. After consulting Holmes and
taking the position as governess she becomes
frightened by the behavior of her employer and the
happenings around her. Holmes's investigation
reveals a father's hiding of his daughter in hopes of
keeping control of her inheritance.

"The Adventure of the Creeping Man"
Holmes comments that he has watched the child to
form a deduction as to the criminal habits of the
father, as in [T]he [Adventure of the] Copper
Beeches, it too can be done with dogs. Watching a
dog tells much about its family.

THE ADVENTURE OF THE CREEPING MAN:
Published in "The Strand": March 1923
Published as part of: "The Case Book of Sherlock Holmes"
Holmes is called upon to investigate why an old
Professor's devoted and loving dog would attack him.
The solution is found in tracing the old Professor's
strange behavior after his engagement to a very
young lady and his wish to regain his youth.

THE ADVENTURE OF THE DANCING MEN:
Published in "The Strand": December 1903
Published as part of: "The Return of Sherlock Holmes"
The story begins with a discussion of Watson
thoughts on investing in South African securities.
Additionally we find that Watson plays billiards
on Thursday nights. The case involves Holmes's
ability to decipher a code of "dancing men" which
has brought fear to the wife of one Hilton Cubitt.
Her past and her father's involvement with the
Chicago underworld come back to haunt Elsie

Patrick. A member of her father's gang, Abe Slaney, was in love with her and followed her to England where he tried to convince he to leave her husband. Abe Slaney kills Hilton Cubitt, while attempting to protect his wife, Elsie, from what he believes to be an attempted robbery.

THE ADVENTURE OF THE DEVIL'S FOOT:

Published in "The Strand": December 1910
Published as part of: "His Last Bow"

Holmes suggest Watson write about the "Cornish Horror" which occurred in the spring of 1897. Watson convinces Holmes to take a vacation during which the mysterious death of a young lady and the onset of insanity in her two brothers leads Holmes on the trail of a criminal who Holmes eventually allows to escape England before the police can act. A family feud, a long lost love, and a strange and powerful drug are all Holmes needs to conclude the case. In so doing, he and Watson are almost overcome by the "devil's foot" drug but for the actions of Watson in dragging himself and Holmes to safety.

THE ADVENTURE OF THE DYING DETECTIVE:

Published in "Collier's: November 22, 1913
Published in "The Strand": December 1913
Published as part of: "His Last Bow"

Holmes pretends to be dying in order to capture a murderer. He keeps the truth from Watson so as to allow Watson to play his role believably. This matter occurs during Watson second year of marriage when Mrs. Hudson comes to Watson's room and informs him of Holmes serious medical condition. Holmes has Watson hide in Holmes's room at Baker Street while he elicits a confession from the murderer.

THE ADVENTURE OF THE EMPTY HOUSE:

Published in "Collier's" September 26, 1903

Published in "The Strand" October 1903

Published as part of: "The Return of Sherlock Holmes"

Occurs in the Spring of 1894 involving the murder of the Honourable Ronald Adair under most unusual and inexplicable circumstances. Watson remarks at the loss, which the community has sustained by the death of Sherlock Holmes. Holmes returns from the "dead" appearing to Watson as an old bookseller, thereafter explaining the reasons for his masquerade.

Holmes explains his part in the battle with Professor Moriarty at the Reichenbach Falls. Holmes solves the murder of Ronald Adair while capturing the "second most dangerous man in London," Colonel Sebastian Moran. After ten years of silence Watson can now tell the story, he having been barred by a positive prohibition from 'his' own lips, which had only been recently withdrawn.

THE ADVENTURE OF THE ENGINEER'S THUMB:

Published in the "Strand" March 1892

Published as part of: "The Adventures of Sherlock Holmes"

Holmes investigation of the severing of engineer Victor Hatherley's thumb leads him to a gang of counterfeiters. Engineer Hatherley had been called upon by the counterfeiters to do some repairs to their press and in his escape from them, he looses his thumb. The counterfeiters escape before Holmes can capture them but their printing press has been destroyed. The Adventure occurred in the summer of 1889 not long after Watson's marriage. Watson had abandoned Holmes and his Baker Street rooms and returned to civil practice.

THE ADVENTURE OF THE GOLDEN PINCE-NEZ:

Published in "The Strand": July 1904

Published as part of: "The Return of Sherlock Holmes"

Homes is able to deduce information from a pince-nez (a pair of glasses) found in the hand of the murdered secretary of a professor. As the case unfolds, the Russian background of the professor comes forth along with his misdeeds of the past which have come back to haunt him. Case occurred during November 1894 and is one of many, which Holmes was involved with during that year.

ADVENTURE OF "GRACE PATERSONS":

"The Five Orange Pips"

An unrecorded case.

Took place in the island of Uffa.

THE ADVENTURE OF THE ILLUSTRIOUS CLIENT:

Published in 'Collier's': November 8, 1924

Published in "The Strand": February/March 1925

Published as part of: "The Case Book of Sherlock Holmes"

Holmes must use unlawful methods to 'steal' a diary and prevent the marriage of a young woman to a vile criminal. The case begins on September 3, 1902 and involves a educated criminal mind, there is 'no more dangerous man in Europe.' Holmes sets up an elaborate plan to obtain a diary detailing the exploits of Baron Gruner. Watson studies Chinese pottery and while he has the attention of Baron Gruner, a collector of Chinese pottery, Holmes breaks into the Baron's house and steals his diary which seals the fate of the Baron and his plans to marry General De Merville's daughter, Violet.

THE ADVENTURE OF THE LION'S MANE:

Published in "Liberty": November 27, 1926
Published in "The Strand": December 1926
Published as part of: "The Case Book of Sherlock Holmes"
This case came to Holmes attention after his
retirement to the South Downs and is told by Holmes
himself, Watson having "passed almost beyond my
ken." Late in July 1907 a man's body is discovered on
a beach near Holmes's retirement home apparently
whipped to death. Later his dog is found in the same
condition in almost the identical area of the beach.
Suspicion falls upon an instructor at a private school
but Holmes is able to reach into his vast memory and
bring forth the reason for the appearance of murder with
a simpler explanation.

THE ADVENTURE OF THE MAZARIN STONE:

Published in "The Strand": October 1921
Published as Part of: "The Case Book of Sherlock Holmes"
This story is told by an anonymous party and
involves Holmes and Watson on the trail of the theft
of the Mazarin Stone, the Crown Diamond, at the
request of the Prime Minister and Home Secretary
and against the wishes of Lord Cantlemere, who does
not believe in nor support Holmes and his methods.
Holmes uses a facsimile of himself to bait the criminals
and retrieve the jewel. He then proceeds to play a
practical joke on Lord Cantlemere while in the process of
returning the jewel to him.

THE ADVENTURE OF THE MISSING THREE-QUARTER:

Published in "The Strand": August 1904
Published as part of: "The Return of Sherlock Holmes"
Holmes becomes involved in the search for a rugby

player who has disappeared the night before a big match. His investigation leads him to suspect the wrong man and later receive a rebuke for meddling in other family's affairs. The case takes place around 1896/97 in February. Things had been very slow for Holmes and Watson prior to this little matter and Watson relates how he has weaned Holmes from his drug mania over a number of years.

THE ADVENTURE OF THE NOBLE BACHELOR:

Published in the "Strand": April 1892
Published as part of: "The Adventures of Sherlock Holmes"
Involves the curious termination of the marriage of Lord St. Simon to Hatty Doran. Was four years old when Watson wrote about it in 1901. According to Watson it took place a few weeks prior to his own marriage.

NOTE: The date provided for this adventure is 1897, however, Watson was married in the fall of 1888, therefore the actual date should have been fall/winter 1888.

THE ADVENTURE OF THE NORWOOD BUILDER:

Published in "Collier's" October 31, 1903
Published in "The Strand" November 1903
Published as part of: "The Return of Sherlock Holmes"
Watson has sold his practice to a young Doctor named Verner and moved back into the Baker Street quarters. Holmes mentions that "London has become a singularly uninteresting city since the death of the late lamented Professor Moriarty. Holmes comes to the assistance of a young solicitor accused of the murder and arson of a wealthy lumberman who has left all his wealth to the young solicitor in his will, which the same young solicitor prepared.

Holmes finds success in the discovery of an incriminating

'thumb print' which he 'knows' was not there the day before. And with this new evidence is able to produce the true criminal.

THE ADVENTURE OF THE RED CIRCLE:
Published in "The Strand": March & April 1911
Published as part of: "His Last Bow"
Holmes's investigation of a strange lodger at Mrs. Warren's home brings him together with Scotland Yard and the Pinkerton Agency of America in the search for a member of the Italian underworld, The Red Circle. Together the three are able to piece together a story of underworld revenge and the attempt of Gennaro and Emilia Lucca to escape their past ties with the criminal world. It is written in two parts.

THE ADVENTURE OF THE RETIRED COLOURMAN:
Published in "Liberty": December 18, 1926
Published in "The Strand": January 1927
Published as part of: "The Case Book of Sherlock Holmes"
An elderly gentleman retains Holmes in 1899 to locate his wife and next-door neighbor, a young doctor with whom he played chess regularly. It appears that the wife and young doctor have stolen the elderly man's monies and run away, but Holmes's deduction concerning the newly painted library of Josiah Amberley proves correct and the old man is confronted with his hideous crime. Holmes sends Watson to investigate the matter early on due to other pressing business and eventually becomes involved with a 'new partner,' one Barker, who has been investigating the case for members of the missing doctor's family. This case is unique in that the criminal comes to Holmes for help, believing that by doing so, suspicion will be thrown off of him.

ADVENTURE OF THE OLD RUSSIAN WOMAN:
"The Musgrave Ritual"
An unrecorded case.

THE ADVENTURE OF THE PARADOL CHAMBER:
"The Five Orange Pips"
An unrecorded case.

THE ADVENTURE OF THE PRIORY SCHOOL:
Published in "Collier's": January 30, 1904
Published in "The Strand": February 1904
Published as part of: "The Return of Sherlock Holmes"
Holmes is called upon to solve the kidnapping of the Duke of Holdernesse's 10-year-old son who has been abducted from the private school he attends. The story involves a bastard son looking to gain the position to which he believes he is entitled and which position his younger half-brother has ascended. Watson is impressed with Holmes's ability to determine the direction a bicycle has traveled by its tracks.

THE ADVENTURE OF THE SECOND STAIN:
Published in "The Strand": December 1904
Published as part of: "The Return of Sherlock Holmes"
Watson informs the reader that Holmes is no longer interested in having his exploits published. Holmes has retired and is studying bee farming on the Sussex Downs. This particular matter involves the "most important international case, which he has ever been called upon to handle." Holmes must retrieve a letter of immense political importance and is able to do so through the lack of a second stain at the exact location of the murder, a rug in the victim's house.

THE ADVENTURE OF SHOSCOMBE OLD PLACE:

Published in "Liberty": March 5, 1927

Published in "The Strand": April 1927

Published as part of: "The Case Book of Sherlock Holmes"

Holmes is asked to look into the strange happenings at Shoscombe Old Place where a brother and sister share a large estate. The brother, Sir Robert Norberton, is heavily in debt and is depending on his best horse in the upcoming Derby to solve his financial difficulties. His sister, Lady Beatrice Falder, is a widow and she owns the estate, stables, and the horses only while she lives, upon her death, her dead husband's family receives the entire estate. She has been ill of late and death cannot be far off. Holmes discovers that Sir Robert is hiding his sister's dead body and trying to keep the image that she is alive until after the Derby so, in the event his horse wins, he will be saved from his financial debt. Holmes decides not to intervene in Sir Robert's plans, and his horse wins, saving him the day.

THE ADVENTURE OF THE SIX NAPOLEONS:

Published in "Collier's": April 30, 1904

Published in "The Strand": May 1904

Published as part of: "The Return of Sherlock Holmes"

Holmes assist Lestrade in this case involving six identical busts of Napoleon. The smashing of the busts after their theft and a murder are all part of the investigation, which involves murder, the Mafia, a young woman's love, and stolen jewels. Holmes provides a little drama in the end by purchasing the final busts and smashing it himself to the shock of Watson and Lestrade. Inside he discovers what he knew would be there, the jewel.

THE ADVENTURE OF THE SOLITARY CYCLIST:

Published in "Collier's": December 26, 1903

Published in "The Strand": January 1904

Published as part of: "The Return of Sherlock Holmes"

Holmes's schedule forces him to send Watson to investigate the case of Miss Violet Smith of Charlington. Watson's work again falls short and Holmes arrives on the scene just in time to witness the forced marriage of Miss Violet Smith to one Mr. Woodley. Holmes is, nevertheless, able to capture the villains and point out the invalidity of the marriage. This case surrounds an attempt by two men. Woodley and Carruthers, and their plan to obtain an inheritance belonging to Miss Smith. Watson dates the case as beginning on April 23, 1895.

THE ADVENTURE OF THE SPECKLED BAND:

Published in the 'Strand' February 1892

Published as part of: "The Adventures of Sherlock Holmes"

Holmes investigates the curious behavior of Dr. Grimesby Roylott in April 1883. The Doctor's daughter is concerned for her safety after her sister dies mysteriously and she is moved into her dead sister's old bedroom. He arranges to spend a night hidden in the room of Dr. Roylott's daughter in order to discover the strange goings on there. After entering the home of Dr. Roylott, without his knowledge, Holmes confronts the deadly Speckled Band, a very poisonous snake, as it makes its way toward the bed where Holmes has been resting.

"The Naval Treaty"

Mentioned in here as Holmes compares his wait for Joseph Harrison during the night with his wait, in the dark, for the "Speckled Band."

THE ADVENTURE OF THE SUSSEX VAMPIRE:

Published in "The Strand": January 1924

Published as part of: "The Case Book of Sherlock Holmes"
Holmes is asked to investigate the strange behavior of Robert Ferguson's wife, her apparent beating of Mr. Ferguson's crippled son and the biting of her baby boy on his neck. Holmes is able to deduce the solution to the problem through the observation of the family dog, which has been mistreated.

THE ADVENTURE OF THE THREE GABLES:

Published in "Liberty": September 18, 1926

Published in "The Strand": October 1926

Published as part of: "The Case Book of Sherlock Holmes"
Strange occurrences at a house of the wife of an early client bring Holmes into the investigation of a burglary and a hidden love affair. The son of Holmes's client has died but having been scorned in a love affair, has written a story based on his encounter and the woman of his love wishes to prevent publication of his book, she now preparing to marry a young Duke.

THE ADVENTURE OF THE THREE GARRIDEBS:

Published in 'Collier's': October 25, 1924

Published in "The Strand": January 1925

Published as part of: "The Case Book of Sherlock Holmes"
In this case, taking place in the latter part of June 1902, Holmes is retained to look into the reality of a large inheritance which is to be split between three men who have a same, singular, last name, Garrideb. Holmes is able to conclude that the 'Three Garridebs' is a ruse to allow the criminal to gain access to a home in Little Ryder Street so as to retrieve something of value, which is hidden there.

THE ADVENTURE OF THE THREE STUDENTS:

Published in "The Strand": June 1904

Published as part of: "The Return of Sherlock Holmes"
During 1895, Holmes and Watson are away from Baker Street while Holmes undertakes research in early English charters. An acquaintance, which serves as an instructor, request Holmes look into the theft of a copy of a scholarship examination. Holmes is faced with determining which of three students was involved and has obtained a copy of the examination prior to the exam date.

THE ADVENTURE OF THE VEILED LODGER:

Published in "Liberty": January 22, 1927

Published in "The Strand": February 1927

Published as part of: "The Case Book of Sherlock Holmes"
Watson opens this story by informing the reader that Holmes has "been in active practice for twenty-three years" and Watson has been with him during seventeen of those years. Watson points out that Holmes's cases are valuable not only to the student of crime but also to the student of social and official scandals of the late Victorian era. Watson also takes a moment to enforce the "discretion and high sense of professional honor which have always distinguished [his] friend" and that this discretion is "still at work in the choice of these memoirs." Watson goes on to say that he "deprecates in the strongest way the attempts which have been made lately to get at and to destroy these papers. The source of these outrages is known, and if they are repeated I have Mr. Holmes's authority for saying the whole story concerning the politician, the lighthouse, and the trained cormorant will be given to the public. There

is at least one reader who will understand." This matter takes Holmes to the lodging house of one Mrs. Merrilow concerning the failure of Mrs. Merrilow to see her lodger more than once in over seven years and now the lodger has requested the landlady to bring Holmes to her. The case begins in late 1896. Holmes is able to see the lodger, Mrs. Ronder, whose face is terribly mutilated from an attack by a lion. After hearing her story Holmes is able to convince her not to commit suicide, asserting that she still has something to offer society.

THE ADVENTURE OF WISTERIA LODGE

AKA "A Reminiscence of Mr. Sherlock Holmes"
Published in "Collier's": August 15, 1908
Published in "The Strand": September/October 1908
Published as part of: "His Last Bow"

Consists of two sections:
"The Singular Experience of Mr. John Scott Eccles"
"The Tiger of San Pedro"

Takes place at the end of March 1892. The case concerns the strange happenings at Wisteria Lodge, where a Mr. Eccles has been invited to spend a few days with a new acquaintance. The disappearance, and subsequent discovery of the murder of Mr. Eccles's host, Mr. Aloysius Garcia, brings Holmes into the bizarre case of revenge reaching across the ocean to Central America

AEROPLANES:

"His Last Bow" "An Epilogue of Sherlock Holmes"

Von Bork, the German spy, had a safe containing pigeonholes bristling with papers and plans, each with its own label. One of these compartments was labeled "Aeroplanes."

AFFAIR OF THE ALUMINUM CRUTCH:
"The Musgrave Ritual"
> An unrecorded case.
> A singular affair.

AFFAIR OF THE VATICAN CAMEOS:
"The Hound of the Baskervilles"
> An unrecorded case.
> Holmes assist the Pope.

AGAR, MOORE:
"The Adventure of the Devil's Foot"
> Dr. Moore, of Harley Street, examined Holmes in
> March of 1897 and suggested he "lay aside all his
> cases and surrender himself to complete rest.

AGATHA:
"The Adventure of Charles Augustus Milverton"
> Engaged to be married to Escott, AKA Sherlock
> Holmes. She is the housemaid of Charles Augustus
> Milverton. Holmes has taken on a disguise to obtain
> information on Milverton and his habits.

AGRA:
"The Sign of Four"
> City in India, protected by the Third Bengal Fusiliers,
> some Sikhs, two troops of cavalry, and a battery of
> artillery. It is a great place, swarming with fanatics
> and fierce devil-worshippers of all sorts.

THE AGRA TREASURE:
"The Red-Headed League"
> Official Police agent Peter Jones states that Holmes
> was "more nearly correct than the official force" in
> the case of the Agra Treasure.

AGRA TREASURE:

"The Sign of Four"

Treasure stolen by Captain Morstan and Major Sholto. Treasure belonging to Achmet, traveling companion of Dost Akbar. It was stolen from Achmet by Dost Akbar, Mahomet Singh, Abdullah Khan, and Jonathan Small at the city of Agra in India during the great mutiny. It consisted of a collection of gems. There were one hundred and forty-three diamonds of the first water, including one known as 'the Great Mogul' the second largest stone in existence. There were ninety-seven very fine emeralds, and one hundred and seventy rubies, some which were small. There were forty carbuncles, two hundred and ten sapphires, sixty-one agates, and a great quantity of beryls, onyxes, cats'-eyes, turquoises, and other stones. Additionally, there were three hundred pearls, ten of which were set in a gold coronet. The treasure was concealed in a safe place until peace again would come to India. The murderers of Achmet are caught and sentenced to Andaman Island where one tells Major Sholto and Captain Marstan of the treasure and its hidden location. Sholto and Marstan locate it in a double cross of the imprisoned murderers. After the death of Major Sholto, his sons searched in vain for the treasure. Its discovery leads to this adventure.

AINSTREE, DR.:

"The Adventure of the Dying Detective"

The greatest living authority upon tropical diseases. Watson knows that he is in London and wants to fetch him to examine Holmes, but Holmes prevents it.

AIREDALE:

"The Adventure of the Lion's Mane"

Fitzroy McPherson's dog, it was found dead near the place where McPherson's body was found a few days after its master's death. Its body had the look of agony in every line of it.

AKBAR, DOST:
> "The Sign of Four"
>> A member of "The Sign of Four" Foster-brother of Abdullah Khan and traveling companion of Achmet. Conspired with Jonathan Small, Abdullah Khan, and Mahomet Singh to kill Achmet and steal his treasure. He is caught, tried, and sentenced with his co-conspirators for the murder of Achmet. He is sent to Andaman Island where his escape with the others fails due to the double-cross of Major Sholto and Captain Marstan, who themselves retrieve the hidden treasure.

ALBEMARLE MANSION:
> "The Adventure of Wisteria Lodge"
> aka "A Reminiscence of Mr. Sherlock Holmes"
>> Home of the Melville family, it is located in Kensington.

ALBERT DOCK:
> "The Adventure of the Cardboard Box"
>> Location, on the Thames, where Lestrade captures Jim Browner.

ALBERT HALL:
> "The Adventure of the Retired Colourman"
>> Music hall in London, Holmes and Watson take in a show when Carina is scheduled to sing.

ALDERSHOT:
> "The Crooked Man"
>> Location of the murder of Colonel Barclay, Holmes and Watson head there from Waterloo by the 11:10 train.

ALDGATE STATION:
"The Adventure of the Bruce-Partington Plans"
Rail Station on the Underground rail system in London. Location of the discovery of the dead body of Arthur Cadogan West. The trains passing through this station are purely Metropolitan, with some from Willesden and outlying junctions.

ALEXANDRIA:
"The Adventure of the Golden Pince-Nez"
Where Ionides, the cigarette maker lives.

ALEXIS:
"The Adventure of the Golden Pince-Nez"
A companion of Anna's, he was sent to work in the salt mines in Siberia as punishment for the killing of a Russian Police Officer. Although he was innocent of the killing of the Russian Police Officer, he was implicated by Sergius, Anna's husband.

ALGAR:
"The Adventure of the Cardboard Box"
A friend of Holmes's serving on the Liverpool force.

ALGERIA:
"The Adventure of the Mazarin Stone"
Count Sylvius used to shoot lions in Algeria.

ALICE:
"The Adventure of the Noble Bachelor"
Maid to Hatty Doran, an American from California, a confidential servant.

ALICIA:
"The Problem of Thor Bridge"
An unrecorded case.
A problem without a solution. The cutter sailed one

morning into a small patch of mist and never emerged, neither the cutter nor her crew were ever heard from again.

ALLAHABAD:
"The Adventure of the Retired Colourman"
> City in north central India. Edmunds was transferred there from the Berkshire Constabulary.

ALLAN BROTHERS':
"The Adventure of Wisteria Lodge"
aka "A Reminiscence of Mr. Sherlock Holmes"
> Chief land agents in the area of Esher and Oxshott, they were the firm, which rented Wisteria Lodge to Mr. Aloysius Garcia.

ALLARDYCE'S:
"The Adventure of Black Peter"
> Butcher shop in London.

ALLEGRO:
"The Adventure of the Noble Bachelor"
> Miss Flora Millat had been a danseuse at the Allegro, becoming good friends with Lord St. Simon.

ALLEN, MRS.:
"The Valley of Fear" Part 1: "The Tragedy of Birlstone"
> A buxom and cheerful person, she was the housekeeper at Manor House. She is a little hard of hearing.

ALPHA INN:
"The Adventure of The Blue Carbuncle"
> Located near the Museum in Bloomsbury and hosted by Windigate, it is a small public house at the corner of one of the streets, which runs down into Holborn.

A group of patrons, Henry Baker included, purchased their goose for Christmas by paying a little each week toward the full purchase price.

ALTAMONT:
"His Last Bow" "An Epilogue of Sherlock Holmes"
Spy working for the German, Von Bork. He is a bitter Irish-American with ill feelings toward England. He has been working for Von Bork for some time and will receive five hundred pounds for delivering the 'Naval Signals' to the German spy. Altamont has a nice taste in wines, with a fancy for Tokay. Began his part in Chicago, graduating from an Irish secret society in Buffalo, he moved to England where he gave serious trouble to the constabulary at Skibbareen and thereby caught the eye of a Von Bork underling. AKA: Sherlock Holmes

THE AMATEUR MENDICANT SOCIETY:
"Five Orange Pips"
An unrecorded case.
Held a luxurious club in the lower vault of furniture warehouse.

AMBERLEY, JOSIAH:
"The Adventure of the Retired Colourman"
A junior partner in the company Brickfall and Amberley, manufacturers of artistic materials. He lives in Lewisham, at The Haven, having retired in 1896. In 1897 he married a woman twenty years his junior, and now, two years later, he is a broken and miserable creature. He plays chess regularly with his next-door neighbor, Dr. Ray Ernest, and believes that Dr. Ray and Mrs. Amberley have run off together. His back was curved as though he carried a heavy

burden, his shoulders and chest were the framework of a giant, though his figure tapered away into a pair of spindled legs. He had an artificial limb. He seeks Holmes assistance in the disappearance of his wife and Dr. Ray Ernest.

AMERICAN ENCYCLOPEDIA:
"The Five Orange Pips"
Reference book used to examine who or what is the Ku Klux Klan.

AMERICAN EXCHANGE, STRAND:
"A Study in Scarlet"
Address to which two letters were addressed to Enoch J. Drebber and Joseph Strangerson with the notice: "to be left till called for."

AMES:
"The Valley of Fear", Part 1: "The Tragedy of Birlstone"
The butler at Manor House. He had been the butler for Sir Charles Chandos for ten years prior to his employ with Mr. Douglas five years ago.

AMSTERDAM:
"The Adventure of the Mazarin Stone"
Count Sylvius intends to move the Crown Diamond out of England and into Amsterdam, Holland to be cut into four pieces by Van Seddar.

ANCIENT ORDER OF FREEMEN:
"The Valley of Fear" Part 2: "The Scowrers"
See 'Eminent Order of Freemen'

ANDAMAN ISLANDER:
"The Adventure of the Golden Pince-Nez"
An unrecorded case.

Took place in the earlier days of Holmes and Watson's career. Watson, in assisting Holmes in "The Adventure of the Golden Pince-nez" saw "the cold winter sun rise over the dreary marshes of the Thames and the long, sullen reaches of the river," which Watson associates with this case.

ANDAMAN ISLANDS:
"The Sign of Four"
> Situated 340 miles to the north of Sumatra, in the Bay of Bengal. Contains convict quarters. Inhabited by aborigines, naturally hideous, having large, misshapen heads, small fierce eyes, and distorted features. They use poison to kill their enemies.

ANDERSON:
"The Adventure of the Lion's Mane"
> The village constable, he was a big, ginger-mustached man of the slow, solid Sussex breed.

ANDERSON MURDERS:
"The Hound of the Baskervilles"
> According to Holmes a situation analogous to that faced in the "Hound of the Baskervilles." One of the most singular and sensational crimes of modern times. Occurred in North Carolina.

ANDOVER `77:
"A Case of Identity"
An unrecorded case.
> Holmes mentions this as a parallel case to that of Miss Mary Sutherland's.

ANDREWS:
"The Valley of Fear" Part 2: "The Scowrers"
> Little more than a boy, frank-faced and cheerful, with

the look of someone out for a holiday. He was one of the assassins sent by Evans Pott to kill Crow Hill manager, Josiah H. Dunn, which he does. He had carried out three killings before this one and was chosen because he does not drink.

ANERLEY ARMS:

"The Adventure of the Norwood Builder"

Where John McFarlane stayed after his meeting with Mr. Jonas Oldacre, the night Mr. Oldacre was murdered.

ANGEL, HOSMER:

"A Case of Identity"

Advertisement appearing in the CHRONICLE describes Mr. Hosmer Angel; " ... five feet seven inches in height; strongly built, sallow complexion, black hair, a little bald in the centre, bushy, black side-whiskers and moustache; tinted glasses, slightly infirmity of speech ... " Very independent about money. He is a cashier in an office in Leadenhall Street. Was to marry Miss Mary Sutherland at St. Saviour's near King's Cross, whereupon they were to have breakfast at the St. Pancras Hotel. He disappeared during the ride to the Church. AKA James Windibank

ANNA:

"The Adventure of the Golden Pince-Nez"

Wife of Professor Coram, she is Russian and asserts that his name is actually Sergius. She was a reformer, a revolutionists, a Nihilists. Some of her companions found their way to the gallows and some to Siberia. She was only twenty when she married Sergius but fell in love with one of the other revolutionaries, Alexis. She was sentenced on the confession of her husband. She had been a member of the Order and

after her release from prison, a member of the
Brotherhood. She entered the Professor's residence to
steal the diaries and letters he possessed which would
free Alexis and was caught by Mr. Willoughby
Smith, whom she stabbed in order to escape. The
Professor who feared she would inform the
Brotherhood of his whereabouts later hid her.

ANNIE:
"The Disappearance of Lady Frances Carfax"
See Fraser.

ANSTRUTHER:
"The Boscombe Valley Mystery"
Doctor friend of Watson's, Watson's wife suggest
Anstruther as someone who will help Watson's
patients while Watson assist Holmes.

ANTHONY:
"The Hound of the Baskervilles"
The manservant at Meripit House, he had been
connected with the Stapletons for several years. He
disappears and it is believed he escaped from the
country. Stapletons confidant.

ANTHROPOLOGICAL JOURNAL:
"The Adventure of the Cardboard Box"
Holmes penned two short monographs on the subject
of the human ear. In particular, how each ear is as a
rule quite distinct and differs from all other ones.

APPLEDORE, CHARLES:
"The Adventure of the Priory School"
Sir Charles is the father-in-law to the Duke of
Holdernesse, his daughter Edith having married the
Duke and borne him a son.

APPLEDORE TOWERS:
"The Adventure of Charles Augustus Milverton"
Home of Charles Augustus Milverton.

ARCADIA:
"The Crooked Man"
Pipe tobacco used by Watson during his bachelor days and in continued use during his married days.

ARCHIE:
"The Red-Headed League"
Accomplice of John Clay's. May also be known as Duncan Ross

ARMITAGE, PERCY:
"The Adventure of the Speckled Band"
Second son of Mr. Armitage, of Crane Water, near Reading. Engaged to Helen Stoner.

ARMSTRONG, LESLIE:
"The Adventure of the Missing Three-quarter"
An unrecorded case, took place in 1894.
Dr. Leslie Armstrong is one of the heads of the medical school at Cambridge and a thinker of European reputation in more than one branch of science. He had a square, massive face, with brooding eyes under thatched brows and the granite molding of an inflexible jaw. He appeared as a man of deep character with an alert mind, grim, ascetic, self-contained, formidable. Holmes believes that if Dr. Leslie Armstrong were to turn his talents to crime he could easily fill the gap left by Moriarty.

ARNSWORTH CASTLE BUSINESS:
>"A Scandal in Bohemia"
>>An unrecorded case.

ASTON:
>"The Adventure of the Three Garridebs"
>>Village in England, near Birmingham, where Howard Garrideb has offices at the Grosvenor Buildings.

ATHENE:
>"The Adventure of Charles Augustus Milverton"
>>A marble bust of Athene sits on a large bookcase in Charles Augustus Milverton's study.

ATHENS:
>"The Greek Interpreter"
>>City in Greece from where Sophy and Paul Kratides originate. Their ordeal brings them to England, Sophy to visit friends and eventually to chum with Harold Latimer, and Paul, to assist his sister in escaping the clutches of Latimer and his partner.

THE ATKINSON BROTHERS:
>"A Scandal in Bohemia"
>>An unrecorded case.
>>Holmes investigated the singular tragedy of the Atkinson Brothers at Trincomalee.

ATWOOD:
>"The Valley of Fear", Part 2: "The Scowrers"
>>Sold his ironworks operation to West Gilmerton General Mining Company instead of paying protection money to the 'Scowrers' to leave him alone.

AVELING:

"The Adventure of the Priory School"
Mathematical master at the Priory School.

AVENGING ANGELS:

"A Study in Scarlet" Part 2 -- "The Country of the Saints"
See "Danite Band"

AUDLEY COURT:

"A Study in Scarlet"
John Rance, the constable who found the body of
Enoch J. Drebber, lives at 46 Audley Court
Kennington Park Gate.

AURORA:

"The Sign of Four"
Steam Launch owned by Mordecai Smith. A trim
little thing, black with two red streaks.

AYRSHIRES:

"The Stock-Broker's Clerk"
Stock selling for 'a hundred and six and a quarter to a
hundred and five and seven-eights.' Mr. Arthur
Pinner ask for this quote as a test of Mr. Hall
Pycroft's knowledge of the financial market.

BACKWATER, LORD:
"Silver Blaze"
>Owner of the racehorse 'Desborough' and the largest training establishment of Mapleton.

BADEN:
"The Disappearance of Lady Frances Carfax"
>When Lady Frances Carfax leaves the Hotel National she heads for the Rhenish spa at Baden. Area of Southwest Germany.

BAIN, SANDY:
"The Adventure of Shoscombe Old Place"
>The jockey from the stables at Shoscombe Old Place, he is to ride Shoscombe Prince in the Derby.

BAKER, HENRY:
"The Adventure of The Blue Carbuncle"
>A large man with rounded shoulders, a massive head, and a broad, intelligent face, sloping down to a pointed beard of grizzled brown. A touch of red in his nose and cheeks, with a slight tremor of his extended hand. He is a man of learning and letters who had had ill-usage at the hands of fortune.

>Owner of the goose, lost and found by Peterson, commissionaire, and found to contain the "Blue Carbuncle".

BAKER STREET:
The lodgings of Sherlock Holmes and Dr. John Watson were located at 221 B Baker Street. Mrs. Hudson was their landlady and young Billy their page. Most of the adventures begin with a

visit by a client to Baker Street and many also involve the use of the lodgings to capture the criminal. Although the rooms are mentioned frequently throughout the numerous recorded adventures they are described in any detail only in "A Study in Scarlet" and "The Adventure of the Empty House."

"A Study in Scarlet"
> Location of a suite of rooms, which has caught the eye of Sherlock Holmes which he, is prepared to share with Watson. 221B Baker Street consists of a couple of comfortable bedrooms and a single large airy sitting-room, cheerfully furnished and illuminated by two broad windows.

"The Adventure of the Empty House"
> Watson describes the lodgings upon his return there after the capture of Colonel Sabastian Moran. The chemical corner and the acid-stained, deal-topped table. Upon a shelf was the row of formidable scrapbooks and books of reference. The diagrams, the violin-case, and the pipe-rack -- even the Persian slipper, which contained the tobacco -- all were still there.

BALDWIN, TED:

"The Valley of Fear", Part 1: "The Tragedy of Birlstone"
> It is his body that the police believe to be that of John Douglas, the face having been hit by a shotgun blast. Ted Baldwin has come to England on the trail of John Douglas to kill him in revenge for the 'Scowrers' but Baldwin, himself, is killed by Douglas instead.

Part 2: "The Scowrers"
> Boss of the 'Scowrers' of Vermissa, they being one and the same as the 'Eminent Order of Freemen' which is run by Black Jack McGinty.

He is in love with Ettie Shafter, daughter of Jacob Shafter owner of the boarding house on Sheridan Street where John McMurdo, a newcomer to Vermissa, is residing. McMurdo is successful in pushing aside Baldwin for Ettie Shafter's affection. This does not endear McMurdo to Baldwin.

He leads the attack on James Stanger, editor/owner of the Vermissa Herald newspaper. Baldwin carried out the execution of William Hales of Stake Royal, with two comrades, as a favor to the Gilmerton Lodge.

He is one of the seven chosen to capture and kill the Pinkerton agent, Birdy Edwards, but he and his comrades are captured instead. He is sentenced to ten years in prison and vows revenge on John McMurdo alias Birdy Edwards upon his release.

BALLARAT:
"The Boscombe Valley Mystery"

In the County of Victoria, Austrlia, Charles McCarthy, in attempting to identify his murderer, spoke to his son, James, who only heard "A RAT." Holmes is able to determine it was the last two syllables of BALLARAT.

BALMORAL, DUKE of:
"Silver Blaze"

Owner of the racehorse 'Iris' which was entered in the Wessex Cup race.

BALMORAL, LORD:
"The Adventure of the Empty House"

He and partner, Godfrey Milner, lost 420 pounds playing cards with Ronald Adair and Colonel Moran some weeks prior to the murder of Ronald Adair.

BANK OF ENGLAND:
"The Adventure of the Three Garridebs"

Rodger Prescott had a printing press hidden under the floor at his rooms on Little Ryder Street and after his death his rooms were rented to one Nathan Garrideb. The printing Press could print Bank of England notes and John Garrideb, aka Killer Evans, knew where the press was and disguised himself in order to get Nathan Garrideb to leave the rooms unattended so he could retrieve the press.

BANNISTER:
"The Adventure of the Three Students"

Servant for ten years of Hilton Soames at the College of St. Luke's. He is a little, white-faced, clean-shaven, grizzly-haired fellow of fifty. He had served as butler to Sir Jabez Gilchrist before coming to the College of St. Luke. He assisted young Gilchrist in obtaining a copy of the Fortescue Scholarship exam prior to the exam date.

BAR OF GOLD:
"The Man With The Twisted Lip"

An opium den located in Upper Swandam Lane. A trap-door is located at the rear of the building, near the corner of Paul's Wharf, which could tell some strange tales of what has passed through it upon the moonless nights.

BARBERTON:
"The Disappearance of Lady Frances Carfax"

Located in South Africa, where the young, Honorable Philip Green made his money after his breakup with Lady Frances Carfax.

BARCAROLE:
"The Adventure of the Mazarin Stone"

A piece of music imitating a song of the Venetian gondoliers written by Hoffman, Holmes plays this piece on his violin while awaiting the decision of Count Sylvius and Sam Merton as to what they intend to do with the Crown Diamond.

BARCELONA:
"The Adventure of Wisteria Lodge"

Aka "A Reminiscence of Mr. Sherlock Holmes"

Believed to be the original landing spot of Don Murillo's ship from Central America after his escape during his people's uprising against him.

BARCLAY, COLONEL JAMES:
"The Crooked Man"

A dashing, jovial old soldier in his usual mood, but there were occasions on which he seem to show himself capable of considerable violence and vindictiveness.

Commanded "The Royal Munsters," having started as a full private, he was raised to commissioned rank for his bravery at the time of the Mutiny in India. He married at the time he was a sergeant, a Miss Nancy Devoy, who was the daughter of a former colour-sergeant in the same corps. He was subject to a singular sort of depression which came upon him at times and lasted for days, additionally, a certain superstition which took the form of a dislike of being left alone, especially after dark, were his only unusual traits. He resided at a villa called 'Lachine' about half a mile from the north camp of his troops. He had a coachman and two maids but no children.

He was found murdered at Aldershot.

He was stationed at Bhurtee with the One Hundred and Seventeenth during the Mutiny. It was here that he competed with Henry Wood for the hand of Nancy Devoy. While Bhurtee was under siege during the Mutiny, Henry Wood volunteered to get help from General Neill and Barclay was to provide the safest route to the General column, but he betrayed Wood resulting in Wood's capture and perceived death at the hands of the rebels. Barclay was then free to marry Miss Devoy.

BARCLAY, NANCY MRS.:

"The Crooked Man"

Wife of Colonel James Barclay of "The Royal Munsters."

Maiden name - Miss Nancy Devoy, daughter of former Colour-Sergeant Devoy, he of the same corps as then Sergeant Barclay.

She was a woman of great beauty, and that even after thirty years of marriage, is still of a striking and queenly appearance. She has been popular with the ladies of the regiment. She was a Roman Catholic and interested herself very much in the establishment of the 'Guild of St. George', which was formed in connection with the Watt Street Chapel.

While in Bhurtee, India, she was whooed by two soldiers, Corporal Wood, whom she loved in return, and Sergeant Barclay, whom her father wished her to marry. Upon the presumed death of Corporal Wood she married Sergeant Barclay. She was the Belle of the One Hundred and Seventeenth of The Royal Munsters.

For additional information: See Henry Wood.

BARDLE, INSPECTOR:
"The Adventure of the Lion's Mane"
> Of the Sussex Constabulary, was a steady, solid, bovine man with thoughtful eyes.

BARELLI, AUGUSTO:
"The Adventure of the Red Circle"
> Father of Emilia Lucca, chief lawyer and once deputy of that area of Italy around Posilippo. He forbid Emilia from marrying Gennaro Lucca, who was in his employ, to no avail, they fled, married at Bari and moved to New York.

BARI:
"The Adventure of the Red Circle"
> Town in Italy where Emilia Barelli and Gennaro Lucca married prior to their move to New York.

BARKER, CECIL JAMES:
"The Valley of Fear", Part 1: "The Tragedy of Birlstone"
> Of Hales Lodge, Hampstead, he was a frequent visitor at the Manor House of Mr. John Douglas. A tall, loose-jointed figure, he was also familiar in the main street of Birlstone village. He was the only friend from the past life of Mr. Douglas.

> An Englishman, he appeared to be a man of considerable wealth and was reputed to be a bachelor. About forty-five, he was tall, straight, broad-chested with a clean-shaven, prizefighter face, thick, strong, black eyebrows, and a pair of masterful black eyes.

> He met and became partners with John Douglas in a successful mining claim at a placed called Benito Canon in California.

BARKER, MR.:

"The Adventure of the Retired Colourman"

Holmes's hated rival on the Surrey shore. A tall, dark, heavily moustached man, he was the individual following Watson at Blackheath Station and London Bridge.

He is a friend of Holmes's working for the family of Dr. Ray Ernest. He catches Holmes escaping Josiah Amberley's home while they both are investigating the disappearance of Mrs. Amberley and Dr. Ray Ernest. He and Holmes pool their information to deduce the true crime and criminal in this case.

BARNES, JOSIAH:

"The Adventure of Shoscombe Old Place"

An old man, he keeps the Green Dragon, three miles away from Shoscombe Old Place in Crendall. He was given Lady Beatrice Falder's favorite spaniel by Sir Robert Norberton just a few days before Holmes arrives.

BARNICOT, DR.:

"The Adventure of the Six Napoleons"

Lives on Kennington Road a few hundred yards from the shop of Morse Hudson. He is a well-known medical practitioner, having one of the largest practices upon the south side of the Thames. His residence and principal consulting room is at Kennington Road but he has a branch surgery and dispensary at Lower Brixton Road, two miles away. He is an admirer of Napoleon and his house is filled with books, pictures, and relics of the French emperor. He purchased two busts of Napoleon from Morse Hudson both identical and by the French sculptor, Devine. Both of his busts were found smashed.

BARRAUD:
>"A Study in Scarlet"
>>Jewelry maker in London, maker of the gold watch, No. 97163, which was owned by Enoch J. Drebber.

BARRETT:
>"The Adventure of the Second Stain"
>>A police constable, he discovered the body of the murdered Eduardo Lucas.

BARRYMORE, ELIZA:
>"The Hound of the Baskervilles"
>>Wife of John Barrymore, older sister of the escaped convict, Selden. She was a large, impassive, heavy-featured woman with a stern set expression of mouth. She is a heavy, solid person, very limited, intensely respectable, and inclined to be puritanical. A very unemotional person, although see seems to have some deep sorrow gnawing within her heart.

BARRYMORE, JOHN:
>"The Hound of the Baskervilles"
>>A man with a full, black beard, he was Sir Charles Baskerville's butler. He is the son of the old caretaker, who has died. His family has looked after Baskerville Hall for four generations. He and his wife, Eliza, are as respectable a couple as any in the county. He was a remarkable-looking man, tall, handsome, with a square black beard and pale, distinguished features. The man is a striking-looking fellow, very well equipped to steal the heart of a country girl. Brother-in-law of escaped convict, Selden.

BARTON'S CROSSING:

"The Valley of Fear", Part 2: "The Scowrers"

Deep in the Vermissa Valley, the coal and iron trains traveled from Stagville through Vermissa and into Bartons Crossing before continuing on to Helmdale and Merton.

BARTON, HILL:

"The Adventure of the Illustrious Client"

Dr. Hill Barton is the disguise Watson will undertake during his visit with Baron Gruner concerning the sale of some valuable Ming dynasty pottery. His address will be 369 Half Moon Street.

BART'S:

"A Study in Scarlet"

Watson began his medical practice at Bart's, nickname for St. Bartholomews Hospital in London. He met a young man, who was a dresser under him, named Stamford, who later introduces Watson to one Sherlock Holmes.

BASIL, CAPTAIN:

"The Adventure of Black Peter"

One of Holmes's disguises which he used to conceal his own formidable identity.

BASKERVILLE, CHARLES, SIR:

"The Hound of the Baskervilles"

Died three months prior to Dr. Mortimer's visit to Sherlock Holmes. His death caused quite a bit of excitement in Devonshire. He was considered as the probable Liberal candidate for Mid-Devon.

Resided at Baskerville Hall for a short period prior to his death (two years), however, during that time, his amiability of character and extreme generosity had won the affection and respect of all who had been brought into contact with him. As was well known, he made large sums of money in South African speculation.

He was childless and a widower and of eccentric habit of mind. He was simple in his personal tastes. His health has been suspect for some time, especially to some affliction of the heart. His death was explained as the result of dyspnoea and cardiac exhaustion. He received a letter from Coombe Tracey the morning of his death, addressed in a woman's hand. The ashes of the letter were found in the back of the grate in the fireplace.

He was at the gate to Baskerville Hall just prior to his death to meet a woman, her initials were L.L.

BASKERVILLE, HENRY, SIR:
"The Hound of the Baskervilles"
Son of Sir Charles Baskerville's younger brother, he has spent considerable time in America, farming in Canada.

The last of the Baskervilles. A small, alert, dark-eyed man about thirty years of age, very sturdily built, with thick black eyebrows and a strong pugnacious face. Was a boy in his teens when his father died. He had lived in a little cottage on the South Coast and from there went straight to a friend in Canada. Had never seen Baskerville Hall before inheriting it.

BASKERVILLE, HUGO:
"The Hound of the Baskervilles"
Had two sons, Roger and John, and a daughter, Elizabeth.

See "Legend of the Hound"

BASKERVILLE, ROGER:

"The Hound of the Baskervilles"

The youngest of three brothers, Sir Charles being the eldest, and the second brother, who died young, was the father of Henry. Roger was the black sheep of the family, the very image of Hugo Baskerville. He made England too hot to hold him and fled to Central America dying there in 1876 of yellow fever.

BASKERVILLE, REAR-ADMIRAL:

"The Hound of the Baskervilles"

Served under Rodney in the West Indies.

BASKERVILLE, WILLIAM:

"The Hound of the Baskervilles"

Chairman of Committees of the House of Commons under Pitt.

BASLE:

"The Final Problem"

Holmes and Watson are to make their way, at their leisure, into Switzerland, via Luxembourg and Basle. The city of Basel in Switzerland may be one and the same.

BASS ROCK:

"The Adventure of the Abbey Grange"

Ship belonging to the Adelaide-Southampton Line sailing between England and South Australia. The Captain was Mr. Jack Crocker and it was scheduled to leave from Southampton in two days.

BATES, MARLOW:

"The Problem of Thor Bridge"

A thin, nervous wisp of a man with frightened eyes and a twitching, hesitating manner. He is manager of Thor

Place, estate of Neil Gibson. Does not like his employer, Mr. Gibson, and has given his notice.

BAXTER, EDITH:
"Silver Blaze"
>
> Maid to John Straker, trainer of Colonel Ross's race horses.

BAYARD:
"Silver Blaze"
>
> Racehorse owned by Colonel Ross and entered along with Colonel Ross's other horse, Silver Blaze, in the Wessex Cup race.

BAYNES, INSPECTOR:
"The Adventure of Wisteria Lodge"
aka "A Reminiscence of Mr. Sherlock Holmes"
>
> Of the Surrey Constabulary. He was a stout, puffy, red man, whose face was only redeemed from grossness by two extraordinarily bright eyes.

BAYSWATER:
"The Adventure of the Missing Three-quarter"
>
> Area of London, one of the bus routes.

BEAUCHAMP ARRIANCE:
"The Adventure of the Devil's Foot"
>
> A lonely wooded area where Dr. Leon Sterndale secluded himself between his journeys to Africa.

BECHER, DR.:
"The Adventure of the Engineer's Thumb"
>
> An Englishman, and there isn't a man in the Eyford parish who has a better-lined waistcoat. He is the owner

of the house where Victor Hatherley is taken to perform work for Colonel Lysander Stark. It is this house, which burns down as Holmes and company, arrive at Eyford Station. Is it possible that Mr. Ferguson and Dr. Becher are one and the same?

BECKENHAM:

"The Greek Interpreter"
Location of "The Myrtles," the house wherein Paul and Sophy Kratides are being held prisoners by Harold Latimer and Wilson Kemp.

BEDDINGTON:

"The Stock-Broker's Clerk"
The famous forger and cracksman, who, with his brother, had onlyrecently emerged from a five year spell of penal servitude. He masquerades as Hall Pycroft in order to rob the financial firm of Mawson & William's. He murders the watchman during the robbery and is caught by the police as he leaves the office of the firm.

BEDDOES:

"The 'Gloria Scott'"
Resides in Hampshire, 'friend' of Mr. Hudson and Justice of the Peace Trevor.

AKA Evans, also see EVANS

BEDFORDSHIRE:

"The Adventure of the Blanched Soldier"
Location of Tuxbury Old Hall, it is north of London.

BEECHER, HENRY WARD:

"The Resident Patient"
An unframed portrait stands upon Watson's books in his rooms at Baker Street. Whenever Watson looks at this

portrait he thinks of Beecher's mission, which he took on
behalf of the North, during the American Civil War.

"The Adventure of the Cardboard Box"
An unframed portrait of Henry Ward Beecher sits on top
of Watson's books. He had performed missions on
behalf of the North during the American Civil War.

BELFAST:
"The Adventure of the Cardboard Box"
Post Office from where the package sent to Miss Susan
Cushing, containing two freshly severed human ears, was
postmarked.

BELGRADE:
"The Adventure of the Second Stain"
A memorandum from Belgrade was in the dispatch-box
belonging to the Right Honourable Trelawney Hope.

BELLAMY, MAUD:
"The Adventure of the Lion's Mane"
Miss Maud Bellamy, of Fulworth, was the beauty of the
neighborhood. The daughter of Tom Bellamy, she had
one brother and lived at The Haven with them, her
mother having died some time ago. She was engaged to
Fitzroy McPherson, but they agreed to keep it a secret,
McPherson fearing his dying uncle would disinherit him
should he learn of the marriage plans. She likewise kept
it from her father and brother.

BELLAMY, TED:
"The Adventure of the Lion's Mane"
Father of Maud Bellamy, he owns all the boats and
bathing-cots at Fulworth. He began as a fisherman but is
now a man of substance. His son William assists him in
running the business. He resides at The Haven, as he

calls his home, with his daughter and son. He is a middle-aged man with a flaming red beard.

BELLAMY, WILLIAM:
"The Adventure of the Lion's Mane"
Son of Ted Ballamy, brother to Maud Bellamy, he helps run his fathers business. He is a powerfully built young man, with a heavy, sullen face. He lives at The Haven with his sister and father.

BELLINGER, LORD:
"The Adventure of the Second Stain"
Austere, high-nosed, eagle-eyed, and dominant, he was twice Premier of Britian.

BELLIVER TOR:
"The Hound of the Baskervilles"
A high rocky hill visible from Baskerville Hall.

BENGAL ARTILLERY:
"The Adventure of the Speckled Band"
Major-General Stoner, father of Helena and Julia Stoner, was a member of this unit.

BENITO CANON:
"The Valley of Fear", Part 1: "The Tragedy of Birlstone"
Area of California where John Douglas and Cecil Barker had a successful mining claim.

BENNETT, TREVOR:
"The Adventure of the Creeping Man"
A tall, handsome youth about thirty, he is the professional assistant to Professor Presbury, lives at the Professor's home, and is engaged to the Professor's daughter.

BENTINCK STREET:
> "The Final Problem"
>> London, at the corner of Bentinck and Welbeck Street a two-horse van furiously driven, whizzed round and almost ran Holmes down. This incident occurs just prior to a brick falling from a building on Vere Street and almost striking Holmes on the head.

BENTLEY'S:
> "The Adventure of the Missing Three-quarter"
>> A private hotel in London.

BENZ:
> "His Last Bow" "An Epilogue of Sherlock Holmes"
>> A 100 horsepower automobile used by Baron Von Herling.

BEPPO:
> "The Adventure of the Six Napoleons"
>> An Italian piece-worker who worked for Morse Hudson doing odd jobs. He also worked for Gelder & Co. and while in its employ, knifed another Italian in the street and ran into the Gelder & Co. building, with the police on his heels, to hide. He was captured there.

BERKELEY SQUARE:
> "The Adventure of the Illustrious Client"
>> Section of London where the castle of General de Merville can be found.

BERKSHIRE:
> "The Adventure of the Retired Colourman"
>> Abbas Parva is a small village in Berkshire, a county west of London.

"The Adventure of Shoscombe Old Place"
> Location of Shoscombe Old Place, a county west of London.

BERKSHIRES:
"A Study in Scarlet"
> See Watson, John

BERLIN:
"His Last Bow" "An Epilogue of Sherlock Holmes"
> Capital of Germany.

BERNSTONE, MRS.:
"The Sign of Four"
> Housekeeper and only woman at Pondicherry Lodge.

BERTILLON, ALPHONSE:
"The Hound of the Baskervilles"
> Dr. J. Mortimer believes that he is the highest expert in Europe to the man of precisely scientific mind and that Sherlock Holmes is second.

> See "Bertillon System."

BERTILLON SYSTEM:
"The Naval Treaty"
> A system of measurement devised by the French anthropologist, Alphonse Bertillon. The system records those dimensions of the human body that are least subject to change; it also notes external physical peculiarities, such as deformities, color, fingerprints, etc. The system allows for the prompt identification of an individual. The system is generally used by authorities for the identification of criminals.

BERYL CORONET:

"The Adventure of the Beryl Coronet"

The most precious public possessions of the empire. There are thirty-nine enormous beryls and the price of the gold chasing is incalculable. It was given to Alexander Holder at his bank in exchange for a loan of 50 thousand pounds.

BEVERLEY, BARON:

"The Adventure of the Priory School"

See Holdernesse, Duke of.

BHURTEE:

"The Crooked Man"

Located in India. For more information see Henry Wood.

BIDDLE:

"The Resident Patient"

One of the Worthingdon Bank Gang, after being released from prison, he and his fellow gang members seek out the gang member who turned on them and testified against them -- Sutton. It is believed he died as a passenger of the ill-fated steamer 'Norah Creina,' which was lost with all hands upon the Portuguese coast, some leagues to the north of Oporto.

BILL:

"The Adventure of The Blue Carbuncle"

Helping boy, small youngster working for Mr. Breckinridge.

BILLY:

>"The Valley of Fear", Part 1: "The Tragedy of Birlstone"
>>Holmes' page.

>"The Adventure of the Mazarin Stone"
>>The young, but very wise and tactful page. He has helped
>>to fill the gap of loneliness and isolation, which
>>surrounded Holmes.

BIRD, SIMMON:

>"The Valley of Fear", Part 2: "The Scowrers"
>>Individual killed by the assassins Lawler and Andrews in
>>their past.

BIRLSTONE:

>"The Valley of Fear", Part 1: "The Tragedy of Birlstone"
>>Located in Sussex, scene of the murder of Mr. Douglas.
>>The village is a small and ancient cluster of half-timbered
>>cottages on the northern border of the county of Sussex.

BIRLSTONE MYSTERY:

>"The Valley of Fear", Part 1: "The Tragedy of Birlstone"
>>Name given by Inspector MacDonald to the murder of
>>Mr. Douglas of Birlstone House. Has been a thorn in the
>>'Scowrers' side, and his murder is being planned, to be
>>carried out by Merton County Lodge members.

BIRLSTONE RIDGE:

>"The Valley of Fear", Part 1: "The Tragedy of Birlstone"
>>Ridge near Manor House from where one has a
>>remarkable view over the Weald.

BIRMINGHAM:

>"The Stock-Broker's Clerk"
>>Destination of Holmes, Watson and Mr. Hall Pycroft,
>>Holmes having persuaded Watson to leave his medical

practice with another doctor and to join them in the case.

"The Adventure of the Three Garridebs"
    Northwest of London, about an hour and a half by train.

"The Adventure of the Three Gables"
    Home to the Bull Ring, a boxing gym.

BISHOPGATE:
"The Sign of Four"
    An unrecorded case.
    A jewelry case in which Holmes assist the police.

BITTERN:
"The Hound of the Baskervilles"
    A very rare bird, practically extinct, in England, believed by Mr. Stapleton to be living on the moor.

BLACK FORMOSA CORRUPTION:
"The Adventure of the Dying Detective"
    An Eastern disease.

BLACK JACK OF BALLARAT:
"The Boscombe Valley Mystery"
    See John Turner and Charles McCarthy

BLACK PEARL OF THE BORGIAS:
"The Adventure of the Six Napoleons"
    The most famous pearl in the existing world. It was 'lost' from the bedroom of the Prince of Colonna at the Dacre Hotel.

    AKA 'The Borgias Pearl.'

BLACK STEVE:
"The Adventure of the Three Gables"
> One of the Spencer John gang, he is a great black, muscular man who is foolish, a blustering baby, and easily cowed. A boxer, he claims to have been at the Bull Ring in Birmingham when young Perkins was killed outside the Holborn Bar, although Holmes believes Steve killed Perkins. He has been sent to warn Holmes to stay away from the Harrow area of London.

> AKA Steve

BLACK SWAN HOTEL:
"The Adventure of the Copper Beeches"
> Hotel in Winchester where Holmes and Watson are requested to meet Violet Hunter. It is an inn of repute in the High Street area, at no distance from the rail station.

BLACK TOR:
"The Hound of the Baskervilles"
> One of the hills surrounding Baskerville Hall.

BLACKHEATH:
"The Adventure of the Missing Three-quarter"
> Town in England.

BLACKHEATH STATION:
"The Adventure of the Retired Colourman"
> Train station with trains to London Bridge. Watson notices that he is being followed by a stranger while on business for Holmes in Lewisham.

BLACKWATER, EARL OF:
"The Adventure of the Priory School"
> His son has attended the Priory School.

BLACKWATER, LORD:

"The Adventure of the Noble Bachelor"

Individual who suggests Holmes to Lord St. Simon. Also, it is his place, near Petersfield, where Lord St. Simon and his new wife are to honeymoon. He attended the wedding of Hatty Doran and Lord St. Simon.

BLACKWELL, EVA:

"The Adventure of Charles Augustus Milverton"

Lady Blackwell is the most beautiful debutante of last season. She is to be married to the Earl of Dovercourt. Charles Augustus Milverton is blackmailing her with several imprudent letters.

BLAKER, FOREMAN:

"The Valley of Fear", Part 2: "The Scowrers"

At a meeting of the Lodge 341 Vermissa, Tiger Cormac and young Wilson volunteer to assist the Merton County Lodge 249. When Wilson inquires as to "what has the man done?" He is told it's none of his business, judgment has already been rendered. Ted Baldwin adds: "folk are getting' out of hand in these parts. It was only last week that three of our men were turned off by Foreman Blaker. It's been owing him a long time and he'll get it full and proper."

BLANDFORD STREET:

"The Adventure of the Empty House"

Street in London, connects with Manchester Street.

BLESSINGTON:

"The Resident Patient"

He lives with Dr. Percy Trevelyan, as a resident patient, in the house he let for himself and the Doctor. He is found murdered in his house, hanging from a cord tied to a hook from which a heavy lamp used to hang.

AKA Sutton, See Worthington Bank Gang.

BLONDIN:
"The Sign of Four"
> Name is mentioned but without any additional
> information.

BLOOMSBURY:
"The Adventure of the Blue Carbuncle"
> Town in England where the Alpha Inn is located.

BLOUNT:
"The Adventure of the Lion's Mane"
> A student at The Gables, he and Sudbury were the two
> individuals to find the dead dog, which had belonged to
> Fitzroy McPherson.

BLUE ANCHOR:
"The Adventure of the Retired Colourman"
> A little pub in Lewisham, where Holmes believed Watson
> could have used his "whispering soft nothings with the
> young lady at the Blue Anchor, and receiving hard
> somethings in exchange." Which in fact Watson failed to
> do.

THE BLUE CARBUNCLE:
"The Adventure of The Blue Carbuncle"
> A jewel that glints and sparkles, not yet 20 years old, it
> was found in the bank of the Amoy River in southern
> China. It has every characteristic of the carbuncle except
> it is blue instead of red. "There have been two murders,
> a vitriol-throwing, a suicide, and several robberies
> brought about for the sake of this forty-grain weight of
> crystallized charcoal."

BLYMER:
"The Adventure of the Mazarin Stone"
Estate of Mrs. Harold. See Harold, Mrs.

BOER WAR:
"The Adventure of the Blanched Soldier"
Had just ended when this case comes to Holmes. The case itself involves two men who had fought in the war.

BOHEMIA, KING OF:
"A Scandal in Bohemia"
"A man ... who could hardly have been less than six feet six inches in height, with the chest and limbs of Hercules. His dress was rich with richness, which would, in England, be looked upon as akin to bad taste. Heavy bands of astrakhan were slashed across the sleeves and fronts of his double-breasted coat, while the deep blue cloak, which was thrown over his shoulders, was lined with flamed-coloured silk and secured at the neck with a brooch, which consisted of a single flaming beryl. Boots which extended halfway up his calves, and which were trimmed at the tops with rich brown fur, completed the impression of barbaric opulence, which was suggested by his whole appearance. He carried a broad-brimmed hat in his hand, while he wore across the upper part of his face, extending down past the cheekbones, a black vizard mask ... From the lower part of the face he appeared to be a man of strong character, with a thick, hanging lip, and a long straight chin suggestive of resolution pushed to the length of obstinacy."

Informed Holmes that "The august person who employs me wishes his agent to be unknown to you". And further states "... I may confess at once that the title by which I have just called myself is not exactly my own."

Discusses possibility of an "immense scandal [which would] seriously compromise one of the reigning families of Europe." "The matter implicates the great House of Ormstein, hereditary kings of Bohemia."

AKA: Wilhelm Gottsreich Sigismond Von Ormstein, Grand Duke of Cassel-Felstein, hereditary King of Bohemia.

AKA: Count Von Kramm

"His Last Bow" "An Epilogue of Sherlock Holmes"
See Heinrich
See Adler, Irene

BOND STREET:
"The Hound of the Baskervilles"
Picture galleries line the street, where Holmes and Watson go to kill some time.

"THE BOOK OF LIFE":
"A Study in Scarlet"
Written by Sherlock Holmes, it attempted to show how much an observant man might learn by an accurate and systematic examination of all that came his way.

BOONE, HUGH:
"The Man With The Twisted Lip"
A sinister cripple living on the second floor of the opium den, Bar of Gold. A shock of orange hair, a pale face disfigured by a horrible scar, which, by its contraction, has turned up the outer edge of his upper lip: (a broad wheal from an old scar ran right across his face from eye to chin, and by its contraction had turned up one side of the upper lip, so that three teeth were exposed in a

perpetual snarl), a bulldog chin, and a pair of very penetrating dark eyes, which present a singular contrast to the colour of his hair. A professional beggar, but to avoid police regulations he pretends to a small trade in wax vestas some little distance down Threadneedle Street collecting money in a greasy leather cap.

AKA Neville St. Clair.
See St. Clair, Neville.

BORGIAS PEARL:
"The Adventure of the Six Napoleons"
"Black Pearl of the Borgias"

BORK, VON:
"His Last Bow" "An Epilogue of Sherlock Holmes"
A German agent of the Kaiser.

BOROUGH:
"The Hound of the Baskervilles"
A section of London, Turpey Street runs through it. Location of the residence of John Clayton, cab driver, cab No. 2704.

BOSCOMBE POOL:
"The Boscombe Valley Mystery"
"A small lake formed by the spreading out of the stream which runs down the Boscombe Valley", it is thickly wooded, with just a fringe of grass and reeds round the edge. "Is a little reed-girt sheet of water some fifty yards across, is situated at the boundary between the Hatherley Farm and the private park of the wealthy Mr. Turner."

BOSCOMBE VALLEY:
"The Boscombe Valley Mystery"
"a country district not very far from Ross, in Herefordshire."

THE BOSCOMBE VALLEY MYSTERY:
Published in "The Strand": October 1891
Published as part of: "The Adventures of Sherlock Holmes"
Holmes and Watson investigate the murder of Charles McCarthy. Holmes is able to conclude who the murderer is but chooses not to turn him into the police due to a serious illness and allows him to live out the short time he has left. The case involves a dark past coming back to haunt the murderer.

BOSWELL:
"A Scandal in Bohemia"
Holmes refers to Dr. Watson as "my Boswell."

BOVINGTON'S:
"The Disappearance of Lady Frances Carfax"
A pawnshop in Westminster Road where an old Spanish pendant had recently been pawned. It had belonged to Lady Frances Carfax.

BOWERY:
"The Adventure of the Red Circle"
Section of New York where Tito Castalotte, of Castalotte and Zamba, is attacked by thugs and saved by Gennaro Lucca.

BRACKENSTALL, EUSTACE:
"The Adventure of the Abbey Grange"
Sir Eustace Brackenstall is one of the richest men in Kent. He is also known as a confirmed drunkard.

BRACKENSTALL, LADY:

"The Adventure of the Abbey Grange"

Wife of Sir Eustace Brackenstall, they have been married about a year, although their marriage has not been a happy one. She has a graceful figure, a womanly presence and beautiful face. She was a blue-eyed blonde. She was brought up in South Australia. Came to England 18 months ago. Maiden name: Miss Mary Fraser of Adelaide.

BRADLEY:

"The Hound of the Baskervilles"

Of Oxford Street, brand of cigarette smoked by Watson.

BRADSTREET, INSPECTOR:

"The Man With The Twisted Lip"

A tall, stout official, wearing a peaked cap and frogged jacket. A member of the force for some twenty-seven years. Arrest Hugh Boone after the disappearance of Neville St. Clair.

"The Adventure of the Engineer's Thumb"

Of Scotland Yard, joins Holmes, Watson, and Victor Hatherley on trip to Eyford to investigate the home of Dr. Becher, where Colonel Lysander Stark, Elsie, and Mr. Ferguson are working on some kind of undertaking.

"The Adventure of The Blue Carbuncle"

From Division B, gave evidence as to the arrest of John Horner on December 22 for the theft of the "Blue Carbuncle".

BRAMBLETYE HOTEL:

"The Adventure of Black Peter"

Hotel where Watson and Holmes stay while investigating the murder of Peter Carey.

BRECKINRIDGE:
"The Adventure of The Blue Carbuncle"
A salesman in Covent Garden.

Proprietor of one of the largest stalls at Covent Garden Market. A horsy-looking man, with a sharp face and trim side-whiskers.

BREWER, SAM:
"The Adventure of Shoscombe Old Place"
A well-known moneylender from Curzon Street. Sir Robert Norberton beat him, nearly to death on Newmarket Heath.

BRIARBRAE:
"The Naval Treaty"
Home of Percy Phelps and his parents. A large detached house standing in extensive grounds within a few minutes walk of the railroad station.

BRICKFALL AND AMBERLEY:
"The Adventure of the Retired Colourman"
Manufacturers of artistic materials, their name appears on paint-boxes. Josiah Amberley is a junior partner in the business.

BRIONY LODGE:
"A Scandal in Bohemia"
"It is a bijou villa, with a garden at the back, but built out in front right up to the road, two stories. Chubb lock to the door. Large sitting-room on the right side, well furnished, with windows almost to the floor, and those preposterous English window fasteners, which a child could open. Behind there was nothing remarkable, save

that the passage window could be reached from the top of the coach-house."

BRISTOL:
"The Boscombe Valley Mystery"
James McCarthy got into the clutches of a barmaid in Bristol and married her at a registry office. She, finding that he was in serious trouble and likely to be hanged, threw him over utterly and wrote to him that she had a husband already in the Bermuda Dockyard.

BRITISH BARROW:
"The Adventure of the Golden Pince-Nez"
An unrecorded case, took place in 1894. A case involving the singular contents of the ancient British barrow.

BRITISH BIRDS:
"The Adventure of the Empty House"
Book offered for sale to Watson by a little old bookseller from his neighborhood.

BRITISH BROKEN HILLS:
"The Stock-Broker's Clerk"
Stock selling for 'seven to seven-and-six.' Mr. Arthur Pinner ask for this quote as a test of Mr. Hall Pycroft's knowledge of the financial market.

BRITISH MEDICAL JOURNAL:
"The Stock-Broker's Clerk"
Watson is reading the Journal when, much to his surprise, he hears Holmes at his door.

"The Adventure of the Blanched Soldier"
Holmes notes that had the man James Dodd saw in the outer cottage been reading the British Medical Journal, it would have helped solve the matter quicker.

BRITISH MUSEUM:

"The Adventure of Wisteria Lodge"
aka "A Reminiscence of Mr. Sherlock Holmes"

> Holmes visits the museum during his investigation into the strange happenings at Wisteria Lodge. He finds and studies the text "Voodooism and the Negroid Religions."

"The Adventure of the Red Circle"

> Great Orme Street is at its northeast side and Howe Street is nearby.

BRIXTON MYSTERY:

"A Study in Scarlet"

> Name the press gave to the affair, which had occurred at 3 Lauriston Gardens, off the Brixton Road, the location of the murder of one Enoch J. Drebber.

BRIXTON WORKHOUSE INFIRMARY:

"The Disappearance of Lady Frances Carfax"

> Infirmary for the poor; Rose Spender, the supposed nurse of Fraser is found their by Fraser and Holy Peters and taken to their home where she dies peacefully.

BROADMOOR:

"The Adventure of the Retired Colourman"

> Mental hospital for criminals, Holmes believes that Josiah Amberley is headed there instead of prison at the conclusion of the case.

BROOK STREET:

"The Resident Patient"

> Street where Dr. Percy Trevelyan resides.

BROOKLYN:
"The Adventure of the Red Circle"
In New York, it is where Gennaro and Emilia Lucca lived in a little house during their time in America.

BROOKS:
"The Adventure of the Bruce-Partington Plans"
One of fifty men Holmes believes has good reason for killing him.

BROTHERHOOD:
"The Adventure of the Golden Pince-Nez"
Group pent on avenging the imprisonment and death of members of the Order by the traitor, Sergius.

BROWN, JOSIAH:
"The Adventure of the Six Napoleons"
Resides at Laburnum Lodge, Laburnum Vale, Chiswick. He is a rotund figure. He purchased a bust of Napoleon from Harding Brothers.

BROWNER, JIM:
"The Adventure of the Cardboard Box"
Husband of Mary (Cushing) Browner, he is a steward aboard the ship 'May Day'.

He was employed on the South American line before his marriage but changed to the Liverpool and London boats to be nearer his wife. He is a big, powerful man, clean-shaven, and very swarthy. His wife allows her sister Sarah to move in with them and Sarah eventually tries to seduce Jim. He rejects Sarah's advances causing her to turn his wife against him and toanother man, Alec Fairbairn.

Jim Browner observes his wife and Fairbairn together, follows and kills hem both, sending Fairbairn's ears to Sarah Cushing just as he had threatened he would if she continued to interfere in his marriage.

BRUCE-PARTINGTON SUBMARINE:
"The Adventure of the Bruce-Partington Plans"

Plans of the submarine were found on the dead body of Arthur Cadogan West. Ten papers were taken from Woolwich, however, only seven were found in the pocket of Arthur Cadogan West. The three most important were stolen.

BRUCE PINKERTON:
"The Resident Patient"

A prize and medal awarded to individuals: Dr. Percy Trevelyan won it for his monograph on nervous lesions.

BRUNTON, RICHARD:
"The Musgrave Ritual"

Butler at the Manor House of Hurlstone. He was a young schoolmaster prior to taking the position as butler, having been hired by Reginald Musgrave's father.

He was a man of great energy and character, well-grown, handsome, with a splendid forehead. He is a bit of a Don Juan. He was married but is now widowed and has been recently engaged to Rachel Howells, a second housemaid at the Manor House of Hurlstone, however he has thrown her over and taken up with the gamekeepers daughter, Janet Tregellis. He was dismissed by Reginal Musgrave when discovered in the library going through private documents of the Musgrave family.

Found dead in the cellar of the Manor House of Hurlstone by Holmes and Reginald Musgrave. Holmes concludes Brunton and Howells were conspirators in the

search of the Musgrave treasure and he further
concludes that Howells was responsible for the death of
Brunton.

BUDA:
"The Adventure of the Devil's Foot"
City in Europe where a laboratory has the only known
specimen of 'devil's root' outside of Africa and not in the
possession of Dr. Leon Sterndale.

BUDA-PESHT:
"The Greek Interpreter"
In Hungry, where the bodies of Harold Latimer and
Wilson Kemp are found with stab wounds. The
Hungarian police believe they killed each other during a
fight.

BUFFALO:
"His Last Bow" "An Epilogue of Sherlock Holmes"
Altamont graduated into an Irish secret society here.

See Altamont.

THE BULL:
"The Adventure of Wisteria Lodge"
aka "A Reminiscence of Mr. Sherlock Holmes"
An Inn where Holmes and Watson take quarters in the
pretty Surrey village of Esher.

BULL, JOHN:
"His Last Bow" "An Epilogue of Sherlock Holmes"
A name used to signify the English people, a
personification of the citizens of England.

BULL RING:

"The Adventure of the Three Gables"

Boxing gym in Birmingham, frequented by the black boxer, Steve.

BURNET, MISS:

"The Adventure of Wisteria Lodge"

aka "A Reminiscence of Mr. Sherlock Holmes"

Governess to Mr. Henderson's two daughters. She is English and about forty years old.

BURNWELL, SIR GEORGE:

"The Adventure of the Beryl Coronet"

Friend of Arthur Holder. A man of the world, has been everywhere, seen everything, a brilliant talker, and a man of great personal beauty. His eyes reveal someone who should not be trusted. Conspires with Mary Holder, Alexander Holder's niece, to steal the Beryl Coronet. Arthur Holder catches him in the act and a piece of the chasing is broken off containing three stones. He flees England with Mary Holder after being confronted by Holmes.

BUSY BEE AND EXCELSIOR:

"The Adventure of the Creeping Man"

English firm with the motto: "We can but try."

CHAPTER C

CAFE ROYAL:
>"The Adventure of the Illustrious Client"
>>Located in Regent Street, it was the seen of a "Murderous Attack Upon Sherlock Holmes."

CAIRNS, PATRICK:
>"The Adventure of Black Peter"
>>A fierce bull-dog face, tangled hair and beard, he had dark eyes, which gleamed behind the cover of thick, tufted, and overhung eyebrows. He was sent to Captain Basil by Sumner, Shipping Agent, having been a harpooner of twenty-six missions.
>>
>>He murdered Peter Carey. Claimed to have done so in self-defense. Witnessed Peter Carey's killing of Neligan at sea after Neligan had been saved by members of the 'Sea Unicorn' while at sea.

CALHOUN, CAPTAIN JAMES:
>"The Five Orange Pips"
>>Address - Bark "Lone Star," Savannah, Georgia. Leader of the gang responsible for the orange pips letters. Watson informs us that it appears that the "Lone Star" was lost at sea, and Calhoun and his two confederates all died.

CAMBERWELL:
>"The Disappearance of Lady Frances Carfax"
>>Miss Dobney, ex-governess for Lady Carfax, lives in Camberwell since her retirement as governess.

>"The Valley of Fear", Part 1: "The Tragedy of Birlstone"
>>Area of London from where Fred Porlock sent Holmes a secret message.

THE CAMBERWELL POISONING:
>"The Five Orange Pips"
>>An unrecorded case. Holmes was able, by winding up the dead man's watch, to prove that it had been wound up two hours before, and that the deceased had gone to bed within that time -- a deduction which was of the greatest importance in clearing up the case.

CAMBRIDGE:
>"The Adventure of the Golden Pince-Nez"
>>University attended by Willoughby Smith.

>"The Adventure of the Missing Three-quarter"
>>Town in England, home of Trinity College.

CAMDEN HOUSE:
>"The Adventure of the Empty House"
>>Located on Baker Street opposite 221B Baker Street.

CAMFORD:
>"The Adventure of the Creeping Man"
>>English town where Professor Presbury is a university professor of physiology. The inn Chequers is also located there.

CAMPDEN HOUSE ROAD:
>"The Adventure of the Six Napoleons"
>>A smashed bust of Napoleon is found in the yard of an empty house on this street in London.

CAMPDEN MANSIONS:
>"The Adventure of the Bruce-Partington Plans"
>>Residence of Louis La Rothiere one of the few men Mycroft Holmes believes could   be able to dispose of the stolen Bruce-Partington papers. Located in Notting Hill.

CANADIAN PACIFIC RAILWAY:
 "The Adventure of Black Peter"
  Notations found in Peter Carey's hut reveal his interest in
  the Canadian Pacific Railway's stock.

CANDAHAR:
 "A Study in Scarlet"
  See Watson, John.

CANTERBURY:
 "The Final Problem"
  Train depot in England.

CANTLEMERE, LORD:
 "The Adventure of the Mazarin Stone"
  A thin, austere figure with a hatchet face and drooping
  mid-Victorian whiskers of a glossy blackness. He is the
  protector of the Crown Diamond and one of the few
  who believe that Holmes's popularity is ill-founded and
  wishes he would fail in his attempt to retrieve the Crown
  Diamond. After Holmes has successfully obtained the
  Crown Diamond, he slips it into the pocket of the
  unsuspecting Lord Cantlemere and suggests arresting his
  Lordship. Lord Cantlemere is completely taken aback
  but Holmes diffuses the situation with acknowledgment
  of his little joke by saying: "My old friend here will tell
  you that I have an impish habit of practical joking. Also
  that I can never resist a dramatic situation."

CAPE TOWN:
 "The Valley of Fear", Part 2: "The Scowrers"
  Destination in South Africa of John and Ivy Douglas
  after the tragedy at Birlstone. John is lost overboard
  during a gale off St. Helena; he never makes it to Cape
  Town.

CAPITAL AND COUNTIES BANK:

"The Man With The Twisted Lip"
>Bank wherein Mr. Neville St. Clair maintained a bank account with a balance of 220 pounds.

"The Adventure of the Priory School"
>Where Holmes banks, it has a branch on Oxford Street.

"The Adventure of the Bruce-Partington Plans"
>It has a branch in Woolwich where Arthur Cadogan West had a checking account.

CARBONARI:

"The Adventure of the Red Circle"
>Criminal organization in Italy, it became closely connected with the 'Red Circle' another Italian criminal organization.

CAREY, PETER:

"The Adventure of Black Peter"
>Captain: he was born in 1845, being 50 years of age. He was a most daring and successful seal and whale fisherman. In 1883 he commanded the steam sealer 'Sea Unicorn' of Dundee. He retired in 1884, traveled for some years and finally settled down at a small place called Woodman's Lee, near Forest Row, in Sussex.
>
>He was a strict Puritan, silent and gloomy. His household consisted of his wife and daughter and two female servants. He was known to flog his wife and daughter regularly.

He was known in the trade as Black Peter, not only due to his swarthy features and the color of his huge beard but for the humours, which were the terror of all around him.

CAREY, MRS.:
"The Adventure of Black Peter"
Wife of Peter Carey, she is a haggard, gray-haired woman.

CARFAX, FRANCES:
"The Disappearance of Lady Frances Carfax"
Lady Frances Carfax is the sole survivor of the direct family of the late Earl of Rufton. She was left with limited means but clings to some old Spanish jewelry, which she is fondly attached. She is a beautiful woman, still in middle age but a rather pathetic figure. She is not more than forty. Lady Carfax is a woman of precise habits, she has written every second week for four years to her long retired governess, but has not done so for the last five weeks. She is discovered in a false bottom of a coffin by Holmes at the home of Holy Peter and Fraser.

CARINA:
"The Adventure of the Retired Colourman"
Opera star that was scheduled to sing at the Albert Hall, Holmes and Watson decide to take in the show.

CARLO:
"The Adventure of the Copper Beeches"
Mastiff belonging to Jephro Rucastle, actually under the control of the groom, Toller.

CARLO:

"The Adventure of the Sussex Vampire"

The Ferguson dog, a spaniel, he has Spinal meningitis. Holmes is curious about the dog and inquires into the dog's illness. The illness appeared to have come on quite quickly, one night, some four months ago. Holmes is able to deduce that the dog was a test case for a poison that was to be used on the Ferguson baby, to kill it.

CARLTON HOUSE TERRACE:

"The Adventure of the Priory School"

Home to the Duke of Holdernesse.

CARNAWAY, JIM:

"The Valley of Fear", Part 2: "The Scowrers"

Was struck down doing the work of the Vermissa Lodge 341 'Eminent Order of Freeman.' His wife receives a pension of sorts from the lodge. He was killed trying to kill Chester Wilcox of Marley Creek.

CARRITON'S:

"The Adventure of the Sussex Vampire"

Name of house in Cheeman's, Lamberley, where homes are known by the names of those who built them.

CARRUTHERS, BOB:

"The Adventure of the Solitary Cyclist"

An older man, he was agreeable. He was dark, sallow, clean-shaven, silent person, but he had polite manners and a pleasant smile. A friend of Ralph Smith of Africa. He requested that Miss Violet Smith teach his ten year old daughter music. Miss Smith would be paid at a rate of a hundred a year. He was doing this at the request of his friend, Ralph Smith, who had died poor but requested his niece be looked after. He is fairly well-to-do, going into the city two or three times a week. He has a keen interest in South African gold shares. He conspires with Roaring Jack Woodley to have Miss Violet Smith marry Woodley so they can have the young lady's inheritance from Ralph Smith. He falls in love with Miss Smith during the plan and attempts to help her in the end. Shoots Roaring Jack Woodley at the conclusion of the marriage ceremony binding Woodley and Miss Violet Smith. Watson has recollection as to what sentence Carruthers received from his trial but believes a few months was all that justice required.

CARRUTHERS, COLONEL:
"The Adventure of Wisteria Lodge"
aka "A Reminiscence of Mr. Sherlock Holmes"
An unrecorded case. Holmes was responsible for locking the Colonel up prior to being presented with "The Adventure of Wisteria Lodge."

CARSTON CASTLE:
"The Adventure of the Priory School"
Home to the Duke of Holdernesse, it is located in Bangor, Wales.

CARSTON, EARL OF:
"The Adventure of the Priory School"
See Holdernesse, Duke of.

CARTER:
"The Valley of Fear", Part 2: "The Scowrers"
A brutal young assassin, he is a member of the Vermissa Lodge of 'Scowrers.'

CARTER:
"The Valley of Fear", Part 2: "The Scowrers"
The treasurer of the Vermissa Lodge of the 'Eminent Order of Freemen', he was a middle-aged man, with an

impassive, rather sulky expression, and yellow parchment skin. A capable organizer, his plotting brain was responsible for the actual details of nearly every outrage planned by the 'Scowrers.' He is one of the seven chosen to capture the Pinkerton man, Birdy Edwards. He was arrested by Captain Marvin and Edwards while waiting with his comrades to capture Edwards and kill him.

CARTWRIGHT:
"The Hound of the Baskervilles"
>Fourteen years old, runner for the district messenger office managed by Mr. Wilson. Cartwright had been helpful to Holmes when Holmes helped Mr. Wilson out some time ago. He was a bright, keen faced young man.

CASTALOTTE, TITO:
"The Adventure of the Red Circle"
>The senior partner of the great firm of Castalotte and Zamba, chief fruit importers of New York. He was attacked by thugs in the Bowery section of New York and saved by Gennaro Lucca, to whom he provides a job and friendship. He refuses to pay money to the 'Red Circle' and in-turn provides information to the police. He is marked for death by Gorgiano and the 'Red Circle' but is warned by Gennaro, who is supposed to kill him.

CASTALOTTE AND ZAMBA:
"The Adventure of the Red Circle"
>Chief fruit importers of New York, Tito Castalotte is the senior partner and after Gennaro Lucca saves his life he provides Gennaro with employment.

CATULLUS:
"The Adventure of the Empty House"
>Book offered for sale to Watson by a little old bookseller from his neighborhood.

CAULFIELD GARDENS:
> "The Adventure of the Bruce-Partington Plans"
>> Number 13 is the home of Hugo Oberstein one of the few men Mycroft Holmes believes could be able to dispose of the stolen Bruce-Partington papers. It is located in Kensington. It is one of those lines of flat-faced pillared, and porticoed houses, which are so prominent a product of the middle Victorian epoch in the West End of London.

CAVENDISH SQUARE:
> "The Resident Patient"
>> Prime medical business location. A specialist who aims high is compelled to start in one of a dozen streets in this quarter, all of which entail enormous rents and furnishing expenses.

CAVENDISH STREET:
> "The Adventure of the Empty House"
>> Street in London.

THE CEDARS:
> "The Man With The Twisted Lip"
>> Home to Mr. Neville St. Clair, where Holmes is staying while looking into the disappearance of Mr. St. Clair. Located near Lee, in Kent.

CHAIRMAN OF COMMITTEES:
> "The Hound of the Baskervilles"
>> Office held by Sir William Baskerville in the House of Commons under Pitt.

CHALDEAN:
> "The Adventure of the Devil's Foot"
>> See Cornish Language.

CHANDOS, CHARLES:
"The Valley of Fear", Part 1: "The Tragedy of Birlstone"
Ames served as butler to Sir Charles for ten years prior to becoming butler for Mr. John Douglas.

THE CHANNEL:
"His Last Bow" "An Epilogue of Sherlock Holmes"
Von Bork, the German spy, had a safe containing pigeon-holes bristling with papers and plans, each with its own label. One of these compartments was labeled "The Channel."

CHARING CROSS:
"The Greek Interpreter"
Section of London.

"The Adventure of the Golden Pince-Nez"
Has a train to the Chatham/Kent area of England.

"The Adventure of Wisteria Lodge"
aka "A Reminiscence of Mr. Sherlock Holmes"
A section of London, has its own post office.

"The Problem of Thor Bridge"
Location of Cox and Co., bank used by Watson to store his papers.

CHARING CROSS HOSPITAL:
"The Hound of the Baskervilles"
Dr. J. Mortimer had been house-surgeon from 1882 to 1884 at Charing Cross Hospital in London.

"The Adventure of the Illustrious Client"
Where Holmes is taken after being beaten, by two men armed with sticks, outside the Cafe Royal.

CHARING CROSS HOTEL:
"The Adventure of the Bruce-Partington Plans"
> Hotel in London where Colonel Walter's is to meet Hugo Oberstein with additional Bruce-Partington papers, however, it is a trap set by Sherlock Holmes and Hugo Oberstein is captured there with the missing Bruce-Partington papers.

CHARING CROSS STATION:
"The Adventure of the Abbey Grange"
> Train station in London.

"The Adventure of the Second Stain"
> Train station in London, Mme. Henri Fournaye was seen there the day after Eduardo Lucas was found murdered.

"The Adventure of the Illustrious Client"
> Train station in London, near Baker Street.

CHARLES THE FIRST:
"The Musgrave Ritual"
> Coins found as part of the Musgrave treasure were coins of Charles the First, he who was executed. He is referred to in the 'Musgrave Ritual' as "Whose was it?" "His who is gone." Of the royal Stuarts, kings of England.

CHARLES THE SECOND:
"The Musgrave Ritual"
> His right-hand man was Sir Ralph Musgrave. He is referred to in the 'Musgrave Ritual' as "He who will come." Of the royal Stuarts, kings of England.

CHARLES STREET:
> "The Naval Treaty"
>> Connects with Whitehall at the offices of the foreign minister, a side door, from the building housing the foreign minister's offices, opens onto Charles Street.

CHARLINGTON HALL:
> "The Adventure of the Solitary Cyclist"
>> A very old residence where Miss Violet Smith stays during the week to teach music to the daughter of Mr. Carruthers. According to a well-known firm in Pall Mall, an elderly gentleman, Mr. Williamson, rented it in March 1895.

CHARLINGTON HEATH:
> "The Adventure of the Solitary Cyclist"
>> Area along the road from Farnham Station to Chiltern Grange, about a mile from Charlington Hall.

CHARLINGTON WOOD:
> "The Adventure of the Solitary Cyclist"
>> Wooded area surrounding Charlington Hall. It is here that the forced marriage of Miss Violet Smith to Mr. Woodly takes place.

CARLTON CLUB:
> "The Adventure of the Illustrious Client"
>> A private club in London.

CHARLTON TERRACE:
> "His Last Bow" "An Epilogue of Sherlock Holmes"
>> Baron Von Herling is headed there after having met with Von Bork about the 'Naval Signals' and their expected arrival.

CHARPENTIER, ALICE:

"A Study in Scarlet"

Daughter of Madame Charpentier, and sister to Navy second-lieutenant, Arthur Charpentier. Her brother comes to her rescue when she is accosted by Mr. Enoch J. Drebber, who later is found murdered.

CHARPENTIER, ARTHUR:

"A Study in Scarlet"

A sub-lieutenant in Her Majesty's navy. Arrested by Gregson as the murderer of Enoch J. Drebber.

CHARPENTIER, MADAME:

"A Study in Scarlet"

Runs a boarding house in Torquay Terrace where Enoch J. Drebber resided. Her son is arrested by Gregson of Scotland Yard for the murder of Enoch J. Drebber.

CHATHAM:

"The Adventure of the Golden Pince-Nez"
Seven miles from Kent.

CHATHAM ROAD:

"The Adventure of the Golden Pince-Nez"

Road, which runs from Chatham to London, it is near the garden gate of Yoxley Old Place.

CHEESEMAN'S:

"The Adventure of the Sussex Vampire"

In Lamberley, Sussex, it is an area of old homes, which are named after the men who built them.

CHESTERFIELD:

"The Adventure of the Priory School"

Town near Machleton, Reuben Hayes is arrested there on the alarm of Holmes.

CHEQUERS:
"The Adventure of the Creeping Man"
An inn in Camford where Holmes and Watson spend the night while investigating the case of Professor Presbury.

CHEQUERS:
"The Adventure of the Sussex Vampire"
Hotel in Lamberley where Holmes and Watson stay while investigating the Ferguson vampire matter.

CHESTERTON:
"The Adventure of the Missing Three-quarter"
A sleepy hollow in England.

CHICAGO:
"His Last Bow" "An Epilogue of Sherlock Holmes"
Where Altamont began his charade.
See Altamont.

"The Valley of Fear", Part 1: "The Tragedy of Birlstone"
Cecil Barker stated that John Douglas knew the city well and had worked there prior to moving to California and then England.

"The Valley of Fear", Part 2: "The Scowrers"
John McMurdo of Chicago has moved to Vermissa in the Vermissa Valley from his home in Chicago after an altercation in which the police became interested.

CHILTERN GRANGE:
"The Adventure of the Solitary Cyclist"
About six miles from Farnham.

CHISELHURST STATION:
"The Adventure of the Abbey Grange"
Located between Charing Cross Station and Kent.

CHRISTIE'S:
"The Adventure of the Three Garridebs"
The auctioneer house in London.

"The Adventure of the Illustrious Client"
Auction house in London.

CHISWICK:
"The Adventure of the Six Napoleons"
Near London.

CHOWDAR, LAL:
"The Sign of Four"
Servant to Major John Sholto, now dead. Assisted the Major in the disposal of the body of Captain Arthur Morstan.

CHRONICLE:
"Silver Blaze"
Newspaper in London, maybe the same as "The Morning Chronicle."

CHUBB'S KEY:
"The Adventure of the Golden Pince-Nez"
A key kept by the Professor on his watch-chain. It opens a wooden bureau and it is not a simple key.

CHURCH OF ST. MONICA:
"A Scandal in Bohemia"
In the Edgeware Road Church where Holmes plays witness to the marriage of IRENE ADLER to Godfrey Norton.

CHURCH ROW:
> "The Adventure of Charles Augustus Milverton"
>> Section of London.

CHURCH STREET:
> "The Adventure of the Empty House"
>> Near Kensington, where a little old man has a bookshop.

> "The Adventure of the Six Napoleons"
>> Street in Stepney where Gelder & Co. is located.

CLAPHAM JUNCTION:
> "Silver Blaze"
>> A train depot.

> "The Greek Interpreter"
>> A mile or so from Wandsworth Common. A train depot with trains heading to Victoria.

CLARIDGE'S HOTEL:
> "His Last Bow" "An Epilogue of Sherlock Holmes"
>> Hotel in London.

> "The Problem of Thor Bridge"
>> Hotel in London where Neil Gibson stays while preparing to meet and retain Sherlock Holmes in the death of Mr. Gibson's wife and the arrest of their governess for the murder.

CLAY, JOHN:
> "The Red-Headed League"
>> A young man: " ... murderer, thief, smasher, and forger." Head of his profession, "His grandfather was a royal duke, and he himself has been to Eton and Oxford. His brain is as cunning as his fingers, ... " Captured

breaking into one of the principal London banks by Holmes in the conclusion to "The Red-Headed League".

CLAYTON, JOHN:
"The Hound of the Baskervilles"

Hansom cab driver, his cab is No. 2704 out of Shipley's Yard, near the Waterloo Station. He lives at 3 Turpey Street, the Borough. Picked up a passenger at half-past nine and was instructed to go to the Northumberland Hotel and then follow the cab of two gentlemen. The passenger claimed to be a detective, Sherlock Holmes.

CLEFT TOR:
"The Hound of the Baskervilles"

About a mile or two from Baskerville Hall, appears to be from where Selden has been signaling the Barrymores after his escape from prison.

CLOTILDE LOTHMAN VON SAXE-MENINGEN:
"A Scandal in Bohemia"

Second daughter of the King of Scandinavia. Her plan to marry WILHELM GOTTSREICH SIGISMOND VON ORMSTEIN is the underlying premise of "A Scandal in Bohemia"

COBB, JOHN:
"The Boscombe Valley Mystery"

The groom at Hatherley Farm.

COBURG SQUARE:
"The Red-Headed League"

Location of Mr. Jabez Wilson's pawnbroker business.
AKA: Saxe-Coburg Square

COCAINE:
> See Holmes, Sherlock
> See Drug Use

COCKSURE, MR.:
> "The Adventure of The Blue Carbuncle"
>> Mr. Breckinridge calls Sherlock Holmes by this name as he checks his books concerning whether or not the goose belonging to Mr. Henry Baker was county or city bred.

COLDSTREAM GUARDS:
> "The Naval Treaty"
>> Military regiment of which Mr. Tangey, commissionaire to the foreign minister, was a member.

COLLEGE OF ST. LUKE'S:
> "The Adventure of the Three Students"
>> School where the Fortescue Scholarship examination is being given. Hilton Soames is a tutor, lecturer, and is the examiner of Greek for the Scholarship exam.

COLONNA, PRINCE OF:
> "The Adventure of the Six Napoleons"
>> He 'lost' the Black Pearl of the Borgias while staying at the Dacre Hotel.

COMMERCIAL ROAD:
> "The Adventure of the Creeping Man"
>> London street where a store belonging to one Dorak is located.

CONK-SINGLETON:
> "The Adventure of the Six Napoleons"
>> An unrecorded case involving forgery which Holmes picks up after clearing up "The Adventure of the Six Napoleons."

CONQUEROR:
>"The Adventure of the Cardboard Box"
>>One of the Liverpool and London boats.

CONTINENTAL GAZETTEER:
>"A Scandal in Bohemia"
>>Book used by Holmes for reference. In "A Scandal in Bohemia" he researches the "contraction" "Eg" to discover it refers to EGRIA a country in Bohemia where German is spoken, is remarkable as "being the scene of the death of Wallenstein, numerous glass-factories and paper-mills".

COOEE:
>"The Boscombe Valley Mystery"
>>An Australian cry used between Australians.

COOK, POLICE-CONSTABLE:
>"The Five Orange Pips"
>>Of H Division, on duty near Waterloo Bridge when he heard the cry for help from John Openshaw. Because the night was extremely dark and stormy it was impossible to effect a rescue.

COOK'S:
>"The Disappearance of Lady Frances Carfax"
>>A local shipping office in Luasanne. Watson is able to obtain information as to Lady Frances Carfax's luggage and where it was sent upon her departure from the Hotel National.

COOLIES:
>"The Adventure of the Dying Detective"
>>A people of Sumatra.

COOMBE TRACEY:
"The Hound of the Baskervilles"
Town near Baskerville Hall where Laura Lyons lives.

THE COPPER BEECHES:
"The Adventure of the Copper Beeches"
Located in Hampshire, five miles on the far side of
Winchester. It is a large square block of house,
whitewashed, but all stained and streaked with damp and
bad weather. There are grounds around it, woods on
three sides, and on the fourth a field, which slopes down
to the Southampton highroad. A clump of copper
beeches immediately in front of the hall door has given
its name to the place.

COPTIC PATRIARCHS:
"The Adventure of the Retired Colourman"
An unrecorded case. It involves two Coptic Patriachs of
the Coptic Church, which is the native Christian Church
of Egypt and Ethiopia.

CORAM, PROFESSOR:
"The Adventure of the Golden Pince-Nez"
An elderly old professor, he had taken the Yoxley Old
Place some years ago. An invalid, he spends much of his
time in bed, hobbling around the house, or being pushed
around the grounds in a Bath chair by his gardener. He is
writing a learned book, an analysis of the documents
found in the Coptic monasteries of Syria and Egypt, and
required a secretary, the first two were not successful, but
the third, Mr. Willoughby Smith, was just right. He was a
member of the Order, a group of revolutionaries,
Nihilists. After the killing of a police officer in Russia, he
turned traitor sending his wife and the man she really

loved, Alexis, to prison in Siberia. He received a reward and with his diaries and letters, materials that would prove Alexis innocent, he fled to England. He hides his wife, Anna, after she kills Mr. Willoughby Smith, who has caught her trying to steal the Professor's diary and letters. She takes a poison, resulting in her death, after she informs Holmes, Watson and Inspector Hopkins of her actions.

CORMAC, TIGER:

"The Valley of Fear", Part 2: "The Scowrers"

A thick-set, dark-faced, brutal-looking young man, whose ferocity had earned him the nickname of 'Tiger.' He, along with Wilson, was chosen to do the job on (beat him up) Andrew Rae, of Rae & Sturmash. He and Wilson were acting on behalf of the Vermissa Lodge 29, Eminent Order of Freemen' on the request of the Merton County Lodge 249.

He is one of the seven chosen to capture the Pinkerton man, Birdy Edwards. Cormac is arrested by Captain Marvin and Birdy Edwards while waiting with his comrades to capture Edwards and kill him.

CORNELIUS, MR.:

"The Adventure of the Norwood Builder"

Was paid large sums of money by Mr. Jonas Oldacre. He was in-fact, Jonas Oldacre, and the transfers of monies were for the purpose of defeating creditors.

AKA Mr. Jonas Oldacre

CORNISH HORROR:

"The Adventure of the Devil's Foot"

Name London papers gave to "The Adventure of the Devil's Foot."

CORNISH LANGUAGE:

"The Adventure of the Devil's Foot"

During his stay near Poldhu Bay, Holmes takes to studying the Cornish language and concludes that it is akin to the Chaldean and had been largely derived from the Phoenician tin traders.

CORNWALL:

"The Adventure of the Devil's Foot"

County in Southwest England where Poldhu Bay is located. Holmes and Watson are vacationing there and become involved in the "Cornish Horror."

COUNTESS OF MORCAR:

"The Adventure of The Blue Carbuncle"

Owner of the "Blue Carbuncle," she was staying at the "Hotel Cosmopolitan" when the jewel robbery occurred on December 22.

COUNTY CONSTABULARY:

"The Hound of the Baskervilles"

According to Mr. Frankland it is in a scandalous state, and is the subject of a lawsuit by Mr. Frankland for not adequately protecting him.

See Frankland v. Regina

COUNTY MONAGHAN:

"The Valley of Fear", Part 2: "The Scowrers"

Located in northeastern Ireland from where John McMurdo claimed he came.

COVENT GARDEN:

"The Adventure of the Red Circle"

A playhouse where playwrite Wagner's play is currently on stage.

COVENT GARDEN MARKET:

"The Adventure of The Blue Carbuncle"

Location of the Breckinridge stall, where geese are sold to the general public. Mr. Breckinridge sold Mr. Windigate the geese he sold to Mr. Henry Baker and friends.

COVENTRY:

"The Adventure of the Solitary Cyclist"

Location of the Midland Electric Company.

COVENTRY, SERGEANT:

"The Problem of Thor Bridge"

Of the local police, he was a tall, thin, cadaverous man, with a secretive and mysterious manner. He had a trick, where he would suddenly sink his voice to a whisper as if he had come upon something of vital importance, though usually his information was common knowledge. Nevertheless, he was not too proud to admit when he needed help.

COWPER:

"A Study in Scarlet", Part 2 -- "The Country of the Saints"

A Mormon to whom Jefferson Hope had rendered services at different times. When Jefferson Hope returns from the mountains after his failed attempt to assist the escape of Lucy and John Ferrier, he confronts Cowper as to what has happened to Lucy and is told: "She was married to young Drebber." "Married yesterday--that's what those flags are for on the Endowment House." He further informs Jefferson Hope that it was Stangerson's son who had shot John Ferrier.

COX AND CO.:
> "The Problem of Thor Bridge"
>> A bank at Charing Cross, its vault contains a travel-worn and battered tin dispatch-box with the name 'John H. Watson, M.D., Late Indian Army,' painted upon the lid. It was filled with papers, nearly all of which consisted of records of the cases which illustrated the curious problems which Sherlock Holmes had at various times come to examine.

CRABBE:
> "The Valley of Fear", Part 2: "The Scowrers"
>> An old man living in Stylestown who is killed by Lander and Egan of the Vermissa Lodge.

CRAVEN STREET:
> "The Hound of the Baskervilles"
>> Location of the Mexborough Private Hotel.

CREDIT LYONNAIS:
> "The Valley of Fear", Part 1: "The Tragedy of Birlstone"
>> Bank where Professor Moriarty keeps the bulk of his wealth.

> "The Adventure of the Mazarin Stone"
>> A stolen check from the robbery of the train de-luxe to the Rivera on February 13, 1892 was forged in the same year on the Credit Lyonnais. Holmes informs Count Sylvius that this is his work, although the Count denies it.

CRIMEAN WAR:
> "The Disappearance of Lady Frances Carfax"
>> Admiral Peter Green commanded the British fleet in the Sea of Azov.

>> See Green, Peter.

CRITERION BAR:
> "A Study in Scarlet"
>> Where Watson meets Stamford, an old military acquaintance, who introduces him to Sherlock Holmes.

CROCKER, JACK:
> "The Adventure of the Abbey Grange"
>> Captain of the 'Bass Rock' of the Adelaide-Southampton Line. He has a magnificent record; nevertheless, he is a wild, desperate man off the deck of his ship. He is hot-headed, excitable, but loyal, honest, and kindhearted. He has been in love with Mary Fraser for some time and visits her just before his ship is scheduled to leave port. During the visit Lady Brackenstall's husband, Sir Eustace, enters cursing her and striking her with a stick. Sir Eustace strikes Jack Crocker who in-turn sticks him with a poker killing him. Holmes allows Crocker to go free after Watson, acting as a British jury, pronounces a 'not guilty' verdict.

CROCKFORD:
> "The Adventure of the Retired Colourman"
>> A directory, which Holmes uses to check up on individuals. He receives a telegram from one J.C. Elman and using the Crockford is able to obtain information on the man, he is the Vicar of Moorsmoor and Little Purlington.

THE CROOKED MAN:
> Published in "The Strand": July 1893
> Published as part of: "Memoirs of Sherlock Holmes"
>> Holmes request Watson's company in an investigation of the death of Colonel Barclay. A few months after Watson's marriage, Homes surprises him at "quarter to twelve" to request that Watson join him in the last stage

of a current problem. Holmes notes that Watson is still smoking "the Arcadia mixture of your bachelor days."

This adventure is noted for the first use of the word "elementary." Holmes deduces that Watson's professional business is busy much to the shock of Watson, wherein Holmes states "elementary."

CROOKSBURY HILL:
"The Adventure of the Solitary Cyclist"
> Located along the road from Franham to Chiltern Grange, between Charlington Heath and Charlington Hall.

CROSBY:
"The Adventure of the Golden Pince-Nez"
> An unrecorded case, took place in 1894. Concerns the terrible death of Crosby, the banker.

CROW HILL:
"The Valley of Fear", Part 2: "The Scowrers"
> A huge business in the strong hands of an energetic and fearless New Englander, Josiah H. Dunn. Under his management, it has been able to keep some order and discipline despite the long reign of terror.

CROWDER, WILLIAM:
"The Boscombe Valley Mystery"
> Gamekeeper in the employ of Mr. John Turner.

CROWN DERBY:
"The Adventure of the Three Gables"
> A tea set, it is somewhat rare, but not so valuable that someone would break into a home to steal it. It is all Mary Maberley tells Holmes she has that may be of value in her home.

CROWN DIAMOND:
>"The Adventure of the Mazarin Stone"
>>It has been stolen by one Count Negretto Sylvius. Also known as the Mazarin Stone, it is large and yellow in color. The protector of the stone is Lord Cantlemere.

CROWN INN:
>"The Adventure of the Speckled Band"
>>Opposite the ancestral home of Grimesly Roylott. Dog-carts are available for travel from here.

CRYSTAL PALACE:
>"The Yellow Face"
>>A short walk from the home of Grant and Effie Munro in Norbury.

CUBITT, HILTON:
>"The Adventure of the Dancing Men"
>>A tall, ruddy, clean-shaven gentleman, with clear eyes and florid cheeks. Resides at Riding Thorpe Manor, Norfolk. Is not a wealthy man, however, his family has been at Riding Thorpe for a matter of five centuries, and there is no better known family in the County of Norfolk. Has been married for a year to Elsie Patrick whom he met at a boardinghouse in Russell Square. Was shot and killed by Abe Slaney.

CUMMINGS, JOYCE:
>"The Problem of Thor Bridge"
>>A rising barrister who was entrusted with the defense of Miss Grace Dunbar.

CUNNINGHAM, ALEC:

"The Reigate Puzzle"

Son of Mr. Cunningham, he was smoking his pipe when he claims he heard the coachman call out for help, and then a shot, he was apparently up stairs prior to the altercation. A dashing young fellow, with a bright, smiling expression. Conspired with his father to kill William Kirwan after Kirwan, having witnessed the Cunninghams' burglary of the Acton estate, got them under his power and proceeded, under threats of exposure, to levy blackmail upon them. He and his father attack Holmes when they realize Holmes has solved the mystery.

CUNNINGHAM, Mr.:

"The Reigate Puzzle"

A Justice of the Peace in the Surrey area, his house is the cite of the murder of his coachman during an attempted burglary. An elderly man, with a strong, deeplined, heavy-eyed face, he has a son, Alec, by his deceased wife. Cunningham is involved in a lawsuit against Old Acton. He conspired with his son Alec to kill William Kirwan after Kirwan, having witnessed the Cunninghams' burglary of the Acton estate, got them under his power and proceeded, under threats of exposure, to levy blackmail upon them. He and his son attack Holmes when they realize Holmes has solved the mystery.

CURZON SQUARE:

"The Adventure of Wisteria Lodge"
aka "A Reminiscence of Mr. Sherlock Holmes"

It is located behind Edmonton Street. A lodging house on Edmonton Street backs up to Curzon Square.

CURZON STREET:
"The Adventure of Shoscombe Old Place"
Home to the moneylenders, Sam Brewer has his lending office there.

CUSACK, CATHERINE:
"The Adventure of The Blue Carbuncle"
Maid to the Countess of Morcar; confederate of James Ryder, he who stole the Blue Carbuncle.

CUSHING, MARY:
"The Adventure of the Cardboard Box"
The youngest sister of Susan and Sarah Cushing she was married to one Jim Browner.

AKA Mary Browner.

CUSHING, SARAH:
"The Adventure of the Cardboard Box"
The middle sister of Susan and Mary Cushing, she lived with Susan until two months ago. She has a temper and is always meddlesome and hard to please. She lives at New Street, Wallington. She lived for a time with her sister Mary and her husband. Her deep love for Jim Browner and his rejections forced her to push her sister Mary to another man, Alec Fairbairn. Jim Browner threatened to send Sarah the ears of Alec Fairbairn if he should ever appear in Browner's house again. The gruesome package sent to Susan Cushing was meant for Sarah, for it contained the ears of Alec Fairbairn.

CUSHING, SUSAN:
"The Adventure of the Cardboard Box"
Miss Susan Cushing has been living on Cross Street in Croydon for the past twenty years, prior to that she made her home in Penge. She is a maiden lady of fifty and has

led a retiring life. She received a gruesome package in the mail, which contained two, freshly severed, human ears. A large woman, with gentle eyes, and grizzled hair curving down over her temples on each side of her face. She is the eldest of three sisters, the other two being Sarah and Mary. Mary is married but Sarah is not. Until two months ago Sarah and Susan shared the same house.

CYANEA:

"The Adventure of the Lion's Mane"

The "Lion's Mane," it was a strange object. It looked like a tangled mass torn from the mane of a lion. Holmes quotes from J.G. Wood's book 'Out of Doors:" "If a bather should see a loose roundish mass of tawny membranes and fibers, something like very large handfuls of lion's mane and silver paper, let him beware, for this is the fearful stinger, Cyanea capillata."

CYCLOPIDES:

"The Hound of the Baskervilles"

A rare butterfly, which Mr. Stapleton is pursuing.

CHAPTER D

D'ALBERT, COUNTESS:
>"The Adventure of Charles Augustus Milverton"
>>While Holmes and Watson are hiding in Charles
>>Augustus Milverton's study, a woman enters with Mr.
>>Milverton. She pretends to have five letters for sale,
>>which compromise the Countess d'Albert. When
>>Milverton recognizes the woman as the Countess
>>d'Albert, she asserts that he has ruined her life but will
>>ruin other lives no more, whereupon she shoots him
>>point blank, and then, while he lay on the floor dying,
>>"grounds her heel into his upturned face."

DACRE:
>"The Adventure of the Six Napoleons"
>>Hotel where the Prince of Colonna was staying when the
>>Black Pearl of the Borgias was 'lost.'

DAILY CHRONICLE:
>"The Adventure of the Cardboard Box"
>>London newspaper, contained an article entitled "A
>>Gruesome Packet" detailing the story about the receipt by
>>Miss Susan Cushing of a package containing two freshly
>>severed human ears.

DAILY GAZETTE:
>"The Adventure of the Red Circle"
>>English newspaper that Mrs. Warren leaves for her
>>strange lodger each morning. Contained stories entitled:
>>"Lady with black boa at Prince's Skating Club"; "Surely
>>Jimmy will not break his mother's heart"; and other
>>articles which Holmes searches through to find a clue
>>concerning Mrs. Warren's mysterious lodger.

THE DAILY NEWS:

"A Study in Scarlet"

An English newspaper reporting on the murder of Enoch J. Drebber. Called the crime a "political one." Made the following observation concerning Scotland Yards Gregson: "A great step had been gained by the discovery of the address of the house at which he (Joseph Stangerson) had boarded -- a result which was entirely due to the acuteness and energy of Mr. Gregson of Scotland Yard."

"The Greek Interpreter"

Mycroft Holmes has an advertisement placed in the London newspaper requesting information concerning the whereabouts of Paul Kratides and/or a Greek woman by the name of Sophy.

DAILY TELEGRAPH:

"A Study in Scarlet"

An English newspaper reporting on the murder of one Enoch J. Drebber. "Remarked that in the history of crime there had seldom been a tragedy which presented stranger features." Suggested that everything in the case "pointed to its   perpetration by political refugees and revolutionists." Admonished the government and advocated a closer watch over foreigners in England.

"The Adventure of the Copper Beeches"

Newspaper Holmes is reading at the beginning of adventure.

"The Adventure of the Norwood Builder"

Carried a story concerning the fire and murder at Lower Norwood: "Mysterious Affair at Lower Norwood. Disappearance of a well Known Builder. Suspicion of Murder and Arson. A clue to the Criminal."

"The Adventure of the Second Stain"
> London newspaper which reported that there was a great likelihood that Eduardo Lucas and one M. Henri Fournaye were one and the same and that Mr. Lucas was killed by his alias's wife.

"The Adventure of the Bruce-Partington Plans"
> English newspaper used by one Pierrot and his contact for the sending of messages.

DAMERY, JAMES:

"The Adventure of the Illustrious Client"
> Colonel Sir James Damery's name is a household word in society. He has a reputation for arranging delicate matters, which are to be kept out of the papers. He is a man of the world with a natural turn for diplomacy. He negotiated with Sir George Lewis over the Hammerford Will case. A very delicate matter. He had a large, bluff, honest personality, broad clean-shaven face, and above all, a pleasant, mellow voice. He was a big, masterful aristocrat.

DANCING MEN:

"The Adventure of the Dancing Men"
> Cryptic characters used to convey secret messages.

THE DANGLING PRUSSIAN:

"His Last Bow" "An Epilogue of Sherlock Holmes"
> As Watson and Holmes transport the German spy, Van Bork, to Scotland Yard, Holmes threatens him with, "you would probably enlarge the two limited titles of our village inns by giving us "The Dangling Prussian" as a signpost" should he cause them any trouble during the trip.

DANITE BAND:

"A Study in Scarlet", Part 2 -- "The Country of the Saints"

Also known as the "Avenging Angels, a sinister and ill-omened organization. The secret police of the Mormons. Strange rumours were bandied about murdered immigrants and rifled camps in regions where Indians had never been seen. Fresh woman appeared in the harems of the Elders--women who pined and wept, and bore upon their faces the traces of an unextinguishable horror. The supply of adult women was running short, and polygamy without a female population on which to draw was a barren doctrine.

DARLINGTON SUBSTITUTION SCANDAL:

"A Scandal in Bohemia"

An unrecorded case.

DARTMOOR:

"Silver Blaze"

Location of the race horse training stables, King's Pyland, owned by Colonel Ross.

DAVENPORT, J.:

"The Greek Interpreter"

Responds to an advertisement placed in the Daily News by Mycroft Holmes concerning the whereabouts of a Greek woman by the name of Sophy. His response directs Mycroft, Sherlock and Watson to 'The Myrtles' in Beckenham. He adds that he has additional information concerning her painful history. He writes from Lower Brixton.

DAVID:

"The Crooked Man"

Jane Stewart, housemaid to the Barclay's of 'Lachine,' overheard Mrs. Barclay utter the word 'David' twice during her argument with Colonel Barclay just before his death. The term comes from David's straying occasionally, in much the same way as Colonel Barclay in the small affair of Uriah and Bathsheba, the story is found in the Bible in the second of Samuel.

DAWSON:
"The Sign of Four"

He and his wife took care of the books of Abel White as well as the general managing of the plantation. He and his wife were killed in the great mutiny of Indians in India.

DAWSON:
"Silver Blaze"

One of the grooms at the Mapleton stables under Silas Brown.

DAWSON AND NELIGAN:
"The Adventure of Black Peter"

West Country bankers that failed for a million, ruining half the county families of Cornwall. Neligan disappeared.

DAY'S MUSIC HALL:
"The Stock-Broker's Clerk"

Harry Pinner suggests Hall Pycroft not overwork himself and spend a couple of hours at the music hall in the evening.

DEEP DENE HOUSE:
"The Adventure of the Norwood Builder"

Home of Mr. Jonas Oldacre, it is located on Sydenham Road in Lower Norwood. A big modern villa of staring brick, standing back in its own grounds, with a laurel-clumped lawn in front of it. To the right and some distance back from the road was the timber-yard, which had been the scene of the fire, which purported to have killed Mr. Oldacre.

de MERVILLE, GENERAL:

"The Adventure of the Illustrious Client"

Sir James Damery is representing the General's interest in this case, for it is the General's daughter that proposes to marry Baron Gruner against the wishes of her father. He is of Khyber fame and lives with his daughter at 104 Berkeley Square in a large castle.

de MERVILLE, VIOLET:

"The Adventure of the Illustrious Client"

Daughter of General de Meville, she is to marry Baron Gruner against the will of her father. She has little concern for the Baron's past and accepts the stories he has told her about his past as true. She is a young, rich, beautiful, accomplished woman in every way, residing with her father at 104 Berkley Square. She met the Baron during a Mediterranean yachting voyage and fell in love with him.

DENNIS, SALLY:

"A Study in Scarlet"

She lives at 3 Mayfield Place, Peckham with her husband Tom Dennis. She has lost her ring, which in response to an advertisement place in the newspaper by Holmes, her mother appears at Baker Street to retrieve it. She is described to Holmes/Watson by "Mrs. Sawyer."

See Mrs. Sawyer.

DENNIS, TOM:
"A Study in Scarlet"

Husband to Sally Dennis, who has lost her ring which is found by Holmes, her mother retrieves it in response to an advertisement place in the evening newspaper by Holmes. He is said to be a smart, clean lad, as long as he's at sea, and no steward in the company more thought of; but when on shore, what with the women and what with liquor shops --- He is described to Holmes/Watson by "Mrs. Sawyer."

See Sawyer, Mrs.

DERBY:
"The Valley of Fear", Part 1: "The Tragedy of Birlstone"

Town in England where it has been reported that the suspected murderer of John Douglas Hargrave, has been seen.

DERBY:
"The Adventure of Shoscombe Old Place"

Major horse race in England, Shoscombe Prince is entered.

DERBYSHIRE, WILLIAM:
"Silver Blaze"

A friend of John Straker's who occasionally had his letters sent to the Straker address. He had purchased some rather expensive clothes for his wife at Madame Lesurier's.

AKA John Straker.

DESBOROUGH:
> "Silver Blaze"
>> Race horse, second favorite to Silver Blaze in the Wessex Cup race. In the charge of Silas Brown at Mapleton stables.

DESMOND, JAMES:
> "The Hound of the Baskervilles"
>> He will inherit the Baskerville estate, along with all the Baskerville money (unless Sir Henry willed the money elsewhere) in the event anything happened to Sir Henry Baskerville. He is an elderly clergyman living in Westmoreland.

DEUTSCHE BANK:
> "The Valley of Fear", Part 1: "The Tragedy of Birlstone"
>> Bank where Professor Moriarty keeps the bulk of his wealth.

DEVINE:
> "The Adventure of the Six Napoleons"
>> French sculptor who designed the busts of Napoleon, which were sold by Morse Hudson and later found, smashed.

DEVIL'S ROOT:
> "The Adventure of the Devil's Foot"
>> The root is shaped like a foot, half human, half goatlike, it is reddish-brown in color, a snuff-like power. It is used as an ordeal poison by the medicine-men in certain areas of West Africa. Other than the specimen possessed by Dr. Leon Sterndale, only one other specimen of it is known to exist in Europe, at a laboratory at Buda. Dr. Leon Sterndale obtained his specimen in the Ubangi country. It was used to kill Mortimer and Brenda Tregennis and drive Owen and George Tregennis insane.

DEVINE, MARY:

"The Disappearance of Lady Frances Carfax"

Miss Mary Devine was the maid of Lady Frances Carfax, she received a check in the amount of fifty pounds from Lady Carfax upon her dismissal. She was engaged to one of the head waiters, Jules Vibart, at the Hotel National. She lives at 11 Rue de Trajan, Montpellier.

DEVON COUNTY CHRONICLE:

"The Hound of the Baskervilles"

Newspaper, which carried account of the death of Sir Charles Baskerville.

DEVOY, NANCY:

"The Crooked Man"

See Mrs. Nancy Barclay.

DIEPPE:

"The Final Problem"

Holmes and Watson travel from Canterbury to Newhaven and over to Dieppe while escaping Professor Moriarty.

THE DINGLE:

"The Adventure of Wisteria Lodge"
aka "A Reminiscence of Mr. Sherlock Holmes"

Home of Lord Harringby, it is located along the road between Wisteria Lodge and Oxshott.

DIOGENES CLUB:

"The Greek Interpreter"

In Pall Mall directly opposite the rooms of Mycroft Holmes, some little distance from the Carlton. The queerest club in London, it is for the convenience of those men in London who, from shyness or misanthropy, have no wish for the company of their fellows. There are

comfortable chairs and the latest periodicals and no
talking is allowed except in the 'Stranger's Room.' Three
violations of the no-talking rule may result in expulsion.
Some of the most unclubable and unsociable men in
town are members. Mycroft Holmes was one of the
founders.

THE DISAPPEARANCE OF LADY FRANCES CARFAX:

Published in "The Strand": December 1911
Published as part of: "His Last Bow"

Holmes sends Watson on a search for the missing Lady
Carfax and appears in disguise later to bring the matter to
its conclusion. Lady Carfax is found in the false bottom
of a coffin just as it is being prepared for burial. Holmes
and Watson chase two criminals known for swindling
elderly individuals out of their monies.

DIXON, JEREMY:

"The Adventure of the Missing Three-quarter"

Lives at Trinity College and raises bloodhounds, Pompey
is one of them and is the dog Holmes wishes to use in
this case.

DIXON, MRS.:

"The Adventure of the Solitary Cyclist"

Housekeeper for Mr. Carruthers, she was a very
respectable, elderly person.

DOBNEY, SUSAN:

"The Disappearance of Lady Frances Carfax"

Miss Susan Dobney consults Holmes when Lady Frances
Carfax, to whom she was governess, stops writing every
other week. It had been their habit to write each other
every second week for four years, but without
explanation, Lady Carfax has not written for five weeks.

DOCTOR'S COMMONS:
"The Adventure of the Speckled Band"
> Holmes goes here to obtain information concerning Dr. Grimesby Roylott.

DODD, JAMES M.:
"The Adventure of the Blanched Soldier"
> He is a big, fresh, sunburned, upstanding Briton, with blue eyes and a short beard. He has served in the Middlesex Corps, Imperial Yeomanry in South Africa. He is presently a stockbroker from Throgmorton Street. He joined the military in January 1901, another youth by the name of Godfrey Emsworth volunteered at the same time in the same unit. They became very close, taking the rough and the smooth together for a hard year of fighting. Godfrey was shot and has not been heard from since. James Dodd is searching for him. Godfrey once pulled him out from under the rifles of the Boers.
>
> He consults Holmes in his search for the missing Godfrey.

DOLORES:
"The Adventure of the Sussex Vampire"
> Maid, and friend, to Mrs. Ferguson, she was with Mrs. Ferguson before her marriage to Robert Ferguson and has come to England with her.

DONNITHORPE:
"The 'Gloria Scott'"
> In Norfolk, location of the home of Justice of the Peace Trevor, father of Victor Trevor, Holmes' college friend. It is a little hamlet just to the north of Langmere, in the country of the Broads.

DORAK:

"The Adventure of the Creeping Man"

An elderly gentleman who keeps a large store on Commercial Road in London. He is agent for Lowenstein, the scientist.

DORAN, MISS HATTY:

"The Adventure of the Noble Bachelor"

The fascinating and only child and daughter of Aloysius Doran, Esq., of San Francisco, California. Has been reported that her dowry will exceed six figures. She is what, in England, one might call a "tomboy" with a strong nature, wild and free, unfettered by any sort of traditions. She is impetuous -- volcanic some might say. She is full of face, a very lovely woman, lustrous black hair, large dark eyes, and an exquisite mouth. She disappeared after the wedding breakfast and it is believed she died. Lestrade has had the Serpentine dragged in search of her body. She is later discovered in the company of her husband, one Frank McQuire, whom she had met and married in the mining fields of the Rockies.

DORKING, COLONEL:

"The Adventure of Charles Augustus Milverton"

See Miss Miles.

DOUGLAS, JOHN:

"The Valley of Fear", Part 1: "The Tragedy of Birlstone"

Murdered by a shotgun blast to the head at his Birlstone home, Manor House. He was a remarkable man both in character and in person. About fifty, he had a strong jaw, rugged face, a grizzling moustache, keen gray eyes, and a wiry, vigorous figure which had lost nothing of the strength and activity of youth. Although he was cheery and genial to all, it was obvious that he had lived his life in a lower social environment than that of Sussex. He had a rich tenor voice and was always willing to sing for a crowd. It was certain he had plenty of money, which he claimed to have gained from the California gold fields. He and his wife had spent much time in America where he had emigrated when he was very young. He met Cecil Barker in California and became partners with him in a successful mining claim at a place called Benito Canon. Mr. Baker was his best man at his wedding five years ago, it was his second marriage, he having been a widower. He was hiding from the Scowrers, and Ted Baldwin was sent to kill him, Douglas succeeds in killing Baldwin instead and uses Baldwin's body in his place to make it appear that he, Douglas, has been murdered.

"The Valley of Fear", Part 2: "The Scowrers"
He is acquitted before the Quarter Sessions as having acted in self-defense. He left England aboard the Palmyra for South Africa but is lost overboard in a gale off St. Helena. It appears to be the work of Professor Moriarty.

AKA Hargrave, See Hargrave
AKA Jack
AKA John McMurdo, See McMurdo, John
AKA Birdy Edwards, See Edwards, Birdy
AKA Steve Wilson, See Wilson, Steve

DOUGLAS, MRS.:
"The Valley of Fear", Part 1: "The Tragedy of Birlstone"
Retiring by disposition, absorbed in her husband and her domestic duties. She was English and had met Mr. Douglas in London. She was a beautiful woman, tall, dark, and slender, some twenty years younger than her husband. She seemed to display extreme uneasiness if her husband was late in returning from any engagements.

DOVERCOURT, EARL OF:
    "The Adventure of Charles Augustus Milverton"
        He is engaged to marry Lady Eva Blackwell.

DOWNING, CONSTABLE:
    "The Adventure of Wisteria Lodge"
    aka "A Reminiscence of Mr. Sherlock Holmes"
        Constable who captured the supposed perpetrator of the
        crime at Wisteria Lodge. This information was reported
        in one of England's newspapers.

DOWNING STREET:
    "The Naval Treaty"
        Political Street in London, home to cabinet ministers.
        Lord Holdhurst has his chambers in Downing Street.

        See Lord Holdhurst.

DOWSON, BARON:
    "The Adventure of the Mazarin Stone"
        An unrecorded case. Old Baron Dowson, in
        complimenting Holmes on his impersonations, stated:
        "what the law had gained the stage had lost". The Baron
        was hanged shortly thereafter.

DREBBER, "ELDER":
    "A Study in Scarlet" Part 2 -- "The Country of the Saints"
        Father of Enoch J. Drebber. One of the four principal
        Elders of the Mormons, one of the "Holy Four" (also
        known as the "Sacred Council of Four") along with
        Johnson, Kemball, and Joseph Stangerson.

DREBBER, ENOCH J.:
    "A Study in Scarlet"
        From Cleveland, Ohio, USA. Was living at 3 Lauriston
        Gardens, off the Brixton Road where he is found

murdered. A man about forty-three/forty-four, middle-
sized, broad-shouldered, with crisp curling black hair, and
a short, stubbly beard.   Holmes determines that he was
murdered by poison. According to the "Standard" (See
Newspapers) "The deceased was an American who had
been residing for some weeks in the metropolis. He
had stayed at the boarding-house of Madame
Charpentier, in Torquay Terrace, Camberwell. He was
accompanied in his travels by his private secretary Mr.
Joseph Stangerson. The Two bade adieu to their landlady
upon Tuesday, the 4th inst., and departed to Euston
Station with the avowed intention of catching the
Liverpool express. They were afterwards seen together
upon the platform. Nothing more is known of them
until Mr. Drebber's body was, as recorded, discovered in
an empty house in the Brixton Road, many miles from
Euston..."

"A Study in Scarlet", Part 2 -- "The Country of the Saints"
A bull-necked youth with coarse, bloated features, he has
seven wives and his father has given him his mills. He
competes with Joseph Stangerson for the hand of Lucy
Ferrier. Is a member of the "Avenging Angels" which
captures Lucy and kills her father. He marries Lucy after
Brigham Young decides in his favor over Joseph
Stangerson during their arguments to the Council of
Four.

DRUG USE:
"The Sign of Four"
The first mention of Holmes' use of drugs. It begins
thus: "Sherlock Holmes took his bottle from the corner
of the mantlepiece, and his hypodermic syringe from its
neat morocco case." "Three times a day for many
months I had witnessed this performance ... " "Which is

it today, I asked, morphine or cocaine? It is cocaine, a seven-percent solution."

"A Case of Identity"
> Watson discovers Holmes in an opium den.

"The Yellow Face"
> Save for the occasional use of cocaine, he had no vices, and he only turned to the drug as a protest against the monotony of existence when cases were scanty and the papers uninteresting.

"The Man with the Twisted Lip"
> When Holmes is spotted by Watson in an opium den, Holmes questions Watson, "I suppose that you imagine that I have added opium-smoking to cocaine injections, and all the other little weaknesses on which you have favoured me with your medical views."

"The Adventure of the Missing Three-Quarter"
> Watson: "For years I had gradually weaned him from that drug mania which had threatened once to check his remarkable career.

"The Adventure of the Dying Detective"
> Watson is summoned to Baker Street by Mrs. Hudson concerning the grave illness of Holmes, on the mantelpiece in his rooms were the following items: "A litter of pipes, tobacco pouches, syringes, penknives, revolver-cartridges, and other debris."

DUCHESS OF BALMORAL:
"The Adventure of the Noble Bachelor"
> Mother of Lord St. Simon, wife of the Duke, was in attendance at the wedding of her son to one Hatty Duran.

THE DUDAS SEPARATION CASE:
"A Case of Identity"
An unrecorded case. Holmes engaged in clearing up some small points. "The husband was a teetotaler, there was no other woman, and the conduct complained of was that he had drifted into the habit of winding up every meal by taking out his false teeth and hurling them at his wife, which, you will allow, is not an action likely to occur to the imagination of the average story-teller."

DUKE OF BALMORAL:
"The Adventure of the Noble Bachelor"
Father of Lord St. Simon, his second son. Was at one time Secretary for Foreign Affairs. Inherited Plantagenet blood by direct descent. Owns/resides at Grosvenor Mansion.

Also see "Silver Blaze" (The Memoirs of Sherlock Holmes) wherein he owns and enters a horse in the famous Wessex Cup race, the horse is named 'Iris.'

DUNBAR, GRACE:
"The Problem of Thor Bridge"
She was a brunette, tall, with a noble figure and commanding presence. Miss Dunbar was governess to the two Gibson children. A very beautiful woman, she was deeply hated by Mrs. Gibson and loved by Mr. Gibson. When confronted by Mr. Gibson she rebuked his advances and vowed to leave his employ if he did not cease in his affections for her. A gun, with a shot having been fired from it, is found on the floor of her wardrobe and the caliber of bullet matches that which killed Mrs. Gibson. She is arrested for the murder of Mrs. Maria Gibson.

DUNDEE:
"The Five Orange Pips"
>> Location in England from where second envelope
>> containing orange pips was sent to Joseph Openshaw,
>> father of John Openshaw.

"The Adventure of Black Peter"
>> Port-of-call for the 'Sea Unicorn.'

THE DUNDEE RECORDS:
"The Five Orange Pips"
>> Reference material for ships, Holmes uses it to find when
>> the "Lone Star," an American ship was last docked in
>> London.

DUNLOP:
"The Adventure of the Priory School"
>> Bicycle tyre, Holmes checks out its track impressions.

DUNN, JOSIAH, H.:
"The Valley of Fear", Part 2: "The Scowrers"
>> Energetic and fearless New Englander, he is the manager
>> of the Crow Hill mine. A tall, loose-framed young man
>> with a clean-shaven, earnest face. He is assassinated by
>> Lawler and Andrews sent to do the job by Evans Pott,
>> County Delegate of the "Eminent Order of Freemen."
>> Dunn is actually shot by Andrews.

DUPIN:
"A Study in Scarlet"
>> Character in stories by Edgar Allen Poe. Watson, in an
>> attempt to compliment Holmes compares him to Dupin.
>> Holmes considers the fellow as "inferior."

DURANDO, SIGNORA VICTOR:

"The Adventure of Wisteria Lodge"
aka "A Reminiscence of Mr. Sherlock Holmes"

Her husband was the San Pedro minister in London. He was recalled by Don Murillo to San Pedro and shot. She has been working to avenge her husband's murder.

AKA Miss Burnet

DUTCHMAN:

"The Adventure of the Mazarin Stone"
Van Seddar.

THE DYNAMICS OF AN ASTEROID:

"The Valley of Fear", Part 1: "The Tragedy of Birlstone"

Book written by Professor Moriarty, it ascends to such rarefied heights of pure mathematics that it is said that there was no man in the scientific press capable of criticizing it.

CHAPTER E

EAGLE COMMERCIAL:
> "The Valley of Fear", Part 1: "The Tragedy of Birlstone"
>> Hotel in Tunbridge Wells, the manager was able to
>> identify the bicycle found near the Manor House, a
>> Rudge-Whitworth, as having belonged to an American
>> who had taken rooms at the hotel, his name was
>> Hargrave.

EAGLE RAVINE:
> "A Study in Scarlet", Part 2 -- "The Country of the Saints"
>> Location where Jefferson Hope had hidden a mule and
>> two horses in preparation of the escape of Lucy and John
>> Ferrier from Salt Lake City to Carson City.

EARL OF MAYNOOTH:
> "The Adventure of the Empty House"
>> Father of 'The Honourable Ronald Adair'. He was
>> governor of one of the Australian colonies.

EAST ANGLIA:
> "The Adventure of the Dancing Men"
>> Area of England on the way from North Walsham to
>> Norfolk, a place of glory and prosperity.

EAST HAM:
> "The Valley of Fear", Part 1: "The Tragedy of Birlstone"
>> Town in England where it has been reported that the
>> suspected murderer of John Douglas, Mr. Hargrave, has
>> been seen and actually arrested.

EAST LONDON:

> "The Five Orange Pips"
>> Location in England from where third envelope containing orange pips was sent to John Openshaw.

EAST RUSTON:

> "The Adventure of the Dancing Men"
>> Village located near Riding Thorpe Manor.

EASTBOURNE:

> "His Last Bow"
>> Holmes lives in retirement in a small farm upon the downs five miles from Eastbourne.

ECCLES, JOHN SCOTT:

> "The Adventure of Wisteria Lodge"
> aka "A Reminiscence of Mr. Sherlock Holmes"
>> Resides at Popham House, Lee. A stout, tall, gray-whiskered and solemnly respectable person with gold-rimmed spectacles, he was a Conservative, a churchman, a good citizen, orthodox and conventional to the last degree. He is a bachelor with a large number of friends.

ECHO:

> "A Study in Scarlet", Part 2 -- "The Country of the Saints"
>> London newspaper which contains the conclusion to the story "A Study in Scarlet": "The public have lost a sensational treat through the sudden death of the man Hope, who was suspected of the murder of Mr. Enoch Drebber and of Mr. Joseph Stangerson. The details of the case will probably be never known now, though we are informed upon good authority that the crime was the result of an old standing and romantic feud, in which love and Mormonism bore a part. It seems that both the victims belonged, in their younger days, to the Latter Day Saints, and Hope, the deceased prisoner, hails also from

Salt Lake City. If the case has had no other effect, it, at least brings out in the most striking manner the efficiency of our detective police force, and will serve as a lesson to all foreigners that they will do wisely to settle their feuds at home, and not carry them on to British soil. It is an open secret that the credit of this smart capture belongs entirely to the well-known Scotland Yard officials, Messrs, Lestrade and Gregson. The man was apprehended, it appears, in the rooms of a certain Mr. Sherlock Holmes, who has himself, as an amateur, shown some talent in the detective line and who, with such instructors, may hope in time to attain to some degree of their skill. It is expected that a testimonial of some sort will be presented to the two officers as a fitting recognition of their services."

ECKERMANN:
>"The Adventure of Wisteria Lodge"
>aka "A Reminiscence of Mr. Sherlock Holmes"
>>Author of "Voodooism and the Negroid Religions" which Holmes found useful in studying while at the British Museum.

EDGWARE ROAD:
>"The Adventure of the Three Garridebs"
>>Runs almost parallel to Baker Street into Bayswater Road/Oxford Street.

EDITH:
>"The Adventure of the Priory School"
>>Duchess of Holdernesse, mother of the kidnapped son of the Duke of Holderness.

>>See Holdernesse, duchess.

EDMONTON STREET:

> "The Adventure of Wisteria Lodge"
> aka "A Reminiscence of Mr. Sherlock Holmes"
>> Street in London on which stands a lodging-house. Don Murillo, his secretary, and his two children entered the lodging-house while being pursued but quickly exited by the rear door into Curzon Square never to be seen again in England.

EDMUNDS:

> "The Adventure of the Retired Colourman"
>> Of the Berkshire Constabulary, thin and yellow-haired, he investigated the Abbas Parva Tragedy and although the inquest ruled death by misadventure, he believed there were still a couple of points, which should have been examined. He dropped by to see Holmes and smoked a pipe with him while retelling the story. A smart lad, he was transferred from the Berkshire Constabulary to Allahabad.

EDWARDS, BIRDY:

> "The Valley of Fear", Part 2: "The Scowrers"
>> A Pinkerton detective, it is believed he is on the trail, and among, the Scowrers.' He is known as the best man in the Pinkerton service. His name is relayed to John McMurdo by Brother Morris who has obtained it from a good friend of his back East who is in the telegraph service. A trap is set by the lodge of Vermissa, 'Eminent Order of Freemen,' to capture and kill him, but he turns the tables and captures Boss McGinty, Ted Baldwin, Carter, the treasurer, Harraway, the secretary, the Willaby brothers, and Tiger Cormac. After serving their time in prison, some of the old members of the 'Scowrers' chase him from Chicago after two attempts on his life, to California where his wife, Ettie (Shafter) Edwards died. He changed his name to Douglas and after hitting it rich

with an English partner, Barker, he moved to England just as the bloodhounds were about to pounce.

AKA John Douglas, See Douglas, John
AKA John McMurdo, See McMurdo, John
AKA Steve Wilson, See Wilson, Steve

EGAN:
"The Valley of Fear", Part 2: "The Scowrers"
He and Lander claim the head money given by the lodge of Vermissa for the killing of old man Crabbe in Stylestown, although no one knows who actually fired the shot.

EGRIA:
"A Scandal in Bohemia"
It is in a German-speaking country--in Bohemia, not far from Carlsbad. Remarkable as being the scene of the death of Wallenstein and for its numerous glass-factories and paper-mills.

EGYPT:
"His Last Bow" "An Epilogue of Sherlock Holmes"
Von Bork, the German spy, had a safe containing pigeon-holes bristling with papers and plans, each with its own label. One of these compartments was labeled "Egypt."

ELEMENTARY:
"A Case of Identity"
First used in "A Case of Identity"
"All this is amusing, though rather elementary, but I must go back to business." Holmes speaking to Watson regarding how and why he was so able to deduce that which Watson could not from their visit by Miss Mary Sutherland.

ELEY'S NO. 2:
> "The Adventure of the Speckled Band"
>> Watson's revolver.

ELISE:
> "The Adventure of the Engineer's Thumb"
>> A pretty woman who spoke in a foreign tongue.

ELMAN, J.C.:
> "The Adventure of the Retired Colourman"
>> He is the Vicar of Moorsmoor and Little Purlington, both which are in Essex. Holmes claims that he has received a telegram from the Vicar with information concerning the disappearance of Mrs. Amberley and Dr. Ray Ernest. He is a big, solemn, rather pompous clergyman. Watson and Josiah Amberley are sent by Holmes to consult with the Vicar, who denies ever sending the telegram.

ELRIGE'S FARM:
> "The Adventure of the Dancing Men"
>> In East Ruston near Riding Thorpe Manor, it serves as an inn. Mr. Abe Slaney resides there.

EMINENT ORDER OF FREEMEN:
> "The Valley of Fear", Part 2: "The Scowrers"
>> It is an order set up for charity and good fellowship. In Vermissa, it is one and the same as 'The Scowrers,' a murder society.
>>
>> AKA 'Ancient Order of Freemen', See 'Ancient Order of Freemen'

EMSWORTH, COLONEL:
> "The Adventure of the Blanched Soldier"
>> Father of Godfrey Emsworth, he was the greatest martinet in the Army during his time. He had been

Crimean V.C. He was a huge, bow-backed, man with a smoky skin and straggling gray beard, red-veined nose jutting out like a vulture's beak and two fierce gray eyes glaring out from under tufted brows. He tries to brush off James Dodd and threatens Holmes until Holmes produces a note with one word on it: 'leprosy.'

EMSWORTH, GODFREY:

"The Adventure of the Blanched Soldier"

Son of Colonel Emsworth, he volunteered for service during the Boer War with the Imperial Yeomanry, Middlesex Corps, Lance Corporal of B Squadron. He became fast friends with one James Dodd and they remained close until Godfrey was struck by a bullet from an elephant gun in action near Diamond Hill outside Pretoria, South Africa. He spent time in a hospital in Southampton, where he sent his last letter to James Dodd. It has been more than six months since he communicated with Dodd. During the war, he pulled Dodd out from under the rifles of the Boers saving his life. He was shot during fighting at Buffelsspruit, outside Pretoria, on the Eastern railway line. He and two others were separated from the rest, the other two were killed. Godfrey made his way to a house and weak with fatigue he fell asleep in what turned out to be a leper's bed in a Leper Hospital. This fear of having contracted leprosy, and wishing to remain with his father as opposed to a leper colony, has kept him hidden. When Holmes uncovers the situation, he brings Sir James Saunders, the noted dermatologist to further examine Godfrey with enlightening results, he does not suffer from leprosy.

ENDOWMENT HOUSE:
>"A Study in Scarlet"
>>House of worship of the Mormons in Salt Lake City. Flags are flown from it to announce the marriage of Lucy Ferrier to the Enoch Drebber as his eighth wife.

ENGLISCHER HOF:
>"The Final Problem"
>>Hotel in Meiringen where Holmes and Watson stay, run by Peter Steiler the elder.

ENGLISCHER HOF:
>"The Disappearance of Lady Frances Carfax"
>>In Baden, it is where Lady Frances Carfax stayed after leaving the Hotel National in Luasanne.

ERNEST, RAY:
>"The Adventure of the Retired Colourman"
>>A young doctor and chess player, he lives near Josiah Amberley and regularly plays chess with him. He is unmarried and may have played the fool with Amberley's wife. He disappears, and is presumed to have fled the country with Mr. Amberley's wife and money. It turns out he has been murdered, along with Mr. Amberley's wife by Mr. Amberley.

ESCOTT:
>"The Adventure of Charles Augustus Milverton"
>>A plumber with a rising business, he is engaged to Charles Augustus Milverton's housemaid, Agatha.
>>
>>AKA Sherlock Holmes (one of his disguises).

ESHER:
"The Adventure of Wisteria Lodge"
aka "A Reminiscence of Mr. Sherlock Holmes"

Town about three miles from Oxshott and two miles
from Wisteria Lodge.

ESMERALDA:
"The Sign of Four"
Vessel of Jonathan Small, outward bound for the Brazils.

ESSEX:
"The Adventure of the Retired Colourman"
English County, it contains Moorsmoor and Little
Purlington.

ESTIMATES:
"The Adventure of the Bruce-Partington Plans"
Department of the British Government through which a
large sum of money was smuggled in order to acquire a
monopoly of the invention of the Bruce-Partington
submarine.

THE ETHEREGE CASE:
"A Case of Identity"
An unrecorded case.
Mrs. Etherege's husband had disappeared and the police
and everyone else had given him up for dead, but
Holmes found him easily.

ETHEREGE, MRS.:
"A Case of Identity"
Her husband was found by Holmes when the "police and
everyone else had given him up for dead." Mrs. Etherege
sends Miss Mary Sutherland to Holmes for help in
finding Mr. Hosmer Angel.

EUSTACE, LORD:
> "The Adventure of the Noble Bachelor"
>> Younger brother of Lord St. Simon, attended the wedding of his brother and Hatty Doran.

EUSTON:
> "The Adventure of the Priory School"
>> London train station.

> "The Adventure of the Blanched Soldier"
>> Trains run from Euston Station London through Bedfordshire.

EVANS:
> "The 'Gloria Scott'"
>> Young fellow, convicted of forgery. Joined other convicts in the taking of the 'Gloria Scott.' Set adrift with James Armitage and others when he refused to take part in the murder of the soldiers on board the ship. Picked up by the 'Hotspur,' the day after the sinking of the 'Gloria Scott,' posing as the survivor of a passenger ship, which had floundered. Changed his name upon his arrival in Sydney, Australia, and headed for the gold fields, returning to England a rich and prosperous man.

>> AKA Beddoes, See Beddoes

EVANS:
> "The Valley of Fear", Part 2: "The Scowrers"
>> One of two policemen killed because he ventured, with his partner, Hunt, to arrest two members of the 'Scowrers.' Both policemen were unarmed and killed in cold blood during the winter of 1875.

EVANS, CARRIE:

"The Adventure of Shoscombe Old Place"

She has been the maid to Lady Beatrice Falder for the last five years. She is married to Mr. Norlett and with him has assisted Sir Robert Norberton in keeping the death of Lady Beatrice Falder a secret until after the running of the Derby.

EVANS, KILLER:

"The Adventure of the Three Garridebs"

He has a sinister and murderous reputation, forty-four years old, he was released from prison in 1901. His record provides the following information: native of Chicago, known to have shot three men in the United States and escaped from the penitentiary through political influence. Arrived in London in 1893. Killed Rodger Prescott during a card game in January 1895 at Waterloo Road, self-defense. A very dangerous man, usually armed. He shoots Watson in the thigh as Holmes and Watson spring their trap upon him as he enters the hidden room with the printing press at the residence of Mr. Garrideb.

AKA James Winter
AKA Morecroft
AKA John Garrideb, See Garrideb, John

EVENING STANDARD:

"The Stock-Broker's Clerk"

According to the 'Evening Standard' a London newspaper, an attempted robbery, resulting in the murder of the watchman, occurred at the offices of Mawson & Williams.

EYFORD:
"The Adventure of the Engineer's Thumb"
Town in Berkshire, near the borders of Oxfordshire and .
within seven miles of Reading. Location where Colonel
Lysander Stark requires Victor Hatherley to go to
perform the engineering work he needs done.

FABER, JOHANN:
"The Adventure of the Three Students"
Maker of unusual pencils, some with soft leads, the outer color being dark blue with the makers name in silver.

FAIRBAIRN, ALEC:
"The Adventure of the Cardboard Box"
He visited the home of Jim and Mary (Cushing) Browner regularly during the time Sarah Cushing was living there. After awhile he began to show his affection for Mary during times her husband was at sea. He was a man with winning ways, dashing, a swaggering chap, smart and curried. He had seen half the world in his travels. He is discovered with Mary (Cushing) Browner by her husband Jim and killed, his ears severed and mailed to Miss Cushing of Croydon.

FAIRBANK:
"The Adventure of the Beryl Coronet"
Located in the southern suburb of Streatham. A good-sized square house of white stone, standing back a little from the road. A double carriagesweep, with a snow-covered lawn, stretched down in front of two large iron gates, which closed the entrance. On the right side was a small wooden thicket, which led into a narrow path between two neat hedges, stretching from the road to the kitchen door, and forming the tradesmen's entrance. On the left ran a lane, which led to the stables, and was not itself within the grounds at all, being a public, though little used, thoroughfare.

FALDER, BEATRICE:
"The Adventure of Shoscombe Old Place"

Lady Beatrice inherited Shoscombe Old Place from her late Husband, Sir James, for the rest of her life. Upon her death, the estate goes to Sir James's brother. Her bother, Sir Robert Norberton, resides with her at Shoscombe Old Place. She has been suffering from a weak heart and dropsy for some time and she relies on her brother. Lately she appears to be drinking like a fish. She dies about two weeks prior to the running of the "Derby" and her body is hidden by her brother until after the "Derby" so as to keep up the appearance that she was still alive.

FALDER, JAMES:
"The Adventure of Shoscombe Old Place"

Sir James Falder is the late husband of Lady Beatrice Falder, he left her a life interest in his estate.

FALER, DENIS:
"The Adventure of Shoscombe Old Place"

Holmes examines the crypt which has been a favorite haunt of Sir Robert Norberton of late and therein discovers graves ranging from very old, Saxon, through a long line of Norman Hugos and Odos, to those of Sir William and Denis Faler of the eighteenth century.

FALER, WILLIAM:
"The Adventure of Shoscombe Old Place"

Holmes examines the crypt which has been a favorite haunt of Sir Robert Norberton of late and therein discovers graves ranging from very old, Saxon, through a long line of Norman Hugos and Odos, to those of Sir William and Denis Faler of the eighteenth century.

FAMILY HERALD:
> "The Problem of Thor Bridge"
>> Periodical, which prints love romances.

FARINTOSH:
> "The Adventure of the Speckled Band"
>> An unrecorded case. Mrs. Farintosh gave Holmes' address to Helen Stoner. He had helped Mrs. Farintosh in her hour of need. The Farintosh case concerned an opal tiara, apparently before Watson's time.

FARQUHAR:
> "The Stock-Broker's Clerk"
>> Doctor from whom Watson purchased his practice.

FERGUSON:
> "The Adventure of the Engineer's Thumb"
>> A short thick man with a chinchilla beard growing out of the creases of his double chin. He is the secretary and manager of Colonel Lysander Stark.

FERGUSON:
> "The Adventure of the Three Gables"
>> A retired sea captain, he owned 'The Three Gables' prior to Mary Maberley.

FERGUSON, JACK:
> "The Adventure of the Sussex Vampire"
>> Son of Robert Ferguson, he was crippled in a childhood accident, a fall which resulted in a twisted spine. He is fifteen and deeply attached to his father, however, he has a deep jealousy and cruel hatred for his baby brother. His jealousy of his brother leads him to prick his baby brother's neck with an arrow dipped in poison, which his stepmother witnesses.

FERGUSON, MR.:
>"The Problem of Thor Bridge"
>>Secretary to Mr. Neil Gibson.

FERGUSON AND MUIRHEAD:
>"The Adventure of the Sussex Vampire"
>>Tea brokers of Mincing Lane, one of its partners, Robert Ferguson, consults Holmes regarding the strange behavior of his wife.

FERGUSON, ROBERT:
>"The Adventure of the Sussex Vampire"
>>He, of Ferguson and Muirhead, tea brokers, of Mincing Lane. He married a Peruvian woman some five years ago, his first wife having died. By his first wife, he has a fifteen-year-old son, little Jack, who was crippled due to an accident in his childhood. There is a second child, a baby, by his second wife. He met his second wife in connection with the importation of nitrates from Peru. Played three-quarter for the Richmond rugby team and remembers Watson from his days of rugby at Blackheath.

FERNWORTHY:
>"The Hound of the Baskervilles"
>>Town near Baskerville Hall, home of Mr. Frankland, who has sued the town for use of an area as a picnic spot. Mr. Frankland is successful in his action.

FERRERS DOCUMENTS:
>"The Adventure of the Priory School"
>>An unrecorded case, which Holmes was involved when, consulted about the matter of the Priory School.

FERRIER, DR.:

"The Naval Treaty"

Lives in Woking near the Phelps family. Is the doctor looking after Percy Phelps during his period of distress after the theft of the naval treaty from the Foreign Office.

FERRIER, JOHN:

"A Study in Scarlet" Part 2 -- "The Country of the Saints"

He and a little girl, Lucy (Ferrier), are all that remain of twenty-one, the others having died of thirst and hunger down in the south, they were traveling to the western part of the United States. He saved the little girl and now claims her as his own. Had a friendship with the father of Jefferson Hope back in St. Louis. Died August 4, 1860 at the hands of the "Avenging Angels" while attempting to flee Salt Lake City with his daughter Lucy and Jefferson Hope.

FERRIER, LUCY:

"A Study in Scarlet" Part 2 -- "The Country of the Saints"

Her mother died while traveling to the west in the United States. Lucy and John Ferrier were the only survivors of twenty-one. She is taken in by John Ferrier and treated as his daughter. Fell in love with Jefferson Hope and fled with him and her father on or about August 2, 1860 from Salt Lake City rather than marry Enoch Drebber's or Joseph Stangerson's sons. She and her father were caught by the "Avenging Angels," she being taken back to Salt Lake City, her father being killed and buried where he stood. She was married to young Drebber, she died within a month of the forced marriage.

FFOLLIOTT, GEORGE:
"The Adventure of Wisteria Lodge"
aka "A Reminiscence of Mr. Sherlock Holmes"

Sir George Ffolliott resides at 'Oxshott Towers', located
along the road between Wisteria Lodge and Oxshott.

FIFTH NORTHUMBERLAND FUSILIERS:
"A Study in Scarlet"
See Watson, John

THE FINAL PROBLEM:
Published in "The Strand": December 1893.
Published as part of: "Memoirs of Sherlock Holmes"
Holmes escapes to Switzerland where Professor Moriarty
has followed him.   Watson begins by telling us that he
began his writings with "A Study in Scarlet" and he had
hoped to end them with "The Naval Treaty" but due to
the recent letters by Colonel James Moriarty, defending
his brother, Watson must "lay the facts before the public
exactly as they occurred."

The facts surrounding "The Final Problem" have been
released in only three accounts in the public press: in the
'Journal de Geneve' on May 6, 1891, the 'Reuter's'
dispatch in the English papers on May 7, 1891, and
finally in the recent letters of Colonel Moriarty. Of these
accounts, the first two were extremely condensed and as
Watson attempts to show, the letters of Colonel Moriarty
are "an absolute perversion of the facts."

Holmes appears at Watson's consulting-room on April
24, 1890 paler and thinner than usual and concerned for
his safety and he request Watson come away with him to
the continent.

Watson introduces Professor Moriarty.

Professor Moriarty's men set fire to Holmes' Baker Street residence, there is, however, little damage. The Adventure follows Holmes and Watson as they travel from London to Switzerland in an attempt to escape Moriarty. The Final Problem closes with the Watson's discovery that Holmes has apparently met his death at the Reichenbach Falls in a battle with Moriarty, Holmes having left Watson a note, which he wrote while Professor Moriarty awaited him. It is believed that Holmes and Moriarty died at the Reichenbach falls on May 4, 1891.

FIRBANK VILLAS:
"The Disappearance of Lady Frances Carfax"
Number 13 is the home of Dr. Hosmer, he being the doctor called to attend to Rose Spender by Fraser and Holy Peters. Rose is dying and has been taken in by Fraser claiming the dying woman had been a servant for them in the past.

FISHER, PENROSE:
"The Adventure of the Dying Detective"
One of the best doctors in London. Watson implores Holmes to consult him or someone about his Sumatra disease.

THE FIVE ORANGE PIPS:
Published in "The Strand": November 1891
Published as part of: "The Adventures of Sherlock Holmes"
Holmes's client falls victim to the long arm of revenge of the Ku Klux Klan in the latter days of September 1887. It is in this case that Holmes states: "I have been beaten four times -- three times by men, and once by a woman."

The case involves the strange appearance of 'orange pips' in an envelope marked KKK and addressed to John Openshaw putting him in a state of fear and causing his nephew to request the assistance of Holmes in discovering the hidden meaning to the 'five orange pips' and the letters KKK.

FLEET STREET:
"The Red-Headed League"
Location of Pope's Court.

FLOWERS, LORD:
"The Adventure of the Second Stain"
A note from Lord Flowers was in the dispatch-box of the Right Honourable Trelawney Hope.

FLUSHING:
"His Last Bow"
"An Epilogue of Sherlock Holmes"
Von Bork's family, he being the German spy, has left London for Flushing prior to Von Bork's flight to the embassy after obtaining the naval signals from his underling, Altamont.

FOLKESTONE COURT:
"The Hound of the Baskervilles"
There have been four burglaries in the area since the arrival of the Stapletons. Holmes believes John Stapleton has been the perpetrator pointing out that the last of the burglaries, here at Folkestone Court, was remarkable for the cold-blooded pistolling of the page, who surprised the masked and solitary burglar.

FORBES, MR.:
"The Naval Treaty"
> Detective from Scotland Yard who undertakes the investigation of the missing naval papers from the Foreign Office. A small, foxy man with a sharp but by no means amiable expression.

FORD:
"His Last Bow"
"An Epilogue of Sherlock Holmes"
> Automobile driven by Watson.

FORDHAM, DR.:
"The 'Gloria Scott'"
> Doctor called upon to administer to Justice of the Peace Trevor after his stroke.

FORDINGHAM:
"The 'Gloria Scott'"
> Located in Hampshire, a letter with its postmark from Fordingham is received by Justice of the Peace Trevor bringing a stroke upon him.

FORDS:
"His Last Bow"
"An Epilogue of Sherlock Holmes"
> Von Bork, the German spy, had a safe containing pigeon-holes bristling with papers and plans, each with its own label. One of these compartments was labeled "Fords." Shallow crossings of rivers which information would be helpful to soldiers and machinery during a war.

FORRESTER, Mrs. CECIL:
"The Sign of Four"
> Lives in Lower Camberwell with Mary Marstan.
> Employer of Mary Morstan, and had once employed the

services of Sherlock Holmes and suggests Mary avail
herself of his powers.

FORRESTER, INSPECTOR:
"The Reigate Puzzle"

The official involved in the murder at the Cunningham
estate and the burglary at the Acton estate. A smart,
keen-faced young fellow.

FORRESTER, THE MATTER OF CECIL:
"The Sign of Four"

An unrecorded case. A domestic complication.

FORTESCUE SCHOLARSHIP:
"The Adventure of the Three Students"

A very valuable scholarship, the examination for which is
being given at the College of St. Luke's.

FORTON OLD HALL:
"The Adventure of Wisteria Lodge"
aka "A Reminiscence of Mr. Sherlock Holmes"

Home to Mr. James Baker Williams, it is located along
the road between Wisteria Lodge and Oxshott.

FOULMIRE:
"The Hound of the Baskervilles"

A moorland farmhouse near Grimpen.

FOURNAYE, HENRI:
"The Adventure of the Second Stain"

Lived in a small villa in the Rue Austerlitz, France, he was
married to Mme. Henri Fournaye, who was of Creole
origin. He played a double live unknown to his wife.

AKA Eduardo Lucas.
See Lucas, Eduardo

FOURNAYE, Mme. HENRI:

"The Adventure of the Second Stain"

Wife of M. Henri Fournaye, she was of Creole origin. She discovered her husband was living a double life and apparently killed him. Returning to France, her servants reported her to the authorities as being insane.

FOWLER. MR.:

"The Adventure of the Copper Beeches"

A very kind-spoken, free-handed gentlemen, a good seaman. A small bearded man. Marries Miss Alice Rucastle and is appointed to a government position in the island of Mauritius.

FRANCO-MIDLAND HARDWARE COMPANY, LIMITED:

"The Stock-Broker's Clerk"

Promoted by Harry Pinner. Located at 126B Corporation Street, Birmingham.

FRANKLAND, MR.:

"The Hound of the Baskervilles"

Of Lafter Hall in Grimpen, four miles to the south of Baskerville Hall. He is an elderly man, red-faced, white-haired, and choleric. His passion is for the British law, and he has spent a large fortune in litigation. He fights for the mere pleasure of fighting and is equally ready to take up either side of a question. He is learned in old manorial and communal rights, and he applies his knowledge sometimes in favour of the villagers of Fernworthy and sometimes against them. He is currently involved in about seven lawsuits. He is curiously employed, being an amateur astronomer, he has an excellent telescope, with which he lies upon the roof of his own house and sweeps the moor all day in the hope of catching a glimpse of the escaped convict. He intends to prosecute Dr. Mortimer for opening a grave without the consent of the next of kin because he dug up a neolithic skull in the barrow on Long Down.

FRANKLAND vs. MORLAND:
"The Hound of the Baskervilles"
>Case of Frankland suing Morland for trespass because he shot in his own warren. Case heard by the Court of Queen's Bench.

FRANKLAND vs. REGINA:
"The Hound of the Baskervilles"
>Case involving Mr. Frankland's lawsuit against the County Constabulary since it has not afforded him protection to which he is entitled. He claimed the Constabulary should have done more in preventing the town's people of Fernworthy from burning him in effigy.

FRASER:
"The Hound of the Baskervilles"
>A consumptive tutor, he with the Vandeleurs ran a successful private school in the east of Yorkshire. After his death the school fell from disrepute into infamy.

FRASER:
"The Disappearance of Lady Frances Carfax"
>Helpmate of Holy Peters, masquerades as Holy Peters wife. She is an Englishwoman, tall, pale, and with ferret eyes.

>AKA Mrs. Shlessinger, Mrs. Peters, Annie.
>See Shlessinger, Mrs.

FRASER, MARY:
"The Adventure of the Abbey Grange"
>See Lady Brackenstall.

FRATTON:
>"His Last Bow"
>"An Epilogue of Sherlock Holmes"
>>Town in England where Altamont lives.

FRENCH REPUBLIC:
>"The Final Problem"
>>An unrecorded case.   The French government engages
>>Holmes upon a matter of supreme importance in 1890.

FRIESLAND:
>"The Adventure of the Norwood Builder"
>>An unrecorded case. Involved the shocking affair of the
>>Dutch steamship, Friesland. Took place just after
>>Watson returned to Baker Street after having been away
>>during his marriage.

FRINTON:
>"The Adventure of the Retired Colourman"
>>Town in Essex near Moorsmoor and Little Purlington.

FULHAM ROAD:
>"The Hound of the Baskervilles"
>>Location of the dog dealers Ross and Mangles.

FULWORTH:
>"The Adventure of the Blanched Soldier"
>>A village near Holmes's retirement home in Sussex, it is
>>on the water, and juts out into the Channel breaking the
>>line of the long ocean beach.

THE GABLES:
      "The Adventure of the Lion's Mane"
            A large place where young men prepare for various professions with a staff of several masters. It is run by Harold Stackhurst.

GANGES:
      "The Sign of Four"
            Jonathan Small lost his leg to a crocodile in the Ganges, a river in Northern India.

GARCIA, ALOYSIUS:
      "The Adventure of Wisteria Lodge"
      aka "A Reminiscence of Mr. Sherlock Holmes"
            A young fellow of Spanish descent, a very good-looking man. He purported to be connected with the Spanish embassy. He was found murdered upon Oxshott Common, nearly a mile from his home.

GARRIDEB, ALEXANDER HAMILTON:
      "The Adventure of the Three Garridebs"
            He made his money in real estate and afterwards in the wheat pit in Chicago. He purchased a great deal of land along the Arkansas River west of Fort Dodge. He was very interested in his own strange name and searched for others with the same last name. When he died, he left a will, which was filed in the State of Kansas and divided his property into three parts. John Garrideb was to receive one-third if he could find two other men with the last name Garrideb to share the remaining two-thirds.

GARRIDEB, HOWARD:

"The Adventure of the Three Garridebs"

His office is located at the Grosvenor Buildings, Aston where he is in the business of the Construction of Agricultural Machinery. He had an advertisement in the local Birmingham newspaper concerning his business.

GARRIDEB, JOHN:

"The Adventure of the Three Garridebs"

Counselor at Law from Moorville, Kansas, U.S.A., he was a short, powerful man with the round, fresh, clean-shaven face characteristic of so many American men of affairs. His eyes were arresting and bespoke a more intense inward life, so bright were they, so alert, so responsive to every change of thought. He was in the law in Topeka, Kansas when he met one Alexander Hamilton Garrideb who left him one-third of his estate if he could locate two other men with last names of Garrideb.

AKA Killer Evans
See Evans, Killer

GARRIDEB, NATHAN:

"The Adventure of the Three Garridebs"

Nathan lives at 136 Little Ryder Street. He was a very tall, loose-jointed, round-backed person, gaunt and bald, about sixty years old. His face was cadaverous, with the dull dead skin of a man to whom exercise was unknown. Large round spectacles and a small projecting goat's beard combined with his stooping attitude to give him an expression of peering curiosity. He is confronted by John Garrideb as the possible inheritor of a large sum of money due to the strangeness of his last name. If he and John can locate one other Garrideb they will all be rich.

GELDER & CO.:
"The Adventure of the Six Napoleons"
> Located on Church Street, Stepney. They are a well-known house in the trade of statutes, etc. and have been for twenty years. It is the source of the six Napoleon busts, which are being smashed one at a time by some unknown criminal.

GEMMI PASS:
"The Final Problem"
> Holmes and Watson pass through it having traveled up the valley of the Rhone, branching off at Leuk. The Pass was still deep in snow. Holmes and Watson, in an attempt to shake off Moriarty, travel to Switzerland wandering up the valley of the Rhone, branching off at Leuk, over the Gemmi Pass, by way of Interlaken, to Meiringen.

GENEVA:
"The Final Problem"
> Holmes and Watson pass through Geneva during their travel to Switzerland wandering up the valley of the Rhone, branching off at Leuk, over the Gemmi Pass, by way of Interlaken, to Meiringen.

GHAZIS:
"A Study in Scarlet"
> See Watson, John

GIBSON, J. NEIL:
"The Problem of Thor Bridge"
> An ex-American Senator from a western state, better known as the greatest gold-mining magnate in the world. He is commonly known as the 'Gold King.' He is the greatest financial power in the world, a man with a most violent and formidable character. He has been living in

England for some time, having purchased a considerable estate in Hampshire five years ago. He was a tall, gaunt man with a craggy figure, cold gray eyes and bristling brows. His wife has died recently from a gunshot wound and the family governess has been accused of the crime. He met his wife while gold hunting in Brazil and after a while they married. After the romance died, he tried everything to destroy her love for him but to no avail, she adored him now as she had twenty years earlier. He has two children, who are educated by a very attractive governess, Miss Dunbar.

GILCHRIST:

"The Adventure of the Three Students"

Resides in a room directly above Hilton Soames at the College of St. Luke's. He is a fine student and athlete, being a member of the Rugby and cricket teams for the college. He received his Blue for the hurdles and long jump. He is a fine, manly fellow, hard-working and industrious. A tall, flaxen-haired, slim young fellow. His father, Sir Jabez Gilchrist, lost the family finances on the turf, leaving the son very poor. He has been preparing for the Fortescue Scholarship exam. He has recently been offered a commission in the Rhodesian Police, and is headed for South Africa. Bannister, Hilton Soames's servant, was butler to young Gilchrist's father. He assists young Gilchrist in obtaining a copy of the Fortescue Scholarship exam prior to the exam date.

GILCHRIST, JABEZ:

"The Adventure of the Three Students"

Sir Gilchrist, a notorious man, whose son attends the College of St. Luke, lost his family fortune on the turf.

GILMERTON MOUNTAINS:
>"The Valley of Fear" Part 2: "The Scowrers"
>>Mountains surrounding Vermissa Valley.

GLASSHOUSE STREET:
>"The Adventure of the Illustrious Client"
>>Street, at the rear of the Cafe Royal, where the two men who beat Sherlock Holmes, ran to escape capture after their attack on Holmes.

GLOBE:
>"The Adventure of the Priory School"
>>English newspaper, carried news of the abduction of the son of the Duke of Holdernesse from the Priory School.

GLORIA SCOTT:
>"The 'Gloria Scott'"
>>Ship which left Falmouth on the 8th of October 1855 and was destroyed at N. Lat 15.20', W. Long. 25.14' on November 6th 1855. This ship had been in the Chinese tea-trade before becoming a convict ship. She was a five-hundred-ton boat, carrying a crew of twenty-six, eighteen soldiers, a captain, three mates, a doctor, a chaplain, four wardens and thirty-eight prisoners. The 'Gloria Scott' departed Falmouth for Australia in October 1855 being a substitute convict ship, all others being used as transports to the Black Sea due to the Crimean War being at its height.

THE "GLORIA SCOTT":
>Published in "The Strand": April 1893
>Published as part of: "Memoirs of Sherlock Holmes"
>>The 'Gloria Scott' is the name of a ship. The first case Holmes was ever engaged. He assists his only college friend's father who's past, eventually, returns to haunt him. Holmes looses his friend's friendship in the end as

Victor Trevor travels to forget the past. Upon Holmes's arrival he shocks his friend's father by the details he is able to gather from the older man's appearance. Holmes receives a great compliment from Mr. Trevor: "it seems to be that all the detectives of fact and of fancy would be children in your hands." This encourages Holmes to consider detection his profession.

"The Musgrave Ritual"
>Mentioned in passing.

"The Resident Patient"
>Mentioned in passing.

"The Adventure of the Sussex Vampire"
>Holmes notes, as he perused one of his large indices, that this case was bad business and Watson has made a record of it, although Holmes was unable to congratulate him upon the result.

GLOUCESTER ROAD:
>"The Adventure of the Bruce-Partington Plans"
>>In Kensington, Goldini's Restaurant is located on Gloucester Road.

GLOUCESTER ROAD STATION:
>"The Adventure of the Bruce-Partington Plans"
>>In Kensington, Lestrade, Mycroft Holmes, Watson and Sherlock Holmes meet there by appointment and proceed to the residence of Hugo Oberstein.

GODNO:
>"The Hound of the Baskervilles"
>>An area in Little Russia where a case, Holmes compares to the 'Hound of the Baskervilles,' occurred in 1866.

GODOLPHIN STREET:
"The Adventure of the Second Stain"
>Number 16 Godolphin Street was the residence of one Eduardo Lucas, secret agent. It was a small select mansion among other old fashioned and secluded rows of eighteen-century houses, which lie between the river and the Abbey. It is almost in the shadow of the great Tower of the Houses of Parliament. It is in Westminster, a short walk from Whitehall Terrace.

GOLD KING:
"The Problem of Thor Bridge"
>See Gibson, Neil.

GOLDINI'S RESTAURANT:
"The Adventure of the Bruce-Partington Plans"
>Restaurant on Gloucester Road, Kensington.

GOODGE STREET:
"The Adventure of The Blue Carbuncle"
>See Peterson.

GORDON, GENERAL:
"The Resident Patient"
>His picture, newly framed, hangs on the wall in Holmes and Watson rooms at Baker Street.

"The Adventure of the Cardboard Box"
>Watson has a newly framed picture of the General hung on the wall in Baker Street.

GORDON SQUARE:
"The Adventure of the Noble Bachelor"
>Number 226 Gordon Square, living quarters of Hatty Doran and Frank Moulton, where Holmes finds them,

after having located the hotel Frank had been residing in prior to his joining Hatty.

GORGIANO, GIUSEPPE:
"The Adventure of the Red Circle"

Member of the Red Circle, an Italian criminal organization. He is at the bottom of fifty murders in America, and has a European fame as well. He has been tracked by Mr. Leverton of the Pinkerton American's Agency from New York to London. He is found murdered with a 'knife driven blade-deep into his body' in a second floor room of a house on Howe Street by Inspector Gregson of Scotland Yard, Mr. Leverton of the Pinkerton's American Agency, and Holmes and Watson. He had fled to New York in order to avoid the Italian police and set up a branch of the 'Red Circle' to force money from older Italian businessmen. He introduced Gennaro Lucca to the 'Red Circle' in Italy and meets him again in New York, forcing Gennaro to join the new branch. After Gorgiano is caught accosting Mrs. Lucca by Gennaro Lucca, he puts Gennaro in the position of having to kill his best friend, Tito Castalotte for not paying for protection, or expose himself and his family to the vengeance of his comrades.

Earned the name "death" in the south of Italy. He being originally from Posilippo, Italy.

AKA Black Gorgiano

GOROT, CHARLES:
"The Naval Treaty"

One of foreign minister Lord Holdhurst's clerks.

GOWER:
"The Valley of Fear" Part 2: "The Scowrers"
Joins Ted Baldwin, Mansel, Scanlan, the two Willabys and
John McMurdo in 'warning' the "Vermissa Herald"
editor/owner James Stanger to curb his stories on the
'Scowrers.'

GRAND HOTEL:
"The Adventure of the Illustrious Client"
Hotel near Charing Cross Station in London.

GRAND NATIONAL:
"The Adventure of Shoscombe Old Place"
Major horse race held in England each year. Once won
by Sir Robert Norberton.

GREYMINSTER, DUKE OF:
"The Adventure of the Blanched Soldier"
Deeply involved in the Abbey School case.

See Abbey School

GRAY'S INN ROAD:
"The Adventure of the Missing Three-quarter"
A street in London near the Bentley's hotel.

THE GREAT ALKALI PLAIN:
"A Study in Scarlet" Part 2 - "The Country of the Saints"
"In the central portion of the great North American
Continent there lies an arid and repulsive desert, which
for many a long year served as a barrier against the
advance of civilization. From the Sierra Nevada to
Nebraska, and from the Yellowstone River in the north
to the Colorado upon the south, is a region of desolation
and silence. Nor is Nature always in one mood
throughout this grim district. It comprises snow-capped

and lofty mountains, and dark and gloomy valleys. There are swift-flowing rivers which dash through jagged canyons; and there are enormous plains, which in winter are white with snow, and in summer are gray with the saline alkali dust. They all preserve, however, the common characteristics of barrenness, inhospitality, and misery."

GREAT GEORGE STREET:

"The Adventure of the Bruce-Partington Plans"

Number 13 is the home of Adolph Meyer, a man Mycroft Holmes believes has the ability to dispose of the Bruce-Partington papers. Located in Westminster.

GREAT ORME STREET:

"The Adventure of the Red Circle"

Street in London where Mrs. Warren's boarding house is located. It is a narrow thoroughfare at the northeast side of the British Museum.

GREAT PETER STREET POST-OFFICE:

"The Sign of Four"

From where Holmes dispatches a telegram to Wiggins, his dirty little lieutenant of the Baker Street Irregulars.

THE GREEK INTERPRETER:

Published in "The Strand": September 1893
Published as part of: "Memoirs of Sherlock Holmes"

Holmes is called upon by his brother Mycroft to solve the problem of the Greek prisoner and his villain captors. Holmes' family history is discussed and we are introduced to his brother Mycroft. Holmes meets a Greek interpreter who has been called upon to interpret for a man who has been bound and tortured. The interpreter is then driven to a desolate area and told not to mention a thing about what has transpired. His consultation with

Holmes also results in his death but Holmes, Watson and Mycroft Holmes arrive in time to save him but not the Greek prisoner.

"The Adventure of the Bruce-Partington Plans"
Watson remembers Holmes description of Mycroft Holmes's position in the British Government.

GREEN DRAGON:
"The Adventure of Shoscombe Old Place"
Pub owned by Mr. Barnes in Crendall.

GREEN, PHILIP:
"The Disappearance of Lady Frances Carfax"
He is a tall, dark, bearded man. The Honorable Philip Green was in love with Lady Frances Carfax but the relationship ended when she discovered his past. He made his way to South Africa and made his money at Barbarton. He now resides in London at the Langham Hotel. He was the son of the famous admiral of the same name who commanded the Sea of Azov fleet in the Crimean War.

GREGORY, INSPECTOR:
"Silver Blaze"
A man who was rapidly making his name in the English detective service. Sent a telegram to Holmes inviting him to assist in the case of the missing 'Silver Blaze.' Holmes believes Gregory lacks one quality, imagination.

GREGSON, TOBIAS:
"A Study in Scarlet"
The smartest of the Scotland Yarders, a tall, white-faced, flaxen-haired man.

"The Greek Interpreter"
>Referred to as "Inspector Gregson," he accompanied
Mycroft, Sherlock, and Watson to The Myrtles to locate
Mr. Melas, Paul Kratides, and Sophy Kratides as well as
Harold Latimer and Wilson Kemp. Only Mr. Melas
and Paul Kratides are present, both being slowly
poisoned by charcoal gas.

"The Adventure of Wisteria Lodge"
aka "A Reminiscence of Mr. Sherlock Holmes"
>An energetic, gallant and within his limitations, a capable
officer with Scotland Yard.

"The Adventure of the Red Circle"
>Holmes and Watson observe signals from a second floor
room of a Howe Street house and upon investigation
meet up with Gregson and a Mr.Leverton of the
Pinkerton's American Agency.

GREUZE, JEAN BAPTISTE:
"The Valley of Fear" Part 1: "The Tragedy of Birlstone"
>A French artist who flourished between 1750 and 1800,
his art has become quite valuable. Professor Moriarty
purchased, in 1865, one of his pictures entitled "La Jeune
Fille a l'Agneau" for one million two hundred thousand
frances (more than forty thousand pounds).

GRIGGS, JIMMY:
"The Adventure of the Retired Colourman"
>The clown in Ronder's wild beast show.

GRIMPEN:
"The Hound of the Baskervilles"
>A small clump of buildings comprises the hamlet of
Grimpen. It is also where Dr. Mortimer is
headquartered. Within a radius of five miles there are

very few buildings: Lafter Hall, Merripit House, two
moorland farmhouses, High Tor and Foulmire. Fourteen
miles away is the great convict prison of Princetown.

GRIMPEN MIRE:
"The Hound of the Baskervilles"
>The moor is mysterious with strange inhabitants, it is
>inscrutable as ever. Tufts of cotton grass grew among the
>slime.

GROSVENOR BUILDINGS:
"The Adventure of the Three Garridebs"
>Address of Howard Garrideb, Constructor of
>Agricultural Machinery, in Aston.

GROSVENOR MIXTURE:
"The Yellow Face"
>A pipe tobacco, expensive at eightpenny an ounce.

GROSVENOR SQUARE:
"The Adventure of the Noble Bachelor"
>An unrecorded case.
>Little problem involving a furniture van.

GRUNER, ADELBERT:
"The Adventure of the Illustrious Client"
>Baron Gruner is a man to whom violence is familiar and
>who will, literally, stick at nothing. There is no more
>dangerous man in Europe. He is known as the Austrian
>murderer. He killed his wife when the so-called
>accident happened in the Splugen Pass. A remarkably
>handsome man, he was of middle size, but built upon
>graceful and active lines. His face was swarthy, almost
>oriental, with large, dark, languorous eyes. His hair and
>moustache were raven black, the latter short, pointed, and
>carefully waxed. He was forty-two years old, though he

looked little over thirty. He met the daughter of General de Merville during a yachting voyage on the Mediterranean. They plan to marry, against the General's wishes, within a month. His residence is Vernon Lodge, near Kingston. A very large house, he has expensive tastes, collecting books, pictures, and Chinese pottery. A horse fancier, he plays polo at Hurlingham. Author of a book on Chinese pottery, he has a complex mind, and according to Holmes, "all great criminals have [a complex mind.]" When visited by Holmes, he issues a threat by telling Holmes that the beating given to the French agent Le Brun was at the Baron's direction, since Le Brun was inquiring into the Baron's affairs. Holmes is attacked by two men presumably on orders of the Baron. The local papers informed the public that he was taking a trip aboard the Cunard boat 'Rurtitania' to the States to settle some financial matters prior to his marriage to Violet de Merville. This information appeared seven days after the attack on Holmes. Watson visits him in the disguise of Dr. Hill Barton to sell him some valuable Chinese Pottery and while there witnesses Holmes theft of the Baron's diary and Miss Kitty Winter tossing vitriol on the Baron's face. The dangerous acid forever scars the Barons face but with the help of his diary, Holmes is able to convince Miss de Merville not to marry the Baron.

GUILD OF ST. GEORGE:

"The Crooked Man"

Established by Mrs. Barclay, wife of Colonel Barclay of 'The Royal Munsters,' in connection with the Watt Street Chapel, part of the Roman Catholic Church. Formed for the purpose of supplying the poor with cast-off clothing.

GUILDFORD ASSIZES:
>"The Adventure of Wisteria Lodge"
>aka "A Reminiscence of Mr. Sherlock Holmes"
>>One of many legal courts in England.

GUION STEAMSHIP COMPANY:
>"A Study in Scarlet"
>>Steamship Company located in London from where mail was sent to "American Exchange, Strand" for Enoch J. Drebber and Joseph Strangerson. Mail was found in the pocket of Enoch J. Drebber by Inspector Gregson while examining the body addressed in this manner.

CHAPTER H

THE HAGUE:
>"A Case of Identity"
>>An unrecorded case.
>>Holmes mentions a parallel case to that of Miss Mary
>>Sutherland's.

HAINES-JOHNSON:
>"The Adventure of the Three Gables"
>>Auctioneer and valuer, he visits Mary Maberley with an
>>offer to purchase her home, 'The Three Gables,' and all
>>its contents. No address is found on his card.

HALES, WILLIAM:
>"The Valley of Fear", Part 2: "The Scowrers"
>>Owner of the Stake Royal, he was one of the best known
>>and most popular mine owners in Gilmerton. He was
>>marked for death because he paid off certain drunken
>>and idle employees who were members of the all-
>>powerful society (the Scowrers of Gilmerton). He is
>>killed by Ted Baldwin and two others as a return favor to
>>Evans Pott for the killing of Josiah Dunn.

HALF MOON STREET:
>"The Adventure of the Illustrious Client"
>>Number 369 is the address of Dr. Hill Barton, the
>>disguised Watson.

HALLAMSHIRE, LORD LIEUTENANT OF:
>"The Adventure of the Priory School"
>>See Holdernesse, Duke of.

HALLIDAY'S PRIVATE HOTEL:
> "A Study in Scarlet"
>> Located in Little George Street. Residence of Joseph Stangerson who is discovered murdered by Mr. Lestrade of Scotland Yard when he goes to discuss the murder of Enoch J. Drebber with him. The Boots (innkeeper/helper) informed Lestrade that Mr. Stangerson was expecting someone, perhaps him (he didn't know who Lestrade was immediately). The cause of death was a stab wound in the left side which it is believed penetrated the heart. On one of the walls was written the word "RACHE."

HAMMERFORD WILL CASE:
> "The Adventure of the Illustrious Client"
>> Case involving the Hammerford Will where negotiations between Sir George Lewis and Sir James Damery resulted in a successful conclusion, a very delicate matter.

HAMMERSMITH:
> "The Adventure of the Second Stain" Town outside London.

HAMMERSMITH BRIDGE:
> "The Adventure of the Six Napoleons"
>> In Chiswick, a short walk from Laburnum Villa.

HAMPSHIRE:
> "The Problem of Thor Bridge"
>> County in southern England, southwest of London.

HAMPSTEAD:
> "The Adventure of Charles Augustus Milverton"
>> Where Charles Augustus Milverton resides, a section of London.

HARBOUR-DEFENSES:

"His Last Bow" "An Epilogue of Sherlock Holmes"

Von Bork, the German spy, had a safe containing pigeon-holes bristling with papers & plans, each with its own label. One compartment was labeled "Harbour-defences."

HARDEN, JOHN VINCENT:

"The Adventure of the Solitary Cyclist"

An unrecorded case.

A very abstruse and complicated problem concerning the persecution of the well known tobacco millionaire.

HARDING BROTHERS:

"The Adventure of the Six Napoleons"

Sellers of statutes and other items. Their offices are located two doors from the High Street Station. Mr. Horace Harker purchased a bust of Napoleon at the Harding Brothers store.

HARDY, CHARLES:

"The Adventure of the Second Stain"

A report from Sir Charles Hardy was in the dispatch-box belonging to the Right Honourable Trelawney Hope.

HARDY, SIR JOHN:

"The Adventure of the Empty House"

Played cards with Ronald Adair, Mr. Murray, and Colonel Moran the evening of Ronald Adair's murder. He was partners with Mr. Murray.

HARDY, MR:

"A Case of Identity"

Foreman for Miss Mary Sutherland's father, helped run the business with Mary's mother after her father's death. Went with Miss Mary Sutherland and her mother to the "gasfitters' ball" where Mary meets Hosmer Angel.

HARE, MR. JOHN:
"A Scandal in Bohemia"

Referenced by Watson in discussing the disguise Holmes undertakes in his attempt to trick IRENE ADLER into revealing her hiding place of the letters she possesses which were written to her by WILHELM GOTTSREICH SIGISMOND VON ORMSTEIN. Holmes disguise is that of a "character of an amiable and simpleminded Nonconformist clergyman. His broad black hat, his baggy trousers, his white tie, his sympathetic smile, and general look of peering and benevolent curiosity were such as Mr. John Hare alone could have equalled."

HARGRAVE:
"The Valley of Fear", Part 1: "The Tragedy of Birlstone"

Named given by an American who owned a Rudge-Whitworth bicycle and stayed at the hotel Eagle Commercial in Tunbridge two days prior to the murder of John Douglas. He as a man five foot nine, fiftyish, slightly grizzled hair, a grayish moustache, curved nose and a fierce and forbidding face.

AKA John Douglas

HARGRAVE, WILSON:
"The Adventure of the Dancing Men"

Friend of Holmes', he is of the New York Police Bureau. Provides Holmes with information on one Abe Slaney.

HARKER, HORACE:
"The Adventure of the Six Napoleons"

Lives at 131 Pitt Street, Kensington. He was an elderly man who worked for the Central Press Syndicate. He had purchased a bust of Napoleon from Harding

Brothers about four months ago, it is discovered smashed alongside a dead man near his front door.

HARLEY STREET:

"The Adventure of Shoscombe Old Place"
Location of the London mental hospital.

"The Adventure of the Devil's Foot"
Where Dr. Moore Agar, who recommends rest for Holmes, resides.

HAROLD, MRS.:

"The Adventure of the Mazarin Stone"
Old Mrs. Harold died leaving her estate (the Blymer estate) to Count Sylvius which he gambled away. Holmes claims that the death of Mrs. Harold was not accidental but arranged by the Count.

HARRAWAY:

"The Valley of Fear", Part 2: "The Scowrers"
A vulture-faced old graybeard, he was secretary of the Vermissa Lodge 341 'Eminent Order of Freemen.' He is one of the seven chosen to capture the Pinkerton man, Birdy Edwards. He was arrested by Captain Marvin and Birdy Edwards while waiting with his comrades to capture Edwards and kill him.

HARRINGBY, LORD:

"The Adventure of Wisteria Lodge"
aka "A Reminiscence of Mr. Sherlock Holmes"
Lives at 'The Dingle' which is located along the road between Wisteria Lodge and Oxshott.

HARRIS, MR.:
"The Stock-Broker's Clerk"

Of Bermondsey, an accountant, actually Holmes.
Holmes, Watson, and Hall Pycroft visit Mr. Pinner at the
office of Franco-Midland Hardware Company, Limited,
Holmes and Watson under alias'.

HARRISON, ANNIE:
"The Naval Treaty"

A striking-looking woman, a little short and thick for
symmetry, but with a beautiful olive complexion, large
dark, Italian eyes, and wealth of deep black hair. She is to
marry Percy Phelps of the Foreign Office. Her brother,
Joseph Harrison, is involved in the theft of the 'Naval
Treaty.'

HARRISON, JOSEPH:
"The Naval Treaty"

A stout man, closer to forty than thirty, with ruddy
cheeks and merry eyes. His sister, Annie Harrison is to
marry Percy Phelps. Has lost heavily in stocks. He has
stolen the treaty but has been unable to retrieve it from
its hiding place, the room wherein Percy Phelps recovers
from his depression over the disappearance of the treaty.
Holmes allows him to flee realizing that the government
would much rather have the matter remain quiet. Holmes
does notify the police but presumes they will find the nest
empty.

HARROW WEALD:
"The Adventure of the Three Gables"

Location of the home of Mary Maberley, The Three
Gables.

HARVEY:

"The Adventure of Shoscombe Old Place"

One of the boys who works for John Mason at Shoscombe Old Place. He found a charred fragment of bone in the central heating furnace in the cellar while cleaning it out.

HARVEY'S:

"The Adventure of the Sussex Vampire"

Name of house in Cheeman's, Lamberley, where homes are known by the names of those who built them.

HARWICH:

"His Last Bow" "An Epilogue of Sherlock Holmes"

Town in England, the lights at night can be seen from the English home of the German spy, Von Bork.

HATHERLEY FARM:

"The Boscombe Valley Mystery"

Farm where Charles McCarthy lived. Given to him, rent-free, by John Turner.

HATHERLEY, VICTOR:

"The Adventure of the Engineer's Thumb"

A quietly dressed man in a suit of heather tweed, with soft cloth cap, round one of his hands he had a handkerchief wrapped, it appears that he has lost his thumb. He was young, not more than twenty-five, with a strong masculine face. He is a hydraulic engineer living at 16A Victoria Street (3rd Floor). A bachelor, residing alone in London, his father and mother are dead, his father having died about two years ago. Did seven years apprenticed to Venner & Matheson, after which he struck out on his own with professional chambers at Victoria Street.

THE HAVEN:
"The Adventure of the Lion's Mane"
A modern house with a corner tower and slate roof in Fulworth. It is home to Ted Bellamy and his son, William, and daughter, Maud.

THE HAVEN HORROR:
"The Adventure of the Retired Colourman"
Name given to crime committed at The Haven, home of Josiah Amberley by the North Surrey Observer.

HAYES, REUBEN:
"The Adventure of the Priory School"
A self-evident villain, he is arrested at Chesterfield in an attempt to escape the clutches of Holmes. He conspired with James Wilder to kidnap Lord Saltire.

HAYLING, JEREMIAH:
"The Adventure of the Engineer's Thumb"
A twenty-six year old hydraulic engineer who disappeared on the 9th inst. (during the summer? of 1888). Left his lodgings at 10 o'clock and has not been heard from since.

HAYMARKET THEATRE:
"The Adventure of the Retired Colourman"
Josiah Amberley had two tickets to the theatre, upper circle seats, the night his wife and young Dr. Roy Ernest disappeared. Mr. Amberley went alone and did not use ticket number 31, B row, since his wife stayed home.

HAYTER, COLONEL:
"The Reigate Puzzle"
An old friend of Watson's who was under his care in Afghanistan. He has taken a house near Reigate in Surrey. A fine old soldier who had seen much of the world. He had a little armory of Eastern weapons.

HAYWARD:

"The Resident Patient"

One of the Worthingdon Bank Gang, after being released from prison, he and his fellow gang members seek out the gang member who turned on them and testified against them -- Sutton. It is believed he died as a passenger of the ill-fated steamer 'Norah Creina,' which was lost with all hands upon the Portuguese coast, some leagues to the north of Oporto.

HEAVY GAME OF THE WESTERN HIMALAYAS:

"The Adventure of the Empty House"
Authored by Colonel Sebastian Moran.

HEBRON, EFFIE (Mrs):

"The Yellow Face"
See Munro, Effie.

HEBRON, JOHN:

"The Yellow Face"

First husband of Effie (Hebron) Munro, they were married in Atlanta, Georgia, USA and had one child, Lucy. He died during the outbreak of yellow-fever. It was an inter-racial marriage, John Hebron was black, Effie Hebron was white.

HEBRON, LUCY:

"The Yellow Face"

Daughter of Effie and John Hebron, "a little coal-black negress. She has been living in a cottage near the home of Grant and Effie (Hebron) Munro without the knowledge of Grant Munro, hence this story.

HEIDEGGER:

"The Adventure of the Priory School"
German master at the Priory School.

HELMDALE:

"The Valley of Fear", Part 2: "The Scowrers"

Deep in the Vermissa Valley, the coal and iron trains traveled from Stagville through Vermissa and Bartons Crossing before continuing to Helmdale and then onto Merton.

HENDERSON, MR.:

"The Adventure of Wisteria Lodge"

aka "A Reminiscence of Mr. Sherlock Holmes"

He resides at 'High Gable' which is located along the road between Wisteria Lodge and Oxshott. He is a man of fifty, strong, active, with iron-gray hair, great bunched black eyebrows, the step of a deer, and the air of an emperor -- a fierce, masterful man, with a red-hot spirit behind his parchment face. He has two children: girls, eleven and thirteen.

AKA Don Murillo, The Tiger of San Pedro.
See Murillo, Don

HEREFORD:

"The Boscombe Valley Mystery"

Town where James McCarthy was being held by police during the investigation of his father's murder. Holmes visited James while he was held there.

HEREFORD ARMS:

"The Boscombe Valley Mystery"

Lodging in Ross where Inspector Lestrade stays while investigating the Boscome Valley Mystery

HERLING, BARON VON:
>"His Last Bow" "An Epilogue of Sherlock Holmes"
>>The chief secretary of the German legation. He is a big man, tall, deep, broad, with a slow, heavy speech.

HEINRICH:
>"His Last Bow" "An Epilogue of Sherlock Holmes"
>>Imperial Envoy for the King of Bohemia and cousin to the German spy, Von Bork.
>>See Adler, Irene

HIGGINS:
>"The Valley of Fear", Part 2: "The Scowrers"
>>Treasurer of the Merton County Lodge 249, 'Ancient Order of Freemen.'

HIGH BARROW:
>"The Hound of the Baskervilles"
>>A parish in the area of Dartmoor.

HIGH GABLE:
>"The Adventure of Wisteria Lodge"
>aka "A Reminiscence of Mr. Sherlock Holmes"
>>Home to Mr. Henderson, it is located along the road between Wisteria Lodge and Oxshott less than a half mile from the scene of the murder of Mr. Garcia. It is the famous old Jacobean grange of High Gable.

HIGH ROAD:
>"The Adventure of the Priory School"
>>Address of the Priory School near Mackleton.

HIGH STREET STATION:
>"The Adventure of the Six Napoleons"
>>Train station in London.

HIGH TOR:

"The Hound of the Baskervilles"
A moorland farmhouse near Grimpen.

HILL, INSPECTOR:

"The Adventure of the Six Napoleons"
Very knowledgeable of the Italian areas of London. Of
Scotland Yard.

HIS LAST BOW:

This compilation of adventures was published between 1908 and
1917. They appeared in book form as "His Last Bow" which
began with a 'preface' stating that the adventures 'involved
Holmes coming out of retirement to assist the British
government in the war against Germany and several previous
experiences so as to complete the volume.' Watson tells us that
Holmes "is still alive and well" but suffers "occasional attacks of
rheumatism." Holmes has lived on a small farm, five miles from
Eastbourne, for the past 'many' years and his retirement is spent
between philosophy and agriculture. The coming of the First
World War brings him out of retirement.

HIS LAST BOW:

"An Epilogue of Sherlock Holmes":
Published in "The Strand": September 1917
Published as part of: "His Last Bow"
This story is not told by Watson but by an anonymous narrator.
Holmes is called out of retirement from the South Downs to
break-up a German spy ring just prior to World War I. He
disguises himself as Altamont, a bitter Irish-American, who is
prepared to turn over British naval documents to the Germans.
Instead he hands the German agent a copy of "The Practical
Handbook of Bee Culture" before capturing him with
chloroform. In the end, he summons Watson to   participate in
the climax and thereafter gives his memorable speech: "There's an
east wind coming, Watson." "I think not, Holmes. It is very

warm." "Good old Watson! You are the one fixed point in a changing age. There's an east wind coming all the same, such a wind as never blew on England yet. It will be cold and bitter, Watson, and a good many of us may wither before its blast. But it's God's own wind none the less, and a cleaner, better, stronger land will lie in the sunshine when the storm has cleared."

HISTON:
"The Adventure of the Missing Three-quarter"
A sleepy hollow in England.

HOBBS, FAIRDALE:
"The Adventure of the Red Circle"
An unrecorded case, Holmes arranged an affair for her a year ago. She is a lodger of Mrs. Warren's.

HOBSON'S PATCH:
"The Valley of Fear", Part 2: "The Scowrers"
Home to Brother Scanlan of the Vermissa Lodge 341. It is a couple of stops on the railroad before Vermissa.

HOFFMAN:
"The Adventure of the Mazarin Stone"
Musician who wrote a 'Barcarole' which Holmes plays on his violin while waiting a decision from Count Sylvius.

HOLBURN BAR:
"The Adventure of the Three Gables"
Young Perkins was killed outside the bar. Holmes believes Black Steve was responsible for the killing of Perkins outside the Holburn Bar.

HOLDER, ALEXANDER:

"The Adventure of the Beryl Coronet"
Of the banking firm of Holder & Stevenson, of Threadneedle Street. A man about 50, tall, portly, and imposing, with a massive, strongly marked face and a commanding figure.

HOLDER, ARTHUR:

"The Adventure of the Beryl Coronet"
Only child of Alexander Holder. He was wild, wayward, and could not be trusted in the handling of large sums of money. He has a charming way and is a member of an aristocratic club where he plays cards and squanders money on the turf. He is spotted with the Beryl Coronet, with three stones missing, by his father who presumes he has sold the gems to pay his gambling debts which his father would not pay. Close friends with Sir George Burnwell. In love with his cousin, Mary Holder whom he has asked to marry him twice, being refused both times. He witnesses his cousin passing the Beryl Coronet out the window to Sir George Burnwell and chases Burnwell down retrieving the Beryl Coronet minus three stones which broke off in the struggle. He refuses to tell his father what he has witnessed, knowing it would break his father's heart.

HOLDER, JOHN:

"The Sign of Four"
Company sergeant under Jonathan Small. A very fine swimmer who saved the life of Jonathan Small after his leg was bitten off by a crocodile in the Ganges.

HOLDER, MARY:

"The Adventure of the Beryl Coronet"
Niece of Alexander Holder, her father having died five years ago, her Uncle has taken her into his family and adopted her. She is sweet, loving, beautiful, a wonderful

manager and housekeeper, yet as tender and quiet and gentle as a woman could be. Arthur Holder has twice asked her to marry him but she has refused. She is twenty-four years old. Falls under the spell of Sir George Burnwell. Conspirator with Sir George Burnwell in the attempted theft of the Beryl Coronet. Her cousin, Arthur, witnesses her assisting Sir George in the theft of the 'Beryl Coronet' yet keeps quiet to protect her. She runs off with Sir George leaving behind her Uncle and cousin after Holmes recovers the missing piece of the Beryl Coronet.

HOLDER & STEVENSON:
"The Adventure of the Beryl Coronet"
A banking firm on Threadneedle Street.
See Holder, Alexander.

HOLDERNESSE, DUCHESS:
"The Adventure of the Priory School"
Married to the Duke of Holdernesse, her name is Edith, she has had a son by the Duke and it is he who has been kidnapped. She has separated from the Duke and is currently residing in the south of France.

HOLDERNESSE, DUKE OF:
"The Adventure of the Priory School"
6th Duke, K.G., P.C. -- Baron Beverley, Earl of Carston -- Lord Lieutenant of Hallamshire since 1900. Married Edith, daughter of Sir Charles Appledore, 1888. Heir and only child, Lord Saltire. Owns about two hundred and fifty thousand acres. Minerals in Lancashire and Wales. Address: Carlton House Terrace; Holdernesse Hall, Hallamshire; Carston Castle, Bangor, Wales. Lord of the Admiralty, 1872; Chief Secretary of State for -- Of late a Cabinet Minister. His marriage has recently ended in a peaceful separation, with is wife moving to the south of

France. Fathered James Wilder, his illegitimate son, before his marriage to the Duchess.

HOLDERNESSE HALL:
"The Adventure of the Priory School"
Home to the Duke of Holdernesse, it is located in Hallamshire.

HOLDHURST, LORD:
"The Naval Treaty"
Great conservative politician, and uncle to Percy Phelps, old schoolmate of Watson's. Became foreign minister bringing his nephew, Percy Phelps, along with him as a clerk. "Cabinet minister and future premier of England," as described by Holmes. He resides in Downing Street.

HOLLAND:
"His Last Bow" "An Epilogue of Sherlock Holmes"
Where Altamont is planning to flee after obtaining his money for handing over the 'Naval Signals' to Von Bork.

"The Adventure of the Mazarin Stone"
See Amsterdam.

HOLLIS:
"His Last Bow" "An Epilogue of Sherlock Holmes"
He was employed by Von Bork to spy for the Germans, captured by the British, Von Bork would offer no help.

HOLLOWAY AND STEELE:
"The Adventure of the Three Garridebs"
House agents for Nathan Garrideb with offices on Edgware Road.

HOLLY, SIR EDWARD:
"The 'Gloria Scott'"

Attacked by a poaching gang which he helped break-up. The gang members had sworn to knife him and Justice of the Peace Trevor in revenge.

HOLMES'S FAILURES:
"A Case of Identity"

Watson remarks "Once only had I know him to fail, in the case of the King of Bohemia and of the Irene Adler photograph ... " "The Five Orange Pips" Holmes states for the record "I have been beaten four times, three times by men, and once by a woman."

HOLMES, MYCROFT:
"The Greek Interpreter"

Holmes' brother, seven years older than Sherlock. Sherlock believes Mycroft has powers of observation better than he. He is very well known in his own circle, and spends much of his time at the Diogenes Club, being there always from quarter to five until twenty to eight. He is one of the Founders of the Club. Unlike Sherlock he will not go out of his way to verify his own solutions, and would rather be considered wrong than take the trouble to prove himself right. He has an extraordinary faculty for figures, and audits the books in some of the government departments. He lodges in Pall Mall, and he walks round the corner into Whitehall every morning and back every evening. Mycroft is a much larger and stouter man than Sherlock, his body is absolutely corpulent, but his face, though massive, had preserved something of the sharpness of expression which was so remarkable in that of his brother. His eyes, which were of a peculiarly light, watery gray, seemed to always retain that far-away, introspective look.

"The Final Problem"
> Mycroft is the coachman who drives the brougham delivering Watson to the train at Victoria as Holmes and Watson attempt to give Moriarty the slip.

"The Adventure of the Empty House"
> Holmes's only confidant in his secret faking of his death.

"The Adventure of the Bruce-Partington Plans"
> Mycroft comes over to see Sherlock at Baker Street, it is only the second time Mycroft has gone to 221B Baker Street. He keeps his own cycle, his Pall Mall lodgings, the Diogenes Club, Whitehall. Sherlock informs Watson that Mycroft "occasionally ... is the British government."
>
> Mycroft draws a salary of four-hundred fifty pounds a year, remains a subordinate, has no ambitions of any kind, will receive neither honor nor title, but remains the most indispensable man in the country. He has the tidiest and most orderly brain, with the greatest capacity for storing facts of any living man. The conclusions of every department are passed to him, and he is the central exchange, the clearinghouse, which makes out the balance. Where other men are specialists, he is omniscience. Again and again his word has decided the national policy of England. He is tall and portly.

HOLMES, SHERLOCK:
> See separate chapter, HOLMES, SHERLOCK, next.

THE HOLY WAR:
"The Adventure of the Empty House"
> Book offered for sale to Watson by a little old bookseller from his neighborhood.

HOMER:
"The Reigate Puzzle"

A copy of Pope's Homer was among the stolen articles from Old Acton's house.

HOPE, HILDA TRELAWNEY:
"The Adventure of the Second Stain"

Lady Hilda Trelawney Hope, youngest daughter of the Duke of Belminster, she was the most lovely woman in London, wife to The Right Honourable Trelawney Hope, Secretary for European Affairs. She steals an important document from her husband which she exchanges for a compromising letter she wrote when she was young. It is her hope to keep the compromising letter from her husband. When she realizes the importance of the document she has stolen she retrieves it allowing Holmes to return it to its rightful place.

HOPE, JEFFERSON:
"A Study in Scarlet"

According to Holmes "the murderer of Enoch Drebber and of Joseph Stangerson."

Part 2, Chapters 1 through 5 of "A Study in Scarlet" tells the story of Jefferson Hope. Some information is listed here.

Originally from St. Louis, met Lucy and John Ferrier while traveling to Salt Lake City, he and his companions had been among the Nevada Mountains prospecting for silver and were returning to Salt Lake City in hope of raising capital enough to work some lodes which they had discovered. He becomes "engaged" to Lucy but does not marry her due to the intervention of the "Sacred Council of Four." On the very night after his capture by Scotland Yard for the murders of Stangerson and Drebber (he, who had married Lucy against her will), he suffers an aneurism, and he was found in the morning stretched upon the floor of the cell, with a placid smile upon his face.

HOPE, TRELAWNEY:

"The Adventure of the Second Stain"
The Right Honourable, Secretary for European Affairs, he was dark, clear-cut, and elegant, not yet of middle-age, and endowed with every beauty of body and of mind, he also had a moustache. His dispatch box is broken into and a valuable document is stolen forcing him to consult Holmes regarding its recovery. He lives in Whitehall Terrace.

HOPKINS, EZEKIAH:

"The Red-Headed League"
American millionaire Founder of the Red-Headed League. His name and information about him is provided by VINCENT SPAULDING to JABEZ WILSON as background to a newspaper advertisement in "The Morning Chronicle" on April 27, 1890.

HOPKINS, STANLEY:

"The Adventure of Black Peter"
A young police inspector for whose future Holmes had high hopes.

"The Adventure of the Golden Pince-Nez"
A young promising detective.

"The Adventure of the Missing Three-quarter"
Inspector with Scotland Yard.

"The Adventure of the Abbey Grange"
> Inspector with Scotland Yard, he request Holmes's assistance in "what promises to be a most remarkable case."

HORNER, JOHN:
"The Adventure of The Blue Carbuncle"
> Plumber accused of stealing the "Blue Carbuncle" from the room of the Countess of Morcar. There is evidence of a prior conviction for robbery.

HORSHAM:
"The Adventure of the Sussex Vampire"
> North of Sussex, in southern England.

HORSOM, DR.:
"The Disappearance of Lady Frances Carfax"
> Of 13 Firbank Villas, he is the doctor called in to tend to Rose Spender by Fraser and Holy Peters in her final days.

HOTEL COSMOPOLITAN:
"The Adventure of The Blue Carbuncle"
> Location of the robbery of the "Blue Carbuncle" on December 22.

HOTEL DIRECTORY:
"The Hound of the Baskervilles"
> Directory listing all the Hotels in England.

HOTEL DULONG:
"The Reigate Puzzle"
> Hotel where Holmes is lying ill at the beginning of the Reigate Puzzle. He sends a telegram to Watson from here. It is located in Lyon.

HOTEL DU LOUVRE:
"The Adventure of the Bruce-Partington Plans"
>Located in Paris, France, it is the residence of Hugo Oberstein when he is not using his Caulfield Gardens, Kensington address.

HOTEL NATIONAL:
"The Disappearance of Lady Frances Carfax"
>Located in Lausanne, it is the Hotel where Lady Frances Carfax stayed and was last heard from. M. Moser is the manager, Jules Vibart is one of the head waiters.

HOTSPUR:
"The 'Gloria Scott'"
>Ship which picks-up the 'survivors' of the sinking 'Gloria Scott,' dropping them at Sydney, Australia.

THE HOUND:
"The Hound of the Baskervilles"
>An enormous coal-black hound, but not such a hound as mortal eyes have ever seen. Fire burst from its open mouth, its eyes glowed with a smouldering glare, its muzzle and hackles and dewlap were outlined in flickering flame. Never in the delirious dream of a disordered brain could anything more savage, more appalling, more hellish be conceived than that dark form and savage face which it bore.

THE HOUND OF THE BASKERVILLES:
Published in "The Strand Magazine"
August 1901 through April 1902.

>The third of four novels. Holmes is consulted concerning the "Legend of the Hound of the Baskervilles" and thereby the safety of Sir Henry Baskerville.

See "Legend of the Hound"

Occurs prior to "The Final Problem" in time, being a reminiscence of Watson.

NOTE: Although this story is dated as occurring from August/September 1889 through November 1889 and Watson has been living at Baker Street, readers will note that in "The Sign of Four" Watson becomes engaged to Mary Morstan in September 1888 and marries her a few months later. "The Crooked Man" occurs a few months after Watson's marriage, late 1888-early 1889, and Holmes visits Watson at his home. "The Naval Treaty" occurs in the July succeeding Watson's marriage, July 1889. "The Adventure of the Engineer's Thumb" takes place not long after Watson's marriage, in the summer of 1889.

HOWE STREET:
"The Adventure of the Red Circle"
> London street near the British Museum and can be seen from some of the houses located on Great Orme Street. Holmes comes upon Inspector Gregson and Mr. Leverton, of Pinkerton's American Agency, at a flat on Howe Street after he, Holmes, has observed a signal from one of the windows on the second floor. The three detectives enter the room to find a murdered man with a "knife driven blade deep into his body."

HOWELLS, RACHEL:
"The Musgrave Ritual"
> Second housemaid at the Manor House of Hurlstone, home to the Musgraves, she was engaged to marry the Butler, Richard Brunton, but he threw her off for the game-keepers daughter, Janet Tregellis. She is a very good girl but of an excitable Welsh temperament. A passionate Celtic woman, she disappeared three days after

the disappearance of Brunton. Holmes concludes she was a co-conspirator with Brunton in the search for the Musgrave treasure.

HUDSON:
"The 'Gloria Scott'"
A little wizened fellow with a cringing manner and a shambling style of walking. His face was thin and brown and crafty, with perpetual smile upon it, which showed an irregular line of yellow teeth, and his crinkled hands were half closed in a way that is distinctive of sailors. He had been a young seaman on-board the 'Gloria Scott' but did not (or so it appears) participate in the conspiracy and take-over of the 'Gloria Scott.' After the sinking of the 'Gloria Scott' he was the lone survivor, eight others having voluntarily left on a small boat prior to the sinking. He was saved by these eight other, included in the group were, James Armitage and Evans. With the knowledge that Armitage and Evans had become successful, he eventually tracked them to England hoping to play off their fears of discovery through blackmail.

HUDSON, MORSE:
"The Adventure of the Six Napoleons"
Owns a place for the sale of pictures and statutes in the Kennington Road. Sold busts of Napoleon.

HUDSON, Mrs:
"The Sign of Four"
Holmes' landlady.

"The Naval Treaty"
Landlady of Holmes and Watson, lives at 221B Baker Street.

"The Adventure of the Empty House"
> Holmes landlady, she kept his lodgings in order during his absence at the request of brother Mycroft.

"The Adventure of the Second Stain"
> Holmes and Watson's landlady.

"The Adventure of Wisteria Lodge"
aka "A Reminiscence of Mr. Sherlock Holmes"
> Landlady for Holmes and Watson.

"The Adventure of the Dying Detective"
> Holmes's landlady, a long suffering woman due to the eccentricities of her lodger.

"The Adventure of the Mazarin Stone"
> Holmes's landlady.

"The Adventure of the Three Garridebs"
> Holmes's landlady.

HUDSON STREET:
"The Crooked Man"
> A busy thoroughfare between Watt Street Chapel and 'Lachine,' home of Colonel and Mrs. Barclay. It is here that Mrs. Barclay meets 'Henry' (Wood), a dreadful-looking creature.

HUNG-WU:
"The Adventure of the Illustrious Client"
> Watson studies Chinese Pottery in preparation for a disguised meeting with Baron Gruner about the sale of a genuine eggshell pottery saucer of the Ming dynasty. In this quest he studies the marks of the Hung-wu.

HUNT:

"The Valley of Fear", Part 2: "The Scowrers"

One of two policemen killed because he ventured, with his partner, Evans, to arrest two members of the 'Scowrers.' Both policemen were unarmed and killed in cold blood during the winter of 1875.

HUNTER, NED:

"Silver Blaze"

One of the three lads under John Straker, Colonel Ross's horse trainer. Was on guard duty, guarding the horses Silver Blaze and Bayard, when a man looking for a tip on the race appeared, he was chased away by Ned.

HUNTER, VIOLET:

"The Adventure of the Copper Beeches"

A young lady, bright, quick face, freckled like a plover's egg with the brisk manner of a woman who has had to make it on her own in the world. She sends a letter to Holmes from Montague Place requesting an appointment concerning whether or not she should take a position of governess which has recently been offered to her. She had previously been employed for five years as governess by Colonel Spence Munro, but he moved two months prior, leaving her without a position. Her accomplishments consist of "a little French, a little German, music, and drawing." She becomes the head of a private school at Walsall.

HURET:

"The Adventure of the Golden Pince-Nez"

An unrecorded case, took place during 1894. Involved the tracking and arrest of the Boulevard assassin. This case won for Holmes an autograph letter of thanks from the French President and the Order of the Legion of Honour.

HURLINGHAM:
>"The Adventure of the Illustrious Client"
>>Polo grounds in London.

HUXTABLE, THORNEYCROFT:
>"The Adventure of the Priory School"
>>M.A., Ph.D. He is a large, pompous, dignified man, the very embodiment of self-possession and solidity. He is the founder and principal of the Priory, a preparatory school near Mackleton. He consults Holmes concerning the kidnapping of the Duke of Holdernesse's son from the Priory school.

HUXTABLE'S SIDELIGHTS ON HORACE:
>"The Adventure of the Priory School"
>>Book written by Dr. Thorneycroft Huxtable, founder and principal of the Priory School.

HYAM, MR.:
>"The Valley of Fear", Part 2: "The Scowrers"
>>Old man allegedly murdered by the Scowrers.

HYAMS:
>"The Adventure of the Norwood Builder"
>>Mr. Jonas Oldacre's tailor.

HYNES, HYNES:
>"The Adventure of Wisteria Lodge"
>aka "A Reminiscence of Mr. Sherlock Holmes"
>>Mr. Hynes is a J.P. and resides at 'Purdey Place' which is located along the road between Wisteria Lodge and Oxshott.

SHERLOCK HOLMES

HOLMES, SHERLOCK
"A Study in Scarlet"

Watson is introduced to Sherlock Holmes by a friend, Stanford, who had been a dresser under Watson at St. Bartholomew's Hospital. Stanford describes Holmes as working at the chemical lab at the hospital, being well up in anatomy and a first-rate chemist. Stamford continues that Holmes is a decent fellow although a "little queer" in his ideas. He tells Watson "perhaps you would not care for him as a constant companion."

Holmes's first words are "I've found it! I've found it!" referring to his development of a new test for bloodstains while Watson and Stamford look on.

Watson agrees to share the Baker Street lodgings with Holmes even after Holmes informs him that he smokes strong tobacco, he always smokes 'ship's.'

Holmes resides at 221B Baker Street, consisting of a couple of comfortable bedrooms and a single large airy sitting-room, cheerfully furnished, and illuminated by two broad windows.

Watson observes that it is rare for Holmes to be up after ten at night. Watson also notices a dreamy, vacant expression in Holmes' eyes to the degree that Watson suspects an addiction to the use of some narcotic. However, Holmes' temperance and cleanliness in his whole like forbid such a notion.

Watson describes Holmes as follows:

"In height he was rather over six feet, and so excessively lean that he seemed to be considerably taller. His eyes were sharp and piercing, save during those intervals of torpor. His thin, hawk-like nose gave his whole expression an air of alertness and decision. His chin, too, had the prominence and squareness which mark the man of determination. His hands were invariably blotted with ink and stained with chemicals, yet he was possessed of extraordinary delicacy of touch."

"His ignorance was as remarkable as his knowledge. Of contemporary literature, philosophy, and politics, he appeared to know next to nothing."

"SHERLOCK HOLMES - his limits"
1. Knowledge of Literature - Nil
2. Knowledge of Philosophy - Nil
3. Knowledge of Astronomy - Nil
4. Knowledge of Politics - Feeble
5. Knowledge of Botany - Variable, well up in belladonna, opium, and poisons generally. Knows nothing of practical gardening.
6. Knowledge of Geology - Practical, but limited. Tells at a glance different soils from each other. After walks has shown me splashes upon his trousers, and told me by their colour and consistence in what part of London he had received them.
7. Knowledge of Chemistry - Profound
8. Knowledge of Anatomy - Accurate, but unsystematic
9. Knowledge of Sensational Literature - Immense, he appears to know every detail of every horror perpetrated in the century.
10. Plays the violin well
11. Is an expert singlestick player, boxer, and swordsman.

12. Has a good practical knowledge of British law.

"The Book of Life"
    Written by Sherlock Holmes, it attempt to show how
    much an observant man might learn by an accurate and
    systematic examination of all that came in his way.

"A Scandal in Bohemia"
    Holmes refers to Dr. Watson as "my Boswell."

"The Sign of Four"
    "UPON THE DISTINCTION BETWEEN THE
    ASHES OF THE VARIOUS TOBACCOS":
    Monograph written by Holmes. Holmes also mentions
    another monograph concerning the tracing of footsteps
    and the use of plaster of paris. Additionally he mentions
    a curious little work upon the influence of a trade upon
    the form of the hand, with lithotypes of the hands of
    slaters, sailors, cork-cutters, compositors, weaver's and
    diamond-polishers.

"A Case of Identity"
    Watson remarks "Once only had I know him to fail, in
    the case of the King of Bohemia and of the Irene Adler
    photograph ... "

"The Five Orange Pips"
    Holmes states for the record "I have been beaten four
    times, three times by men, and once by a woman."

"The Man with the Twisted Lip"
    Watson discovers Holmes in an opium den while
    searching for a friend.

"The Adventure of the Engineer's Thumb"
>His before-breakfast pipe was composed of all the plugs and dottles left from his smokes of the day before which had been carefully dried and collected on the corner of the mantelpiece.

"Silver Blaze"
>Here is the first mention of the "deerstalker" hat that Holmes wears: "his ear-flapped traveling-cap."

"The 'Gloria Scott'"
>This case involves Holmes association with one of his two friends from his college days, Victor Trevor.

>It is Holmes's first case.

"The Musgrave Ritual"
>His method of thought was the neatest and most methodical of mankind. He affected a certain quiet primness of dress. In his personal habits, he was one of the most untidy men that ever drove a fellow-lodger to distraction. He kept his cigars in the coal-scuttle, his tobacco in the toe of a Persian slipper, and his unanswered correspondence transfixed by a jack-knife into the very centre of his wooded mantelpiece. He would sit in an armchair with his hair-trigger pistol and a hundred Boxer cartridges and proceed to adorn the opposite wall with a patriotic V.R. done in bullet-pockets. The chambers were always filled full of chemicals and of criminal relics. He had a horror of destroying documents, especially those which were connected with his past cases. He kept all his papers in a large tin box. When Holmes first came to London he had rooms in Montague Street, just round the corner from the British Museum.

>This case involves Holmes association with one of his

two friends from his college days, Reginald Musgrave.
Holmes informs Watson that this was his third case.

"The Greek Interpreter"

He was an isolated phenomenon, a brain without a heart,
as deficient in human sympathy as he was preeminent in
intelligence. His aversion to women and his
disinclination to form new friendships were both typical
of his unemotional character, but not more so than his
complete suppression of every reference to his own
people. His brother Mycroft Holmes is seven years his
senior and, according to Sherlock, the one with the
greater powers of observation. See Holmes, Mycroft.

Of his family he says, "My ancestors were country
squires, who appear to have led much the same life as is
natural to their class. His grandmother is the sister of
Vernet, the French artist.

"The Final Problem"

After Watson's marriage and subsequent start in private
practice, the very intimate relations which had existed
between Holmes and Watson became, to some extent,
modified. Holmes still came to Watson from time to
time when he desired a companion in his investigations,
but those occasions grew more and more seldom, until
Watson found that in the year 1890 there were only three
cases of which Watson retained any record.

It was believed that Holmes died, along with Moriarty,
locked in each other's arms, reeling over the Reichenbach
falls on May 4, 1891.

"The Adventure of the Empty House"

Holmes returns to London, in 1894, disguised as an old book-seller, after allowing the world to believe he died in 1891.

"The Adventure of the Priory School"

He is familiar with forty-two different impressions left by tyres.

"The Adventure of the Cardboard Box"

Watson tells us that Holmes has purchased a 'Stradivarius' violin, worth about 500 guineas at a Jew's broker's in Tottenham Court Road for 55 shillings. Holmes informs Watson that he wrote two monographs, which appeared a year earlier in 'Anthropological Journal,' on the human ear and how each and every ear is distinct and differs from all other ones.

"The Adventure of the Red Circle"

He was accessible upon the side of flattery and on the side of kindliness.

"The Adventure of the Bruce-Partington Plans"

Has recently made the music of the Middle-Ages his hobby. He is rewarded by Queen Victoria for his success in recovering the submarine plans which are the basis of this case.

"The Adventure of the Dying Detective"

He was incredibly untidy, addicted to music at strange hours, he practiced with his revolver in his rooms, he conducted malodorous scientific experiments and there was forever an atmosphere of violence and danger surrounding him.

He had a remarkable gentleness and courtesy in his dealings with women. Although he disliked and distrusted the female sex, he was always a chivalrous opponent.

Watson is summoned to Baker Street by Mrs. Hudson concerning the grave illness of Holmes, on the mantelpiece in his rooms were the following items: "A litter of pipes, tobacco pouches, syringes, penknives, revolver-cartridges, and other debris."

"The Adventure of the Devil's Foot"
He has never been known to write where a telegram would serve. "His health was not a matter in which he himself took the faintest interest, for his mental detachment was absolute..."

"His Last Bow" "An Epilogue of Sherlock Holmes"
PRACTICAL HANDBOOK OF BEE CULTURE WITH SOME OBSERVATIONS UPON THE SEGREGATION OF THE QUEEN:
Book written by Sherlock Holmes, he presents it to the German spy, Von Bork as the 'Naval Signals' before chloroforming him.

"The Valley of Fear", Part 1: "The Tragedy of Birlstone"
Admits to Inspector MacDonald that he has never met Professor Moriarty.

"The Adventure of the Mazarin Stone"
"I am a brain. The rest of me is a mere appendix."

"The Adventure of the Creeping Man"
He was always of the opinion that Watson should publish the singular facts of the case of Professor Presbury, if for

no other reason than to dispel the ugly rumors, which agitated the university some twenty years ago.

"The Adventure of the Three Garridebs"
Refused a knighthood in June 1902 for services rendered to England. When Watson is shot by Killer Evans, Holmes responds, after examining Watson's wound, "By the Lord, it is well for you. If you had killed

Watson, you would not have got out of this room alive. Watson believes it to be "the one and only time I caught a glimpse of a great heart as well as of a great brain. All my years of humble but single-minded service culminated in that moment of revelation." "It was worth a wound – it was worth many wounds - to know the depth of loyalty and love which lay behind that cold mask." Holmes directs Watson to "give the Yard a call" after they have captured Killer Evans. It is the first time Holmes uses a telephone.

"The Adventure of the Illustrious Client"
Watson believes this case to be the "supreme moment of my friend's career." Holmes had a weakness for the Turkish bath. Holmes's view towards women can be seen in the following quote: "Woman's heart and mind are insoluble puzzles to the male." Holmes is beaten by two men armed with sticks outside the Cafe Royal in Regent Street as a warning for his meddling in the affairs of Baron Gruner. Morphine is given to him by Sir Leslie Oakshott, the famous surgeon, for his injuries sustained in the attack.

"The Adventure of the Blanched Soldier"
Holmes writes this adventure himself and states: "The good Watson had at that time [January 1903] deserted me

for a wife, the only selfish action which I can recall in our association. I was alone."

"The Adventure of the Lion's Mane"
Holmes wrote this adventure himself. He has retired and this case is authored by him, Watson having "passed beyond [his] ken," except for an occasional week-end visit. He lives with his housekeeper and bees in Sussex upon the southern slope of the downs with a commanding view of the Channel.

"The Adventure of the Retired Colourman"
His eyes are gray, bright and keen as rapiers. Sends Watson to investigate this case because of other pressing business. When Watson reports as to his findings, Holmes replies: "[you] have missed everything of importance." Holmes then attempts to soothe Watson with: "Don't be hurt, my dear fellow. You know that I am quite impersonal. No one else would have done better. Some possibly not so well."

"The Adventure of the Veiled Lodger"
Holmes has been engaged in private practice for some 23 years, of which Watson has been with him for 17 years.

"The Adventure of Shoscombe Old Place"
His use of the microscope and its application to solving crimes is revealed as he discusses the St. Pancras case.

HOLMES'S DRUG USE:
"The Sign of Four"
The first mention of Holmes' use of drugs. It begins thus: "Sherlock Holmes took his bottle from the corner of the mantlepiece, and his hypodermic syringe from its neat morocco case. With his long, white, nervous fingers he adjusted the delicate needle and rolled back his left

shirtcuff. For some little time his eyes rested thoughtfully upon the sinewy forearm and wrist, all dotted and scarred with innumerable puncture-marks. Finally, he thrust the sharp point home, pressed down the tiny piston, and sank back into the velvet-lined armchair with a long sigh of satisfaction."

"Three times a day for many months I had witnessed this performance ... "

"Which is it today, I asked, morphine or cocaine? It is cocaine, a seven-percent solution."

"A Case of Identity"
Watson discovers Holmes in an opium den.

"The Yellow Face"
Save for the occasional use of cocaine, he had no vices, and he only turned to the drug as a protest against the monotony of existence when cases were scanty and the papers uninteresting.

"The Man with the Twisted Lip"
Watson, while searching an opium den for the husband of his wife's friend Kate, discovers Sherlock Holmes in the very opium den he is searching. As they exit the den, Holmes questions Watson, "I suppose that you imagine that I have added opium-smoking to cocaine injections, and all the other little weaknesses on which you have favoured me with your medical views."

"The Adventure of the Missing Three-Quarter"
Watson: "For years I had gradually weaned him from that drug mania which had threatened once to check his remarkable career.

"The Adventure of the Dying Detective"

Watson is summoned to Baker Street by Mrs. Hudson concerning the grave illness of Holmes, on the mantelpiece in his rooms were the following items: "A litter of pipes, tobacco pouches, syringes, penknives, revolver-cartridges, and other debris."

CHAPTER I

I'M SITTING ON THE STILE, MARY:
"The Valley of Fear" Part 2: "The Scowrers"

>Song sung by John McMurdo to the great thrill of his
>new Lodge, "Eminent Order of Freemen", of Vermissa.

IMPERIAL THEATRE:
"The Adventure of the Solitary Cyclist"
>Miss Violet Smith's father James conducted the orchestra
>here before his death.

IMPERIAL TOKAY:
"His Last Bow" "An Epilogue of Sherlock Holmes"
>An expensive wine favored by Altamont and in supply at
>the English home of the German spy, Von Bork.

IMPERIAL YEOMANRY:
"The Adventure of the Blanched Soldier"
>British division stationed in South Africa during the Boer
>War. James Dodd and Godfrey Emsworth were mates in
>the Middlesex Corps of the Imperial Yeomanry.

INDIA:
"A Study in Scarlet"
>See Watson, James

INSPECTOR:
For a list of Inspectors See POLICE.

INTERLAKEN:
"The Final Problem"
>Holmes and Watson make their way by Interlaken, a
>town in Switzerland during their escape from England.

Holmes and Watson, in an attempt to shake off Moriarty, travel to Switzerland wandering up the valley of the Rhone, branching off at Leuk, over the Gemmi Pass, by way of Interlaken, to Meiringen.

IRELAND:

"His Last Bow"   "An Epilogue of Sherlock Holmes"
Von Bork, the German spy, had a safe containing pigeon-holes bristling with papers and plans, each with its own label. One of these compartments was labeled "Ireland."

IRIS:

"Silver Blaze"
Race horse owned by the Duke of Balmoral and entered in the Wessex Cup race.

IRON DIKE COMPANY:

"The Valley of Fear" Part 2: "The Scowrers"
One of the many iron mining companies in Vermissa Valley. Its chief foreman is Chester Wilcox, who has been marked for death by the 'Scowrers' of Vermissa. One attempt on his life has already failed.

IRONHILL:

"The Valley of Fear" Part 2: "The Scowrers"
Area in the Vermissa Valley and home to Jack Knox.

ITALIAN QUARTER:

"The Adventure of the Six Napoleons"
Section of London.

IONIDES:

"The Adventure of the Golden Pince-Nez"
He is of Alexandria and prepares cigarettes for Professor Coram.

CHAPTER J

JACKSON:
> "The Crooked Man"
>> Doctor friend of Watson's, he takes over Watson's practice so Watson can join Holmes on this adventure.

THE JACKSON PRIZE FOR COMPARATIVE PATHOLOGY:
> "The Hound of the Baskervilles"
>> Prize awarded in the medical profession and won by Dr. J. Mortimer for his essay 'Is Disease a Reversion?'

JACOBS:
> "The Adventure of the Second Stain"
>> Butler for the Trelawney Hope home.

JAMES:
> "The Hound of the Baskervilles"
>> Son of the village grocer and postmaster. Delivered telegrams for his father. Lived in Grimpen.

JAMES, BILLY:
> "The Valley of Fear", Part 2: "The Scowrers"
>> Little Billy was allegedly murdered by the Scowrers.

JAMES, JACK:
> "His Last Bow"
> "An Epilogue of Sherlock Holmes"
>> An American citizen sentenced to Portland prison as a German spy. He worked for Von Bork who wouldn't help him when he got caught.

JENKINS:
>"The Valley of Fear", Part 2: "The Scowrers"
>>During the winter of 1875 he was killed by the 'Scowrers' of Vermissa, soon thereafter his brother was also killed by the 'Scowrers.'

JEZAIL:
>"A Study in Scarlet"
>>See Watson, John

JOHANNESBURG:
>"The Adventure of the Solitary Cyclist"
>>Major town in South Africa, it is where Ralph Smith was reported to have died.

JOHN:
>"The Adventure of the Missing Three-quarter"
>>The butler of Dr. Leslie Armstrong, a pompous man.

JOHN UNDERWOOD AND SONS:
>"A Study in Scarlet"
>>Makers of fine hat wear, located at 129 Camberwell Road. Makes of the hat found next to the dead body of Enoch J. Drebber.

JOHNSON:
>"A Study in Scarlet", Part 2 -- "The Country of the Saints"
>>One of the four principal Elders of the Mormons, one of the "Holy Four" (also known as the "Sacred Council of Four") along with Kemball, Stangerson, and Drebber.

JOHNSON:
>"The Adventure of the Missing Three-quarter"
>>Plays for the Oxford rugby team, he is a flier.

JOHNSON, SHINWELL:
"The Adventure of the Illustrious Client"
> He joined forces with Holmes during the first years of the 1900's. He had made his name as a very dangerous criminal and served two years at Parkhurst before repenting and allying himself, as a valuable assistant, to Holmes. A huge, coarse, red-faced, scorbutic man, he had a pair of vivid black eyes, which were the only external sign of the very cunning, mind within.

> AKA Porky Shinwell

JOHNSON, SIDNEY:
"The Adventure of the Bruce-Partington Plans"
> The senior clerk and draughtsman at Woolwich Arsenal, he has one of the two keys to the safe containing the Bruce-Partington papers. He is forty, married, with five children. He is a silent, morose man, unpopular with his colleagues, but a hard worker with an excellent record.

JOHNSON, THEOPHILUS:
"The Hound of the Baskervilles"
> Had his family signed in at the Northumberland Hotel after the arrival of Sir Henry Baskerville. He stays at the Northumberland on many occasions. Is about the same age as Holmes, a coal-owner and very active gentleman.

JOINT, THE:
"The Adventure of the Dancing Men"
> Gang of seven in Chicago, headed by Elsie Patrick's father. Made their money by dishonest means.

JONES, ATHELNEY:

"The Sign of Four"

Inspector, Scotland Yard, a very stout, portly man, red-faced, burly, and plethoric, with a pair of very small twinkling eyes.

JONES, PETER:

"The Red-Headed League"

Official Police agent of Scotland Yard. He makes note of past Holmes successes where Holmes "has been more nearly correct than the official force." Jones cites "that business of the Sholto murder and the Agra treasure" as references.

JOSEF, FRANZ:

"His Last Bow" "An Epilogue of Sherlock Holmes"

Owner of the Schoenbrunn Palace where he has a special wine cellar from which the German spy, Von Bork, brought a few bottles of Imperial Tokay.

JOURNAL de GENEVE:

"The Final Problem"

French newspaper, which carried a condensed version of the facts of "The Final Problem" on May 6, 1891. Watson's version, "The Final Problem,"   is to lay the true facts before the public.

JUSTICE OF THE PEACE TREVOR:

"The 'Gloria Scott'"

Father of Victor Trevor, only college friend of Sherlock Holmes. A man of some wealth and a landed proprietor. A widower with one son, Victor, his daughter died of diphtheria while on a visit to Birmingham. A man of little culture but with considerable amount of rude strength, both physically and mentally. He knew hardly any books but had traveled far eeing much of the world, remembering all that he had learned. Physically, he was a thick-set, burly man with a shock of grizzled hair, a brown, weather-beaten face, and blue eyes, which were keen to the verge of fierceness. He had a reputation for kindness and charity on the countryside, and was noted for the leniency of his sentences from the bench. Made all his money in the gold fields of New Zealand.

AKA James Armitage.
See ARMITAGE, JAMES

CHAPTER K

KEMBALL:

"A Study in Scarlet", Part 2 -- "The Country of the Saints"
One of the four principal Elders of the Mormons, one of the "Holy Four" (also known as the "Sacred Council of Four") along with Johnson, Stangerson, and Drebber.

KEMP, WILSON:

"The Greek Interpreter"
A man of the foulest antecedents. Partner with Harold Latimer in the kidnapping of Sophy Kratides. Had a little pointed beard, was thready and ill-nourished. As he spoke, his lips and eyelids were continually twitching like a man with St. Vitus's dance. His eyes were steel gray and glistening coldly with malignant, inexorable cruelty in their depths. Believed to have been killed by Latimer and to have killed Latimer in Buda-Pesht, Hungary. Holmes, however, believes Sophy killed both of them to avenge her brothers death and her imprisonment.

KENNINGTON PARK GATE:

"A Study in Scarlet"
John Rance, the constable who found the body of Enoch J. Drebber, lives at 46 Audley Court Kennington Park Gate.

KENNINGTON ROAD:

"The Adventure of the Six Napoleons"
Street in London where Morse Hudson owns a place for the sale of pictures and statutes. A bust of Napoleon was discovered broken upon the floor as a stranger fled the scene.

"The Disappearance of Lady Frances Carfax"
>Fraser (Mrs. Shlessinger) pawns a piece of jewelry and next heads up Kennington Road stopping at an undertaker's shop, Stimpson and Co.

KENSINGTON:
"The Adventure of the Empty House"
>Where Watson lives since the death of Holmes at the Reichenback Falls.

"The Adventure of the Six Napoleons"
>Section of London, Pitt Street is located there.

"The Adventure of Wisteria Lodge"
aka "A Reminiscence of Mr. Sherlock Holmes"
>Town where Albemarle Mansion, home of the Melville family, is located.

"The Adventure of the Bruce-Partington Plans"
>Town in England, Hugo Oberstein lives at 13 Caulfield Gardens, Kensington. Goldini's Restaurant is located on Gloucester Road, Kensington.

"The Adventure of the Dying Detective"
>Separated from Notting Hill by Lower Burke Street.

KENSINGTON OUTRAGE:
"The Adventure of the Six Napoleons"
>'Kensington Outrage. Murder by a Madman' headlines which appeared in news-bills in London following the discovery of a murder at the door to Mr. Horace Harker's home.

KENT:

"The Adventure of the Golden Pince-Nez"
Seven miles from Chatham and three from the railway line, it is the location of Yoxley Old Place.

"The Adventure of the Abbey Grange"
Town in England, location of the Abbey Grange.

"The Valley of Fear", Part 1: "The Tragedy of Birlstone"
English county wherein Tunbridge Wells is located.

"The Adventure of the Lion's Mane"
It is off the coast of Kent that the famous observer, J.G. Wood, encountered the "Lion's Mane," cyanea capillata.

See Cyanea.

KENT, MR.:

"The Adventure of the Blanched Soldier"
A small bearded man, he was a surgeon who was willing to keep quiet and stay with Godfrey Emsworth thereby keeping Mr. Emsworth's medical malady from the public.

KENTISH TRAIN:

"The Adventure of the Abbey Grange"
Train from Charing Cross Station to Kent.

KESWICK:

"A Study in Scarlet"
Individual who lives at 13 Duncan Street, Houndsditch. which, is the address given to Holmes by Mrs. Sawyer as her residence. When Holmes investigates he discovers that Mr. Keswick is a respectable paperhanger and had no knowledge of anyone named Sawyer or Dennis.

KHALIFA:

    "The Adventure of the Empty House"

        At Khartoum, Holmes spent a short but interesting visit, the results of which he sent to the Foreign Office. His visit here took place during that time he was allowing the public to presume he had died at the Reichenbach Falls with Professor Moriarty.

KHAN, ABDULLAH:

    "The Sign of Four"

        A member of "The Sign of Four". Under the command of Jonathan Small in Agra during the great mutiny. A fierce looking chap who had borne arms against the British at Chilian Wallah. Conspired with Jonathan Small, Dost Akbar, and Mahomet Singh to kill Achmet and steal his treasure. He is caught, tried, and sentenced with his co-conspirators for the murder of Achmet. He is sent to Andaman Island where his escape with the others fails due to the double-cross of Major Sholto and Captain Marstan, two guards the prisoners had trusted. The two guards retrieve the treasure of Achmet for themselves.

KIMBERLEY:

    "The Adventure of the Solitary Cyclist"

        Located in South Africa, area where Roaring Jack Woodley is well known.

KING EDWARDS STREET:

    "The Red-Headed League"

        New Offices of William Morris, solicitor, are located at 17 King Edwards Street, after having moved from 7 Pope's Court, Fleet Street. Actually, it is the location of a manufacturer of artificial knee-caps and there is not sign of Mr. Morris's office.

KING OF PROOSIA:
> "The Adventure of The Blue Carbuncle"
>> Name Mr. Breckinridge calls a little man (John Ryder) who is looking for a particular goose sold to Mr. Breckinridge by Mrs. Oakshott.

KING, MRS.:
> "The Adventure of the Dancing Men"
>> The cook at Riding Thorpe Manor.

KING'S COLLEGE HOSPITAL:
> "The Resident Patient"
>> Dr. Percy Trevelyan occupied a minor position doing research into the pathology of catalespy.

KING'S CROSS STATION:
> "The Adventure of the Missing Three-quarter"
>> A train depot in London from where one might get a train to Cambridge.

KING'S PYLAND:
> "Silver Blaze"
>> Training stables for the horses of Colonel Ross.

KINGSTON:
> "The Adventure of the Illustrious Client"
>> The home of Baron Gruner, Vernon Lodge, is located in Kingston, a village southwest of London proper.

KIRWAN, WILLIAM:
> "The Reigate Puzzle"
>> Coachman for the Cunningham's, murdered while attempting to thwart a burglary. Had been in the service of Mr. Cunningham for years and was a good servant.

KLEIN:

    "The Adventure of the Three Gables"

        German sugar king, he was married to Isadora Klein, a
        beautiful Spanish woman, prior to his death.

KLEIN, ISADORA:

    "The Adventure of the Three Gables"

        Lives in Grosvenor Square, she was the celebrated
        beauty, of pure Spanish blood of the master
        Conquistadors. Her people have been leaders in
        Pernambuco for generations. She was tall, queenly, a
        perfect figure, a lovely mask-like face, with two
        wonderful Spanish eyes. She married the old German
        sugar king, Klein, and found herself a very wealthy
        widow. She had several lovers, Douglas Maberley, one of
        the most handsome men in London, was one of them.
        She is about to marry the young Duke of Lomond. Her
        greatest concern is to retrieve the second of two copies
        of Douglas Maberley's manuscript about his affair with
        her. She, having broken off the relationship, broke his
        heart, hence his book.

KLOPMAN:

    "His Last Bow"
    "An Epilogue of Sherlock Holmes"

        A Nihilist, tried to murder Count Von und Zu
        Grafenstein but was foiled by Holmes.

        See Und Zu Grafenstein, Count Von.

KNELLER:

    "The Hound of the Baskervilles"

        Artist responsible for some of the family portraits of the
        Baskervilles.

KNOX, JACK:

"The Valley of Fear", Part 2: "The Scowrers"

John McMurdo quizzes Lawler and Andrews, the assassins, about whom they plan to kill and McMurdo suggest that it might be Jack Knox of Ironhill.

KRATIDES, PAUL:

"The Greek Interpreter"

Brother of Sophy Kratides. He comes from a wealthy Grecian family. In an attempt to locate his sister in London, he travels from Athens and becomes the captive of Harold Latimer. Mr. Melas is used in an attempt to persuade Kratides to sign over his and his sister's property. Mr. Melas seeks to help him and goes to Mycroft Holmes. He was deadly pale and terribly emaciated, with protruding, brilliant eyes of a man whose spirit was greater than his strength, when seen by Mr. Melas for the first time. Latimer and his partner, Kemp, attempt to kill him by charcoal gas. They ssucceed; he dies before Holmes can reach him.

KRATIDES, SOPHY:

"The Greek Interpreter"

Sister of Paul Kratides. She comes from a wealthy Grecian family. While visiting London she falls under the spell of Harold Latimer. She became a prisoner of Latimer's as he tried to persuade her brother to sign over his and her property. She was tall and graceful, with black hair. It is believed by Sherlock Holmes that to avenge the death of her brother and her own imprisonment she killed both Latimer and Kemp in Buda-Pesht, Hungary.

KU KLUX KLAN:

"The Five Orange Pips"

Described in detail by Holmes as he reads from the American Encyclopedia.

KYBER:

"The Adventure of the Illustrious Client"

West of Kabol, Afghanistan. General de Merville was famous for his exploits in Kyber.

CHAPTER L

LABURNUM LODGE:
"The Adventure of the Six Napoleons"
See Laburnum Villa.

LABURNUM VALE:
"The Adventure of the Six Napoleons"
Located in Chiswick, it is home to Josiah Brown's
residence, Laburnam Villa.

LABURNUM VILLA:
"The Adventure of the Six Napoleons"
Home to Josiah Brown, located in Laburnum Vale,
Chiswick.

LACHINE:
"The Crooked Man"
Villa residence of Colonel and Mrs. Barclay, located in
Aldershot and scene of the murder of Colonel Barclay.

LADY DAY:
"The Resident Patient"
British holiday, also the day Dr. Percy Trevelyan moved
into his new house to begin his practice.

LAMBERLEY:
"The Adventure of the Sussex Vampire"
It is in Sussex, south of Horsham.

LANCASTER, JAMES:
"The Adventure of Black Peter"
A little Ribston pippin of a man, with ruddy cheeks and
fluffy white side-whiskers. He has been sent to Captain
Basil by Sumner, Shipping Agent.

LANCET:

"The Adventure of the Blanched Soldier"

Holmes notes that had the man James Dodd saw in the outer cottage been reading the Lancet, it would have helped solve the matter quicker.

LANDER:

"The Valley of Fear", Part 2: "The Scowrers"

Member of the 'Scowrers' of Vermissa, he and Egan claim the head money given by the lodge of Vermissa for the killing of old man Crabbe in Stylestown, although no one knows who actually fired the shot.

LANGHAM HOTEL:

"The Disappearance of Lady Frances Carfax"

A hotel in London, it is the residence of the Honorable Philip Green.

LANGUR:

"The Adventure of the Creeping Man"

Black-faced, a crawler and climber, it is the great black-faced monkey of the Himalayan slopes. Langur is the biggest and most human of the climbing monkeys.

LANNER:

"The Resident Patient"

A smart-looking police-inspector, he is investigating the murder (suicide) of one Blessingtom in the Cavendish Square quarter.

LARBEY, MRS.:

"The Valley of Fear", Part 2: "The Scowrers"

Shot while nursing her husband who had been beaten almost to death on the orders of Boss McGinty in the winter of 1875.

La ROTHIERE, LOUIS:
"The Adventure of the Second Stain"
A secret agent known to Holmes. Lives in the West End of London. A bold man.

"The Adventure of the Bruce-Partington Plans"
One of the few men Mycroft Holmes believes could be able to dispose of the stolen Bruce-Partington papers. He resides at Campden Mansions, Notting Hill.

LATIMER, HAROLD:
"The Greek Interpreter"
A fashionably dressed young man. He provides information that he lives in Kensington. Became involved with Sophy Kratides. Once getting her under his spell he tried to get her to sign over her property to him. In an attempt to kill Paul Kratides and Mr. Melas, he uses charcoal gas. Kradites dies but Melas is saved by Holmes. Believed to have been killed by Latimer and to have killed Latimer in Buda-Pesht, Hungary. Holmes, however, believes Sophy killed both of them to avenge her brothers death and her imprisonment.

LATIMER'S:
"The Disappearance of Lady Frances Carfax"
A shoe store on Oxford Street where Watson has purchased a pair of English boots.

LAURISTON GARDENS:
"A Study in Scarlet"
Number 3 is the location of the discovery of the dead body of one Enoch J. Drebber. It wore an ill-omen and minatory look. It was one of four, which stood back some little way from the street, two being occupied and two empty. The latter looked out with three tiers of

vacant melancholy windows, which were blank and dreary, save that here and there a "To Let" card had developed like a cataract upon the bleared panes. A small garden sprinkled over with scattered eruption of sickly plants separated each of these houses from the street, and was traversed by a narrow pathway, yellowish in colour, and consisting apparently of a mixture of clay and of gravel. The whole place was very sloppy from the rain, which had fallen through the night. The garden was bounded by a three-foot brick wall with a fringe of wood rails upon the top.

LAUSANNE:
"The Disappearance of Lady Frances Carfax"
In France, where Holmes sends Watson to search for the missing Lady Frances Carfax. Location of the Hotel National, where Lady Frances Carfax stayed and was last heard from.

LAWLER:
"The Valley of Fear", Part 2: "The Scowrers"
An elderly man, shrewd, silent, and self-contained, his ragged, grizzled beard help give him the general appearance of an itinerant preacher. He is one of the assassins sent by Evans Pott to kill the manager of Crow Hill, Josiah H. Dunn. He kills the mine engineer, Menzies, while his partner, Andrews, kills Dunn. He had carried out fourteen killings before this one and was chosen because he does not drink.

LEADENHALL STREET:
"A Case of Identity"
Location of the office where Mr. Hosmer Angel works as a cashier.

LEADENHALL STREET POST OFFICE:
>"A Case of Identity"
>>Where Miss Mary Sutherland sends all her mail to Mr. Hosmer Angel, he not wanting it to go to his place of business.

LE BRUN:
>"The Adventure of the Illustrious Client"
>>French agent, he was looking into the affairs of Baron Gruner when he was beaten by some Apaches in the Montmartre district and crippled for life. The beating was at the direction of Baron Gruner.

LECOQ:
>"A Study in Scarlet"
>>Character in the works of Gaboriau. Watson questions Holmes on his opinion of Lecoq's work and Holmes refers to him as "a miserable bungler" his only redeeming quality is his energy.

LEE:
>"The Adventure of Wisteria Lodge"
>aka "A Reminiscence of Mr. Sherlock Holmes"
>>Town in England wherein Popham House is located, home to Mr. John Scott Eccles.

LEE:
>"The Valley of Fear", Part 2: "The Scowrers"
>>Sold his mining operation to the State & Merton County Railroad Company instead of paying the 'Scowrers' to leave him alone.

LEEDS MERCURY:

"The Hound of the Baskervilles"

English newspaper (London), Holmes remarks that he once confused it with the Western Morning News due to the similarity of their print.

LEGEND OF THE HOUND:

"The Hound of the Baskervilles"

In the time of the Great Rebellion this Manor of Baskerville was held by Hugo of that name. There was in him a certain wanton and cruel humour, which made his name a byword through the West. It chanced that this Hugo came to love the daughter of a yeoman who held lands near the Baskerville estate. The young maiden, being discreet and of good repute, would ever avoid him, for she feared his evil name. One Michaelmas (the feastday of St. Michael, September 29th) this Hugo, with five or six of his idle and wicked companions, stole down upon the farm and carried off the maiden, her father and brothers being from home, as he well knew. They brought her to the Hall and she was placed in an upper chamber, while Hugo and his friends sat down to a long carouse, as was their nightly custom. She, through the use of ivy covered walls, climbed down the outside wall and made her escape across the moor, there being three leagues between the Hall and her father's farm. Hugo, carrying food and wine, and with other worse things on his mind to his captive, discovered the cage empty, the bird escaped. He became enraged, and swearing his soul to the Powers of Evil if he might overtake the wench, set out after her. Hugo's friends set out after him and meeting a night shepherd upon the moorlands asked if Hugo had passed-by; the shepherd, at first unable to speak, finally stated that he had seen "the unhappy maiden with the hounds upon her track, but more than that, had seen Hugo Baskerville, upon his black mare, and there ran mute behind him such a hound of hell as God forbid should ever be at my heels." Hugo's friends finally came upon the hounds, having heard their whimpering. The moon was shining bright upon the clearing, and there in the center lay the unhappy maid where she had fallen, dead of fear and of fatigue. But it was not the sight of her body, nor yet was it that of the body of Hugo Baskerville lying near her, which raised the hair upon the heads of these three daredevil roysterers, but it was that, standing over Hugo, and plucking at his throat, there stood a foul thing, a great, black beast, shaped like a hound, yet larger than any hound that ever mortal eye has rested upon. And even as they looked, the thing tore out the throat of Hugo Baskerville.

LEICESTER:
"The Valley of Fear", Part 1: "The Tragedy of Birlstone"
Town in England where it has been reported that the suspected murderer of John Douglas, Mr. Hargrave, has been seen and actually arrested.

LEONARDO:
"The Adventure of the Retired Colourman"
The strong man in Ronder's wild beast show. He began to have more and more contact with Ronder's wife as the show went down hill. He had a deep love for Eugenia Ronder and she came to him for comfort after beatings by her husband. It was Leonardo who conspired with Eugenia Ronder to kill Ronder but everything went wrong at the last moment resulting in the Abbas Parva Tragedy. He killed Ronder, after opening the lion cage, and panicked when the lion attacked Eugenia Ronder, his confidant and lover.

He drowned in late 1896 while bathing near Margate.

LEPIDOPTERA:
"The Hound of the Baskervilles"

A butterfly characterized by two pairs of broad, membranous wings covered with very fine scales, often brightly covered. Mr. Stapleton has a collection of them, which he believes to be the most complete one in the south-west of England.

LES HUGUENOTS:
"The Hound of the Baskervilles"

Holmes has a box (seats) for 'Les Huguenots', which he suggests he and Watson take in after dinner at the conclusion of "The Hound of the Baskervilles."

LESTRADE:
"A Study in Scarlet"

A little sallow, rat-faced, dark-eyed fellow. A well known detective has come to Holmes after having got himself in a fog over a forgery case. Lean and ferret-like.

"The Boscombe Valley Mystery"

Of Scotland Yard

Refers this case to Holmes being rather puzzled. "A lean, ferret-like man, furtive and sly-looking" with a light brown dustcoat and leather-leggings.

"The Adventure of the Nobel Bachelor."

He is investigating the disappearance of Hatty Doran, wife to be of Lord St. Simon.

"The Hound of the Baskervilles"

Comes to Baskerville Hall with an unsigned warrant upon Holmes request.

"The Adventure of the Empty House"
>Assist Holmes in the arrest of Colonel Sebastian Moran after Moran shoots at a wax bust of Holmes believing it to be Holmes himself.

"The Adventure of the Norwood Builder"
>In charge of the criminal investigation involving the incident at Norwood, the arson and murder of Mr. Jonas Oldacre.

"The Adventure of Charles Augustus Milverton"
>He implores Holmes to assist him in the investigation of the murder of Charles Augustus Milverton but Holmes states: "Well, I'm afraid I can't help you, Lestrade. The fact is that I knew this fellow Milverton, and I considered him one of the most dangerous men in London, and that I think there are certain crimes which the law cannot touch, and which therefore, to some extent, justify private revenge ... My sympathies are with the criminals rather than with the victim, and I will not handle this case."

"The Adventure of the Six Napoleons"
>Of Scotland Yard, comes to Holmes for help in investigating the smashing of busts of Napoleon.

"The Adventure of the Cardboard Box"
>Investigates the gruesome package, containing the severed human ears, sent to Miss Susan Cushing. Referred to in an article contained in the 'Daily Chronicle' as "one of the very smartest of our detective officers."

"The Adventure of the Bruce-Partington Plans"
>Arrives with Mycroft Holmes at 221B Baker Street to consult Sherlock Holmes on the disappearance of the Bruce-Partington plans.

"The Disappearance of Lady Frances Carfax"
>Holmes consults Lestrade in his search for Holy Peters, Fraser, and Lady Frances Carfax in London to no avail.

"The Adventure of the Three Garridebs"
>Holmes consults Lestrade concerning the background of one Killer Evans.

>aka John Garrideb.

LESURIER, MADAME:
"Silver Blaze"
>Milliner of Bond Street, sold some rather expensive garments to one William Derbyshire for his wife.

LEUK:
"The Final Problem"
>Holmes and Watson, having wandered for a week up the valley of the Rhone, branched off at Leuk on their way over Gemmi Pass. Leuk is a small town in Switzerland. Holmes and Watson, in an attempt to shake off Moriarty, travel to Switzerland wandering up the valley of the Rhone, branching off at Leuk, over the Gemmi Pass, by way of Interlaken, to Meiringen.

LEVERSTOKE, LORD:
"The Adventure of the Priory School"
>His son has attended the Priory School.

LEVERTON, MR.:
"The Adventure of the Red Circle"

Of the Pinkerton's American Agency, he is on the trail of "Gorgiano of the Red Circle" and has trailed him to London. He is with Inspector Gregson, about to investigate a house on Howe Street, when Holmes joins them in response to a signal Holmes saw from the second floor window. He is a quiet, businesslike young man, with a clean-shaven, hatchet face. He has been known as the hero of the Long Island cave mystery.

Le VILLARD, FRANCOIS:
"The Sign of Four"

An unrecorded case.

French detective who is helped by Holmes, the case involved a will, he is also translating some of Holmes' monographs from English to French.

LEWIS, GEORGE:
"The Adventure of the Illustrious Client"

Sir George Lewis was involved in some negotiations with Sir James Damery concerning the Hammerford Will case. A very delicate matter.

LEWISHAM:
"The Adventure of the Retired Colourman"

Josiah Amberley has retired to Lewisham where he lives in The Haven, his house.

LEWISHAM GANG:
"The Adventure of the Abbey Grange"

A gang of burglars consisting of the three Randalls, the father and two sons. They are alleged to have done a job in Sydenham a fortnight before the death of Sir Eustace Brackenstall, for which they appear responsible. They are, nevertheless, arrested in New York a few days later dispelling the notion they killed Sir Eustace.

LEXINGTON, MRS.:
"The Adventure of the Norwood Builder"
Mr. Jonas Oldacre's housekeeper, she was a little, dark, silent person, with suspicious and sidelong eyes.

LHASSA:
"The Adventure of the Empty House"
While on his travels through Tibet, after his fight with Professor Moriarty at the Reichenbach Falls, and being presumed dead, Holmes visits with the head lama.

LIGHT BLUES:
"The Adventure of the Missing Three-quarter"
Name of the Trinity College rugby team.

LIME STREET:
"The Adventure of the Mazarin Stone"
Street in London where Van Seddar is to be met and given the Crown Diamond which he will take to Amsterdam for cutting.

LITTLE PURLINGTON:
"The Adventure of the Retired Colourman"
Site of the Vicarage of J.C. Elman, Vicar of Moorsmoor and Little Purlington. It is in Essex near Frinton, east of London. It is on a branch line, and not an easy place to reach. Holmes sends Watson and Josiah Amberley to Little Purlington to consult with the Vicar, J.C. Elman, concerning a telegram he sent Holmes about information on the disappearance of Mrs. Amberley and Dr. Ray Ernest. When Watson and Amberley arrive, the Vicar denies ever sending a telegram to Holmes.

LITTLE RYDER STREET:
"The Adventure of the Three Garridebs"
> One of the smaller offshoots from the Edgware Road,
> within a stone throw of old Tyburn Tree of evil memory.

LIVERPOOL:
"The Adventure of the Cardboard Box"
> City in England.

"The Valley of Fear", Part 1: "The Tragedy of Birlstone"
> Town in England where it has been reported that the
> suspected murderer of John Douglas, Hargrave, has been
> seen and actually arrested.

"The Adventure of the Mazarin Stone"
> Where Count Sylvius intends to tell Holmes the Crown
> Diamond can be found while he turns it over to Van
> Seddar in Lime Street instead.

LIVERPOOL, DUBLIN, AND LONDON STEAM PACKET COMPANY:
"The Adventure of the Cardboard Box"
> Owner of the ship 'May Day' on which Jim Browner
served as steward.

LIVERPOOL STREET:
"The Adventure of the Dancing Men"
> Street in London.

"The Adventure of the Retired Colourman"
> Watson and Josiah Amberley take a train from Liverpool
> Street to Little Purlington to consult with the Vicar of the
> area, J.C. Elman concerning information on the
> disappearance of Mrs. Amberley and Dr. Ray Ernest.

LLOYD'S REGISTERS:

"The Five Orange Pips"

Reference material for Holmes -- contains files of old papers, following the future career of every vessel which touched at Pondicherry in January & February 1883. The "Lone Star" is reported as one such ship which Holmes takes note of.

LOMAX:

"The Adventure of the Illustrious Client"

Sublibrarian of the London Library, he is a friend of Holmes.

LOMOND, DUKE OF:

"The Adventure of the Three Gables"

A young man, he is engaged to marry an older woman, one Isadora Klein.

LONDON BRIDGE:

"The Man With The Twisted Lip"

See Upper Swandam Lane.

"The Adventure of the Bruce-Partington Plans"

The London Bridge Underground railway station is considerably past Aldgate Station where the body of Arthur Cadogan West was found.

"The Adventure of the Retired Colourman"

Train station in London. Watson has noticed that he is being followed, and has been since departing Blackheath. Watson has been to Lewisham on business for Holmes and is returning with his report.

LONDON LIBRARY:
"The Adventure of the Illustrious Client"
> Located in St. James Square, the sublibrarian is a friend of Holmes's, one Lomax.

LONDON UNIVERSITY:
"A Study in Scarlet"
> Where Dr. John Watson took his medical degree.

"The Resident Patient"
> College from which Dr. Percy Trevelyan graduated.

LONG ISLAND CAVE MYSTERY:
"The Adventure of the Red Circle"
> Case solved by Mr. Leverton of the Pinkerton's American Agency and noted by Sherlock Holmes in his meeting Mr. Leverton.

LOPEZ:
"The Adventure of Wisteria Lodge"
aka "A Reminiscence of Mr. Sherlock Holmes"
> Mr. Lucas was known by this name during his days of 'greatness," before running away with Don Murillo.

> See Lucas.

LORD STREET:
"The Adventure of Black Peter"
> In Brixton, Number 46 Lord Street is the address of Inspector Stanley Hopkins.

THE LOSS OF THE "SOPHY ANDERSON":
"The Five Orange Pips"
> An unrecorded case. A British bark.

LOWENSTEIN, H.:
"The Adventure of the Creeping Man"
An obscure scientist who was striving in some unknown way for the secret of rejuvenescence and the elixir of life. He has been sending supplies to his agent, Dorak, in London for Professor Presbury.

LOWER BRIXTON:
"The Greek Interpreter"
From where a J. Davenport writes in response to Mycroft's advertisement in the Daily News regarding information about a young Greek woman.

LOWER BRIXTON ROAD:
"The Adventure of the Six Napoleons"
Street in London located two miles from Kennington Road. It is the site of Dr. Barnicot's branch surgery and dispensary.

LOWER BURKE STREET:
"The Adventure of the Dying Detective"
A line of houses lying in the vague borderland between Notting Hill and Kensington.

LOWER GILL MOOR:
"The Adventure of the Priory School"
Located between the Priory school and Holdernesse Hall near Mackleton. It is a great rolling moor extending for ten miles.

LOWER GROVE ROAD:
"The Adventure of the Six Napoleons"
Located in Reading, a Mr. Sandeford, who purchased a bust of Napoleon from Harding Brothers, lives there.

LOWER NORWOOD:
"The Adventure of the Norwood Builder"
Where Mr. Jonas Oldacre lived on Sydenham Road.

LUCAS, EDUARDO:
"The Adventure of the Second Stain"
A secret agent, he is found murdered at his residence, 16 Godolphin Street. He was well known in society circles due to his personality and reputation as one of the best amateur tenors in the country. He was 34 and unmarried. AKA M. Henri Fournaye.

LUCAS, MR.:
"The Adventure of Wisteria Lodge"
aka "A Reminiscence of Mr. Sherlock Holmes"
Friend and secretary to Mr. Henderson. He resides at High Gable. He is a foreigner, chocolate brown, wily, suave, and catlike, with a poisonous gentleness of speech.

AKA Lopez
See Lopez

LUCCA, EMILIA:
"The Adventure of the Red Circle"
From New York, she is a tall beautiful woman with dark eyes, a pretty Italian. She is married to Gennaro Lucca. Holmes discerns that she has been the mysterious lodger of Mrs. Warren and has been in hiding. She is called to the second floor room of a house on Howe Street where Holmes, Watson, Inspector Gregson, and Mr. Leverton of Pinkerton's American Agency are waiting. Holmes has used a code, which Mrs. Lucca and her husband were employing and Holmes deciphered. She was born in Posilippo, near Naples, the daughter of Augusto Barelli. Her marriage to Gennaro was against her fathers will. They were married at Bari fled to New York where they

had lived for the past four years.

LUCCA, GENNARO:
"The Adventure of the Red Circle"

A middle-sized man, dark, and bearded, youngish, not over thirty, very smartly dressed, he spoke good English but was obviously a foreigner. Husband of Emila Lucca, he rented a room in Mrs. Warren's boarding house and hid his wife there without anyone's knowledge, she becoming the mysterious lodger. He had married Emila, at Bari, against her fathers will and fled to New York with her. He had been employed by Emilia's father prior to their flight. He saved a man, Tito Castalotte, from muggers in the Bowery section of New York and as a reward got a job with Tito Castalotte's fruit importing business in New York. Before his marriage, during his rough and tumble times, he met one Gorgiano who invited him to join a Neapolitan society called the 'Red Circle' which was allied to the old Carbonari. After moving to New York he believed he was free of the 'Red Circle' until Gorgiano appeared, having fled Italy to avoid the police. Gennaro was forced to join a branch of the 'Red Circle' in New York under Gorgiano. When Gennaro fails to follow through on orders of the 'Red Circle' Gorgiano vows to punish Gennaro and his family. They eventually meet in London where Gorgiano meets his own death at the hands of Gennaro.

LUCERNE:
"The Adventure of the Three Gables"

Italy, the luggage of Douglas Maberley has a label from Lucerne upon it. The luggage is piled in a corner of a room at 'The Three Gables' having been returned to Mr. Maberley's mother's house after his death.

LUXEMBOURG:
"The Final Problem"

Holmes and Watson are to make their way, at their leisure, into Switzerland, via Luxembourg and Basle.

LYCEUM THEATRE:
"The Sign of Four"

Location where Mary Morstan is to meet someone, an unknown friend, at seven-o'clock. This information is obtained from a letter she has received and revealed to Holmes the day she received it.

LYNCH, JUDGE:
"The Valley of Fear", Part 2: "The Scowrers"

Local judge in Vermissa Valley.

LYNCH, VICTOR:
"The Adventure of the Sussex Vampire"

A forger, his name is listed under the "V's" in Holmes's index. May be an unrecorded case or simply accumulated information for reference.

LYON:
"The Reigate Puzzle"

Location of the Hotel Dulong, where Holmes is lying ill and telegraphs Watson.

NO. 31 LYON PLACE, CAMBERWELL:
"A Case of Identity"

Address of Miss Mary Sutherland.

LYONS:
"The Hound of the Baskervilles"

Married Laura Frankland without the consent of her father. He was an artist who did sketchings of the moor. He deserted Laura, his wife, after their marriage.

LYONS, LAURA:
"The Hound of the Baskervilles"

Daughter of Frankland, she married an artist named Lyons who deserted her. Her father refused to have anything to do with her since she married without his consent. The town's people did something to enable her to earn an honest living; she was set up in a typewriting business. Her eyes and hair were of the same rich hazel colour, and her cheeks, though considerably freckled, were flushed with the exquisite bloom of the brunette, the dainty pink which lurks at the heart of the sulphur rose.

MABERLEY, DOUGLAS:
>"The Adventure of the Three Gables"
>
>>Son of Mortimer and Mary Maberley, he was attached to Rome where he died recently of pneumonia. He had had an affair with Isadora Klein and when she ended the relationship he wrote a book detailing their love affair. Her attempts to retrieve his copy of the book is the theme of "The Adventure of the Three Gables."

MABERLEY, MARY:
>"The Adventure of the Three Gables"
>
>>Widow of Mortimer Maberley, one of Holmes's early clients. She consults Holmes over a strange request to buy her home and its contents. She has only lived in the

house for one year and the buyer insist that the purchase must include everything that is in the house, less a few of her personal items. After her visit to Holmes she discovers there has been a burglary at her house. Her son, Douglas, died recently of pneumonia in Rome, where he was attache.

MABERLEY, MORTIMER:
"The Adventure of the Three Gables"
Husband to Mary and father to Douglas, he died some time ago. He was one of Holmes's early clients. An unrecorded case. His widow consults Holmes in the strange matter of the proposed sale and eventual burglary of her home in the "Adventure of the Three Gables."

MacKINNON, INSPECTOR:
"The Adventure of the Retired Colourman"
Policeman who works with Holmes to capture the criminal, Josiah Amberley. MacKinnon receives all the publicity in the local media after the case is concluded.

MACKLETON:
"The Adventure of the Priory School"
Located in the north of England, the Priory School can be found there.

MacDONALD, ALEC:
"The Valley of Fear" Part 1: "The Tragedy of Birlstone"
Inspector with Scotland Yard, he was a young but trusted member of the force. He was tall, with a bony figure which gave promise of exceptional physical strength, while his large cranium and deep-set eyes spoke no less clearly of the keen intelligence which twinkled out from behind his bushy eyebrows. He had a hard Aberdonian accent.

MacNAMARA, WIDOW:

"The Valley of Fear" Part 2: "The Scowrers"

After John McMurdo reveals to Jacob Shafter that he is a member of the 'Eminent Order of Freemen' Shafter request he leave his boarding house on Sheridan Street. McMurdo and Scanlan, whom McMurdo first met on the train to Vermissa, take lodgings on the extreme outskirts of town, with Widow MacNamara, an easy-going old Irishwoman who left them to themselves. Her boarding house is used to house two assassins, Lawler and Andrews, from the Gilmerton lodge of the "Ancient Order of Freemen,' prior to the murder of Josiah Dunn and Menzies. It is in her boarding house that Birdy Edwards has set a trap which results in the capture of Boss McGinty, Ted Baldwin, Tiger Cormac, Harraway, Carter, and the Willaby brothers.

MACPHAIL:

"The Adventure of the Creeping Man"

Professor Presbury's coachman, he lives over the stables.

MacPHERSON:

"The Adventure of the Second Stain"

A constable, he was a very big man, assigned to guard the murder scene of Eduardo Lucas.

MADRID:

"The Adventure of the Second Stain"

A letter from Madrid was in the dispatch-box of the Right Honorable Trelawney Hope.

"The Adventure of Wisteria Lodge"
aka "A Reminiscence of Mr. Sherlock Holmes"

One of the stops made by Don Murillo after his escape from Central America, following the uprising of his people against him, in an attempt to hide from his past and his pursuers.

MAFIA:
"The Adventure of the Six Napoleons"
A secret political society of Italians which enforces its decrees by murder.

MAIWAND:
"A Study in Scarlet"
See Watson, John

MAJOR FREEBODY:
"The Five Orange Pips"
Friend of Joseph Openshaw's, commander of fort upon Portsdown Hill, who is killed while walking home after a visit with Major Freebody.

THE MAN WITH THE TWISTED LIP:
Published in "The Strand": December 1891
Published as part of: "The Adventures of Sherlock Holmes"
Holmes solves the mystery of the disappearance of Neville St. Clair. Mrs. St. Clair swears that she has seen her husband above an opium den and   believes he is being held against his will. Holmes unravels the mystery and reveals that no true crime has been committed. Watson's wife calls him by the name "James." Watson discovers Holmes in an opium den. Holmes questions Watson, "I suppose that you imagine that I have added opium-smoking to cocaine injections, and all the other little weaknesses on which you have favoured me with your medical views."

"The Adventure of The Blue Carbuncle"
Mentioned in passing.

MANCHESTER STREET:
>"The Adventure of the Empty House"
>>Street in London, connects with Blandford Street.

MANDERS:
>"The Valley of Fear" Part 2: "The Scowrers"
>>A reckless youngster chosen to join John McMurdo and
>>Reilly in settling the Chester Wilcox matter.

MANOR HOUSE:
>"The Greek Interpreter"
>>An unrecorded case.
>>Case where Mycroft Holmes expected Sherlock Holmes
>>to seek his assistance, Mycroft believing Sherlock to be
>>out of his depth.
>>See Adams

MANOR HOUSE:
>"The Valley of Fear" Part 1: "The Tragedy of Birlstone"
>>Dates back to the first crusade, the original house was
>>built by Hugo de Capus as a fortalice in the centre of the
>>estate, which had been granted to him by the Red King.
>>It was destroyed by fire in 1543 and a brick   country
>>house rose from its ashes. It had many gables and small
>>diamond-paned windows and was guarded by two moats,
>>the outer having been allowed to dry up was now used as
>>a kitchen garden. The inner moat was forty feet in width
>>but only a few feet deep, the ground floor windows were
>>within a foot of the surface of the water. The only
>>approach to the house was over a drawbridge which was
>>raised every evening and lowered every morning, the
>>Manor House was converted into an island each night.
>>The House was erected in the fifth year of the reign of
>>James I and is one of the finest surviving examples of the
>>moated Jacobean residence. King Charles and the

George II were hidden here during periods of their reign and Civil Wars.

MANOR HOUSE CASE:

"The Greek Interpreter"
> An unrecorded case.
> The guilty party is a man named Adams. Mycroft Holmes, Sherlock's brother, believed Sherlock, being out of his depth, would have consulted him.

MANOR HOUSE OF HURLSTONE:

"The Musgrave Ritual"
> Home of the Musgraves, located in western Sussex, it is the oldest inhabited building in the county.

MANSEL:

"The Valley of Fear"   Part 2: "The Scowrers"
> Joins Ted Baldwin, Gower, Scanlan, the two Willabys and John McMurdo in 'warning' the "Vermissa Herald" editor/owner James Stanger to curb his stories on the 'Scowrers.'

MAPLETON:

"Silver Blaze"
> Race horse training establishment of Lord Backwater, managed by Silas Brown, home to Desborough, the second favorite in the upcoming Wessex Cup race.

MARGATE:

"The Adventure of the Second Stain"
> An unrecorded case.
> Holmes suspected a woman at Margate because "the motives of women are so inscrutable." He compares the motives of the woman at Margate with those of Lady Hilda Trelawney Hope's visit to Baker Street in the present case.

"The Adventure of the Retired Colourman"
> On the coast, east of London, it is in Kent and the scene
> of the drowning of Leonardo, strongman for Ronder's
> wild beast show.

MARKET SQUARE:
"The Valley of Fear"   Part 2: "The Scowrers"
> Boss McGinty's Union House, through continued
> expansion, threatened to swallow-up one whole side of
> Market Square.

MARQUESS OF MONTALVA:
"The Adventure of Wisteria Lodge"
aka "A Reminiscence of Mr. Sherlock Holmes"
> Found murdered in his room with his secretary, Signor
> Rulli at the Hotel Escurial in Madrid. The murderers were
> never found and the crime was ascribed to Nihilism. It is
> widely believed that he was also know as Don Murillo but
> proof was never forthcoming.

MARSHAM:
"The Adventure of the Abbey Grange"
> Area of Kent, England.

MARTHA:
"His Last Bow"
"An Epilogue of Sherlock Holmes"
> A dear old ruddy-faced woman, the last remaining servant
> of the German spy, Von Bork, the rest having been sent
> away, as he prepares to depart himself. She actually worked
> for Sherlock Holmes in her position as servant to Von Bork

MARTIN, INSPECTOR:
"The Adventure of the Dancing Men"
> From Norwich, of the Norfolk Constabulary.

MARTIN, LIEUTENANT:
>"The 'Gloria Scott'"
>>One of the soldiers responsible for guarding the convicts
>>on the 'Gloria Scott' during its trip to the prison camps of
>>Australia..

MARVIN, TEDDY:
>"The Valley of Fear" Part 2: "The Scowrers"
>>Captain Marvin is head of the Mine Constabulary, a
>>special body of security personnel employed by the
>>railways and colliery owners to supplement the efforts of
>>the ordinary civil police who were helpless in the face of
>>the organized ruffianism which terrorized the Vermissa
>>Valley. Originally of the Chicago Central police
>>department. He is aware of John McMurdo's past in
>>Chicago, in particular, the murder of Jonas Pinto, and the
>>counterfeiting. He assist Birdy Edwards in the capture of
>>Boss McGinty, Tiger Cormac, Ted Baldwin, Harraway,
>>Carter, and the Willaby brothers at Widow MacNamara's
>>boarding house.

MARX AND CO.:
>"The Adventure of Wisteria Lodge"
>aka "A Reminiscence of Mr. Sherlock Holmes"
>>Clothing company located in High Holborn. The clothing
>>found in closets at Wisteria Lodge bore the stamp "Marx
>>and Co., High Holborn."

MARY:
>"The Five Orange Pips"
>>Elisa Openshaw's maid.

MARY:

"The Adventure of the Three Gables"

Maid at 'The Three Gables,' she screams for the police after hearing noises during the break-in.

MARY JANE:

"A Scandal in Bohemia"

Watson's servant girl described by Holmes as "most clumsy and careless". Fired by Watson as "she is incorrigible." Watson's wife had given Mary Jane her notice.

MASON:

"The Adventure of the Bruce-Partington Plans"

A plate-layer who discovered the dead body of Arthur Cadogan West just outside Aldgate Station on the Underground rail system in London.

MASON:

"The Valley of Fear"   Part 2: "The Scowrers"

Sold his ironworks operation to West Gilmerton General Mining Company instead of paying the 'Scowrers' protection money to leave him alone.

MASON, JOHN:

"The Adventure of Shoscombe Old Place"

Head trainer at Shoscombe Old Place. He consults Holmes on the strange behavior of Sir Robert Norberton at Shoscombe Old Place. A tall, clean-shaven man with a firm, austere expression, it is his belief that his master has gone mad.

MASON, MRS.:

"The Adventure of the Sussex Vampire"

The nurse for the Ferguson family.

MASON, WHITE:

"The Valley of Fear"   Part 1: "The Tragedy of Birlstone"
  The local police officer of Birlstone and personal friend
  of Inspector MacDonald. He was a quiet, comfortable-
  looking person, clean-shaven, with a ruddy face, stoutish
  body, and powerful bandy legs.

MASONIC TIE-PIN:

"The Adventure of the Retired Colourman"
  The man that has been following Watson from
  Blackheath Station to London Bridge was wearing a
  Masonic tie-pin.

MATHEWS:

"The Adventure of the Empty House"
  An unrecorded case.
  He knocked out Holmes's left canine in the waiting-room
  at Charing Cross.

MATILDA BRIGGS:

"The Adventure of the Sussex Vampire"
  An unrecorded case.
  Holmes assisted the firm of Morrison, Morrison, and
  Dodd, machinery assessors, in this matter. Matilda Briggs
  was a ship and it was associated with the giant rat of
  Sumatra. Holmes notes that the world is not yet
  prepared for this story.

MAUDSLEY:

"The Adventure of The Blue Carbuncle"
  Friend of John Ryder's living in Kilburn; had done time
  in Pentonville for some crime. He would be able to show
  John Ryder how to turn the stolen jewel (the Blue
  Carbuncle) into money.

MAURITIUS:
>"The Adventure of the Copper Beeches"
>>An island in the Indian Ocean off the east coast of Madagascar, where Mr. Fowler took a government appointment after his marriage to Miss Rucastle.

MAWSON & WILLIAM'S:
>"The Stock-Broker's Clerk"
>>Famous financial house, stock-broking firm in Lombard Street, it is about the richest house in London. Offers a position to Hall Pycroft. According to the 'Evening Standard' a London newspaper, an attempted robbery resulting in the murder of the watchman occurred at its office. The criminal was captured, he using the named Hall Pycroft when in fact his name was Beddington.

MAX LINDER & CO.:
>"The Valley of Fear"   Part 2: "The Scowrers"
>>Business in Vermissa Valley which pays the Vermissa Lodge, 'Eminent Order of Freemen,' "The Scowrers," protection money to be left alone.

MAY DAY:
>"The Adventure of the Cardboard Box"
>>One of the Liverpool and London boats on which Jim Browner, husband of Mary Cushing, served as steward. It is owned by the 'Liverpool, Dublin and London Steam Packet Company.'

MAZARIN STONE:
>"The Adventure of the Mazarin Stone"
>>See Crown Diamond.

McCARTHY, CHARLES:

"The Boscombe Valley Mystery"

An ex-Australian, letting the Hatherly farm from Mr. John Turner, where he lives with his only son, James. Fond of sports, he was frequently seen at the race-meetings of the neighborhood. Was the wagon-driver of a gold convoy traveling from Ballarat to Melbourne which was robbed by "Black Jack of Ballarat" also know as John Turner and who spared the life of Charles McCarthy.

McCARTHY, JAMES:

"The Boscombe Valley Mystery"

He is the 18 year old son of the murdered Charles McCarthy, he is accused of the murder and eventually acquitted. Fell into the clutches of a barmaid in Bristol and married her at the registry office. The barmaid threw him over upon hearing of his troubles with the law following the death of his father, asserting she already had a husband in the Bermuda Dockyard.

McFARLANE, JOHN HECTOR:

"The Adventure of the Norwood Builder"

Young man, a bachelor, a solicitor, a Freemason, and an asthmatic. He was flaxen-haired and handsome, in a washed-out negative fashion, with frightened blue eyes, and a clean-shaven face, with a weak, sensitive mouth. His age may have been about twenty-seven, his dress and bearing that of a gentleman. He is a junior partner of Graham and McFarlane, of 426 Gresham Buildings, E.C. He lives with his parents at Torrington Lodge, Blackheath. He is accused of the murder of Jonas Oldacre and the arson of Oldacre's home. He had written Oldacres will which left everything to McFarlane himself. He consults Holmes claiming his innocence.

McGINTY, BLACK JACK:

"The Valley of Fear"   Part 2: "The Scowrers"
See McGinty, Jack.

McGINTY, BOSS:

"The Valley of Fear"   Part 2: "The Scowrers"
See McGinty, Jack.

McGINTY, JACK:

"The Valley of Fear"   Part 2: "The Scowrers"
Bodymaster of the Vermissa Lodge of the 'Eminent Order
of Freemen', Lodge 341. He can be found at the Union
House and is commonly known as Boss McGinty or Black
Jack McGinty. He is head of the 'Scowrers' and gives the
orders as to whom is going to be killed, beaten, and/or
blackmailed. He is one of the seven who are to capture the
Pinkerton man, Birdy Edwards. He was arrested by
Captain Marvin and Birdy Edwards while waiting with his
comrades to capture Edwards and kill him. He meets his
end upon the scaffold.

AKA Boss McGinty
AKA Black Jack McGinty

McLAREN, MILES:

"The Adventure of the Three Students"
Lives three floors above Hilton Soames at the College of
St. Luke. He is a brilliant fellow when he chooses to be,
one of the brightest intellects of the university, however,
he is wayward, dissipated, and unprincipled. He is about
five foot six in height. In his first year, he was almost
expelled over a card scandal. He has been idling all this
term and cannot be looking forward to the Fortescue
Scholarship exam.

McMURDO:

"The Sign of Four"

Ex-prize-fighter and body-guard to Major Sholto and after the Major's death, his son, Bartholomew's body-guard. The porter or gatekeeper according to the STANDARD, a London newspaper. Accused, along with Thaddeus Sholto, of the murder of Bartholomew Sholto.

McMURDO, JOHN:

"The Valley of Fear"   Part 2: "The Scowrers"

Brother John McMurdo of Lodge 29 Eminent Order of Freemen, Chicago, he is a fresh-complexioned, middle-sized young man, around thirty. Gregarious in his habits and communicative in his nature, he is known to have a quick wit and a ready smile, this pleasant, brown-haired young Irishman. He was made a Brother in Lodge 29 Chicago June 24, 1872, his Bodymaster being James H. Scott and his district ruler was Bartholomew Wilson. After arriving in Vermissa, he takes a room at the boarding house of Jacob Shafter on Sheridan Street, falling in love with Jacob's daughter, Ettie. After informing the boarding house owner that he is a member of the 'Eminent Order of Freemen' he is asked to leave the lodgings and find another residence. McMurdo moves to lodgings at Widow MacNamara's on the extreme outskirts of town. He is joined there by fellow brother, Scanlan, who has also moved to Vermissa. He informed all who knew him that he had worked in a planing mill in Chicago but due to his being an educated man he obtains employment as a bookkeeper in Vermissa. He carried a newspaper clipping revealing the shooting of one Jonas Pinto in Chicago, allegedly by him. They were involved in counterfeiting American dollars. He becomes a member of the Vermissa Lodge 341, "Eminent Order of Freemen' and takes part in a 'warning' given to "Vermissa Herald" owner/editor James Stanger. He is later arrested and acquitted of any involvement in the assault on Stanger. He is assigned the 'job' of settling the Chester Wilcox matter, which will involve killing the entire family. Wilcox is warned of the impending attack and flees. Nevertheless, sometime later, newspapers report that he has been shot. Members of the Vermissa 'Scowrers' believe McMurdo to have been responsible. During the 'reign of terror,' the winter of 1875, he was appointed Inner Deacon of the Lodge of Vermissa. He comes into possession of a telegraph message revealing a Pinkerton detective is on the trail of the 'Scowrers' and he informs the lodge of this information. He, with seven others, Boss McGinty, Ted Baldwin, Tiger Cormac, Carter, Harraway and the Willaby brothers set a trap for the Pinkerton, Birdy Edwards at Widow MacNamara's. At the moment the trap is to be sprung Boss McGinty asks McMurdo "Is Birdy Edwards here?" McMurdo responds "Yes, Birdy Edwards is here. I am Birdy Edwards." And the seven leaders of the 'Scowrers' are arrested by Captain Marvin and his police force.

AKA John Douglas, See Douglas, John
AKA Hargrave, See Hargrave
AKA Birdy Edwards, See Edwards, Birdy
AKA Steve Wilson, See Wilson, Steve

McMURDO THE SCOWRER:
"The Valley of Fear"   Part 2: "The Scowrers"
Name given to John McMurdo by one of the boarders at Jacob Shafter boarding house.
See McMurdo, John.

McPHERSON, FITZROY:
"The Adventure of the Lion's Mane"

The science master at The Gables, he was a fine upstanding young man whose life had been crippled by heart trouble after a bout with rheumatic fever. Nevertheless, he was a natural athlete and excelled in areas that did not put too great a strain on his heart. He was engaged to Maud Bellamy, but kept it secret fearing his old uncle, who was said to be dying, might disinherit him for marrying against his wishes. He is discovered by Holmes and Harold Stackhurst running from the ocean edge like a drunken man. He let out a terrible cry and fell on his face, his last words were 'the Lion's Mane.' His back was covered with dark red lines as though he had been terribly flogged by a thin wire scourge.

McQUIRE:
"The Adventure of the Noble Bachelor"

Owner of a mining camp where Miss Hatty Doran and Mr. Frank Moulton met, while Hatty's father was working a claim.

MECCA:
"The Adventure of the Empty House"

Persia; Holmes traveled to Mecca after his visit to Tibet, these travels occuring after his fight with Professor Moriarty at the Reichenbach Falls, in an attempt to keep the world thinking he was dead.

MEEK, FASPER:
"The Adventure of the Dying Detective"

One of the best doctors in London. Watson implores Holmes to consult someone about his Sumatra disease and suggest Fasper Meek.

MEIRINGEN:
> "The Final Problem"
>> Final destination of Holmes and Watson in their attempt to avoid Moriarty. Having traveled to Switzerland wandering up the valley of the Rhone, branching off at Leuk, over the Gemmi Pass, by way of Interlaken, they are heading to Meiringen.

MELAS, MR.:
> "The Greek Interpreter"
>> Of Greek extraction, he is a remarkable linguist, earning a living partly as an interpreter in the law courts and partly as a guide to any wealthy Orientals who may visit the Northumberland hotels. He lodges on the floor above Mycroft Holmes in Pall Mall and is a slight acquaintance. He is short and stout, with coal-black hair, he has the speech of an educated Englishman. After an extraordinary adventure involving his translation skills, he consults Mycroft Holmes, who inturn calls in Sherlock Holmes to investigate Mr. Melas's strange tale, a tale of secrecy, foreign prisoners, and money. He is poisoned by Latimer and his partner, Kemp, with charcoal gas but is saved by Holmes.

MELVILLE:
> "The Adventure of Wisteria Lodge"
> aka "A Reminiscence of Mr. Sherlock Holmes"
>> A retired brewer living at Albermarle Mansion, Kensington. He is a friend of Mr. John Scott Eccles, his family introducing Mr. Eccles to one Mr. Garcia.

MENZIES:
> "The Valley of Fear"   Part 2: "The Scowrers"
>> Mine engineer for the Crow Hill mine, he is a great bearded Scotchman. When he comes to the aid of Josiah

Dunn, who has been shot by the assassins Lawler and Andrews, he is shot by Lawler.

MERCER:
"The Adventure of the Creeping Man"
Holmes's general utility man who looks up routine business. He has come about since Watson's time.

MEREDITH, GEORGE:
"The Boscombe Valley Mystery"
No additional information is provide by Watson as to who is Mr. Meredith.

MEREER:
"The 'Gloria Scott'"
The second mate on the 'Gloria Scott' and a conspirator in the over-throw of the captain and soldiers, during the ship's trip to Australia and the prison camps.

MERIVALE:
"The Adventure of Shoscombe Old Place"
He is of Scotland Yard and has asked Holmes to look into the St. Pancras case, an unrecorded case.

MERRIDEW:
"The Adventure of the Empty House"
An unrecorded case. Of abominable memory, contained in Holmes's index of biographies under the letter "M".

MERRILOW, MRS.:
"The Adventure of the Retired Colourman"
An elderly, motherly woman, she ran a boarding house in South Brixton. She comes to Holmes at the request of one of her lodgers, an individual she has only seen once in seven years.

MERROW, LORD:
"The Adventure of the Second Stain"
A letter from Lord Merrow was in the dispatch-box belonging to The Right Honourable Trelawney Hope.

MERRYWEATHER, MR.:
"The Red-Headed League"
He is a bank director, in fact, the chairman of directors of "the City branch of one of the principal London banks. His bank "had occasion some months ago to strengthen our resources and borrowed for that purpose 30,000 napoleons [French gold] from the Bank of France." It is his Bank which is to be robbed by tunneling from the pawn shop of Jabez Wilson.

MERTON COUNTY:
"The Valley of Fear"   Part 2: "The Scowrers"
Deep in the Vermissa Valley, the coal and iron trains traveled from Stagville through Vermissa and Bartons Crossing continuing on to Helmdale and the purely agricultural county of Merton. At the far end of Vermissa Valley, it is home to Lodge 249 'Ancient Order of Freemen.'

MERTON, SAM:
"The Adventure of the Mazarin Stone"
A great big silly, bull-headed gudgeon, a boxer, he has been used by Count Negretto Sylvius in the theft of the Crown Diamond. Holmes believes he isn't really a bad fellow.

METROPOLITAN STATION:
"The Adventure of the Beryl Coronet"
Train station near the Baker Street lodgings of Holmes and Watson.

MEUNIER, OSCAR:
> "The Adventure of the Empty House"
>> Molded a bust, in wax, of Holmes.

MEYER, ADOLPH:
> "The Adventure of the Bruce-Partington Plans"
>> One of the few men Mycroft Holmes believes is able to dispose of the stolen Bruce-Partington papers. He resides at 13 Great George Street, Westminster.

MEYERS:
> "The Hound of the Baskervilles"
>> Of Toronto, boot maker. Where Sir Henry Baskerville's boots were purchased.

MEXBOROUGH PRIVATE HOTEL:
> "The Hound of the Baskervilles"
>> Located in Craven Street, where the Stapletons resided while John Stapleton followed Dr. Mortimer and Sir Henry Baskerville. Mrs. Stapleton was a prisoner in the room.

MICHAEL:
> "The Adventure of the Sussex Vampire"
>> A stablehand at the Ferguson residence, he lives in the house in servant quarters.

MIDDLESEX:
> "The Yellow Face"
>> Effie (Hebron) Munro returns to live with a maiden Aunt at Pinner, in Middlesex, after the death of her husband and child in America.

MIDDLESEX CORPS:

"The Adventure of the Blanched Soldier"

Division of the Imperial Yeomanry stationed in South Africa during the Boer War. James Dodd and Godfrey Emsworth were mates in this corps.

MIDDLETON:

"The Hound of the Baskervilles"

Involved in a lawsuit with Mr. Frankland concerning a right of way. Frankland is successful in winning a right of way right through old Middleton's park, within a hundred yards of his front door.

MIDIANITES:

"The Disappearance of Lady Frances Carfax"

Dr. Shlessinger is preparing a map of the Holy Land with particular attention to the kingdom of the Midianits, upon which he is writing a monograph.

MIDLAND ELECTRIC COMPANY:

"The Adventure of the Solitary Cyclist"

Of Coventry, it is the company for which Cyril Morton, boyfriend of Miss Violet Smith, is employed.

MILANO:

"The Adventure of the Three Gables"

Italy, the luggage of Douglas Maberley has a label from Milano upon it. The luggage is piled in a corner of a room at 'The Three Gables' having been returned to his mother after his death.

MILES, MISS:

"The Adventure of Charles Augustus Milverton"

The Honorable Miss Miles was to marry Colonel Dorking, however, two days before the scheduled marriage was to take place it was called off. Charles

Augustus Milverton released some letters written by Miss Miles when she refused to pay him a large sum of money for them and it was these letters which led to the canceling of the marriage.

MILLAR, MISS FLORA:

"The Adventure of the Noble Bachelor"

She caused a disturbance at the wedding breakfast of Hatty Doran and Lord St. Simon. She was formally a danseuse at the Allegro and had been very, very friendly with Lord St. Simon. She is later seen with Hatty Doran after the wedding and prior to her disappearance. Flora is arrested when Hatty Doran disappears.

MILLER HILL:

"The Valley of Fear"   Part 2: "The Scowrers"

An ill-kept public park in the center of Vermissa. In Summer it is a favorite spot for people but in Winter it is desolate. It commands a view of the entire Valley. It is here that John McMurdo has been summoned by Brother Morris to discuss the criminal ways of the Lodge of which they are both members.

MILMAN:

"The Valley of Fear"   Part 2: "The Scowrers"

Allegedly murdered by the Scowrers.

MILNER, GODFREY:

"The Adventure of the Empty House"

He and partner, Lord Balmoral, lost 420 pounds playing cards with Ronald Adair and Colonel Moran some weeks prior to the murder of Ronald Adair.

MILVERTON, CHARLES AUGUSTUS:

"The Adventure of Charles Augustus Milverton"

The worst man in London. A man of fifty, he has a large, intellectual head, a round, plump, hairless face, a perpetual frozen smile, and two keen gray eyes, which gleam brightly from behind broad, gold-rimmed glasses. There is something of Mr. Pickwick's benevolence in his appearance. He is the King of all Blackmailers. He purchases letters which compromise people of wealth and position and then with a smiling face and a heart of marble, he will squeeze and squeeze until he has drained them dry. He obtains his wares not only from treacherous valets and maids, but frequently from genteel ruffians, who have gained the confidence and affection of trusting woman. He has been known to hold a card back for years in order to play it at the moment when the stake is best worth winning. He is in possession of some imprudent letters written by Lady Eva Blackwell which he is threatening to send to her fiance, the Earl of Dovercourt, unless she pays him a large sum of money. He is murdered in his study, by an unnamed woman, as Holmes and Watson look on from their hiding place.

MINCING LANE:

"The Adventure of the Sussex Vampire"

Location of the offices of Ferguson and Muirhead, tea brokers.

MINE CONSTABULARY:

"The Valley of Fear"   Part 2: "The Scowrers"

Captain Marvin is head of the Mine Constabulary, a special body of police raised by the railways and colliery owners to supplement the efforts of the ordinary civil police who were helpless in the face of the organized ruffianism which terrorized the Vermissa Valley.

MING DYNASTY:
"The Adventure of the Illustrious Client"
Holmes provides Watson with a genuine piece of Ming Dynasty pottery to show Baron Gruner as part of the plan to defeat the criminal in his attempt to marry Violet de Merville.

MINORIES:
"The Adventure of the Mazarin Stone"
Section of London where the craftsman, Straubenzee, has his workshop.

MISSION OF HOLLAND:
"A Scandal in Bohemia"
An unrecorded case. Holmes accomplished a matter delicately and successfully for the reigning family of Holland.

MITTON, JOHN:
"The Adventure of the Second Stain"
Valet to Eduardo Lucas.

MOFFAT:
"The Resident Patient"
One of the Worthingdon Bank Gang; after being released from prison, he and his fellow gang members seek out the gang member who turned on traitor and testified against them -- one Sutton. It is believed he died as a passenger of the ill-fated steamer 'Norah Creina,' which was lost with all hands upon the Portuguese coast, some leagues to the north of Oporto.

MOLESEY MYSTERY:
"The Adventure of the Empty House"
A case handled by Lestrade while Holmes was presumed to be dead.

MONOGRAPHS:

Sherlock Holmes wrote several monographs only one of which we have the actual title. He tells us the subject matter of some of the others, they are listed below with subject matter as title:

*Upon the Distinction Between the Ashes of the Various Tobaccos

In this monograph Holmes enumerates a hundred and forty forms of cigar, cigarette, and pipe tobacco, with colored plates illustrating the difference in the ash.

* The Tracing of Footsteps

This monograph includes some remarks upon the uses of plaster of Paris as a preserver of impresses.

* The Influence of a Trade Upon the Form of Hand

This monograph contains lithotypes of the hands of slaters, sailors, cork-cutters, compositors, weavers and diamond-polishers.

MONTAGUE PLACE:

"The Adventure of the Copper Beeches"

A letter, sent to Holmes by Violet Hunter, is dated from 'Montague Place.'

MONTAGUE STREET:

"The Musgrave Ritual"

Street where Holmes took rooms when he first came to London. It is here that Reginald Musgrave consults Holmes concerning the strange occurrences at the Musgrave ancestral home.

MONTGOMERY, INSPECTOR:
"The Adventure of the Cardboard Box"
Inspector who took down Jim Browner's statement (confession) at the Shadwell Police Station.

MONTMARTRE DISTRICT:
"The Adventure of the Illustrious Client"
Section of Paris.

MONTPELLIER:
"The Adventure of the Empty House"
France; Holmes spent time at a laboratory here conducting research into the coal-tar derivatives.

"Disappearance of Lady Frances Carfax"
Mary Devine, maid to Lady Frances Carfax lives at Number 11 Rue de Trajan, Montpellier.

MME. MONTPENSIER:
"The Hound of the Baskervilles"
An unrecorded case.
Holmes defends Mme. Montpensier from a charge of murder which hung over her in connection with the death of her step-daughter, Mlle. Carere, who was discovered six months later alive and married in New York. Takes place right after "The Hound of the Baskervilles."

THE MOOR:
"The Hound of the Baskervilles"
It is a wonderful place, undulating downs, long green rollers, with crests of jagged granite foaming up into fantastic surges. It is vast, barren and mysterious.

MOORHOUSE:
> "The Adventure of the Missing Three-quarter"
>> Plays for Trinity College's rugby team. He is a first reserve, trained as a half and he always edges right in on to the scrum instead of keeping out on the touchline.

MOORSMOOR:
> "The Adventure of the Retired Colourman"
>> With Little Purlington, it is the area of the Vicarage of J.C. Elman. It is east of London, near Frinton in Essex.

MOORVILLE:
> "The Adventure of the Three Garridebs"
>> Town in Kansas, U.S.A. where John Garrideb practices law.

MORAN, AUGUSTUS, SIR:
> "The Adventure of the Empty House"
>> Father of Colonel Sebastian Moran. Once British Minister to Persia.

MORAN, PATIENCE:
> "The Boscombe Valley Mystery"
>> The daughter of the lodge-keeper of the Boscombe Valley estate Witness to a fight between Charles and James McCarthy, just prior to the death of Charles McCarthy.

MORAN, COLONEL SEBASTIAN:
> "The Adventure of the Empty House"
>> Was very fond of cards, it is presumed he was caught at cheating by his partner, Ronald Adair, who he then killed with an expanding bullet from an air-gun. He had a tremendously virile and yet sinister face with the brow of a philosopher above and the jaw of a sensualist below. His cruel blue eyes, with drooping, cynical lids, fierce,

aggressive nose, and threatening, deep-lined brow revealed Nature's plainest danger-signals. Once of Her Majesty's Indian Army, and the best heavy-game shot that the Eastern Empire has ever produced. His bag of tigers remains unrivalled. From Holmes "index of biographies": Moran, Sebastian, Colonel. Unemployed. Formerly 1st Bangalore Pioneers. Born London, 1840. Son of Sir Augustus Moran, C.B., once British Minister to Persia. Educated Eton and Oxford. Served in Jowaki Campaign, Afghan Campaign, Charasiab (despatches), Sherpur, and Cabul. Author of 'Heavy Game of the Western Himalayas' (1881); 'Three Months in the Jungle' (1884). Address: Conduit Street. Clubs: The Anglo-Indian, the Tankerville, the Bagatelle Card Club. Holmes has written in the margin of his "Index": 'The second most dangerous man in London' Made India too hot to hold him although there was no open scandal. Holmes believes him to be responsible for the death of Mrs. Stewart, of Lauder, in 1887. Holmes believes it was Moran, who with Professor Moriarty, followed Watson and Holmes to Switzerland and threw a few large stones at Holmes while he was clinging above the Reichenbach Falls. He is Professor Moriarty's confidant. Colonel Moran is captured by Holmes and Watson after he fires his air-gun at a wax bust of Holmes, believing it to be Holmes sitting in his rooms in Baker Street. The gun and the expanding bullet, which Holmes retrieves from his room is evidence that Colonel Moran killed Ronald Adair.

"His Last Bow" "An Epilogue of Sherlock Holmes"
  The German spy, Von Bork, threatens to "get level" with Holmes and he, Holmes, comments on how often he has heard the same phrase, even from the Colonel, yet he continues to live and keep his bees upon the South Downs.

"The Valley of Fear" Part 1: "The Tragedy of Birlstone"
>Colonel Sebastian Moran is Professor Moriarty's chief of staff.

"The Adventure of the Illustrious Client"
>Holmes wonders whether Baron Gruner is as dangerous as the living Colonel Sebastian Moran.

MORECROFT:

"The Adventure of the Three Garridebs"
>See Evans, Killer

MORGAN:

"The Adventure of the Empty House"
>An unrecorded case. The poisoner, contained in Holmes's index of biographies under the letter "M".

MORIARTY, JAMES (COLONEL):

"The Final Problem"
>Brother of Professor Moriarty, his letters purporting to tell the facts of "The Final Problem" lead to Watson's taking pen in hand and writing "The Final Problem" to tell the true facts.

MORIARTY, PROFESSOR:

>See separate chapter entitled Moriarty, Professor.

MORLAND, JOHN:

"The Hound of the Baskervilles"
>Sued by Mr. Frankland for trespass because he shot in his own warren. Frankland won -- Frankland v. Morland, Court of Queen's Bench.

THE MORNING CHRONICLE:
"The Red-Headed League"
The April 27, 1890 edition carried an announcement:

"TO THE RED-HEADED LEAGUE:
On account of the bequest of the late Ezekiah Hopkins, of Lebanon, Pennsylvania, U.S.A., there is now another vacancy open which entitles a member of the League to a salary of œÀ4 a week for purely nominal services. All red-headed men who are sound in body and mind, and above the age of twenty-one years, are eligible. Apply in person on Monday, at eleven o'clock, to Duncan Ross, at the offices of the League, 7 Pope's Court, Fleet Street.

"A Case of Identity"
Miss Mary Sutherland causes an advertisement to be printed in the Saturday edition describing her missing fiance, Mr. Hosmer Angel.
See: Angel, Hosmer.

MORNING POST:
"The Adventure of the Noble Bachelor"
London newspaper which reported the ongoings associated with the marriage of Lord St. Simon and Hatty Doran.

"The Adventure of the Illustrious Client"
London newspaper which carried the announcement that Miss Violet de Merville's marriage to Baron Adelbert Gruner would not take place. It also carried notice of the police-court hearings concerned with the proceedings against Miss Kitty Winter on the charge of vitriol-throwing.

MORPHINE:
>"The Adventure of the Illustrious Client"
>>Holmes receives some morphine, by Sir Leslie Oakshott, the famous surgeon, after he is beaten by two armed men in front of the Cafe Royal in Regent Street.

MORPHY, ALICE:
>"The Adventure of the Creeping Man"
>>A very perfect girl both in mind and body, she is engaged to Professor Presbury. She is much younger than the Professor.

MORPHY, PROFESSOR:
>"The Adventure of the Creeping Man"
>>Colleague of Professor Presbury's, he has the chair of comparative anatomy. Professor Morphy's daughter, Alice, is engaged to Professor Presbury.

MORRIS:
>"The Valley of Fear"   Part 2: "The Scowrers"
>>An elderly, clean-shaven man with a kindly face and a good brow, a brother in the Lodge, 'Eminent Order of Freemen' but he is concerned that the 'Scowrers' are forcing all the little mine owners out thereby bringing in the 'big' companies who will be a greater threat to the Lodge. Bodymaster McGinty refers to him as 'Mr. Standback' when he questions the planning of an attack on the local newspaper owner, James Stanger. Through an old friend in Philadelphia he intercepts a telegraph meant for Birdy Edwards, an undercover Pinkerton detective, investigating the 'Scowrers.' He gives this information to John McMurdo.

MORRIS, WILLIAM:
>"The Red-Headed League"
>>See DUNCAN ROSS

MORRISON, ANNIE:

"The Reigate Puzzle"

A note which Mr. Cunningham and his son, Alec put together to attract William Kirwan, their coachman, to his death, mentions the name 'Annie Morrison.' She does not appear in the story and Holmes states that "we do not yet know what the relations may have been between Alec Cunningham, William Kirwan, and Annie Morrison." Whatever the relationship, the note brought Kirwan to his death.

MORRISON, MISS:

"The Crooked Man"

A young lady who lived in the villa next to 'Lachine,' home to Colonel and Mrs, Barclay. A little ethereal slip of a girl, with timid eyes and blond hair, but by no means wanting in shrewdness and common sense.

MORRISON, MORRISON, AND DODD:

"The Adventure of the Sussex Vampire"

Offices at 46 Old Jewry, they are in the business of assessing machinery and have had occasion to seek help from Sherlock Holmes in the past, as in the case of Matilda Briggs. They have been approached by Robert Ferguson concerning vampires and they have recommended that Holmes be consulted.

MORSTAN, ARTHUR:

"The Sign of Four"

Captain Morstan is the father of Mary Morstan. Officer in an Indian regiment, he was the senior captain of his regiment, the Thirty-fourth Bombay Infantry. Had been to the Andaman Islands. In 1878 he received 12 months leave and wrote his daughter he would be staying at the Langham Hotel. He disappeared upon the third of

December 1878. His only known friend was a Major Sholto, of his own regiment. It is later discovered that he died of a heart attack while arguing with Major Sholto over the Agra treasure. He and Sholto had double-crossed four convicts, retrieved the Arga Treasure for themselves, and planned to live happily thereafter. See: Agra Treasure

MORSTAN, MISS MARY:
"The Sign of Four"

She was a blonde young lady, small, dainty, well gloved and dressed in the most perfect taste. There was, however, a plainness and simplicity about her costume which bore with it a suggestion of limited means. She had large blue eyes which were singularly spiritual and sympathetic. Lives with Mrs. Cecil Forrester in Lower Camberwell. Marries Dr. Watson some time after the conclusion of her case. See: Watson, John

MORTIMER:
"The Adventure of the Golden Pince-Nez"

The gardener for Professor Coram, he pushes the Professor around the grounds of Yoxley Old Place in a Bath chair. He is an army pensioner, an old Crimean man of excellent character. He resides in a three room cottage at the end of the garden.

MORTIMER, JAMES:
"The Hound of the Baskervilles"

M.R.C.S., 1882, Grimpen, Dartmoor, Devon. House surgeon, from 1882 to 1884, at Charing Cross Hospital. Winner of the Jackson prize for Comparative Pathology, with essay entitled 'Is Disease a Reversion?' Corresponding member of the Swedish Pathological Society. Author of 'Some Freaks of Atavism' (Lancet, 1882), 'Do We Progress?' (Journal of Psychology, March

1883). Medical Officer for the parishes of Grimpen, Thorsley, and High Barrow. [From Holmes' Medical Directory] A very tall, thin man, with a long nose like a beak, which jutted out between two keen, gray eyes, set closely together and sparkling brightly from behind a pair of gold-rimmed glasses. Though young, his long back was already bowed, and he walked with a forward thrust of his head and a general air of peering benevolence. Personal friend and medical attendant to Sir Charles Baskerville, he consults Holmes, prior to the arrival of Sir Henry Baskerville, concerning the Legend of the "Hound of the Baskervilles."

MORTON:

"The Adventure of the Missing Three-quarter"
Plays for the Oxford rugby team, he is a flier.

MORTON, CYRIL:

"The Adventure of the Solitary Cyclist"
An electrical engineer, he is the boyfriend of Miss Violet Smith, with plans to marry her at the end of the summer of 1895. Watson notes that Cryil does indeed marry Miss Violet Smith and he becomes the senior partner of Morton & Kennedy, the famous Westminster electricians.

MORTON, INSPECTOR:

"The Adventure of the Dying Detective"
Of Scotland Yard, he meets Watson as Watson is fetching Mr. Culverton Smith and asked about Holmes health. Had it not been too fiendish, Watson believes he saw "exultation in Morton's face."

MORTON & KENNEDY:

"The Adventure of the Solitary Cyclist"
Famous Westminster electricians, Cyril Morton being the senior partner and husband of Miss Violet Smith.

MOSER, M.:
"The Disappearance of Lady Frances Carfax"
Manager of the Hotel National.

MOULTON, FRANCIS HAY (FRANK):
"The Adventure of the Noble Bachelor"
Husband of Hatty Doran. Married her while in the mining fields of the Rockies, locates her in England just prior to her arranged marriage to Lord   St. Simon. She had believed he was killed by Apache Indians in New Mexico. An American, he was small, wiry, sunburnt man, clean-shaven, with sharp face and alert manner.

MOUNT-JAMES, LORD:
"The Adventure of the Missing Three-quarter"
One of the richest men in England and the uncle of Godfrey Staunton.

MOUNTS BAY:
"The Adventure of the Devil's Foot"
A sinister semicircle, a death trap of sailing vessels, with its fringe of black cliffs and surge swept reefs on which many a seaman had met his end.

MUNRO, EFFIE:
"The Yellow Face"
Married to Grant Munro who met her when she was twenty-five and widowed. Her previous married name was Mrs. Hebron. She had left England when she was young, traveling to America where she met a man named John Hebron whom she married. She has told everyone that they had one child, who along with Mr. Hebron, died during the outbreak of yellow-fever. After the alleged death of her husband and child, she returned to England to live with a maiden Aunt at Pinner, in Middlesex.

Her marriage to Grant Munro appears to be breaking up due to her strange behavior which leads her husband to consult Holmes. It turns out that she has been harboring a "colored" girl who is in fact her child. Her first husband, Mr. Hebron, was a black man and together they had a child, a girl, who did not die, as Effie claimed, in the outbreak of yellow fever. Effie's longing for the child has resulted in the bringing the child to England.

MUNRO, GRANT:
"The Yellow Face"
> Has been married for three years. His wife's name is Effie. He appears to be around thirty but is actually older. Consults Holmes on a domestic matter. He is a hop merchant with an income of seven or eight hundred, and he and Effie live in an eighty-pound villa at Norbury.

MUNRO, SPENCE (COLONEL):
"The Adventure of the Copper Beeches"
> Previous employer of Violet Hunter. He has moved to Halifax, Nova Scotia taking his children with him and thereby releasing Miss Hunter from her duties.

MURCHER, HENRY:
"A Study in Scarlet"
> Had the Holland Grove beat the night of the discovery of the body of Enoch J. Drebber. He met John Rance at the corner of Henrietta Street just prior to John Rance's discovery of the body.

MURDEROUS ATTACK UPON SHERLOCK HOLMES:
"The Adventure of the Illustrious Client"
> Headlines in newspaper spotted by Watson on his way to Baker Street from the Charing Cross Station. Holmes was attacked outside the Cafe Royal and beaten about the head by two men armed with sticks. He was taken to

Charing Cross Hospital and was later transported to his rooms at Baker Street. The attackers ran through the Cafe Royal and out to Glasshouse Street behind it, they were never found. For six days the public was under the impression that Holmes was at death's door.

MURDOCH, IAN:

"The Adventure of the Lion's Mane"

Mathematics instructor at The Gables, he was tall, dark, and thin, a taciturn and aloof man, he had no friends. He has an argument with Harold Stackhurst concerning the formers presence at The Haven. Stackhurst, displeased with Murdoch's impertinence, gives him notice as to his position at The Gables. His preparations to depart the area, his appearance of affection for McPherson's lady, Maud Bellamy, and his typical, everyday behavior, place him in the position as prime suspect in the death of McPherson. He goes swimming in the general area where McPherson was found and encounters a strange object which attacks him. He is able to escape to Holmes's residence, through the help of Harold Stackhurst, and is discovered to have the same 'criss-cross, reticulated pattern of red, inflamed lines' on his shoulder that had been the death-mark of Fitzroy McPherson.

MURDOCH, JAMES:

"The Valley of Fear"   Part 2: "The Scowrers"

Mutilated by the 'Scowrers' in the winter of 1875.

MURILLO, DON:

"The Adventure of Wisteria Lodge"

aka "A Reminiscence of Mr. Sherlock Holmes"

He was known as the most lewd and bloodthirsty tyrant that ever governed any country. His name was a terror through all Central America. Strong, fearless, and energetic, he was able to control his people for ten or twelve years until the people rose up against him and he fled. He arrived at Barcelona by ship in 1886, from there he moved to Madrid, then Rome, Paris and finally Wisteria Lodge. He is still pursued for his past acts and his children's governess is secretly one of his pursuers. He realizes she is a spy before she can harm him and he escapes before being caught by Holmes or the police to places unknown.

AKA Mr. Henderson
AKA The Tiger of San Pedro
AKA Juan Murillo

EX-PRESIDENT MURILLO:
"The Adventure of the Norwood Builder"
>An unrecorded case. A case which involved the papers of ex-President Murillo, it having taken place soon after Watson's return to Baker Street sometime after his marriage.

MURILLO, JUAN:
"The Adventure of Wisteria Lodge"
aka "A Reminiscence of Mr. Sherlock Holmes"
>See Murillo, Don.

MURPHY:
"The Hound of the Baskervilles"
>A Gypsy horse-trader, he was on the moor the night Sir Charles Baskerville died, and by his own confession, "the worse for drink."

MURPHY:
    "The Valley of Fear"   Part 2: "The Scowrers"
        Friend of John McMurdo's in Chicago who
        recommended the boarding house on Sheridan Street in
        Vermissa, owned by Jacob Shafter.

MURPHY, MAJOR:
    "The Crooked Man"
        Individual from whom Holmes obtains most of his
        information concerning Colonel and Mrs. Barclay of 'The
        Royal Munsters.' Requested Holmes help in the murder
        of Colonel Barclay at 'Lachine.'

MURRAY:
    "A Study in Scarlet"
        Watson's orderly, threw Watson across a pack-horse and
        succeeded in bringing him safely to the British lines while
        Watson was serving in India.

MURRAY, MR.:
    "The Adventure of the Empty House"
        Played cards with Ronald Adair, Sir John Hardy, and
        Colonel Moran the evening of Ronald Adair's murder.

        He was the partner of Sir John Hardy against Adair and
        Moran.

MUSEUM OF THE COLLEGE OF SURGEONS:
    "The Hound of the Baskervilles"
        Located in London, Dr. Mortimer spent a day in pure
        amusement and visited the museum.

MUSGRAVE, REGINALD:
    "The Musgrave Ritual"
        Attended college with Holmes, with some slight
        acquaintance between the two. He was not very popular

and what was set down as pride was really an attempt to cover extreme natural difference. He was a man of an exceedingly aristocratic type, thin, high-nosed, and large-eyed, with languid and yet courtly manners. He was indeed a scion of one of the very oldest families in the kingdom, though his branch was a cadet one which had separated from the northern Musgraves some time in the sixteenth century and had established itself in western Sussex, where the Manor House of Hurlstone is perhaps the oldest inhabited building in the county. Holmes, upon seeing the man, associated him with gray archways and mullioned windows and all the venerable wreckage of a feudal keep. His father died about two years before he consults Holmes over the disappearance of his butler and other strange happenings at his home.

THE MUSGRAVE RITUAL:

Published in "The Strand": May 1893

Published as part of: "Memoirs of Sherlock Holmes"

Holmes describes the adventure as "something a little 'recherché'." Involves a strange family ritual and the Crown of the Kings of England. From a small wooden box with a sliding lid he produced - a crumpled piece of paper, an old-fashioned brass key, a peg of wood with a ball of string attached to it, and three rusty old disc of metal; all that he had left to remind him of the adventure of the Musgrave Ritual. Case brought to Holmes by a old fellow-student, it was his third case. His old friend Reginald Musgrave was concerned with the disappearance of his butler and other strange happenings at his home. Holmes tells Watson of this adventure during Watson's attempt to have Holmes tidy-up their lodgings.

MUSGRAVE RITUAL:

"The Musgrave Ritual"

The 'Musgrave Ritual' is a sort of ceremony peculiar to the Musgrave family, which each Musgrave for centuries past has gone through on his coming of age. It reads in question and answer format as follows:

"Whose was it? His who is gone.
Who shall have it? He who will come.
Where was the sun? Over the oak.
Where was the shadow? Under the elm.
How was it stepped? North by ten and by ten, east by five and by five, south by two and by two, west by one and by one, and so under.
What shall we give for it? All that is ours.
Why should we give it? For the sake of the trust."

It was written, as can be best determined, in the middle of the 17th century. Holmes is able to deduce that the ritual is actually directions to a hidden treasure, the crown jewels of Charles I.

THE MYRTLES:

"The Greek Interpreter"

Located in Beckenham it is a large, dark house standing back from the road in its own grounds. It is here that Sophy and Paul Kratides are being held by Harold Latimer and Wilson Kemp.

MORIARTY

MORIARTY, PROFESSOR JAMES:
"The Final Problem"

His first appearance.

He pervades London, and no one has heard of him, he is on a pinnacle in the records of crime. His career has been an extraordinary one. He is of good birth and excellent education, endowed by nature with a phenomenal mathematical faculty. At the age of twenty-one he wrote a treatise on the binomial theorem, which has a European vogue. He thereby won the mathematical chair at one of England's smaller universities with a brilliant career ahead of him. He had hereditary tendencies of the most diabolical kind. A criminal strain ran in his blood, which, instead of being modified, was increased and rendered infinitely more dangerous by his extraordinary mental powers. Dark rumors gathered around him and he was forced to resign his chair, he came down to London, where he set up as an army coach. He is the Napoleon of crime; he is the organizer of half that is evil and of nearly all that is undetected in London. He is a genius, a philosopher, an abstract thinker. He has the brain of the first order.

Reichenbach Falls: It is here that Watson believes Holmes and Moriarty met their death on May 4, 1891: "an examination by experts leaves little doubt that a personal contest between the two men ended, as it could hardly fail to end in such a situation, in their reeling over, locked in each other's arms. Any attempt at recovering the bodies was absolutely hopeless, and there, deep down in that dreadful cauldron of swirling water and seething foam, will lie for all time the most dangerous criminal and the foremost champion of the law of their generation.

"The Adventure of the Empty House"
>Holmes tells Watson of his battle with Moriarty at the
>Reichenbach Falls: "He drew no weapon, but rushed me
>and threw his long arms around me."

"The Adventure of the Norwood Builder"
>Holmes mentions "London has become a singularly
>uninteresting city since the death of the late lamented
>Professor Moriarty.

"His Last Bow", "An Epilogue of Sherlock Holmes"
>The German spy, Von Bork, threatens to "get level" with
>Holmes and he, Holmes, comments on how often he has
>heard the same phrase, even from the late Professor, yet
>he continues to live and keep his bees upon the
>South Downs.

"The Valley of Fear", Part 1: "The Tragedy of Birlstone"
>The greatest schemer of all time, the organizer of every
>deviltry, the controlling brain of the underworld, a brain
>that might have made or marred the destiny of nations.

>The celebrated author of "The Dynamics of an Asteroid."

>He has a younger brother who is employed as a
>stationmaster in the west of England.

>The Professor purchased a painting by the French artist,
>Jean Baptiste Greuze, for forty thousand pounds in 1865,
>a tremendous price considering he is not a wealthy man
>and his professor chair pays only seven hundred pounds
>per year. The bulk of his wealth is hidden away in
>the Deutsche Bank or the Credit Lyonnais. He has
>twenty or more banking accounts.

>John Douglas is lost overboard during a gale off St.

Helena on his way to Cape Town South Africa and the accident has Moriarty's signature.

"The Adventure of the Illustrious Client"
Holmes wonders whether Baron Gruner is as dangerous a fellow as the late Professor.

CHAPTER N

NAPLES:
> "The Adventure of the Red Circle"
>> Italian city near Posilippo.

NAPOLEON:
> "The Adventure of the Six Napoleons"
>> The First; it is copies of his bust which are being stolen and smashed.

NAPOLEON OF CRIME:
> "The Final Problem"
>> See Professor Moriarty.

NARA:
> "The Adventure of the Illustrious Client"
>> See Shomu, Emperor.

NARBONNE:
> "The Final Problem"
>> Holmes sent a note to Watson dated from Narbonne, France in early 1891.

NAVAL SIGNALS:
> "His Last Bow" "An Epilogue of Sherlock Holmes"
>> Von Bork, the German spy, had a safe containing pigeon-holes bristling with papers and plans, each with its own label. One of these compartments was labeled "Naval Signals." This compartment is out of date, the British government having discovered that enemy spies had knowledge of their naval signals, the signals were changed. Von Bork is awaiting the new signals and then he is scheduled to make his escape from England.

THE NAVAL TREATY:

Published in "The Strand": October/November 1893

Published as part of: "Memoirs of Sherlock Holmes"

Holmes is consulted to located a stolen naval treaty before it can be sold to enemies of England. A friend of Watson's needs help, he being the individual from whom the treaty was stolen. Occurs in the July immediately succeeding Watson's marriage. This case, at one time, promised to be of national importance and is marked by several incidents that give it a quite unique character. Another example of Holmes allowing the criminal time to escape before contacting the police.

Also mentioned in "The Final Problem" as the point at which Watson intended to end his writings about Holmes.

NEAL:

"The Valley of Fear", Part 1: "The Tragedy of Birlstone"

An outfitter, in Vermissa, U.S.A. Maker of an overcoat Holmes finds attached to a dumb-bell in the moat surrounding the Manor House.

NED, Uncle:

"A Case of Identity"

Uncle of Miss Mary Sutherland, he was from Auckland, New Zealand. He left her 2500 pounds in New Zealand stock, however, she can only touch the interest, which pays 4 1/2 percent. No mention is made as to whether he is her mother or fathers brother or brother-in-law.

THE NEGRO:

"Silver Blaze"

Race horse owned by Mr. Heath Newton and entered in the Wessex Cup race.

NEILL, GENERAL:

"The Crooked Man"

His column was moving up-country while Bhurtee was under siege and Henry Wood volunteered to warn him of the danger at Bhurtee but he never reached the General, having been captured by the rebels. The General, nevertheless, successfully relieved Bhurtee upon his arrival.

NELIGAN:

"The Adventure of Black Peter"

Of Dawson and Neligan, the failed bankers of the West Country. He disappeared in his little yacht, headed for Norway, just before a warrant for his arrest was issued. He was rescued at sea by Peter Carey and the ship 'Sea Unicorn' but is thrown overboard by Carey who keeps the valuable documents Neligan was carrying with him. Patrick Cairns, unseen by Carey, witnesses the murder of Neligan.

NELIGAN, JOHN HOPLEY:

"The Adventure of Black Peter"

A young man, frail and thin, about twenty years old. Son on Neligan of Dawson and Neligan the West Country bankers. He has been trying to clear his father's name and had discovered that some of the securities his father had taken with him on his trip to Norway had reappeared on the London market, the seller one Peter Carey. In his attempt to review the old logbooks of the 'Sea Unicorn' he losses his own notebook which is discovered at the scene of the killing of Peter Carey. He is arrested by Stanley Hopkins, his initials being found upon the notebook located at the scene of the murder.

NETHER WALSLING:

"The Adventure of Wisteria Lodge"
aka "A Reminiscence of Mr. Sherlock Holmes"

>Home to the Reverend Joshua Stone, it is located along
>the road between Wisteria Lodge and Oxshott.

NETLEY:

"A Study in Scarlet"
>Where Dr. John Watson took the course prescribed for
>surgeons after earning his medical degree.

NEW BRITIAN:

"The Adventure of the Cardboard Box"
>Town in England, Alec Fairbairn and Mary (Cushing)
>Browner take a train there for a social day. They are
>followed, unknowingly, by Mary's husband, Jim, who
>eventually catches up with them and kills them on a lake.

NEW FOREST:

"The Resident Patient"
>Holiday/vacation spot, Watson wishes he were there but
>for a depleted bank account.

NEW STREET:

"The Stock-Broker's Clerk"
>Location of hotel where Hall Pycroft stays in
>Birmingham while tending to his new position with
>Franco-Midland Hardware Company, Limited.

NEW YORK:

"His Last Bow" "An Epilogue of Sherlock Holmes"
>Planned destination of Altamont after finishing his work
>for the German spy, Von Bork.

NEW ZEALAND CONSOLIDATED:
"The Stock-Broker's Clerk"
Stock selling for 'a hundred and four.' Mr. Arthur Pinner ask for this quote as a test of Mr. Hall Pycroft's knowledge of the financial market.

NEWGATE CALENDAR:
"The Adventure of the Three Garridebs"
Calendar of release dates of criminals from the Newgate prison. Holmes carries a portable Newgate Calendar in his memory.

NEWHAVEN:
"The Final Problem"
Holmes and Watson make a cross-country journey from Canterbury to escape Moriarty during their trip to Switzerland.

NEWMARKET HEATH:
"The Adventure of Shoscombe Old Place"
Place where Sir Robert Norberton beat Sam Brewer, almost killing him.

NEWSPAPERS:
"The Adventure of the Blue Carbuncle"
Holmes places and ad in several London Newspapers: Globe, Pall Mall, St. Jame's Star, Evening News Standard, Echo.

* CHRONICLE:
"Silver Blaze"
Newspaper in London, maybe the same as "The Morning Chronicle."

* DAILY CHRONICLE:
"The Adventure of the Cardboard Box"

London newspaper, contained an article entitled "A Gruesome Packet" detailing the story about the receipt by Miss Susan Cushing of a package containing two freshly severed human ears.

* THE MORNING CHRONICLE:

"The Red-Headed League"
The April 27, 1890 edition carried an announcement: TO THE RED-HEADED LEAGUE: On account of the bequest of the late Ezekiah Hopkins, of Lebanon, Pennsylvania, U.S.A., there is now another vacancy open which entitles a member of the League to a salary of 4£ a week for purely nominal services. All red-headed men who are sound in body and mind, and above the age of twenty-one years, are eligible. Apply in person on Monday, at eleven o'clock, to Duncan Ross, at the offices of the League, 7 Pope's Court, Fleet Street.

"A Case of Identity"
Miss Mary Sutherland causes an advertisement to be printed in the Saturday edition describing her missing fiance, Mr. Hosmer Angel. See Angel, Hosmer

* DAILY GAZETTE:

"The Adventure of the Red Circle"
English newspaper which Mrs. Warren leaves for her strange lodger each morning. Contained stories entitled: "Lady with black boa at Prince's Skating Club"; Surley Jimmy will not break his mother's heart"; and other articles which Holmes searches through to find a clue concerning Mrs. Warren's mysterious lodger.

* THE DAILY NEWS:

"A Study in Scarlet"
An English newspaper reporting on the murder of Enoch J. Drebber. Called the crime a "political one." Made the

following observation concerning Scotland Yards Gregson: "A great step had been gained by the discovery of the address of the house at which he (Joseph Stangerson) had boarded -- a result which was entirely due to the acuteness and energy of Mr. Gregson of Scotland Yard."

"The Greek Interpreter"
Mycroft Holmes has an advertisement placed in the London newspaper requesting information concerning the whereabouts of Paul Kratides and/or a Greek woman by the name of Sophy.

* DAILY TELEGRAPH:

"A Study in Scarlet"
An English newspaper reporting on the murder of one Enoch J. Drebber. "Remarked that in the history of crime there had seldom been a tragedy which presented stranger features." Suggested that everything in the case "pointed to its perpetration by political refugees and revolutionists." Admonished the government and advocated a closer watch over foreigners in England.

"The Adventure of the Copper Beeches"
Newspaper Holmes is reading at beginning of the adventure.

"The Adventure of the Norwood Builder"
Carried a story concerning the fire and murder at Lower Norwood: "Mysterious Affair at Lower Norwood. Disappearance of a well Known Builder. Suspicion of Murder and Arson. A clue to the Criminal."

"The Adventure of the Second Stain"
London newspaper which reported that there was a great likelihood that Eduardo Lucas and M. Henri Fournaye

were one and the same and that Mr. Lucas was killed by his alias's wife.

* TELEGRAPH:

"Silver Blaze"
Newspaper in London, may be the same as "The Daily Telegraph."

* DEVON COUNTY CHRONICLE:

"The Hound of the Baskervilles"
Newspaper which carried account of the death of Sir Charles Baskerville.

* ECHO:

"A Study in Scarlet", Part 2 --"The Country of the Saints"
London newspaper which contains the conclusion to the story "A Study in Scarlet;" "The public have lost a sensational treat through the sudden death of the man Hope, who was suspected of the murder of Mr. Enoch Drebber and of Mr. Joseph Stangerson. The details of the case will probably be never known now, through we are informed upon good authority that the crime was the result of an oldstanding and romantic feud, in which love and Mormonism bore a part. It seems that both the victims belonged, in their younger days, to the Latter Day Saints, and Hope, the deceased prisoner, hails also from Salt Lake City. If the case has had no other effect, it, at least brings out in the most striking manner the efficiency of our detective police force, and will serve as a lesson to all foreigners that they will do wisely to settle their feuds at home, and not carry them on to British soil. It is an open secret that the credit of this smart capture belongs entirely to the well-known Scotland Yard officials, . Messrs, Lestrade and Gregson. The man was apprehended, it appears, in the rooms of a certain Mr. Sherlock Holmes, who has himself, as an amateur, shown

some talent in the detective line and who, with such
instructors, may hope in time to attain to some degree of
their skill. It is expected that a testimonial of some sort
will be presented to the two officers as a fitting
recognition of their services."

* GLOBE:

"The Adventure of the Priory School"
English newspaper, carried news of the abduction of the
son of the Duke of Holdernesse from the Priory School.

* JOURNAL de GENEVE:

"The Final Problem"
French newspaper which carried a condensed version of
the facts of "The Final Problem" on May 6, 1891.
Watson's version, "The Final Problem," is to lay the true
facts before the public.

* LEEDS MERCURY:

"The Hound of the Baskervilles"
English newspaper (London), Holmes remarks that he
once confused it with the Western Morning News due to
the similarity of their print.

* MORNING POST:

"The Adventure of the Noble Bachelor"
London newspaper that reported the ongoings associated
with the marriage of Lord St. Simon and Hatty Doran.

"The Adventure of the Illustrious Client"
London newspaper which carried the announcement that
Miss Violet de Merville's marriage to Baron Adelbert
Gruner would not take place. It also carried notice of the
police-court hearings concerned with the proceedings
against Miss Kitty Winter on the charge of vitriol-
throwing.

* NORTH SURREY OBSERVER:

"The Adventure of the Retired Colourman"
A bi-weekly newspaper which contained flaming
headlines which began: "The Haven Horror" and ended
with "Brilliant Police Investigation." It gave credit to the
'remarkable acumen' by which Inspector MacKinnon was
able to conclude the case.

* SPECTATOR:

"The Adventure of the Blanched Soldier"
A British weekly newspaper.

* THE STANDARD:

"A Study in Scarlet"
An English newspaper which reported on the murder of
Enoch J. Drebber. "Commented upon the fact that the
lawless outrages of the sort usually occurred under a
Liberal administration." Went on to describe the known
information of Mr. Enoch J. Drebber and his secretary
Joseph Stangerson before the death of Mr. Drebber and
the disappearance of Mr. Stangerson. Commented on
Scotland Yard's Mr. Lestrade and Mr. Gregson: "We are
glad to learn that Mr. Lestrade and Mr. Gregson, of
Scotland Yard, are both engaged upon the case, and it is
confidently anticipated that these well-known officers will
speedily throw light upon the matter."

Also see Enoch J. Drebber.

"The Sign of Four"
A London newspaper which printed an account of the
"Mysterious Business at Upper Norwood" regarding the
murder of Bartholomew Sholto. According to the
STANDARD, a London newspaper, one McMurdo, an

ex-prize-fighter, was the porter or gatekeeper for
Bartholomew Sholto.

* EVENING STANDARD:
"The Stock-Broker's Clerk"
According to the 'Evening Standard', a London
newspaper, an attempted robbery, resulting in the murder
of the watchman, occurred at the offices of Mawson &
Williams.

* TIMES:
"The Sign of Four"
London newspaper containing an advertisement asking
for the address of Mary Morstan and asking her to come
forward.

"The Hound of the Baskervilles"
London newspaper from which words are cut and pasted
together to send a message to Sir Henry Baskerville at the
Northumberland Hotel. Holmes remarks that "a Times
leader [print] is entirely distinctive." One could not
confuse it with another newspaper.

"The Adventure of the Solitary Cyclist"
London newspaper, contained an advertisement, in
December 1884, inquiring as to the whereabouts of the
Smith Family, in particular, the Miss Violet Smith Family.

"The Adventure of the Missing Three-quarter"
English newspaper.

* WESTERN MORNING NEWS:
"The Hound of the Baskervilles"
English newspaper (London), Holmes remarks that he
once confused it with the Leeds Mercury due to the
similarity of their print.

NEWTON, HEATH:
>"Silver Blaze"
>>Owner of the race horse 'The Negro' which was entered in the Wessex Cup race.

NIAGARA:
>"The Adventure of the Cardboard Box"
>>Jim Browner describes the noises he heard in his ears the day he discovered his wife with Alec Fairbairn as "all Niagara whizzing and buzzing in my ears." A reference to Niagara Falls.

NICHOLSON FAMILY:
>"The Valley of Fear", Part 2: "The Scowrers"
>>Allegedly murdered by the Scowrers.

NIHILIST:
>"The Adventure of the Six Napoleons"
>>Anarchist group. Morse Hudson believes they are responsible for the smashing of the busts of Napoleon.

NIMES:
>"The Final Problem"
>>Holmes sent a note to Watson dated from Nimes, France in early 1891.

No. 2704:
>"The Hound of the Baskervilles"
>>Number of the hansom cab which follows Sir Henry Baskerville and Dr. Mortimer during a walk from the Northumberland Hotel, with Holmes and Watson closely watching from afar.

NONPAREIL CLUB:

"The Hound of the Baskervilles"

An unrecorded case. Holmes exposes the atrocious conduct of Colonel Upwood in connection with the famous card scandal of the Nonpareil Club. Takes place right after "The Hound of the Baskervilles."

NORAH CREINA:

"The Resident Patient"

Steamer lost at sea, with all hands on board, near the Portuguese coast, some leagues to the north of Oporto. Believed to be carrying the three remaining members of the 'Worthingdon Bank Gang.'

NORBERTON, ROBERT:

"The Adventure of Shoscombe Old Place"

Sir Robert lives with his widowed sister at Shoscombe Old Place. He is known as being a dangerous man, having once horsewhipped Sam Brewer, the well-known money lender, nearly killing him. He is about the most dare-devil rider in England, having finished second in the Grand National a few years earlier. He was huge in stature and fierce in manner, a strong, heavily moustached face with angry eyes. Sir Robert is heavily in debt and dependent upon the success of Shoscombe Prince in the upcoming Derby. However, the horse is owned, as is Shoscombe Old Place, by his sister, only while she is alive. When she dies, the estate and Shoscombe Prince go to her late husband's brother. Such a fate would ruin Sir Robert. Upon his sister's death he hides her body and continues to pretend that she is alive so Shoscombe Prince may run in the Derby and pull Sir Robert free from debt. Holmes refuses to interfere once he knows the truth. Sir Robert is successful. Shoscombe Prince wins the Derby and Sir Robert won a substantial amount of money, and retired to an old age.

NORBURY:
> "The Yellow Face"
>> Location of the home of Grant and Effie Munro.

NORFOLK:
> "The Adventure of the Dancing Men"
>> County in England, location of the home of Hilton Cubitt, Riding Thorpe Manor. Located near the German Ocean, it is on the coast.

NORLETT, MR.:
> "The Adventure of Shoscombe Old Place"
>> Husband of Carrie (Evans) Norlett, confidential maid to Lady Beatrice Falder. He has assisted Sir Robert Norberton in keeping the death of Lady Beatrice Falder a secret until after the running of the Derby.

NORLETT, MRS.:
> "The Adventure of Shoscombe Old Place"
>> See Evans, Carrie.

NORMAN CONQUEST:
> "The Musgrave Ritual"
>> Believed to be the time when the Musgrave Ritual was written.

NORMAN HUGOS:
> "The Adventure of Shoscombe Old Place"
>> Holmes examines the crypt which has been a favorite haunt of Sir Robert Norberton of late and therein discovers graves ranging from very old, through a long line of Norman Hugos and Odos, to those of the eighteenth century.

NORTH SURREY OBSERVER:
> "The Adventure of the Retired Colourman"
>> A bi-weekly newspaper which contained flaming headlines which began: "The Haven Horror" and ended with "Brilliant Police Investigation." It gave credit to the 'remarkable acumen' by which Inspector MacKinnon was able to conclude the case.

NORTH WALSHAM:
> "The Adventure of the Dancing Men"
>> Train Station in Norfolk.

NORTHERN WEI DYNASTY:
> "The Adventure of the Illustrious Client"
>> Baron Gruner test Dr. Hill Barton by requesting information on the Northern Wei dynasties place in the history of ceramics.

NORTHUMBERLAND AVENUE:
> "The Adventure of the Illustrious Client"
>> An establishment on this street has a Turkish bath, for which Watson and Holmes have a weakness.

NORTHUMBERLAND HOTEL:
> "The Hound of the Baskervilles"
>> Hotel in London where Sir Henry Baskerville stays after his voyage from Canada and prior to his trip to Baskerville Hall.

NORTON, IRENE (ADLER):
> "A Scandal in Bohemia"
>> AKA Irene Adler

NORTON, GODFREY:
> "A Scandal in Bohemia"
>> A lawyer, he is a member of the Inner Temple. Marries

IRENE ADLER at the Church of St Monica in the Edgeware Road with a disguised Holmes as a witness.

NORWAY:
"The Adventure of Black Peter"
Where Neligan, of Dawson and Neligan, was headed after the failure of his bank when he is rescued at sea by Peter Carey and the 'Sea Unicorn' during a violet storm. It is also the address Holmes gives Inspector Stanley Hopkins, at the conclusion of the story, as to where he and Watson can be reached if needed for the trial of Patrick Cairns.

NORWOOD DISAPPEARANCE CASE:
"The Adventure of the Norwood Builder"
Name Holmes gives to the case when he believes they have come up empty: "it will not figure in that chronicle of our successes."

NOTTING HILL:
"The Adventure of the Red Circle"
Area of London known for its rough inhabitants, a down trodden area.

"The Adventure of the Bruce-Partington Plans"
A section of London wherein is located Campden Mansions.

"The Adventure of the Dying Detective"
Separated from Kensington by Lower Burke Street.

NOTTINGHAM:
"The Valley of Fear", Part 1: "The Tragedy of Birlstone"
Town in England where it has been reported that the suspected murderer of John Douglas, Hargrave, has been seen.

CHAPTER O

OAKINGTON:
"The Adventure of the Missing Three-quarter"
A sleepy hollow in England.

OAKSHOTT, LESLIE:
"The Adventure of the Illustrious Client"
Sir Leslie Oakshott is a famous surgeon who has been
tending to Holmes's wounds after the attack on him in
Regent Street.

OAKSHOTT, MRS.:
"The Adventure of The Blue Carbuncle"
Lives at 117 Brixton Road. She is an "egg and poultry
supplier." She sold Mr. Breckinridge the geese he sold to
Mr. Windigate, who in-turn sold them to Mr. Henry
Baker and friends. She is the sister of James Ryder, Head
attendant at the Hotel Cosmopolitan, and had promised
him the choice of her geese for Christmas.

OBERSTEIN:
"The Adventure of the Second Stain"
A secret agent known to Holmes. Lives in the West End
of London. A bold man. See Oberstein, Hugo

OBERSTEIN, HUGO:
"The Adventure of the Bruce-Partington Plans"
One of the few men Mycroft Holmes believes could be
able to dispose of the stolen Bruce-Partington papers.
He resides at 13 Caulfield Gardens, Kensington. He
moves to the Hotel du Louvre in Paris using the

Kensington address for meetings with Colonel Walter. He has agreed to pay Colonel Valentine Walter a substantial sum to pay off his stock exchange debts in exchange for the Bruce-Partington papers. After the Colonel is captured, Holmes uses the Colonel to lay a trap which successfully snares Hugo and the missing Bruce-Partington papers.
See Oberstein

ODLEY'S:
"The Adventure of the Sussex Vampire"
Name of house in Cheeman's, Lamberley, where homes are known by the names of those who built them.

ODOS:
"The Adventure of Shoscombe Old Place"
Holmes examines the crypt which has been a favorite haunt of Sir Robert Norberton of late and therein discovers graves ranging from very old, Saxon, through a long line of Norman Hugos, to those of Sir William and Denis Faler of the eighteenth century.

OFFICIAL REGISTRY:
"The Hound of the Baskervilles"
Contains the name and addresses of all hansom cabmen, it is from where Holmes obtains the name of the driver of Cab No. 2704.

OLD DEER PARK:
"The Adventure of the Sussex Vampire"
Rugby filed in England.

OLD JEWRY:
"The Adventure of the Sussex Vampire"
Address of Morrison, Morrison, and Dodd, machinery assessors.

OLDACRE, JONAS:

"The Adventure of the Norwood Builder"

Of Lower Norwood, believed to have been murdered and then burned in a fire at his small timber-yard at the rear of his house. He was a well known resident of Lower Norwood and had been a builder for many years. A bachelor, he was fifty-two years old and lived at Deep Dene House, at the Sydenham end of the road of the same name.   He was a strange little ferret-like man, with white eyelashes and keen gray eyes. He has a reputation of being a man of eccentric habits, secretive and retiring, he has practically withdrawn from the lumber business. It is said he amassed a considerable wealth.   He wrote a will leaving his entire estate to John McFarlane, his lawyer. Holmes discovers that Mr. Oldacre is deeply in debt and has been withdrawing large sums of money, paying it to one Mr. Cornelius. He is discovered hiding in a false room in his own house when Holmes starts a small fire and yells 'FIRE.'   AKA Mr. Cornelius.

OLDMORE, MRS.:

"The Hound of the Baskervilles"

She signed in at the Northumberland Hotel after Sir Henry Baskerville, she is an invalid with her maid. Her husband was once mayor of Gloucester.

ON THE BANKS OF ALLAN WATER:

"The Valley of Fear"   Part 2: "The Scowrers"

Song sung by John McMurdo to the great thrill of his new Lodge, 'Eminent Order of Freemen,' Vermissa.

OPENSHAW, ELIAS:

"The Five Orange Pips"

Uncle of John Openshaw he emigrated to America when he was a young man and became a planter in Florida, fought in Jackson's army, and afterwards under Hood, where he rose to be a colonel. He returned to his plantation after the war and remained there till 1869 or 1870 when he returned to Europe and took a small estate in Sussex, near Horsham. A singular man, fierce and quick-tempered, very foul mouthed when angry, and a most retiring disposition. He drank a great deal of brandy and smoked very heavily, but was not social and had no friends, not even his own brother. Took a fancy to John Openshaw, imploring his father, Joseph, to let young John live with him. Received a letter on March 10, 1883 with 5 orange pips in an envelope, he died seven weeks later on the night of May 2nd.

OPENSHAW, JOHN:

"The Five Orange Pips"

Young visitor, 22, well-groomed and trimly clad, with something of refinement and delicacy in his bearing, he is from Horsham. Has heard of Holmes through another case, that of Major Prendergast and the ankerville Club scandal. His uncle Elias took a fancy to him, so John moved in to live with his Uncle. Received an envelope with 5 orange pips inside in September 1887, two years and eight months following the death of his father after he too received an envelope with 5 orange pips. During a dark and stormy night fell into the water near Waterloo Bridge and died. It was believed he was chasing the train from Waterloo Station, missed the path and went over the edge. An envelope in his pocket identified him and his address.

OPENSHAW, JOSEPH:

"The Five Orange Pips"

Brother of Elias Openshaw and father of John Openshaw, died in January 1885 after receiving and envelope containing 5 orange pips. He was returning from a visit to a friends, Major Freebody, of Fareham, who was in command of one of the forts upon Portsdown Hill, when he fell into a chalk-pit shattering his skull. It had been twilight and the area was unknown to him. Had a small factory at Coventry and was the patentee of the Openshaw unbreakable bicycle tire. Was able to sell his business and retire on the proceeds.

OPORTO:
"The Resident Patient"
Area on the Portuguese coast where it is believed that the steamer 'Norah Creina' was lost with all hands on board.

ORDER, THE:
"The Adventure of the Golden Pince-Nez"
A group of Russian revolutionaries, Nihilists, reformers. Sergius, Anna, and Alexis were all members. Most of their membership was arrested after the killing of a Russian police officer on the evidence of Sergius. Sergius moved to England and took the name Professor Coram.

ORDER OF THE LEGION OF HONOUR:
"The Adventure of the Golden Pince-Nez"
See 'Huret' under "Unrecorded Cases"

ORONTES:
"A Study in Scarlet"
See Watson, John

OTHER ADVENTURES:
See "Unrecorded Cases"

OUT OF DOORS:
>"The Adventure of the Lion's Mane"
>>Book written by the famous observer, J.G. Wood, in
>>which he describes his personal encounter with the
>>"Lion's Mane," Cyanea capillata.
>>See Cyanea.

OVERTON, CYRIL:
>"The Adventure of the Missing Three-quarter"
>>Of Trinity College, Cambridge. He was an enormous
>>young man, sixteen stone of solid bone and muscle.
>>Skipper of the College rugby team. He was first reserve
>>for England against Wales.

OXFORD STREET:
>"The Hound of the Baskervilles"
>>London street near Baker Street. Location of Bradley's, a
>>maker of cigarettes in London: brand smoked by Watson.

>"The Greek Interpreter"
>>Street in London.

>"The Final Problem"
>>Holmes went to transact some business in Oxford Street,
>>his life is threatened along the way by a two-horse van
>>and a falling brick.

>"The Adventure of the Empty House"
>>At the end of Park Lane.

>"The Adventure of the Priory School"
>>Location of the branch office of The Capitals and
>>Counties Bank.

>"The Adventure of Charles Augustus Milverton"
>>Street in London.

"The Adventure of the Golden Pince-Nez"
Street in London.

"The Disappearance of Lady Frances Carfax"
Location of the shoe store Latimer's.

OXSHOTT:
"The Adventure of Wisteria Lodge"
aka "A Reminiscence of Mr. Sherlock Holmes"
Town about three miles from Esher and one mile from
Wisteria Lodge.

OXSHOTT COMMON:
"The Adventure of Wisteria Lodge"
aka "A Reminiscence of Mr. Sherlock Holmes"
Mr. Aloysius Garcia was found murdered there. See
Oxshott.

THE OXSHOTT MYSTERY:
"The Adventure of Wisteria Lodge"
aka "A Reminiscence of Mr. Sherlock Holmes"
Name given, by the newspapers, to the strange
happenings at Wisteria Lodge.

OXSHOTT TOWERS:
"The Adventure of Wisteria Lodge"
aka "A Reminiscence of Mr. Sherlock Holmes"
Home to Sir George Ffolliott, it is located along the road
between Wisteria Lodge and Oxshott.

CHAPTER P

PADDINGTON STATION:
> "The Boscombe Valley Mystery"
>> Where Holmes and Watson meet to begin their work in the "Boscombe Valley Mystery"

> "The Adventure of the Engineer's Thumb"
>> Watson lives no very great distance away where he practices medicine after his marriage.

> "The Stock-Broker's Clerk"
>> Watson purchased the medical practice of 'Old Farquhar' in the Paddington district.

> "Silver Blaze"
>> Holmes and Watson set out for Dartmoor and the King's Pyland stables.

> "The Hound of the Baskervilles"
>> Train depot.

PAGANINI:
> "The Adventure of the Cardboard Box"
>> An extraordinary man, a great musician.

PALL MALL:
> "The Greek Interpreter"
>> Location of the rooms of Mycroft Holmes and the
Diogenes Club.

> "The Final Problem"
>> Holmes takes refuge in his brothers rooms at Pall Mall after a close call with a two-horse van at the corners of Bentinck Street and Welbeck Street and the falling of a

brick from a building on Vere Street nearly hitting him on the head.

"The Adventure of the Solitary Cyclist"
Firms which rent real estate are located here.

PALMER:
"The Adventure of the Priory School"
Bicycle tyre used by the German master, Heidegger.

PALMYRA:
"The Valley of Fear", Part 2: "The Scowrers"
Ship which John Douglas and his wife Ivy took to South Africa, John is lost overboard during a gale off St. Helena and never reaches Cape Town, South Africa.

PARIS:
"The Final Problem"
Where Holmes believes Moriarty will head in pursuit of Holmes and Watson, they being on their way to Switzerland.

"The Adventure of Wisteria Lodge"
aka "A Reminiscence of Mr. Sherlock Holmes"
In an attempt to hide from his past and his pursuers, Don Murillo resides in Paris for a brief period during his escape from Central America after the uprising of his people against him.

PARK LANE:
"The Adventure of the Empty House"
Number 427 is the address of Ronald Adair, his mother, Lady Maynooth, and his sister. It is a frequented thoroughfare.

PARK LANE MYSTERY:

"The Adventure of the Empty House"

Name newspapers gave to the murder of Ronald Adair whose residence was on Park Lane.

PARKER:

"The Adventure of the Dancing Men"

Vicar of the parish of which Hilton Cubitt is a member. He was staying at the boardinghouse in Russell Square while Hilton Cubitt and Elsie Patrick were there.

PARR, LUCY:

"The Adventure of the Beryl Coronet"

Second waiting-maid in the service of Alexander Holder. Had only been in his service for a few months when Mr. Holder consulted Holmes. She came with excellent character and is a very pretty girl who has attracted admirers who have occasionally hung around the place.

PATRICK, ELSIE:

"The Adventure of the Dancing Men"

An American young lady, she met Hilton Cubitt at a boardinghouse in Russell Square and later married him. She was originally from Chicago where her father was involved in dishonest undertakings which she wished to escape. Abe Slaney, one of her father's gang members grew up with her and was in love with her. She did not return his favors. Shot herself in the head, in an attempted suicide, after witnessing the killing of her husband by Abe Slaney. She dedicated herself to helping the poor and maintaining Riding Thorpe Manor after her recovery.

PATRICK, OLD:
> "The Adventure of the Dancing Men"
>> Boss of the 'Joint,' he invented the 'dancing men" code. Father of Elsie Patrick.

PATTINS, HUGH:
> "The Adventure of Black Peter"
>> A long, dried-up creature, with lank hair and sallow cheeks. He has been sent to Captain Basil by Sumner, Shipping Agent.

PAUL'S WHARF:
> "The Man With The Twisted Lip"
>> Located near rear of the Bar of Gold opium den.

PEACE, CHARLIE:
> "The Adventure of the Illustrious Client"
>> An old friend of Holmes's, he was a great criminal with a complex mind and a violin virtuoso.

PEAK COUNTRY:
> "The Adventure of the Priory School"
>> Area surrounding the Priory School.

PEKING:
> "The Adventure of the Illustrious Client"
>> Holmes tells Watson that Peking is the only place one is likely to find a complete set of Ming dynasty egg-shell pottery of the kind Watson will take to Baron Gruner to sell, as part of Holmes' plan.

PENANG LAWYER:
> "The Hound of the Baskervilles"
>> A fine, thick piece of wood, bulbous-headed, the stick carried by Dr. J. Mortimer.

PENGE:
>"The Adventure of the Cardboard Box"
>>Town in England. Miss Susan Cushing lived there before moving to Croydon twenty years ago.

PENNSYLVANIA SMALL ARMS COMPANY:
>"The Valley of Fear", Part 1: "The Tragedy of Birlstone"
>>A well known American firearms company.

PERKINS:
>"The Hound of the Baskervilles"
>>The groom/coachman at Baskerville Hall, he was a hard-faced, gnarled little fellow.

PERKINS:
>"The Adventure of the Three Gables"
>>Killed outside the Holborn Bar and Holmes suspects a black boxer, Steve, as the culprit.

PERSANO, ISADORE:
>"The Problem of Thor Bridge"
>>An unrecorded case.
>>A problem without a solution. He was a well known journalist and duellist, he was found stark staring mad with a match box in front of him which contained a remarkable worm said to be unknown to science.

PERSHORE:
>"The Sign of Four"
>>Birthplace of Jonathan Small, in Worcestershire.

PESHAWAR:
>"A Study in Scarlet"
>>See Watson, John

PETER:
"The Adventure of the Solitary Cyclist"
The groom of Charlington Hall, he is a lad of seventeen.

PETERS, HENRY:
"The Disappearance of Lady Frances Carfax"
Of Adelaide, Australia.
AKA Holy Peters, Rev. Dr. Shlessinger.
See Shlessinger, Dr.

PETERS, HOLY:
"The Disappearance of Lady Frances Carfax"
One of the most unscrupulous rascals that Australia has ever produced. His specialty is playing upon lonely ladies and their religious beliefs. He works with a partner, his so-called wife, named Fraser. He has a physical peculiarity: he was badly bitten in the ear in a saloon-fight at Adelaide in 1889.
AKA Rev. Dr. Shlessinger, See Shlessinger, Dr.

PETERS, MRS.:
"The Disappearance of Lady Frances Carfax"
See Fraser.

PETERSON:
"The Adventure of The Blue Carbuncle"
Commissionaire, it was he who found the goose which held the Blue Carbuncle in Tottenham Court Road at the corner of Goodge Street.

PHELPS, PERCY:
"The Naval Treaty"
A friend from Watson's school days with whom he had been very close, although he was two classes ahead of Watson. A brilliant boy, he won a scholarship to Cambridge where he continued a triumphant career. He

was very well connected, his mother's brother being Lord Holdhurst. He had a good position with the Foreign Office. The Naval treaty Documents have been stolen from his office.

Nickname - "Tadpole"

PHILADELPHIA MINT:
"The Valley of Fear", Part 2: "The Scowrers"
John McMurdo has in his possession dollars that have never passed through the Philadelphia mint, he counterfeited them while in Chicago with Jonas Pinto.

PHILLIMORE, JAMES:
"The Problem of Thor Bridge"
An unrecorded case.
A problem without a solution. He stepped back into his own house to get his umbrella and was never seen again.

PHOENICIAN TIN TRADERS:
"The Adventure of the Devil's Foot"
See Cornish Language.

PIKE, LANGDALE:
"The Adventure of the Three Gables"
Holmes's book of reference upon all matters of social scandal. He sits in a bow window of a St. James Street club and receives and disseminates all the gossip of the metropolis.

PINKERTON:
"The Valley of Fear", Part 2: "The Scowrers"
American detective force, they are involved in the investigation of the 'Scowrers.' John McMurdo has uncovered the information that one Birdy Edwards is at

work collecting evidence against the members of the 'Eminent Order of Freemen.'
AKA Steve Wilson

PINKERTON'S AMERICAN AGENCY:

"The Adventure of the Red Circle"

American private police force of which Mr. Leverton is a member. It is involved in the search for Gorgiano of the Red Circle, an Italian criminal organization.

PINNER:

"The Yellow Face"

Located in Middlesex, where Effie (Hebron) Munro returns to live with her maiden Aunt after she returned from America.

PINNER, ARTHUR:

"The Stock-Broker's Clerk"

Financial Agent, hires Hall Pycroft to manage Franco-Midland Hardware Company, Limited. A smallish, dark man his tooth was stuffed with gold. Brother to Harry Pinner.

AKA Harry Pinner.

Actually, the brother of Beddington, the famous forger and cracksman. He usually assisted him in his crimes. Commits suicide after meeting Holmes and Watson (alias Harris and Price), having seen a newspaper story revealing the capture of his brother by police. He had spent five years in penal servitude, having recently been released.

PINNER, HARRY:
    "The Stock-Broker's Clerk"
        Brother of Arthur Pinner and promoter of the Franco-
        Midland Hardware Company, Limited. His tooth was
        stuffed with gold.
        AKA Arthur Pinner, See Pinner, Arthur.

PINTO, JONAS:
    "The Valley of Fear", Part 2: "The Scowrers"
        Shot in the Lake Saloon, Market Street, Chicago during
        the first week of 1874. He was helping John McMurdo
        to make and pass counterfeit coins when McMurdo shot
        him. A newsclipping account of this shooting was
        provided to Boss McGinty by John McMurdo as an
        explanation as to McMurdo's presence in Vermissa.

PINTO, MARIA:
    "The Problem of Thor Bridge"
        Maria (Pinto) Gibson was the wife of Neil Gibson. They
        have two children, cared for by a governess. Mrs. Gibson
        met her husband in Brazil while he was gold hunting.
        She was the daughter of a government official at Manaos.
        She had been very beautiful but was now beyond her
        prime. She was found at Thor Bridge with a   bullet
        through her brain.

PITT:
    "The Hound of the Baskervilles"
        Prime Minister under whom Sir William Baskerville
        served as Chairman of Committees in the House of
        Commons.

PITT STREET:
    "The Adventure of the Six Napoleons"
        Located in Kensington, it is a quiet little backwater just
        beside one of the briskest currents of London life. No.
        131 was one of a row, all flatchested, respectable, and

most unromantic dwellings.   Home to Mr. Horace
Harker.

PLYMOUTH:
"The Hound of the Baskervilles"
> Town in England, furnishers and decorators from
> Plymouth are called upon to restore the grandeur of the
> Baskerville family by Sir Henry Baskerville.

"Silver Blaze"
> Holmes suggest he met Mrs. Straker in Plymouth at a
> garden-party some little time ago, she denies it.

PLYMOUTH HOTEL:
"The Adventure of the Devil's Foot"
> Hotel in which Dr. Leon Sterndale stayed the night of the
> mysterious happenings at Tredannick Wartha.

POE:
"The Adventure of the Cardboard Box"
> Edgar Allen Poe, one of his sketches involves an
> individual being able to "follow the unspoken thoughts of
> his companion" an idea with which Watson expresses
> incredulity, but which Holmes reveals as simple.

POLDHU BAY:
"The Adventure of the Devil's Foot"
> At the further extremity of the Cornish peninsula where
> Holmes and Watson take a small cottage for a rest filled
> vacation for Holmes.

POLICE:
The individuals listed here are members of Scotland Yard and
various other law enforcement agencies. Information about them
can be found by searching their last name elsewhere in this book.

BARDLE, INSPECTOR
BAYNES, INSPECTOR
BRADSTREET, INSPECTOR
EDWARS, BIRDY
FORRESTER, INSPECTOR
GREGORY, INSPECTOR
GREGSON, TOBIAS
HILL, INSPECTOR
HOPKINS, STANLEY
JONES, ATHELNEY
LANNER
LESTRADE
LEVERTON, MR.
MacKINNON, INSPECTOR
MacDONALD, ALEC
MARTIN, INSPECTOR
MARVIN, TEDDY
MASON, WHITE
MERIVALE
MONTGOMERY, INSPECTOR
MORTON, INSPECTOR
PATTERSON, INSPECTOR
PETERSON
POLLOCK, CONSTABLE
TUSON, SERGEANT
WALTERS
WILSON, SERGEANT
WILSON, STEVE

POLLOCK, CONSTABLE:
"The Stock-Broker's Clerk"
Assists Sergeant Tuson in the capture of Beddington just
after the robbery and murder at Mawson & William's.

POLLOCK, FRED:
"The Valley of Fear", Part 1: "The Tragedy of Birlstone"
> A nom-de-plume, led on by some aspirations towards
> right, and encouraged by the judicious stimulation of ten
> pound notes from Holmes, he has assisted Holmes with
> information from the criminal underworld.

POLYPHONIC MOTETS OF LASSUS:
"The Adventure of the Bruce-Partington Plans"
> A monograph which Holmes undertakes to read while
> awaiting additional information concerning the Bruce-
> Partington papers.

POMPEY:
"The Adventure of the Missing Three-quarter"
> The pride of the local draghounds, a staunch on a scent.

PONDICHERRY:
"The Five Orange Pips"
> Location in England from where the first envelope
> containing orange pips was sent to Elias Openshaw,
> brother of Joseph Openshaw, uncle of John Openshaw.

PONDICHERRY LODGE:
"The Sign of Four"
> Home of Major Sholto and his twin sons, Thaddeus and
> Batholomew.

POPE'S COURT, FLEET STREET:
"The Red-Headed League"
> Number 7 is the offices of the "Red-Headed League,"
> also known as the temporary office of William Morris,
> solicitor.

POPHAM HOUSE:
"The Adventure of Wisteria Lodge"
aka "A Reminiscence of Mr. Sherlock Holmes"
    Residence of Mr. John Scott Eccles, it is in Lee.

PORTER, MRS.:
"The Adventure of the Devil's Foot"
    An elderly woman, she is the cook and housekeeper at
    Tregannick Wartha. It is she who discovers the dead
    body of Brenda Tregannis and Owen and George
    Tregennis in a state of insanity.

PORTSMOUTH:
"A Study in Scarlet"
    Port Watson arrives at on his return from India.

"His Last Bow" "An Epilogue of Sherlock Holmes"
    Altamont sends a telegram from Portsmouth, announcing
    his impending arrival with the 'Naval Signals,' to the
    German spy Von Bork.

Also the location of an English jail.

PORTSMOUTH FORTS:
"His Last Bow" "An Epilogue of Sherlock Holmes"
    Von Bork, the German spy, had a safe containing pigeon-
    holes bristling with papers and plans, each with its own
    label. One of these compartments was labeled
    "Portsmouth forts."

POSILIPPO:
"The Adventure of the Red Circle"
    Town in Italy near Naples where Emilia Lucca was born.
    Also home to Gennaro Lucca and Giuseppe Gorgiano.

POTT, EVANS:
"The Valley of Fear", Part 2: "The Scowrers"

County Delegate, he lives at Hobson's Patch, Gilmerton and has power over several different lodges of the 'Eminent Order of Freemen.' He used his power in sudden and arbitrary ways and even Boss McGinty felt some repulsion and fear towards him. Pott's was a sly, little gray-haired rat of a man, with a slinking gait and a sidelong glance that was charged with malice. He sends two assassins to kill the Crow Hill manager.

POULTNEY SQUARE:
"The Disappearance of Lady Frances Carfax"

Section of London where Holmes finds Holy Peters, his wife, and a coffin. He examines the coffin finding nothing but returns later realizing his error and finds Lady Carfax in the false bottom of the coffin.

PRACTICAL HANDBOOK OF BEE CULTURE WITH SOME OBSERVATIONS UPON THE SEGREGATION OF THE QUEEN:
"His Last Bow" "An Epilogue of Sherlock Holmes"

Book written by Sherlock Holmes, he presents it to the German spy, Von Bork as the 'Naval Signals' before chloroforming him.

PRAGUE:
"The Adventure of the Creeping Man"

Mr. Bennett, Professor Presbury's assistant received a letter from a fellow-student expressing pleasure in seeing Professor Presbury in Prague, although he had not the opportunity to speak with him. Mr. Bennett had been unaware the Professor had been to Prague. A letter to Professor Presbury with an Austrian stamp and postmarked Prague contained information regarding the strange behavior of the Professor. It included references to Langur.

MAJOR PRENDERGAST AND THE TANKERVILLE SCANDAL:
"The Five Orange Pips"

An unrecorded case. The Major was wrongfully accused of cheating at cards and was saved by Holmes.

PRENDERGAST, JACK:
"The 'Gloria Scott'"

A young man with a clear, hairless face, a long, thin nose, and rather nutcracker jaws. He carried his head very jauntily in the air, had a swaggering style of walking, and was, above all else, remarkable for his extraordinary height. He was a man of good family and of great ability, but of incurably vicious habits. By an ingenious system of fraud, he had obtained huge sums of money from the leading London merchants, a quarter of a million never having been recovered. Arrested, tried, found guilty, he was sentenced to Australia. Along the way he became the boatmate of James Armitage aboard the 'Gloria Scott.' He leads a breakout of the convicts during the 'Gloria Scott's' voyage to Australia. He dies in the explosion which sinks the 'Gloria Scott'.

PRESBURY, EDITH:
"The Adventure of the Creeping Man"

A bright, handsome girl of a conventional English type, she is engaged to Trevor Bennett her father's assistant.

PRESBURY, PROFESSOR:
"The Adventure of the Creeping Man"

The famous Camford physiologist, he owns a wolfhound, Roy, that has attacked him several times. He is a man of European reputation, a widower with one daughter,

Edith. A man very virile and positive, one might almost say he had a combative character. At sixty-one years old he became engaged to the daughter of Professor Morphy, a very young woman and although there is no objection from the girls family, there is great disapproval from his own daughter. His strange behavior has led Mr. Trevor Bennett, his assistant, to consult Holmes. The Professor has been obtaining a special serum from H. Lowenstein through his agent Dorak in London.

PRESCOTT, RODGER:
"The Adventure of the Three Garridebs"

A famous forger and coiner from Chicago, he was shot and killed by Killer Evans during a card game in a night-club in the Waterloo Road area in January 1895. He fits the description of a man who had rented the same rooms as Nathan Garrideb now rents five years earlier. That man's name was Waldron and he vanished and nothing more has been heard from him.

PRICE, MR.:
"The Stock-Broker's Clerk"

Of Bermingham, a clerk, actually Watson. Holmes, Watson, and Hall Pycroft visit Mr. Pinner at the office of Franco-Midland Hardware Company, Limited, Holmes and Watson under alias'.

PRINCETOWN:
"The Hound of the Baskervilles"

Location of the convict prison, it lies about fourteen miles from Grimpen.

PRINGLE, MRS.:
"The Adventure of the Second Stain"

Elderly housekeeper for Eduardo Lucas.

PRIORY SCHOOL:
>"The Adventure of the Priory School"
>>Located near Machleton, in northern England, it is the best and most select preparatory school in England. The principal and founder is one Dr. Thorneycroft Huxtable.

THE PROBLEM OF THOR BRIDGE:
>Published in "The Strand": February/March 1922
>Published as part of: "The Case Book of Sherlock Holmes"
>>An American millionaire retains Holmes's services to exonerate his children's young and beautiful governess of the murder of their mother, his wife. Holmes is willing to take the case because of the young woman, though he loathes the American himself. The matter commences in October. Holmes is able to determine that the dead woman committed suicide while trying to make it appear that she was murdered.

PROSPER, FRANCIS:
>"The Adventure of the Beryl Coronet"
>>The green-grocer who brings vegetables to the Holder household at Fairbank. He has a wooden leg.

PRUSSIC ACID:
>"The Adventure of the Retired Colourman"
>>A poison, with an almondy odor, which Eugenia Ronder planned to use to end her own life. Holmes talks her out of it and she sends him the bottle of poison as a sign of his success.

PUGILIST:
>"Silver Blaze"
>>Race horse owned by Colonel Wardlaw and entered in the Wessex Cup race.

PUNJABEES:
    "The Sign of Four"
        Mahomet Singh and Abdullah Khan were both
        Punjabees, natives of the Punjab region of northwest
        India.

PURDEY PLACE:
    "The Adventure of Wisteria Lodge"
    aka "A Reminiscence of Mr. Sherlock Holmes"
        Home to Mr. Hynes Hynes, it is located along the road
        between Wisteria Lodge and Oxshott.

PYCROFT, HALL:
    "The Stock-Broker's Clerk"
        Well-built, fresh-complexioned young fellow, with a
        frank, honest face and a slight, crisp, yellow moustache.
        He was a smart young City man, of the class who have
        been labeled cockneys, but who provide England with its
        crack volunteer regiments, and who turn out more fine
        athletes and sportsmen than any body of men in these
        islands.

        Used to have a billet at Coxan & Woodhouse's, of Draper
        Gardens, for five years, was let go due to the Venezuelan
        loan failure, but given a 'ripping good testimonial' by old
        Coxon. After much searching he located a new position
        with Mawson & Williams of Lombard Street, however,
        on the night he received his promise of employment he
        was visited by one Arthur Pinner, Financial Agent, on the
        recommendation of Parker, past manager of Coxon's.
        Pinner offers him the position of manager of 'Franco-
        Midland Hardware Company, Limited' which he accepts.

CHAPTER Q

QUEEN ANNE:
> "The Reigate Puzzle"
>> Style of house of the Cunningham estate. The date of Malplaquet was upon the lintel of the door. It was a fine old house.

QUEEN ANNE STREET:
> "The Adventure of the Illustrious Client"
>> Watson has his own rooms on Queen Anne Street.

QUARTER SESSIONS:
> "The Valley of Fear"   Part 2: "The Scowrers"
>> English court which acquits John Douglas of the murder of Ted Baldwin as having been an act of self-defense.

RACHE:

"A Study in Scarlet"

Word appears on wall written in blood in the darkest corner of the room where Enoch J. Drebber is found murdered. Lestrade believes it was written by the dying man and is to mean a female - RACHEL. Holmes points out that it is the German word for "revenge."

RAE, ANDREW:

"The Valley of Fear", Part 2: "The Scowrers"

Of Rae & Sturmash, coal owners, located near Merton County. Division Master Windle of Merton Lodge 249, 'Ancient Order of Freemen' has requested a job be done on Andrew Rae by the Vermissa Lodge as repayment for a past favor.

RAGGED SHAW:

"The Adventure of the Priory School"

A grove of trees situated between the Priory School and Lower Gill Moor.

RAILWAY ARMS:

"The Adventure of the Retired Colourman"

Small pub in Little Purlington from where Watson telephones Holmes and informs him that the Vicar, J.C. Elman denies ever sending Holmes a telegram about information on the disappearance of Mrs. Amberley and Dr. Ray Ernest.

RALPH:

"The Adventure of the Blanched Soldier"

An old man, he is the butler at Tuxbury Old Hall.

RANCE, JOHN:
>"A Study in Scarlet"
>>The constable who found the body of Enoch J. Drebber.
>>He resides at 46 Audley Court Kennington Park Gate.

RAPHAEL:
>"The Adventure of the Three Gables"
>>Holmes wonders if Mary Maberley might have some
>>valuable artwork by Raphael in her home that thieves
>>might want.

RAS, DAULAT:
>"The Adventure of the Three Students"
>>An Indian student who attends the College of St. Luke's
>>and lives on the second floor above Hilton Soames. He
>>is preparing to take the examination for the Fortescue
>>Scholarship. He is a silent, little, hook-nosed fellow.
>>Quiet and inscrutable, he is steady, methodical and well
>>up on his work, Greek being his weak subject.

RASPER:
>"Silver Blaze"
>>Race horse owned by Lord Singleford and entered in the
>>Wessex Cup race.

RATCLIFF HIGHWAY:
>"The Adventure of Black Peter"
>>Location of the Sumner, Shipping Agent, an individual
>>who finds sailors for departing ships.

READING:
>"The Adventure of the Six Napoleons"
>>Town outside London.

RED BULL INN:
>"The Adventure of the Priory School"
>>Located on the High Road near the Priory School in Mackleton.

RED CIRCLE:
>"The Adventure of the Red Circle"
>>A secret Neapolitan society, it was allied with the old Carbonari. Once an individual became a member there was no leaving the organization. It raised funds by blackmailing wealthy Italians and threatening them with violence if they refused to pay. An Italian criminal organization.

THE RED-HEADED LEAGUE:
>Published in "The Strand": August 1891
>Published as part of: "The Adventures of Sherlock Holmes"
>>Holmes is called upon by Jabez Wilson as to the sudden dissolution of the Red-Headed League. Holmes feels that Mr. Wilson has nothing to be upset about considering he has reaped a benefit and realized no actual loss. Nevertheless, Holmes is intrigued by the facts and is eventually able to thwart the notorious criminal John Clay.

RED-HEADED LEAGUE:
>"The Red-Headed League"
>>Organization set up by the late EZEKIAH HOPKINS, of Lebanon, Pennsylvania, U.S.A. Members of the League are entitled to a salary of 4 pounds a week for purely nominal services. Vacancies are filled by "red-headed men who are sound in body and mind, and above the age of twenty-one years" Only red-headed men are eligible. In "The Red-Headed League" application was to be made to "Duncan Ross, at the offices of the League, 7 Pope's Court, Fleet Street." The League was

dissolved on October 9, 1890 with the following notice:
"The Red-Headed League Is Dissolved October 9, 1890"
attached to the door of the League offices written on a
white square of card-board.

RED LEECH:
"The Adventure of the Golden Pince-Nez"
An unrecorded case, took place in 1894.
A repulsive story.

RED REPUBLICANS:
"The Adventure of the Six Napoleons"
Anarchist group. Morse Hudson believes they are
responsible for the smashing of the busts of Napoleon.

REDRUTH:
"The Adventure of the Devil's Foot"
The Tregennis family at one time owned tin-mines in
Redruth, from which came the source of their wealth.

REGENT CIRCUS:
"The Adventure of Charles Augustus Milverton"
Section of London.

"The Greek Interpreter"
Area near St. James, in London.

REGENT STREET:
"The Boscombe Valley Mystery"
Street where John Turner meets up with his past. It is
here that he meets Charles McCarthy with hardly a coat
to his back or boot to his foot. Charles and his son
James follow John Turner home and, with the threat of
going to the police about John Turner's past, convince
Turner it is better that he "have the keeping of us."

"The Hound of the Baskervilles"
>London street off Oxford Street near Baker Street.

"The Adventure of the Illustrious Client"
>A "Murderous Attack Upon Sherlock Holmes" took place outside the Cafe Royal in Regent Street.

REICHENBACH FALLS:
"The Final Problem"
>Located in Switzerland it is a fearful place, the torrent, swollen by the melting snow, plunges into a tremendous abyss, from which the spray rolls up like the smoke from a burning house. The shaft into which the river hurls itself is an immense chasm, lined by glistening coal-black rock, and narrowing into a creaming, boiling pit of incalculable depth, which brims over and shoots the stream onward over its jagged lip. The long sweep of green water roaring forever down, and the thick flickering curtain of spray hissing forever upward, turn a man giddy with their constant whirl and clamour.

>It is here that Watson believes Holmes and Moriarty met their death on May 4, 1891: "an examination by experts leaves little doubt that a personal contest between the two men ended, as it could hardly fail to end in such a situation, in their reeling over, locked in each other's arms. Any attempt at recovering the bodies was absolutely hopeless, and there, deep down in that dreadful cauldron of swirling water and seething foam, will lie for all time the most dangerous criminal and the foremost champion of the law of their generation."

THE REIGATE PUZZLE:

> AKA The Reigate Squire
> AKA The Reigate Squires
> Published in "The Strand": June 1893
> Published as part of: "Memoirs of Sherlock Holmes"
>> April 14, 1887, Watson receives a telegram from Lyons informing him that Holmes is lying ill in the Hotel Dulong. Holmes investigates a local murder mystery when he and Watson visit a friend of Watson's house near Reigate in Surrey so as to give Holmes a chance to recuperate from his illness.

REILLY:

> "The Valley of Fear", Part 2: "The Scowrers"
>> Lawyer for the 'Scowrers' he successfully defends John McMurdo and others involved in the 'warning' provided to James Stanger of the "Vermissa Herald."

REILLY:

> "The Valley of Fear", Part 2: "The Scowrers"
>> A reckless youngster chosen to join John McMurdo and Manders in settling the Chester Wilcox matter.

REMINGTON:

> "The Hound of the Baskervilles"
>> Typewriter used by Laura Lyons in her typewriting business.

THE RESIDENT PATIENT:

> Published in "The Strand": August 1893
> Published as part of: "Memoirs of Sherlock Holmes"
>> Holmes is consulted by a young physician after his rooms are disturbed, although Holmes refuses to help him initially, he will not express why he is in fear. Holmes steps in after the murder of the young doctor's 'resident patient.' Begins on a rainy day in October.

REUTER'S:
> "The Final Problem"
>> Dispatch service for English newspapers, it provided a condenses version of the facts of "The Final Problem" on May 7, 1891. Watson's version, "The Final Problem," is to lay the true facts before the public.

REYNOLDS:
> "The Hound of the Baskervilles"
>> Artist responsible for some of the family portraits of the Baskervilles.

RHENISH SPA:
> "The Disappearance of Lady Frances Carfax"
>> In Baden, where Lady Frances Carfax heads after leaving the Hotel National.

RHODESIAN POLICE:
> "The Adventure of the Three Students"
>> Young Gilchrist has been offered a commission with the Rhodesian Police nd is leaving the College of St. Luke to do so.

RHONE:
> "The Final Problem"
>> Valley of the Rhone, Holmes and Watson wandered up the valley for a week during their trip to Switzerland. Holmes and Watson, in an attempt to shake off Moriarty, travel to Switzerland wandering up the valley of the Rhone, branching off at Leuk, over the Gemmi Pass, by way of Interlaken, to Meiringen.

RICHARDS, DR.:

"The Adventure of the Devil's Foot"

Dr. Richards is summoned to Tredannick Wartha upon the call of the housekeeper, Mrs. Porter when she discovers the horrible scene of death and madness.

RICHMOND:

"The Valley of Fear", Part 1: "The Tragedy of Birlstone"

Town in England where it has been reported that the suspected murderer of John Douglas, Hargrave, has been seen.

RICOLETTI:

"The Musgrave Ritual"

An unrecorded case.

A full account of Ricoletti of the club-foot, and his abominable wife.

RIDING THORPE MANOR:

"The Adventure of the Dancing Men"

Home of Hilton Cubitt, the Manor has been in his family for five centuries. It is in Norfolk. Has two old brick and timber gables which projected from a grove of trees.

The RING:

"A Case of Identity"

" ... from the reigning family of Holland ... " Holmes served the reigning family of Holland in a matter of such delicacy that he cannot confide it even to Watson.

RIPLEY:

"The Naval Treaty"

A small village near Surrey.

ROCK OF GILBRALTAR:
> "The Adventure of the Abbey Grange"
>> Ship belonging to the Adelaide-Southampton Line sailing between England and South Australia.

RODNEY:
> "The Hound of the Baskervilles"
>> British Admiral under whom served Rear-Admiral Baskerville in the West Indies.

ROMAN CATHOLIC CHURCH:
> "The Crooked Man"
>> Mrs. Barclay, the Colonels wife, is a member and she dedicates much time to the establishment of the 'Guild of St. George,' which was formed in connection with the Watt Street Chapel.

ROME:
> "The Adventure of Wisteria Lodge"
> aka "A Reminiscence of Mr. Sherlock Holmes"
>> One of the stops made by Don Murillo after his escape from Central America after the uprising of his people against him in an attempt to hide from his past and his pursuers.

RONDER:
> "The Adventure of the Retired Colourman"
>> It was a household word, he was the rival of Wombwell and of Sanger, one of the greatest showman of his day. He and his wife ran a wild beast show. A huge porcine person, he was violent and treated his wife with great disrespect, beating her regularly. He became a drinker and his show went on the downgrade. He was a man of many enemies.

RONDER, EUGENIA:

"The Adventure of the Retired Colourman"

Wife of Ronder, she was very beautiful. However, as the show declined, Ronder beat his wife pushing her to Leonardo, who loved her, for comfort. She conspired with Leonardo to kill her husband and make it look like one of the lions did it, but things went wrong, Ronder was killed by Leonardo but Sahara King attacked Eugenia disfiguring her face forever. When she was attacked, she screamed "Coward!, Coward!" in reference to Leonardo's fleeing the scene in a panic when she herself, his lover, was attacked. At the inquest it was determined that the lion had attacked both Ronder and Eugenia and Leonardo was never discovered. She has called Holmes to bear her soul prior to committing suicide, which Holmes talks her out of. She sends the poison she was to use to Holmes.

ROSENLAUI:

"The Final Problem"

A small hamlet outside of Meiringen, just beyond the Reichenbach falls.

ROSS:

"The Boscombe Valley Mystery"

A pretty little country-town

ROSS AND MANGLES:

"The Hound of the Baskervilles"

Dealers in dogs, with offices at Fulham Road, London. From whom John Stapleton purchased the strongest and most savage dog in their possession, the hound.

ROSS, COLONEL:
> "Silver Blaze"
>> Holmes assist the locale police who are trying to help Colonel Ross, owner of "Silver Blaze," a horse entered in the Wessex Cup race and favored to win. He is   also the owner of the King's Pyland stables and is a well known sportsman.

ROSS, DUNCAN:
> "The Red-Headed League"
>> He is a co-conspiarator with the criminal Vincent Spaulding/John Clay.
>>
>> AKA: WILLIAM MORRIS; a solicitor using the premises at No. 4 Pope's Court on a temporary basis before moving to his new offices at 17 King Edward Street near St. Paul's. He did not undertake space at the new address which was "a manufactory of artificial knee-caps, and no one in it had ever heard of either Mr. William Morris or Mr. Duncan Ross."
>>
>> One of the "pensioners upon the fund left by our noble benefactor [Ezekiah Hopkins]" Accepts Jabez Wilson to fill the vacancy in the Red-Headed League.

ROSYTHE:
> "His Last Bow" "An Epilogue of Sherlock Holmes"
>> Von Bork, the German spy, had a safe containing pigeon-holes bristling with papers and plans, each with its own label. One of these compartments was labeled "Rosythe."

ROTHERHITHE:
"The Adventure of the Dying Detective"
> A back alley near the river in London where Holmes had been working among Chinese sailors prior to his illness.

ROTTERDAM:
"His Last Bow" "An Epilogue of Sherlock Holmes"
> City in Holland where Altamont plans to get a ship to New York in his plan to flee England and Europe.

ROUNDHAY, MR.:
"The Adventure of the Devil's Foot"
> Vicar of the parish of Tredannick Wollas, he was something of an archaeologist, a middle aged man, portly and affable, with a considerable fund of local lore. He was a bachelor.

ROY:
"The Adventure of the Creeping Man"
> Professor Presbury's wolfhound. A dog of very good behavior and disposition, it has attacked its master on several occasions, July 2, July 11, and July 20.

THE ROYAL MUNSTERS:
"The Crooked Man"
> The most famous Irish regiments in the British Army. It did wonders in the Crimea and the Mutiny. It was commanded by one James Barclay, a gallant veteran. The first battalion (the old One Hundred and Seventeenth) has been stationed at Aldershot for some years. Married officers live out of the barracks.

ROYLOTT, DR. GRIMESBY:
"The Adventure of the Speckled Band"
> Stepfather of Henen and Julia Stoner. Last survivor of one of the oldest Saxon families in England, the Roylotts

of Stroke Moran. A tall man with a large face, seared with a thousand wrinkles, burned yellow with the sun and marked with every evil passion. His deep-set, bile-shot eyes, and his high thin, fleshless nose, gave him somewhat the resemblance of a fierce old bird of prey.

Obtained an advance from a relative enabling him to take his medical degree. He went to Calcutta, where he established a large practice due to his skill and character. He is a man of immense strength and absolutely uncontrollable in his anger. It was his anger that brought about his downfall in Calcutta when, some robberies had been perpetrated in his house, he beat his native butler to death, narrowly escaping capital sentence, he suffered a long term of imprisonment, returning to England a morose and disappointed man. He married Mrs. Stoner, the young widow of Major-General Stoner, while in India. Abandoned his attempts to practice medicine after the death of Mrs. Stoner, moving to his ancestral home with the children.

RUCASTLE, ALICE:
"The Adventure of the Copper Beeches"
Daughter of Jephro Rucastle, she is now living in Philadelphia. The story about her is: she is about twenty years old, has moved to Philadelphia due to an unreasoning aversion to her stepmother. She is actually kept prisoner by her father so he can have his way with her inheritance. Marries Mr. Fowler at end of adventure.

RUCASTLE, EDWARD:
"The Adventure of the Copper Beeches"
Son of Mr. and Mrs. Rucastle, it is he for whom Violet Hunter has been employed as governess.

RUCASTLE, JEPHRO:

"The Adventure of the Copper Beeches"

A prodigiously stout man with a very smiling face and a great heavy chin which rolled down in fold upon fold over his throat with glasses on his nose. He appears to be about forty-five and resides at the 'Copper Beeches' in Hampshire. A widower, he has one child by his first wife, he has remarried, to a younger woman, and has had a son by her. Offers employment to Violet Hunter at the rate of 100 pounds per year, to serve as governess at the 'Copper Beeches.' He is attacked by his own mastiff being severely injured but saved by Watson's shooting of the dog.

RUCASTLE, MRS.:

"The Adventure of the Copper Beeches"

Silent, pale-faced woman, much younger than her husband, not more than thirty. Has been married about seven years, she has one child, a boy, Edward.

RUDGE-WHITWORTH:

"The Valley of Fear" Part 1: "The Tragedy of Birlstone"

A bicycle believed to belong to the murdered of Mr. John Douglas, it was found about a hundred yards from the front door of Manor House.

RUE DE TRAJAN:

"The Disappearance of Lady Frances Carfax"

Number 11 Rue de Trajan in Montpellier is the address of Mary Devine, maid to Lady Frances Carfax.

RUFTON, EARL OF:

"The Disappearance of Lady Frances Carfax"

Ancestor of Lady Frances Carfax, she is his sole surviving descendent.

RULLI, SIGNOR:

> "The Adventure of Wisteria Lodge"
> aka "A Reminiscence of Mr. Sherlock Holmes"
>> Found murdered in his room with the Marquess of
>> Montalva at the Hotel Escurial in Madrid. The murderers
>> were never found and the crime was ascribed to Nihilism.
>> It is widely believed that he was also know as Mr. Lucas
>> but proof was never forthcoming.

RUSSEL, CLARK:

> "The Five Orange Pips"
>> Author of fine sea-stories which Watson is reading when
>> a visitor arrives to see Holmes.

RUSSELL SQUARE:

> "The Adventure of the Dancing Men"
>> In London, location of a boardinghouse where Hilton
>> Cubitt stayed and met Elsie Patrick.

RUSSIAN-GERMAN GRAIN TAXES:

> "The Adventure of the Second Stain"
>> A note pertaining to the taxes was in the dispatch-box of
>> the Right Honourable Trelawney Hope.

RYDER, JAMES:

> "The Adventure of The Blue Carbuncle"
>> Upper attendant at the Hotel Cosmopolitan.

SAFFRON HILL:
>"The Adventure of the Six Napoleons"
>Section of London, heavy in Italian population.

SAHARA KING:
>"The Adventure of the Retired Colourman"
>Name of the lion, in Ronder's wild beast show, which
>was believed to have killed Ronder and maimed his wife.
>Originally from North Africa, he was used in exhibitions.

ST. CLAIR, MRS.:
>"The Man With The Twisted Lip"
>See Aberdeen Shipping Company.

ST. CLAIR, NEVILLE:
>"The Man With The Twisted Lip"
>Lives at The Cedars, near Lee, in Kent. Came to Lee in
>1894 appearing to have plenty of money, made friends in
>the neighborhood, married the daughter of the local
>brewer in 1987 and has two children but no occupation,
>but supposedly was interested in several companies and
>went to town every morning returning in the evening.
>He is thirty-seven years of age, of temperate habits, a
>good husband, a very affectionate father, and a man who
>was popular with all who knew him. He had debts of 88
>pounds 10 shillings and a bank account of 220 pounds.
>His father was a school-master in Chesterfield, where he
>received an excellent education. He travelled in his
>youth, took the stage, and finally became a reporter with
>a London newspaper.
>AKA Hugh Boone, See Boone, Hugh.

ST. GEORGE'S:

"The Adventure of the Noble Bachelor"

Location of the marriage of Lord St. Simon and Hatty Doran, located in Hanover Square.

ST. JAMES:

"The Greek Interpreter"

Area in London near Pall Mall.

ST. JAMES SQUARE:

"The Adventure of the Illustrious Client"

In central London, it is the home to the London Library.

ST. JAMES STREET:

"The Adventure of the Three Gables"

In central London

ST. OLIVER'S PRIVATE SCHOOL:

"The Hound of the Baskervilles"

Private school in York run by Mr. and Mrs. Vandeleur.

ST. PANCRAS:

"The Adventure of Shoscombe Old Place"

An unrecorded case. Not actually one of Holmes's but one Merivale of Scotland Yard ask Holmes to look into. A cap was found beside a dead policeman, however, the accused denied that he was his. Holmes, using his microscope, is able to determine that threads from a tweed coat reveal gray masses of dust, epithelial scales and blobs, in the center, which are glue. The presence of glue is important because the accused is a picture-frame maker who habitually handles glue and Holmes has found glue in the tweed cap linking the accused to the crime.

ST. PANCRAS HOTEL:
"A Case of Identity"
Hotel where Miss Mary Sutherland and Mr. Hosmer
Angel were to have breakfast after their wedding.

ST. SAVIOUR'S:
"A Case of Identity"
Church near King's Cross wherein Miss Mary Sutherland
was to wed Mr. Hosmer Angel.

ST. SIMON, LADY CLARA:
"The Adventure of the Noble Bachelor"
Younger sister of Lord St. Simon, attended his wedding
to Hatty Doran.

ST. SIMON, LORD ROBERT WALSINGHAM DE VERE:
"The Adventure of the Noble Bachelor"
Sent letter to Holmes on the advice of Lord Blackwater
regarding a strange occurrence at his wedding. Second
son of the Duke of Balmoral, born in 1846, he is
currently 41. He was Under-Secretary for the
colonies in a late administration. Was to marry Miss
Hatty Doran, the only daughter of Aloysius Doran, Esq.
of San Francisco, California, USA. He has no property
of his own save the small estate of Birchmoor. He has a
pleasant, cultured face, high-nosed and pale, with
something perhaps of petulance about the mouth, and
with the steady, well-opened eye of a man whose pleasant
lot it had ever been to command and to be obeyed. His
manner was brisk, and yet his general appearance gave an
undue impression of age, for he had a slight forward
stoop and a little bend of the knees as he walked. He
wore golden eyeglasses.

SALTIRE, LORD:
>   "The Adventure of the Priory School"
>>   Son, and only heir, of the Duke of Holdernesse. He has
>>   been sent to the Priory School from where he was
>>   kidnapped. He is 10 years old and although close to his
>>   mother remains in his father's custody upon the breakup
>>   of his parents marriage.

SANGER:
>   "The Adventure of the Retired Colourman"
>>   A showman and rival of Ronder's wild beast show.

SAN PEDRO:
>   "The Adventure of Wisteria Lodge"
>>   aka "A Reminiscence of Mr. Sherlock Holmes"
>>   Country in Central America governed by Don Murillo.
>>   The people of San Pedro rose up against and overthrew
>>   Don Murillo after ten or so years.

SANDEFORD, MR.:
>   "The Adventure of the Six Napoleons"
>>   Of Lower Grove Road, Reading. He was an elderly red-
>>   faced man with grizzled side-whiskers. He purchased a
>>   bust of Napoleon from Harding Brothers.

SANDERS, IKEY:
>   "The Adventure of the Mazarin Stone"
>>   Jeweler who refused to cut up the Crown Diamond for
>>   Count Sylvius, he has informed Holmes of the request
>>   and the person who made the request.

SAUNDERS:
>   "The Adventure of the Dancing Men"
>>   The housemaid at Riding Thorpe Manor.

SAUNDERS, JAMES:
"The Adventure of the Blanched Soldier"
Sir James Saunders is a noted dermatologist who Holmes has helped in the past and has agreed to examine Godfrey Emsworth. He notes that the boy is not suffering from leprosy but ichthyosis, a scale-like affection of the skin, unsightly, obstinate, but possibly curable, and certainly noninfectious.

SAUNDERS, MRS.:
"The Adventure of the Three Garridebs"
She cares for the house in which Nathan Garrideb lives.

SAVAGE, VICTOR:
"The Adventure of the Dying Detective"
Nephew of Culverton Smith, he was a strong, hearty young fellow who died four days after contracting the disease of the coolies of Sumatra. He was poisoned by his uncle Culverton Smith but Holmes was unable to prove it.

SAWYER, MRS.:
"A Study in Scarlet"
A very old and wrinkled woman. Mother of Sally Dennis, it is she who retrieves Sally's lost ring from Holmes in response to an advertisement in the newspaper. She resides at 13 Duncan Street, Houndsditch. Holmes follows her when she leaves Baker Street and although fooled, determines she was most likely a young man.

SAXE-COBURG SQUARE:
"The Red-Headed League"
See Coburg Square

SAXON:

"The Adventure of Shoscombe Old Place"

Holmes examines the crypt which has been a favorite haunt of Sir Robert Norberton of late and therein discovers graves ranging from very old, one which was Saxon, to those of the eighteenth century.

SCANDINAVIAN ROYAL FAMILY:

"The Final Problem"

An unrecorded case.

Holmes is of assistance to the royal family of Scandinavia during 1890.

SCANLAN, MIKE:

"The Valley of Fear" Part 2: "The Scowrers"

Brother Scanlan is the first member of the Eminent Order of Freemen, Lodge 341, Vermissa Valley, to meet the newcomer, John McMurdo. Their initial meeting takes place on a train to Vermissa. He lives at Hobson's Patch and is a small, sharp-faced, nervous, black-eyed man. Takes part in the 'warning' attack on James Stanger, owner/editor of the 'Vermissa Herald.' Eventually he moves in with John McMurdo at Widow MacNamara's place. He informs McMurdo he doesn't have the stomach for murder and is sent away during the capture of the 'Scowrers.'

SCHOENBRUNN PALACE:

"His Last Bow"

"An Epilogue of Sherlock Holmes"

Home to Franz Josef, it has a special wine cellar, from which the German spy, Von Bork, acquired a few bottles of Imperial Tokay.

SCOTLAND YARD:

The English police department, it investigates all criminal matters of a serious nature or which it believes it should become involved with. Has countrywide jurisdiction and is usually concerned with major cases.

For a list of Inspectors See POLICE.

SCOTLAND YARD MUSEUM:

"The Adventure of the Empty House"

Where the famous air-gun of Von Herder will be displayed. It having been ordered by Professor Moriarty and used, in an attempt to kill Sherlock Holmes, by Colonel Sebastian Moran.

SCOTT, JAMES H.:

"The Valley of Fear" Part 2: "The Scowrers"

Bodymaster of Chicago Lodge 29 of the Eminent Order of Freemen of which John McMurdo was a member.

SCOWRERS:

"The Valley of Fear" Part 2: "The Scowrers"

A gang of murderers, as reported in the news in Chicago and other parts of the country. One and the same as the 'Eminent Order of Freemen' in Vermissa. It is known as a murder society in the Vermissa Valley.

AKA 'Eminent Order of Freemen,'

AKA 'Society of Freemen'

See 'Eminent Order of Freemen'

SCOWRERS OF GILMERTON:

"The Valley of Fear"   Part 2: "The Scowrers"

Lodge of 'Ancient Order of Freemen' in Gilmerton run by Evans Pott.

SEA OF AZOV:
> "The Disappearance of Lady Frances Carfax"
>> Sea touching the Black Sea in the area of Crimea. The British fleet during the Crimean War was commanded by the Honorable Peter Green's father of the same name.

SEA UNICORN:
> "The Adventure of Black Peter"
>> Steam sealer commanded by Captain Peter Carey in 1883; of Dundee.

SELDEN:
> "The Hound of the Baskervilles"
>> Known as the Notting Hill murderer, he escaped from the convict prison in Princetown and is hiding in the moor near Grimpen. Younger brother of Eliza Barrymore, servant at Baskerville Hall. The peculiar ferocity of the crime and the wanton brutality which had marked all the actions of the assassin had interested Holmes. Selden's death sentence had been commuted to life due to some doubts as to his complete sanity, so atrocious was his conduct. Is planning to make his way to South America. He had an evil yellow face, a terrible animal face, all seamed and scored with vile passions. Foul with mire, with a bristling beard and hung with matted hair, it might well have belonged to one of those old savages who dwelt in the burrows on the hillsides. He had small cunning eyes which peered fiercely to right and left through the darkness like a crafty and savage animal. Killed by the Hound on the moor while wearing clothes belonging to Sir Henry Baskerville.

SERGIUS:
> "The Adventure of the Golden Pince-Nez"
>> Married to Anna, he was fifty when they married. A Russian reformer, revolutionary, a Nihilists, he sacrificed

his wife and compatriots for his own skin and reaped a reward in the process. He maintained diaries and other materials which would have proved Alexis innocent of the crimes for which he was sentenced to Siberia. He moved to England under the name Professor Coram. AKA Professor Coram.

SERPENTINE AVENUE:
"A Scandal in Bohemia"

Street where home of Irene Adler is located. Her address is: Briony Lodge, Serpentine Avenue, St. John's Woods. See Briony Lodge

SHADWELL POLICE STATION:
"The Adventure of the Cardboard Box"

Police station where Jim Browner gave his statement (confession) to Inspector Montgomery.

SHAFTER, ETTIE:
"The Valley of Fear" Part 2: "The Scowrers"

Daughter of Jacob Shafter owner of the boarding house on Sheridan Street Vermissa. She is a young and beautiful woman, German type, blonde, with beautiful dark eyes. Until the arrival of John McMurdo she has been seeing Ted Baldwin, who expects to marry her. However, after McMurdo arrives, she begins to favor him over Baldwin. Marries Birdy Edwards ten days after the arrest of the 'Scowrers' of Vermissa with Jacob Shafter as a witness in Chicago. She dies in California about ten or so years later.

SHAFTER, JACOB:
"The Valley of Fear" Part 2: "The Scowrers"

Owner of a boarding house on Sheridan Street in Vermissa which was recommended to John McMurdo by a friend in Chicago. A very honest man, his wife died some time ago and he and his one daughter, Ettie, run the boarding house.

SHAFTESBURY AVENUE:
>"The Greek Interpreter"
>>Street in London.

SHAKESPEARE:
>"The Adventure of the Three Gables"
>>Holmes wonders if Mary Maberley might have a first folio Shakespeare in her home that thieves might want.

SHERMAN:
>"The Sign of Four"
>>Bird-stuffer who lives at No. 3 Pinchin Lane, down near the water's edge at Lambeth, third house on the right-hand side.

SHETLAND HEIGHTS:
>"The Adventure of Black Peter"
>>Where the 'Sea Unicorn' put in after picking Neligan up at sea.

SHINWELL, PORKY:
>"The Adventure of the Illustrious Client"
>>See Johnson, Shinwell.

SHIPLEY'S YARD:
>"The Hound of the Baskervilles"
>>Near Waterloo Station, where John Clayton gets his cab, No. 2704.

SHLESSINGER, DR.:
>"The Disappearance of Lady Frances Carfax"
>>The Reverend Doctor Shlessinger is a missionary from South America who is staying at Englischer Hof with his

wife recovering from some disease he contracted in the exercise of his duties. He was preparing a map of the Holy Land, with special reference to the kingdom of the Midianites, upon which he was writing a monograph. AKA Holy Peters. See Peters, Holy.

SHLESSINGER, MRS.:
"The Disappearance of Lady Frances Carfax"
>She is staying with her husband at Englischer Hof nursing him as he recovers from a disease he contracted in his missionary work.
>AKA Fraser. See Fraser.

SHOLTO, BATHOLOMEW:
"The Sign of Four"
>Son of Major Sholto and twin brother of Thaddeus Sholto. Found murdered by Holmes, Watson, Thaddeus, and Mary Marstan at his residence at Pondicherry Lodge.

THE SHOLTO MURDER:
"The Red-Headed League"
>Appears to refer to the murder of the Sholto's in "The Sign of Four." Holmes "more nearly correct than the official force" - Spoken by Official Police agent Peter Jones.

SHOLTO, Major JOHN:
"The Sign of Four"
>Friend of Captain Morstan and member of the same regiment, the Thirty-fourth Bombay Infantry. He died on the twenty-eighth of April 1882. He was late of Pondicherry Lodge in Upper Norwood. He and Captain Morstan were in command of the troops at the Andaman Islands. He had twin sons, Thaddeus and Bartholomew. He alone knew the fate of Arthur Morstan.

SHOLTO, THADDEUS:
>"The Sign of Four"
>>A little man, he asserts that Captain Morstan died of a bad heart.

SHOMU, EMPEROR:
>"The Adventure of the Illustrious Client"
>>Associated with the Shoso-in near Nara, Baron Gruner request Dr. Hill Barton provide information on this as a test of his authenticity.

SHOSCOMBE OLD PLACE:
>"The Adventure of Shoscombe Old Place"
>>It is the center of Shoscombe Park and home to the famous Shoscombe stud and training quarters. It is also known for its Shoscombe spaniels, the most exclusive breed of dog in England. They are of special pride to Lady Beatrice Falder, present owner of Shoscombe Old Place.

SHOSCOMBE PRINCE:
>"The Adventure of Shoscombe Old Place"
>>Colt belonging to the Shoscombe Old Place estate and scheduled to run in the Derby. It is one of the best colts in England and Sir Robert Norberton is betting his future on the horse. The colt has a half-brother which Sir Robert has been running for all to see as if Shoscombe Prince were running himself. One can't tell the difference between the two, but Shoscombe Prince is quicker by two lengths in a furlong.

SHOSO-IN:
>"The Adventure of the Illustrious Client"
>>See Shomu, Emperor.

SHUMAN:

"The Valley of Fear"   Part 2: "The Scowrers"
Sold his ironworks operation to West Gilmerton General Mining Company instead of paying the 'Scowrers' to leave him alone.

SIERRA BLANCO:

"A Study in Scarlet"   Part 2 -- "The Country of the Saints"
It is said that "in the whole world there can be no more dreary view than that from the northern slope of the Sierra Blanco.

SIGERSON:

"The Adventure of the Empty House"
Name used by Holmes while traveling through Tibet after his fight with Professor Moriarty at the Reichenbach Falls. A Norwegian who wrote of his explorations.

THE SIGN OF FOUR:

Published October 1890
The Second of the four novels
AKA 'The Sign of the Four' The second story.
Holmes is consulted by Mary Morstan about the disappearance of her father. The first mention of Holmes' use of drugs. It begins thus: "Sherlock Holmes took his bottle from the corner of the mantelpiece, and his hypodermic syringe from its neat morocco case." "Three times a day for many months I had witnessed this performance ... " "Which is it today, I asked, morphine or cocaine? It is cocaine, a seven-percent solution."

At the conclusion of the case Watson states: "The division seems rather unfair, you have done all the work in this business. I get a wife out of it, Jones gets the credit, pray what remains for you?" Holmes responds:

'For me there still remains the cocaine-bottle.' And he stretched his long white hand up for it."

It is also in "The Sign of Four" that we have the reference to Holmes being a detective: "... I have chosen my own particular profession, or rather created it, for I am the only one in the world. The only unofficial detective, I said, raising my eyebrows. The only unofficial consulting detective, he answered." Holmes goes on to say: "I am the last and highest court of appeal in detection. When Gregson, or Lestrade, or Athelney Jones are out of their depths -- which , by the way, is their normal state -- the matter is laid before me."

This case takes place in 1888, ten years since the disappearance of Captain Morstan and involves the strange appearance of a boxed pearl being delivered to Mary Morstan every year. She consults Holmes when she receives a strange note to meet her unknown friend.

"A Case of Identity"
Mentioned in passing.

"The Adventure of the Cardboard Box"
Holmes compares "A Study in Scarlet" and "The Sign of Four" to the present case in that each case must be reasoned backward from effects to causes.

SIKH:
"The Sign of Four"
A member of a Hindu religious sect in northern India.

SILVER BLAZE:
>   Published in "The Strand": December 1892
>   Published as part of: "The Memoirs of Sherlock Holmes"
>>   Holmes is called upon to look into the death of John
>>   Straker and the disappearance of the racehorse 'Silver
>>   Blaze.'
>
>>   First mention of Holmes' hat: "his ear-flapped travelling-
>>   cap."

SILVESTER'S:
>   "The Disappearance of Lady Frances Carfax"
>>   Bank where Lady Frances Carfax does her banking.

SIMPSON:
>   "The Crooked Man"
>>   A small street Arab, one of Holmes' young spies.

SIMPSON, FITZROY:
>   "Silver Blaze"
>>   A man of excellent birth and education, who squandered
>>   a fortune upon the turf, and who lives now by doing a
>>   little quiet and genteel book-making in the sporting clubs
>>   of London. Arrested for the disappearance of the race
>>   horse Silver Blaze and the murder of John Straker.

SIMPSON'S:
>   "The Adventure of the Dying Detective"
>>   A London restaurant.
>
>   "The Adventure of the Illustrious Client"
>>   Restaurant in the Strand where Holmes and Watson meet
>>   to map strategy.

SINCLAIR, ADMIRAL:

"The Adventure of the Bruce-Partington Plans"

Lives at Barclay Square, has testified that Sir James Walter was at his house the night the Bruce-Partington papers were stolen.

SINGH, MAHOMET:

"The Sign of Four"

A member of "The Sign of Four" Under the command of Jonathan Small in Agra during the great mutiny. A fierce looking chap who had borne arms against the British at Chilian Wallah. Conspired with Jonathan Small, Abdullah Khan, and Dost Akbar to kill Achmet and steal his treasure. He is caught, tried, and sentenced with his co-conspirators for the murder of Achmet. He is sent to Andaman Island where is escape with the others fails due to the double-cross of Major Sholto and Captain Marstan, who themselves retrieve the treasure.

SINGLEFORD, LORD:

"Silver Blaze"

Owner of the race horse 'Rasper' which was entered in the Wessex Cup race.

SKIBBAREEN:

"His Last Bow"

"An Epilogue of Sherlock Holmes"

Altamont gave the constabulary some serious trouble here, before being spied by an underling of the German spy, Von Bork.

See Altamont.

SLANEY, ABE:

"The Adventure of the Dancing Men"

Resides at Elrige's Farm, East Ruston, Norfolk. The most dangerous crook in Chicago. A Tall, handsome, swarthy fellow, with a bristling black beard and a great, aggressive hooked nose. Writer of the 'dancing men' coded messages. Shot and killed Hilton Cliff while leaving Riding   Thorpe Manor. Slaney had come to Riding Thorpe to see Elsie Patrick, whom he loved, when she spurned him he tried to pull her out a window with him and along came Hilton pulling a revolver and firing at and missing Slaney. He was condemned to death at the winter assizes at Norfolk, but his penalty was later changed to penal servitude.

SLATER:
> "The Adventure of Black Peter"
>> A stonemason reported that he had seen the shadow of a man other than Peter Carey on the blind.

SLOANE, HANS:
> "The Adventure of the Three Garridebs"
>> Great collector of scientific artifacts.

SMALL, JONATHAN:
> "The Sign of Four"
>> A member of "The Sign of Four" An Englishman in prison where Major Sholto and Captain Marstan were guards. He drew the map which was in the possession of Captain Marstan and signed "The Sign of Four." He has a wooden-leg due to an accident, while in the army, with a crocodile in the Ganges, his life being saved by his company sergeant, John Holder. Originally from Worcestershire, born near Pershore, joined the Third Buffs headed for India. While in Agra, during the great mutiny in India, two Sikh troopers were placed under his command to guard the gates during certain hours. They were Mahomet Singh and Abdullah Khan. He conspired with these men and Khan's foster-brother to kill Achmet and steal his treasure. He and his co-conspirators are

caught, tried and sentenced for the murder of Achmet and sent to Andaman Island. He tells Major Sholto and Captain Marstan of the treasure and its whereabouts in hopes of gaining his and his friends escape but Sholto and Marstan double-cross them.

SMITH, CULVERTON:

"The Adventure of the Dying Detective"

He resides at 13 Lower Burke Street and is the man who is best versed in the disease suffered by Holmes. He is not a medical man but a planter. He is a well known resident of Sumatra presently visiting London. An outbreak of the disease upon his plantation caused him to study it with far reaching consequences. He had a great yellow face, coarse grained and greasy, with a heavy, double-chin, and two sullen, menacing gray eyes. He had an enormous skull which was bald and yet he was small and frail. He was small, twisted in the shoulders and back like one who had suffered from rickets as a child. He comes, at Watson's request, to administer to the dying Holmes and while doing so relates that it was he who sent the mysterious box with the needle and spring attachment to Holmes in an attempt to poison him with the coolie disease of Sumatra as he had his nephew, Victor Savage. Holmes arrest him for the murder of Victor Savage and the attempted murder of Sherlock Holmes after revealing his charade.

SMITH, JAMES:

"The Adventure of the Solitary Cyclist"

Father of Miss Violet Smith, he conducted the orchestra at the old Imperial Theatre. He died recently leaving his wife and daughter very poor.

SMITH, MORDECAI:

"The Sign of Four"
> Hired out boats from the wharf by the hour or day. His wife informs Holmes that he has been gone for some time and she is concerned. He has a son Jack, aged about 6, and another son Jim who has traveled with his father. Mordecai and Jim are missing.

SMITH-MORTIMER:

"The Adventure of the Golden Pince-Nez"
> An unrecorded case, took place in 1894.
> The famous Smith-Mortimer succession case.

SMITH, RALPH:

"The Adventure of the Solitary Cyclist"
> Brother of James Smith and Uncle to Miss Violet Smith, he left for Africa twenty-five years ago. Made a fortune in South Africa, which would be inherited by Miss Violet Smith and her mother.

SMITH, VIOLET:

"The Adventure of the Solitary Cyclist"
> Comes to Holmes on April 23, 1895. She is a young and beautiful lady, tall, graceful and queenly. She teaches music near Farnham, on the borders of Surrey. Her father died leaving she and her mother very poor. Her only other relative being a Ralph Smith of Africa, from whom she has had no word in some twenty-five years. Bob Carruthers and Roaring Jack Woodley conspire to force her to marry Woodley so they can obtain her inheritance due her from her dying uncle Ralph Smith. Carruthers falls in love with her during the plan, and even though she turns him down he works to save her from Woodley. She is engaged to Cyril Morton whom she marries at the end of the summer of 1895. She inherited a large fortune from her uncle Ralph Smith.

SMITH & WESSON:
>"The Valley of Fear"   Part 2: "The Scowrers"
>>Revolver carried by John McMurdo.

SMITH, WILLOUGHBY:
>"The Adventure of the Golden Pince-Nez"
>>A very young man, he was secretary to Professor Coram
>>at Yoxley Old Place until his death. His work consisted
>>of writing all his employer's dictation during the morning,
>>and the evenings were spent in research of references and
>>passages bearing upon the next days work. He was from
>>Uppingham and studied at Cambridge. He was a fine
>>young man with nothing against him.

SNUFFBOX:
>"A Case of Identity"
>>"Of old gold, with a great amethyst in the centre of the
>>lid" A souvenir from the King of Bohemia.

SOAMES, CATHCART:
>"The Adventure of the Priory School"
>>Sir Cathcart's son has attended the Priory School.

SOAMES, HILTON:
>"The Adventure of the Three Students"
>>An acquaintance of Holmes and Watson, he is a tutor and
>>lecturer at the College of St. Luke's. He is a tall, spare
>>man, of a nervous and excitable temperament. He is one
>>of the examiners for the Fortescue Scholarship, his
>>subject being Greek. He has one servant, Bannister, who
>>has looked after his rooms for ten years.

SOCIETY OF FREEMEN:
>"The Valley of Fear"   Part 2: "The Scowrers"
>>See 'Scowrers'

SOTHEBY'S:
>"The Adventure of the Three Garridebs"
>>The auctioneer house in London.

>"The Adventure of the Illustrious Client"
>>Auction house in London.

SOUTH AFRICA:
>"The Adventure of the Three Students"
>>Where young Gilchrist is headed to join the Rhodesian Police.

>"The Disappearance of Lady Frances Carfax"
>>Where the young, Honorable Philip Green went after his breakup from Lady Frances Carfax.

SOUTH AFRICAN WAR:
>"The Adventure of the Three Garridebs"
>>Ended around June 1902.

SOUTHAMPTON:
>"The Adventure of the Copper Beeches"
>>Location of marriage of Miss Alice Rucastle and Mr. Fowler.

>"The Hound of the Baskervilles"
>>Port where Sir Henry Baskerville arrives after his trip from Canada.

SOUTHAMPTON:

"The Valley of Fear"   Part 1: "The Tragedy of Birlstone"
Town in England where it has been reported that the
suspected murderer of John Douglas, Hargrave, has been
seen.

SOUTHERTON, LORD:

"The Adventure of the Copper Beeches"
Owns the woods which are on three sides of the Copper
Beeches as part of his preserve.

SOUTHSEA:

"The Resident Patient"
Holiday/vacation spot, Watson wishes he were there but
for a depleted bank account.

SPARKING PLUGS:

"His Last Bow"   "An Epilogue of Sherlock Holmes"
Code name given to the 'Naval Signals' but Von Bork and
his spy Altamont.

SPAULDING, VINCENT:

"The Red-Headed League"
Works for Jabez Wilson in the pawnbrokers business for
half wages, smart and "not such a youth", has his faults --
"Never was such a fellow for photography" Points out
advertisement concerning The Red-Headed League in
paper to Mr Jabez Wilson. Explains how league came
about and suggest Mr. Wilson apply for the vacancy. See
Clay, John

THE SPECKLED BAND:

"The Adventure of the Speckled Band"
A swamp alder, the deadliest snake in India.

SPECTATOR:
"The Adventure of the Blanched Soldier"
A British weekly newspaper.

SPENCER JOHN GANG:
"The Adventure of the Three Gables"
The black boxer, Steve, and Barney Stockdale are members. It specializes in assaults, intimidation and the like.

SPENDER, ROSE:
"The Disappearance of Lady Frances Carfax"
The body of Rose Spender is discovered in a coffin in the home of Holy Peters and his partner Fraser. They claim she is an old nurse of Fraser's whom they found in the Brixton Workhouse Infirmary. She was taken from the Infirmary by Peters and Fraser to their home until she died under the care of Dr. Horsom of senile decay.

SPLUGEN PASS:
"The Adventure of the Illustrious Client"
In southern Switzerland, it was the scene of an 'accident' which claimed the life of Baron Gruner's wife. The death was suspicious and an investigation was thwarted by the mysterious death of a witness.

STACKHURST, HAROLD:
"The Adventure of the Lion's Mane"
He has a well known coaching establishment, The Gables, within half a mile of Holmes's retirement home in Sussex. He was a well-known rowing Blue in his day and an excellent all-round scholar.

STAGVILLE:
>"The Valley of Fear" Part 2: "The Scowrers"
>>On the plain to Vermissa at the head of the valley. Coal-trains connect coal-mining and iron-working settlements between the two towns, then continuing into the valley to BArtons Crossing, Helmdale, and finally Merton.

STAMFORD, ARCHIE:
>"The Adventure of the Solitary Cyclist"
>>The Forger captured by Holmes and Watson near Farnham. An unrecorded case.

THE STANDARD:
>"A Study in Scarlet"
>>An English newspaper which reported on the murder of Enoch J. Drebber. "Commented upon the fact that the lawless outrages of the sort usually occurred under a Liberal administration." Went on to describe the known information of Mr. Enoch J. Drebber and his secretary Joseph Stangerson before the death of Mr. Drebber and the disappearance of Mr. Stangerson. Commented on Scotland Yard's Mr. Lestrade and Mr. Gregson: "We are glad to learn that Mr. Lestrade and Mr. Gregson, of Scotland Yard, are both engaged upon the case, and it is confidently anticipated that these well-known officers will speedily throw light upon the matter."
>>Also see Enoch J. Drebber.

>"The Sign of Four"
>>A London newspaper which printed an account of the "Mysterious Business at Upper Norwood" regarding the murder of Bartholomew Sholto.

"The Sign of Four"
>According to the STANDARD, a London newspaper, one McMurdo, an ex-prize-fighter, was the porter or gatekeeper for Bartholomew Sholto.

STANFORD:

"A Study in Scarlet"
>A 'dresser' under Watson at Bart's. Introduces Watson to a fellow who is working at the chemical laboratory at the hospital, one Sherlock Holmes.

STANGER, JAMES:

"The Valley of Fear"   Part 2: "The Scowrers"
>Owner of the Vermissa newspaper, "Vermissa Herald." He is an old man, well respected in the township and district. His newspaper stands for all that is solid in the valley. His paper has run an editorial about the 'Scowrers' aka "Eminent Order of Freemen' blasting their "reign of terror' in the valley. He is 'marked' for a 'warning' by Bodymaster McGinty, his death possibly bringing about too much trouble.

STANGERSON, "ELDER":

"A Study in Scarlet"   Part 2 -- "The Country of the Saints"
>One of the four principal Elders of the Mormons, one of the "Holy Four" (also known as the "Sacred Council of Four") along with Johnson, Kemball, and Enoch Drebber.

>It is in his wagon that Lucy Ferrier is transported to safety in Salt Lake City after she and John Ferrier are found in the Sierra Balnco dying. It is his son that is found murdered in London by Lestrade.

STANGERSON, JOSEPH:

"A Study in Scarlet"
Appears to be the private secretary of the deceased, Enoch J. Drebber. His whereabouts are unknown. Is found to have been murdered at Halliday's Private Hotel through the investigation of Mr. Lestrade of Scotland Yard.

"A Study in Scarlet" Part 2 -- "The Country of the Saints"
Son of the "Elder" Stangerson. He had a long pale face, he has four wives with great prospects in the future for he shall inherit his fathers tanning yard and leather factory. He is older than Enoch Drebber and is higher in the Church. He competed for the hand of Lucy Ferrier with Enoch Drebber but Brigham Young decide in favor of Drebber during arguments before the Council of Four. Was a member of the "Avenging Angels," having ridden with them in their search for Lucy and John Ferrier. He asserts he killed John Ferrier and that should give him a better claim for Lucy Ferrier in his argument before the Council of Four. A Mormon by the name of COWDER informs Jefferson Hope that it was Joseph Stangerson that killed John Ferrier.

STAPHOUSE FAMILY:

"The Valley of Fear" Part 2: "The Scowrers"
Their house was blown up killing the entire family, the work of the 'Scowrers' during the winter of 1875.

STAPLES:

"The Adventure of the Dying Detective"
Butler for Culverton Smith.

STAPLETON, BERYL, MISS:

"The Hound of the Baskervilles"

Supposed sister of Mr. Stapleton, she was described to Watson as "being a beauty." She was darker than a brunette, slim, elegant, and tall. She had a proud finely cut face, so regular that it might have seemed impassive were it not for the sensitive mouth and the beautiful dark, eager eyes. She had a perfect figure. She is found by Holmes and Watson tied to a post, so swathed and muffled in the sheets which had been used to secure it that one could not for a moment tell whether it was that of a man or a woman. She was virtually a prisoner of John Stapleton, being in complete fear of him, a fear founded upon brutal treatment. She sent the message to Sir Henry Baskerville warning him to fear for his life. Actually, she is the wife of John Stapleton, having married him in South America where they met. Her name was Beryl Garcia, which she later changed to Vandeleur when she fled with her husband to England. East of Yorkshire, she and her husband ran a private school until after the death of the tutor.

AKA Beryl Garcia, Mrs. Vandeleur.

STAPLETON, JOHN MR.:

"The Hound of the Baskervilles"

A naturalist Of Merripit House in Grimpen, he has been in the area for only two years, villagers refer to him as a newcomer. He arrived shortly after Sir Charles Baskerville. He was neutral tinted, with light hair and gray eyes. Son of Roger Baskerville, he was born in South America, married Beryl Garcia (see Beryl Stapleton), a beauty of Costa Rica. He was involved in purloining a considerable sum of public money, changed his name to Vandeleur and fled to England, where he established a school in the east of Yorkshire.

AKA Vandeleur

STARK, COLONEL LYSANDER:
"The Adventure of the Engineer's Thumb"

A thin man, his whole face sharpened away into nose and chin, and the skin of his cheeks was drawn quite tense over his outstanding bones. His eye was bright, his step brisk, and his bearing assured. He was plainly but neatly dressed, and his age nearer forty than thirty. Has a German accent in his speech. Has had Victor Hatherley recommended to him to perform some work. He can not say who it is that made the recommendation.

STARR, LYSANDER, DR.:
"The Adventure of the Three Garridebs"

Holmes claims to have known this individual from Topeka, Kansas, who, Holmes asserts, was mayor in 1890. Holmes asks John Garrideb if he is familiar with the man and John responds "His name is still honored." Holmes tells Watson that there is no such man as Dr. Lysander Starr and the John Garrideb is up to no good.

STATE & MERTON COUNTY RAILROAD COMPANY:
"The Valley of Fear"   Part 2: "The Scowrers"

Purchased the mining business of Archie Swindon. It also purchased the mining businesses of Todman and Lee which were put up for sale due to the 'Scowrers' blackmail demands a year earlier.

STAUNTON, ARTHUR H.:
"The Adventure of the Missing Three-quarter"

A rising young forger.

STAUNTON, GODFREY:
"The Adventure of the Missing Three-quarter"

Plays for Trinity College's rugby team, he is the teams 'three-quarter' and has been described as the hinge of the team. He is a crack three-quarter for Cambridge, Blackheath, and five Internationals. He is an orphan, his nearest relative being Lord Mount-James, one of the richest men in England. He has disappeared. He had married a young woman in London and was trying to keep it from his Uncle. She dies due to a dangerous illness, consumption of the most virulent kind.

STAUNTON, HENRY:

"The Adventure of the Missing Three-quarter"
A criminal Holmes helped to hang.
An unrecorded case.

STEILER, PETER:

"The Final Problem"

The elder. Keeper of the Englischer Hof, hotel where Holmes and Watson stay while in Meiringen. He is an intelligent man who speaks perfect English, having served for three years as waiter at the Grosvenor Hotel in London. It is he who advices Holmes and Watson to cross the hills and spend the night at the hamlet of Rosenlaui, with strict instructions not to pass the falls of Reichenbach without stopping to see them.

STEINER:

"His Last Bow"

"An Epilogue of Sherlock Holmes"
Employed by the German spy, Von Bork, he and all his papers are presently in the Portsmouth jail. His capture has shaken Von Bork.

STENDALS:

"The Valley of Fear"   Part 2: "The Scowrers"
Murdered by the "Scowrers' during the winter of 1875.

STEPHENS:

"The Adventure of Shoscombe Old Place"
The butler at Shoscombe Old Place.

STEPNEY:

"The Adventure of the Six Napoleons"
Section of London wherein Gelder & Co. is located.

STERNDALE, LEON:

"The Adventure of the Devil's Foot"
Dr. Leon Sterndale, the great lion-hunter and explorer, had a huge body, craggy and deeply seamed face with fierce eyes and a hawk-like nose. His hair was grizzled and his beard, golden at the fringes and white near the lips, revealed a nicotine stain from his perpetual cigar. He was deeply in love with Brenda Tregennis and concluding her bother Mortimer was responsible for her death, brought death to Mortimer in the same way Mortimer had brought it upon Brenda. Holmes allows him to go to Africa, Holmes believing he might very well have done the same thing.

STEVENS, BERT:

"The Adventure of the Norwood Builder"
A terrible murderer who wanted Holmes to get him off in 1887. He was a mild-mannered, Sunday-school young man. Holmes and Watson discuss the appearance of an individual and its relationship to his guilt or innocence.

STEVENSON:

"The Adventure of the Missing Three-quarter"
Plays for Trinity College's rugby team. He is fast enough to be a three-quarter but lacks the ability to drop from the twenty-five line.

STEWART, JANE:
>"The Crooked Man"
>>The housemaid at 'Lachine' home of Colonel and Mrs. Barclay.

STEWART, MRS:
>"The Adventure of the Empty House"
>>Of Lauder, Holmes believes Colonel Sebastian Moran was responsible for her death in 1887.

STIMPSON AND COMPANY:
>"The Disappearance of Lady Frances Carfax"
>>Undertakers with offices on Kennington Road. They have been retained to handle the death of Rose Spender by the Peters.

THE STOCK-BROKER'S CLERK:
>Published in "The Strand": March 1893
>Published as part of:"Memoirs of Sherlock Holmes"
>>Involves the curious behavior of the employer of a stock-broker's clerk assigning him useless and long assignments. "shortly after my marriage I had bought a connection in the Paddington district" from an old doctor with St. Vitus's dance by the name of Farquhar. Due to the fact that the practice had fallen from 1200 a year to about 300 a year, Watson was kept very closely at work for the first three months and saw little of Holmes.

STOCKDALE, BARNEY:
>"The Adventure of the Three Gables"
>>Member of the Spencer John Gang, he has been working for Isadora Klein to retrieve a manuscript written by Douglas Maberley. He is the husband of Susan, one of the maids to Mary Maberley of 'The Three Gables.'

STOKE MORAN:
>"The Adventure of the Speckled Band"
>>On the western border of Surrey, location of the ancestral home of the Roylotts, (Dr. Grimesby Roylott).

STONE, REV. JOSHUA:
>"The Adventure of Wisteria Lodge"
>aka "A Reminiscence of Mr. Sherlock Holmes"
>>He resides at 'Nether Walsling' which is located along the road between Wisteria Lodge and Oxshott.

STONER, HELEN:
>"The Adventure of the Speckled Band"
>>Lives with her stepfather, Dr. Grimesby Roylott, was two years old when her mother married Dr. Roylott. She has a twin sister, Julia, who died about 1881. Helen is engaged to marry Percy Armitage. Thirty years old, or thereabouts, but her hair is shot with premature gray.

STONER, JULIA:
>"The Adventure of the Speckled Band"
>>Twin sister of Helen Stoner. Lived with her sister and stepfather until her untimely death at the age of thirty, her hair having already begun to whiten.

STONER, MAJOR-GENERAL:
>"The Adventure of the Speckled Band"
>>Father of Helen and Julia Stoner. Of the Bengal Artillery.

STOPER, MISS:
>"The Adventure of the Copper Beeches"
>>Manages the Westaway agency. See: Westaway's.

STRADIVARIUS:
"The Adventure of the Cardboard Box"

> Great violin maker, Holmes purchases one of his violins
> for 55 shillings, knowing it to be worth 500 guineas, from
> a Jew's broker's in Tottenham Court Road.

STRAKER, JOHN:
"Silver Blaze"

> Horse trainer, a retired jockey who rode in Colonel Ross's
> colours before he became too heavy for the weighing-
> chair. He has served the Colonel for five years as jockey
> and seven as trainer. He is married, living two-hundred
> yards from the stables. He has no children, keeps one
> maidservant, and is comfortably off. He has three lads
> under him. Is killed by 'Silver Blaze' as he attempts to cut
> the horses tendon.
> AKA William Derbyshire.

THE STRAND:
"A Study in Scarlet"

> A private hotel where Watson resides after returning
> from the Afgan war.

"The Adventure of the Missing Three-quarter"

> A hotel in London.

STRAND:
"The Adventure of the Missing Three-quarter"

> A section of England.

"The Adventure of the Illustrious Client"

> Location of Simpson's, a restaurant visited by Holmes
> and Watson.

STRASBOURG:

"The Final Problem"

Stop along the way as Holmes and Watson make their way, at their leisure, into Switzerland, via Luxembourg and Basle.

STRAUBENZEE:

"The Adventure of the Mazarin Stone"

Owns a workshop in the Minories, he is the man who made the air-gun, which Holmes believes to be a 'very pretty bit of work.'

STRAUSS, HERMAN:

"The Valley of Fear"   Part 2: "The Scowrers"

John McMurdo quizzes Lawler and Andrews, the Assassins, about whom they plan to kill and McMurdo suggest it might be Strauss.

STREATHAM:

"The Adventure of the Copper Beeches"

A southern suburb where Fairbank, Alexander Holder's home, is located.

STUARTS:

"The Musgrave Ritual"

Royalty, kings of England, Charles the First and Charles the Second. It is the ancient crown of the kings of England, belonging to the Stuart line, which is discovered to be the Musgrave treasure.

STYLESTOWN:

"The Valley of Fear"   Part 2: "The Scowrers"

Town where old man Crabbe lived before he was killed by Lander and Egan. It is in the Vermissa Valley.

SUDBURY:
"The Adventure of the Lion's Mane"
A student at The Gables, he and Blount were the two individuals to find the dead dog which had belonged to Fitzroy McPherson.

SULTAN OF TURKEY:
"The Adventure of the Blanched Soldier"
An unrecorded case.
Holmes notes that this case is presently pressing and immediate action is necessary as political consequences of the gravest kind might arise from its neglect.

SUMATRA:
"The Adventure of the Dying Detective"
Holmes claims to suffer a coolie disease from Sumatra that is horribly contagious by touch. It is a Far East disease of the Chinese and is infallibly deadly. The Dutch know of the disease but have made little of it.

SUMATRA, GIANT RAT OF:
"The Adventure of the Sussex Vampire"
An unrecorded case.
Holmes assisted the firm of Morrison, Morrison, and Dodd, machinery assessors, in this matter. Matilda Briggs was a ship and it was associated with the giant rat of Sumatra. Holmes notes that the world is not yet prepared for this story.

SUMNER:
"The Adventure of Black Peter"
Shipping Agent located at Ratcliff Highway.

SUNG:

"The Adventure of the Illustrious Client"

    Watson studies Chinese Pottery in preparation for a disguised meeting with Baron Gruner about the sale of a genuine eggshell pottery saucer of the Ming dynasty. In this quest he studies the primitive period of the Sung.

SURREY:

"The Naval Treaty"
"The Reigate Puzzle"
"The Adventure of the Solitary Cyclist"

    A county in England.

SURREY CONSTABULARY:

"The Adventure of Wisteria Lodge"
aka "A Reminiscence of Mr. Sherlock Holmes"

    Department of Inspector Baynes, covers the area in which Esher and Oxshott are located, as well as Wisteria Lodge.

SURRY FAMILY:

"The Adventure of the Speckled Band"

    Of the Roylotts of Stroke Moran. Family was at one time among the richest in England, with estates extending over the borders into Berkshire in the north, and Hampshire in the west. During the last century, four successive heirs were of a dissolute and wasteful disposition and the family ruin was eventually completed by a gambler in the days of the Regency. Nothing has been left but a few acres and the two-hundred year old house, burdened by a heavy mortgage.

SUSAN:

"The Adventure of the Three Gables"

    Maid to Mary Maberley, Holmes catches her listening in on his conversation with Mary Maberley and rightly deduces that she tipped off Barney Stockdale that Holmes was consulted by Mrs. Maberley. Susan quits after the confrontation with Holmes at 'The Three Gables.' She is the wife of Barney Stockdale.

SUSSEX:
"The Musgrave Ritual"
Location of the Manor House of Hurlstone, home to the Musgraves.

"The Adventure of Black Peter"
Location of Woodman's Lee, home of Peter Carey, near Forest Row.

"The Valley of Fear"   Part 1: "The Tragedy of Birlstone"
Location of Birlstone and the scene of the murder of Mr. Douglas.

"The Adventure of the Sussex Vampire"
County in England wherein lies Lamberley.

"The Adventure of the Lion's Mane"
Location of Holmes's retirement home.

SUSSEX CONSTABULARY:
"The Valley of Fear"   Part 1: "The Tragedy of Birlstone"
Police officer in charge of the Birlstone station is Sargeant Wilson.

SUTHERLAND, MISS MARY:
"A Case of Identity"
A large woman with a heavy fur boa round her neck, and a large curling red feather in a broad-brimmed slate-coloured straw hat which was tilted in a coquettish Duchess of Devonshire fashion over her ear. "Her jacket was black, with black beads sewn upon it, and a fringe of

little black jet ornaments. Her dress was brown, rather darker than coffee colour, with a little purple plush at the neck and sleeves. Her gloves were grayish and were worn through at the right forefinger. She had small round, hanging gold earrings, and a general air of being fairly well-to-do in a vulgar, comfortable, easy-going way." Lives at "no. 31 Lyon Place, Camberwell." She is involved in a love matter where she is not so angry as perplexed or grieved. She is near-sighted and has been doing much typing. Her father was a plumber in the Tottenham Court Road and he left a tidy business behind him [when he died] which [her] mother carried on with Mr. Hardy, the foreman." She sold the business when Mr. Windibank came along. Her own income is derived from stocks left to her by her uncle Ned, she can only touch the interest. She is "engaged" to one HOSMER ANGEL who has disappeared. She met him at the "gasfitters' ball."

"The Adventure of The Blue Carbuncle"
>Mentioned in passing.

"The Adventure of the Copper Beeches"
>Mentioned in passing.

SUTRO, MR.:
>"The Adventure of the Three Gables"
>>Lawyer for Mrs. Mary Maberley, he lives in Harrow.

SUTTON:
>"The Resident Patient"
>>One of the Worthingdon Bank Gang, after their arrest, he turned traitor and testified against the other four. He changed his name in an attempt to hide from his 'old gang' to Blessington.
>>AKA Blessington, See Blessington.

SWEDISH PATHOLOGICAL SOCIETY:
>"The Hound of the Baskervilles"
>>Dr. J. Mortimer is a corresponding member.

SWINDON, ARCHIE:
>>"The Valley of Fear"   Part 2: "The Scowrers"
>>Ran a mine business in Vermissa Valley but sold out
>>rather than pay the 'Scowrers' any money to leave him
>>alone.

SWITZERLAND:
>"The Adventure of the Final Problem"
>>Site of the Reichenbach Falls. Holmes and Watson flee
>>Moriarty from England to Switzerland and it is here that
>>Holmes and Professor Moriarty fall into the Falls.

SYDENHAM:
>"The Adventure of the Norwood Builder"
>>Location of Deep Dene House in Lower Norwood.

>"The Adventure of the Abbey Grange"
>>Located near the town of Kent. Location of the
>>residence of Mr. Jack Crocker.

SYLVIUS, NEGRETTO:
>"The Adventure of the Mazarin Stone"
>>Count Negretto Sylvius, of 136 Moorside Gardens, has
>>stolen the Crown Diamond. He is a famous game-shot,
>>sportsman, and man-about-town. A big, swarthy fellow,
>>he had a dark moustache with a cruel, thin-lipped mouth,
>>and a long curved nose like the beak of an eagle.

CHAPTER T

TADPOLE:
> "The Naval Treaty"
>> Nickname for Percy Phelps.
>> See Phelps, Percy

TANG:
> "The Adventure of the Illustrious Client"
>> Baron Gruner shows Dr. Hill Barton, Watson in disguise, a little specimen from the seventh century.

TANG-YING:
> "The Adventure of the Illustrious Client"
>> Watson studies Chinese Pottery in preparation for a disguised meeting with Baron Gruner about the sale of a genuine eggshell pottery saucer of the Ming dynasty. In this quest he studies the writings of the Tang-ying.

TANGEY, MR.:
> "The Naval Treaty"
>> Commissionaire at the Foreign Office. Lives at 16 Ivy Lane, Brixton with his wife and daughter. He is an old soldier, had been a member of the Coldstream Guards.

TANGEY, MRS.:
> "The Naval Treaty"
>> Wife of the Foreign Office commissionaire, tall and elderly, she lives at 16 Ivy Lane, Brixton. She also works at the Foreign Office. She is a bad lot and a drinker.

TAPANULI FEVER:
> "The Adventure of the Dying Detective"
>> An Eastern disease.

TARLETON:
> "The Musgrave Ritual"
>> An unrecorded case. Case of the Tarleton murders.

TAVERNIER:
> "The Adventure of the Mazarin Stone"
>> French modeller, very good at waxworks, he the facsimile of Holmes that sits in a chair by the window.

TEDDY:
> "The Crooked Man"
>> A beautiful reddish-brown creature, thin and lithe, with legs of a stoat, a long, thin nose, and a pair of the finest red eyes that were ever in an animals head -- a mongoose. A pet belonging to Henry Wood.

TELEGRAPH:
> "Silver Blaze"
>> Newspaper in London, maybe the same as "The Daily Telegraph."

THAMES:
> "The Adventure of the Cardboard Box"
>> River port in England, scene where Jim Browner is arrested by Lestrade.

THIRD BUFFS:
> "The Sign of Four"
>> Jonathan Small was a member of this military unit when it was sent to India.

THOR BRIDGE:
> "The Problem of Thor Bridge"
>> A single broad span of stone with balustraded sides, carries the drive over the narrowest part of a deep, reed-girt sheet of water to the estate of Neil Gibson,

Thor Place, Hampshire.

THOR PLACE:
"The Problem of Thor Bridge"
In Hampshire, it is the estate of Mr. Neil Gibson. A widespread, half-timbered house, half Tudor and half Georgian, sitting upon the crest of a hill.

THORSLEY:
"The Hound of the Baskervilles"
A parish in the area of Dartmoor.

THREADNEEDLE STREET:
"The Man With The Twisted Lip"
Location where professional beggar Hugh Boone plied his trade.
See Hugh Boone.

"The Adventure of the Beryl Coronet"
In London, location of the banking firm of Holder & Stevenson.

THE THREE GABLES:
"The Adventure of the Three Gables"
Home of Mary Maberley, it is a brick and timber villa, standing in its own acre of undeveloped grassland. Three small projections above the upper windows made a feeble attempt to justify its name. Mary Maberley has lived here for more than a year.

THREE MONTHS IN THE JUNGLE:
"The Adventure of the Empty House"
Authored by Colonel Sebastian Moran.

THUCYDIDES:
> "The Adventure of the Three Students"
>> Students partaking of the Fortescue Scholarship examination will be required to translate a half a chapter of Thucydides.

TIBET:
> "The Adventure of the Empty House"
>> Where Homes travels for two years after his fight with Professor Moriarty at the Reichenbach Falls.

TIMES:
> "The Sign of Four"
>> London newspaper containing an advertisement asking for the address of Mary Morstan and asking her to come forward.

> "The Hound of the Baskervilles"
>> London newspaper from which words are cut and pasted together to send a message to Sir Henry Baskerville at the Northumberland Hotel. Holmes remarks that "a Times leader [print] is entirely distinctive." One could not confuse it with another newspaper.

> "The Adventure of the Solitary Cyclist"
>> London newspaper, contained an advertisement, in December 1884, inquiring as to the whereabouts of the Smith Family, in particular, the Miss Violet Smith Family.

> "The Adventure of the Missing Three-quarter"
>> English newspaper.

> "His Last Bow" "An Epilogue of Sherlock Holmes"
>> English newspaper.

TOBACCO:

"The Boscombe Valley Mystery"

Holmes informs Watson that he has dedicated some time in the study of different varieties of pipe, cigar, and cigarette tobacco and their ashes.

TOBY:

"The Sign of Four"

A dog owned by Sherman residing at No. 7. He was an ugly, long-haired, lop-eared creature, with a very clumsy, waddling gait.

TODMAN:

"The Valley of Fear", Part 2: "The Scowrers"

Sold his mining operation to the State & Merton County Railroad Company instead of paying the 'Scowrers' to leave him alone.

TOLLER:

"The Adventure of the Copper Beeches"

One of the servants, the groom, the other being his wife, for the Rucastle's at the Copper Beeches. A rough, uncouth man, with grizzled hair and whiskers, and a perpetual smell of drink. His wife is a very tall and strong woman with a sour face. A most unpleasant couple.

TONGA:

"The Sign of Four"

An aborigine from the Andaman Islands, murderer of Major Sholto. Faithful mate to Jonathan Small, helped him escape Andaman Island, was a fine boatman.

TOPEKA:
>The Adventure of the Three Garridebs"
>>City in Kansas, U.S.A. where John Garrideb met
>>Alexander Hamilton Garrideb.

TOSCA, CARDINAL:
>"The Adventure of Black Peter"
>>An unrecorded case handled by Holmes in 1895,
>>involving the sudden death of the Cardinal, at the express
>>desire of His Holiness the Pope.

TOTTENHAM COURT ROAD:
>"A Case of Identity"
>>Location of Miss Mary Sutherland's father's plumbing
>>business.

>"The Adventure of The Blue Carbuncle"
>>See Peterson.

>"The Adventure of the Cardboard Box"
>>Street in London, location of a Jew's Broker from which
>>Holmes purchases a 'Stradivarius' for 55 shillings
>>knowing the instrument to be worth 500 guineas.

TRAFALGAR SQUARE:
>"The Hound of the Baskervilles"
>>Location where John Clayton picked up his passenger,
>>the passenger requesting he be taken to the
>>Northumberland Hotel and then following the cab of
>>two gentleman.

TRAVISTOCK:
>"Silver Blaze"
>>Lies two miles to the west of Dartmoor.

THE TREATY:

"The Naval Treaty"

Defined the position of Great Britian towards the Triple Alliance, and foreshadowed the policy which Britian would pursue in the event of a French fleet gaining a complete ascendency over that of Italy in the Mediterranean. It was a Naval Treaty. It was a long document, written in French, and containing twenty-six separate articles. French and Russian embassies would be very interested in obtaining a copy of the treaty.

TREDANNICK WARTHA:

"The Adventure of the Devil's Foot"

Family home to the Tregennis's, Owen, George, Brenda, and Mortimer. It was the scene of the horrible death of Brenda, and insanity of Owen and George.

TREDANNICK WOLLAS:

"The Adventure of the Devil's Foot"

A hamlet in Cornwall where the cottages of a couple hundred inhabitants cluster around an ancient, moss-covered church.

TREGELLIS, JANET:

"The Musgrave Ritual"

Daughter of the head game-keeper at the Manor House of Hurlstone, home to the Musgraves. She took up with the Butler, Richard Brunton, after he had broken off his engagement to the second housemaid, Rachel Howells.

TREGENNIS, BRENDA:

"The Adventure of the Devil's Foot"

She had been a very beautiful girl, though now reaching middle-age, her dark, clear-cut face was still very handsome. She had played cards with her brothers dying at the table sometime after half-past ten that evening.

TREGENNIS, GEORGE:

"The Adventure of the Devil's Foot"

He was involved in the family business, tin-miners at
Redruth, until the company was sold. Elder brother of
Owen and Mortimer Tregennis, he is discovered in a state
of insanity the morning after having played cards with his
two brothers and sister in their family house, Tredannick
Wartha. He is taken with Owen to Helston to be looked
after.

TREGENNIS, MORTIMER:

"The Adventure of the Devil's Foot"

An independent gentleman, he was thin, dark, spectacled,
with a stoop which gave the impression of a physical
deformity. He lodged with the vicar, Mr. Roundhay. His
money came from the family business, tin-mining, which
was sold profitably. He had two brothers, Owen and
George, and a sister Brenda. There had been a family
quarrel and Mortimer was on the outside for some time,
but it appeared to have been settled. He had played cards
with them, at the family home, Tredannick Wartha, the
night of the horrible incident, which claimed the life of
his sister and caused insanity in his two brothers. He dies
in much the same fashion as his sister shortly thereafter.
He had quizzed Dr. Leon Sterndale on the qualities of
'devil's root' and stole some of the doctors specimen
which he used to kill his sister and injure his brothers.
Dr. Sterndale retaliates with some of the poison to bring
about the death of Mortimer.

THE TREPOFF MURDER:

"A Scandal in Bohemia"

An unrecorded case. Holmes summoned to Odessa.

TREVELYAN, DR. PERCY:
> "The Resident Patient"
>> Lives at 403 Brook Street, he is the author of a monograph upon obscure nervous lesions. He is a pale, taper-faced man with sandy whiskers, about 34 or 35 years old, although his haggard expression and unhealthy hue told of a life which had sapped his strength and robbed him of his youth. Graduated from London University and from there devoted himself to research, occupying a minor position in King's College Hospital. His research dealt with the pathology of catalepsy and he won the 'Bruce Pinkerton' prize and metal for his monograph on nervous lesions. He takes up professional consulting in the Cavendish Square quarter with the help of one Blessington who provides the house, maid, cook and a page.

TREVOR, JUSTICE OF THE PEACE:
> "The 'Gloria Scott'"
>> See "Justice of the Peace Trevor"

TRINITY COLLEGE:
> "The Adventure of the Missing Three-quarter"
>> Located in Cambridge, has a first rate rugby team coached by Cyril Overton.

TRIPLE ALLIANCE:
> "The Naval Treaty"
>> See 'The Treaty'

TRUMPINGTON:
> "The Adventure of the Missing Three-quarter"
>> A village in England near where Dr. Leslie Armstrong has a lonely cottage which he provided for use by Godfrey Staunton and his wife.

TUNBRIDGE WELLS:
> "The Adventure of Black Peter"
>> Train Station with trains to London, located ten miles from Woodman's Lee, Forest Row.
>
> "The Valley of Fear", Part 1: "The Tragedy of Birlstone"
>> Ten to twelve miles east of Birlstone in the county of Kent.

TURNER, ALICE:
> "The Boscombe Valley Mystery"
>> Daughter of John Turner, 18 years old, "most lovely young woman that I have ever seen in my life" (Watson), violet eyes, parted lips, pink flush upon her cheeks. James McCarthy and Alice were like brother and sister and it was the elder McCarthy's wish that they should marry - neither Alice nor James believed they were ready to do so.

TURNER, JOHN:
> "The Boscombe Valley Mystery"
>> Murderer of Charles McCarthy, but due to his declining health, Holmes lets him off. Made his money in Australia, in the gold mines, returning to the "old country" some years ago, largest landed proprietor in Boscombe Valley. He also owns the farm, Hatherley, which he lets to one Charles McCarthy. After McCarthy's death, he has been seeing Dr. Willows, his nervous system being shattered.
>>
>> "a strange and impressive figure, slow limping step and bowed shoulders but his hard, deep-lined, craggy features, and his enormous limbs showed that he was possessed of unusual strength of body and character. His tangled beard, grizzled hair, and outstanding drooping eyebrows combined to give an air of dignity and power to

his appearance, but his face was of an ashen white, while his lips and the corners of his nostrils were tinged with a shade of blue. He was obviously in the grip of some deadly and chronic disease."

Has one daughter, his wife having died soon after the birth of the girl. He dies seven months after the case is solved by Holmes.

AKA Black Jack of Ballarat (See Charles McCarthy)

TURNER, MRS.:
"A Scandal in Bohemia"
As per Watson: "our landlady".

TURPEY STREET:
"The Hound of the Baskervilles"
Located in the Borough where Jon Clayton lives, he the cab driver of can N0. 2704.

TUSON, SERGEANT:
"The Stock-Broker's Clerk"
Of the City police, he captures Beddington, with the help of Constable Pollock, just after the robbery and murder at Mawson & William's.

TUSSAUD, MADAME:
"The Adventure of the Mazarin Stone"
Sam Merton states: "A fake, is it? Well, strike me! Madame Tussaud ain't in it. It's the living spit of him, gown and all." In reference to the wax model of Holmes made by Travernier.

May be a reference to the Asiatic silkworm, tussah, and its cocoon.

TUXBURY OLD HALL:

"The Adventure of the Blanched Soldier"

Home to Colonel Emsworth, it is inaccessible, five miles from anywhere. A great wandering house, it stands in a considerable park and is of all sorts of ages and styles. The house begins on a half-timbered Elizabethian foundation and ends in a Victorian portico. Inside it is all panelling and tapestry and half-effaced old pictures, a house of shadows and mystery.

TYBURN TREE:

"The Adventure of the Three Garridebs"

Of evil memory, it is within a short distance from Little Ryder Street.

UBANGI COUNTRY:
"The Adventure of the Devil's Foot"
Area of Africa where the great lion-hunter Dr. Leon
Sterndale obtained some 'devil's foot,' a very powerful
poison.

UND ZU GRAFENSTEIN, COUNT VON:
"His Last Bow"
"An Epilogue of Sherlock Holmes"
Holmes informs the German spy, Von Bork, that his
capture is not Holmes's first involvement with Von
Bork's family. It was Holmes who saved from murder,
by the Nihilist Klopman, Count Von und Zu
Grafenstein, Von Bork's mother's elder brother.

UNION BAR:
"The Valley of Fear" Part 2: "The Scowrers"
Bar at the Union House where dozens of men will swear
Ted Baldwin, John McMurdo, the two Willabys, Mansel,
Mike Scanlan, and Gower were during the attack on
James Stanger of the "Vermissa Herald."

UNION HOUSE:
"The Valley of Fear" Part 2: "The Scowrers"
Located in Vermissa it is the headquarters of the
Vermissa Lodge 341, Eminent Order of Freemen, Jack
McGinty, Bodymaster. It was a saloon which rose almost
to the dignity of being a hotel. During the reign of Black
Jack McGinty, it grew in size, almost swallowing-up one
whole side of Market Square.

UNRECORDED CASES:

Unrecorded Cases are those which Sherlock Holmes undertook either while separated from   Dr. Watson or which Watson saw fit not to report in his chronicles. Many are mentioned simply in passing, others are given some particular detail. In any event, all references are listed and where detail exist it is included.

* ABBEY SCHOOL:

"The Adventure of the Blanched Soldier"

Holmes was clearing this case up when James Dodd requested he look into the strange disappearance of Godfrey Emsworth. Holmes notes that Watson wrote of this case in which the Duke of Greyminster was so deeply involved.

* ABERGAVENNY MURDER:

"The Adventure of the Priory School"

Holmes must remain in London due to the upcoming Abergavenny murder trial, and only a very important issue could call him away from London at this time.

* ADDLETON TRAGEDY:

"The Adventure of the Golden Pince-Nez"

No details are provided.

* ADVENTURE OF "GRACE PATERSONS":

"The Five Orange Pips"

Took place in the island of Uffa

* ADVENTURE OF THE OLD RUSSIAN WOMAN:

"The Musgrave Ritual"

No details are provided.

* **THE ADVENTURE OF THE PARADOL CHAMBER**:
  "The Five Orange Pips"
  No details are provided.

* **AFFAIR OF THE ALUMINUM CRUTCH**:
  "The Musgrave Ritual"
  A singular affair.

* **AFFAIR OF THE VATICAN CAMEOS**:
  "The Hound of the Baskervilles"
  Holmes assist the Pope.

* **ALICIA**:
  "The Problem of Thor Bridge"
  A problem without a solution. The cutter sailed one morning into a small patch of mist and never emerged, neither the cutter nor her crew were ever heard from again.

* **THE AMATEUR MENDICANT SOCIETY**:
  "The Five Orange Pips"
  Held a luxurious club in the lower vault of furniture warehouse.

* **ANDOVER `77**:
  "A Case of Identity"
  Holmes mentions a parallel case to that of Miss Mary Sutherland's.

* **ARNSWORTH CASTLE BUSINESS**:
  "A Scandal in Bohemia"
  No details are provided.

* THE ATKINSON BROTHERS:

>"A Scandel in Bohemia"
>>Holmes investigated the singular tragedy of the
>>Atkinson Brothers at Trincomalee.

* BISHOPGATE:

>"The Sign of Four"
>>A jewelry case in which Holmes assist the police.

* BRITISH BARROW:

>"The Adventure of the Golden Pince-Nez"
>>Took place in 1894, it involved the singular
>>contents of the ancient British barrow.

* THE CAMBERWELL POISONING:

>"The Five Orange Pips"
>>Holmes was able, by winding up the dead man's
>>watch, to prove that it had been wound up two
>>hours before, and that the deceased had gone to
>>bed within that time -- a deduction which was of
>>the greatest importance in clearing up the case.

* COPTIC PATRIARCHS:

>"The Adventure of the Retired Colourman"
>>It involves two Coptic Patriachs of the Coptic
>>Church which is native Christian Church of
>>Egypt and Ethiopia.

* CROSBY:

>"The Adventure of the Golden Pince-Nez"
>>Took place in 1894, and concerned the terrible
>>death of Crosby, the banker.

* DARLINGTON SUBSTITUTION SCANDAL:

>"A Scandal in Bohemia"
>>No details are provided.

* DOWSON, BARON:
"The Adventure of the Mazarin Stone"

Old Baron Dowson told Holmes that "what the law had gained the stage had lost" in complimenting Holmes on his impersonations. The Baron was hanged shortly thereafter.

* THE DUDAS SEPARATION CASE:
"A Case of Identity"

Holmes engaged in clearing up some small points. "The husband was a teetotaler, there was no other woman, and the conduct complained of was that he had drifted into the habit of winding up every meal by taking out his false teeth and hurling them at his wife, which, you will allow, is not an action likely to occur to the imagination of the average story-teller."

* THE ETHEREGE CASE:
"A Case of Identity"

Mrs. Etherege's husband had disappeared and the police and everyone else had given him up for dead, but Holmes found him easily.

* FARINTOSH:
"The Adventure of the Speckled-Band"

Mrs. Farintosh gave Holmes' address to Helen Stoner. He had helped Mrs. Farintosh in her hour of need. The Farintosh case concerned an opal tiara, apparently before Watson's time.

* **FERRERS DOCUMENTS**:
  "The Adventure of the Priory School"
  > Holmes is currently involved in this case when his assistance is requested in "The Adventure of the Priory School."

* **Mrs. CECIL FORRESTER**:
  "The Sign of Four"
  > A domestic complication.

* **FRENCH REPUBLIC**:
  "The Final Problem"
  > Holmes is engaged by the French government upon a matter of supreme importance during 1890.

* **FRIESLAND**:
  "The Adventure of the Norwood Builder"
  > Involved the shocking affair of the Dutch steamship, Friesland. Took place just after Watson returned to Baker Street after having been away during his marriage.

* **GROSVENOR SQUARE**:
  "The Adventure of the Noble Bachelor"
  > Little problem involving a furniture van.

* **THE HAGUE**:
  "A Case of Identity"
  > Holmes mentions a parallel case to that of Miss Mary Sutherland's.

* **HARDEN, JOHN VINCENT**:
    "The Adventure of the Solitary Cyclist"
    A very abstruse and complicated problem
    concerning the peculiar persecution of the well
    known tobacco millionaire.

* **Le VILLARD, FRANCOIS**:
    "The Sign of Four"
    French detective who is helped by Holmes, the
    case involved a will, he is also translating some of
    Holmes' monographs from English to French.

* **THE LOSS OF THE "SOPHY ANDERSON"**:
    "The Five Orange Pips"
    A British bark

* **LYNCH, VICTOR**:
    "The Adventure of the Sussex Vampire"
    A forger, his name is listed under the "V's" in
    Holmes's index. May be an unrecorded case or
    simply accumulated information for reference.

* **MABERLEY, MORTMER**:
    "The Adventure of the Three Gables"
    One of Holmes's early clients, his widow
    consults Holmes in the strange matter of the
    proposed sale and eventual burglary of her home.

* **MANOR HOUSE CASE**:
    "The Greek Interpreter"
    The guilty party is a man named Adams.
    Mycroft Holmes, Sherlock's brother, believed
    Sherlock would have consulted him, Sherlock
    being out of his depth.

*** MAJOR PRENDERGAST AND THE
    TANKERVILLE SCANDAL**:
> "The Five Orange Pips"
>> The Major was wrongfully accused of cheating at cards and was saved by Holmes.

* MARGATE:
> "The Adventure of the Second Stain"
>> Holmes suspected a woman at Margate for the same reason he questions Lady Hilda Trelawney Hope's visit to Baker Street. Holmes states: "the motives of women are so inscrutable."

* MATHEWS:
> "The Adventure of the Empty House"
>> He knocked out Holmes's left canine in the waiting-room at Charing Cross.

* MATILDA BRIGGS:
> "The Adventure of the Sussex Vampire"
>> Holmes assisted the firm of Morrison, Morrison, and Dodd, machinery assessors, in this matter. Matilda Briggs was a ship and it was associated with the giant rat of Sumatra. Holmes notes that the world is not yet prepared for this story.

* MERRIDEW:
> "The Adventure of the Empty House"
>> Of abominable memory, contained in Holmes 'index of biographies' under the letter "M".

* MISSION OF HOLLAND:
> "A Scandel in Bohemia"
>> Holmes accomplished a matter delicately and successfully for the reigning family of Holland.

* MME. MONTPENSIER:

"The Hound of the Baskervilles"

Holmes defends Mme. Montpensier from a charge of murder which hung over her in connection with the death of her step-daughter, Mlle. Carere, who was discovered six months later alive and married in New York. Takes place right after "The Hound of the Baskervilles."

* MORGAN:

"The Adventure of the Empty House"

The poisoner, contained in Holmes 'index of biographies' under the letter "M".

* EX-PRESIDENT MURILLO:

"The Adventure of the Norwood Builder"

A case which involved the papers of ex-President Murillo, it having taken place soon after Watson's return to Baker Street sometime after his marriage.

* NONPAREIL CLUB:

"The Hound of the Baskervilles"

Holmes exposes the atrocious conduct of Colonel Upwood in connection with the famous card scandal of the Nonpareil Club. Takes place right after "The Hound of the Baskervilles."

* PERSANO, ISADORE:

"The Problem of Thor Bridge"

A problem without a solution. He was a well known journalist and duelist, he was found stark staring mad with a match box in front of him which contained a remarkable worm said to be unknown to science.

* **PHILLIMORE, JAMES**:
>"The Problem of Thor Bridge"
>>A problem without a solution. He stepped back into his own house to get his umbrella and was never seen again.

* **RED LEECH**:
>"The Adventure of the Golden Pince-Nez"
>>Took place in 1894, it was a very repulsive story.

* **RICOLETTI**:
>"The Musgrave Ritual"
>>A full account of Ricoletti of the club-foot, and his abominable wife.

* **ST. PANCRAS**:
>"The Adventure of Shoscombe Old Place"
>>Not actually one of Holmes's but one Merivale of Scotland Yard ask Holmes to look into. A cap was found beside a dead policeman, however, the accused denied that he was his. Holmes, using his microscope, is able to determine that threads from a tweed coat reveal gray masses of dust, epithelial scales and blobs, in the center, which are glue. The presence of glue is important because the accused is a picture-frame maker who habitually handles glue and Holmes has found glue in the tweed cap linking the accused to the crime.

* **SCANDINAVIAN ROYAL FAMILY**:
>"The Final Problem"
>>Holmes is of assistance to the royal family of Scandinavia during 1890.

* **STAMFORD, ARCHIE**:
    "The Adventure of the Solitary Cyclist"
        The Forger captured by Holmes and Watson near Farnham.

* **SULTAN OF TURKEY**:
    "The Adventure of the Blanched Soldier"
        Holmes notes that this case is presently pressing and immediate action is necessary as political consequences of the gravest kind might arise from its neglect.

* **TARLETON**:
    "The Musgrave Ritual"
        Case of the Tarleton murders.

* **THE TREPOFF MURDER**:
    "A Scandel in Bohemia"
        Holmes summoned to Odessa.

* **VAMBERRY**:
    "The Musgrave Ritual"
        Vamberry was a wine merchant.

* **VAMPIRES IN TRANSYLVANIA**:
    "The Adventure of the Sussex Vampire"
        May be an unrecorded case or simply accumulated information for reference.

* **VAMPIRISM IN HUNGARY**:
    "The Adventure of the Sussex Vampire"
        May be an unrecorded case or simply accumulated information for reference.

* VANDERBILT AND THE YEGGMAN:

"The Adventure of the Sussex Vampire"

An unrecorded case which Holmes has noted in his giant index.

* VENOMOUS LIZARD:

"The Adventure of the Sussex Vampire"

This case, which involved a venomous lizard or gila. Holmes notes it was a remarkable case.

* VIGOR:

"The Adventure of the Sussex Vampire"

The Hammersmith wonder. May be an unrecorded case or simply accumulated information for reference.

* VITTORIA:

"The Adventure of the Sussex Vampire"

The circus belle. May be an unrecorded case or simply accumulated information for reference.

* COLONEL WARBURTON'S MADNESS:

"The Adventure of the Engineer's Thumb"

One of two cases Watson introduced to Holmes.

* WILSON MATTER:

"The Hound of the Baskervilles"

Mr. Wilson, manager of the district messenger office is helped by Holmes who saves Wilson's good name and perhaps his life. One of the messenger boys, Cartwright, helps Holmes out during his investigation.

"UPON THE DISTINCTION BETWEEN THE ASHES OF THE VARIOUSTOBACCOS":

"The Sign of Four"

Monograph written by Holmes. He enumerates a hundred and forty forms of cigar, cigarette, and pipe tobacco, with colored plates illustrating the difference in the ash.

UPPER SWANDAM LANE:

"The Man With The Twisted Lip"

A vile alley lurking behind the high wharfs which line the north side of the river to the east of London Bridge.

UPPINGHAM:

"The Adventure of the Golden Pince-Nez"

Town in England, Willoughby Smith grew up there.

CHAPTER V

THE VALLEY OF FEAR:

Published in "The Strand": September 1914 thru May 1915

Is written in two parts:

Part 1 - "The Tragedy of Birlstone"

Holmes is called upon to investigate the death of a man at his home in Sussex. Holmes is able to determine that the dead man isn't whom they are told he is and that Moriarty is involved.

Although Moriarty is foiled at first, the Epilogue informs us that he has succeeded in the end.

Part 2 - "The Scowrers"

This section of the book takes the reader to the coal fields of Pennsylvania and the wars between the mine owners and the criminal brotherhood, The Scowrers. It begins in February 1875 and the tie-in between Part 1 and Part 2 lies in the undercover detective who becomes a Scowrer so as to bring the criminals to justice. It is this detective which Moriarty hunts on behalf of his American friends.

VALLEY OF FEAR:

"The Valley of Fear" Part 1: "The Tragedy of Birlstone"

Vermissa Valley, coal mining fields in America. See Vermissa.

VAMBERRY:

"The Musgrave Ritual"

An unrecorded case. Vamberry was a wine merchant.

VAMPIRES IN TRANSYLVANIA:
"The Adventure of the Sussex Vampire"
>
> May be an unrecorded case or simply accumulated information for reference.

VAMPIRISM IN HUNGARY:
"The Adventure of the Sussex Vampire"
>
> May be an unrecorded case or simply accumulated information for reference.

VAN DEHER:
"The Valley of Fear" Part 2: "The Scowrers"
>
> Sold his ironworks operation to West Gilmerton General Mining Company instead of paying the 'Scowrers' to leave him alone.

VAN SEDDAR:
"The Adventure of the Mazarin Stone"
>
> Jeweler in Amsterdam who is willing to cut the Crown Diamond into four pieces for further sale.

VAN SHORST:
"The Valley of Fear" Part 2: "The Scowrers"
>
> Allegedly murdered by the Scowrers.

VANDELEUR, MR.:
"The Hound of the Baskervilles"
>
> Ran St. Oliver's private school in York with his wife, Holmes has obtained a photo of the two of them. AKA Stapleton.

VANDELEUR, MRS.:
"The Hound of the Baskervilles"
>
> Ran St. Oliver's private school in York with her husband, Holmes has obtained a photo of the two of them. AKA Mrs. Stapleton.

VANDERBILT AND THE YEGGMAN:
"The Adventure of the Sussex Vampire"
An unrecorded case which Holmes has noted in his giant index.

VENNER & MATHESON:
"The Adventure of the Engineer's Thumb"
Well known engineering firm of Greenwich, where Victor Hatherley did his apprentice work for seven years.

VENOMOUS LIZARD:
"The Adventure of the Sussex Vampire"
An unrecorded case which involved a venomous lizard or Gila. Holmes notes that it was a remarkable case.

VENUCCI, PIETRO:
"The Adventure of the Six Napoleons"
Originally from Naples, he is one of the greatest cut-throats in London. He is connected with the Mafia. Found murdered on the doorstep of Horace Harker. Brother of Lucretia Venucci.

VENUCCI, LUCRETIA:
"The Adventure of the Six Napoleons"
Sister of Pietro Venucci. Maid to the Princess of Colonna. Suspicion fell upon her when the Borgias Pearl was first discovered to be 'lost.'

VERE STREET:
"The Final Problem"
London, a brick mysteriously falls from the roof nearly striking Holmes on the head. This incident occurs just after he is almost run down by a two-horse van at the corner of Welbeck Street and Bentinck Street.

VERMISSA:
>"The Valley of Fear" Part 1: "The Tragedy of Birlstone"
>>A flourishing little town at the head of one of the best known coal and iron valleys in the United States, it is the central township of Vermissa Valley.

VERMISSA VALLEY:
>"The Valley of Fear" Part 1: "The Tragedy of Birlstone"
>>See Vermissa, Valley of Fear.

VERNER, DR.:
>"The Adventure of the Norwood Builder"
>>Young doctor who purchases Dr. Watson's practice. Watson discovers that he is a distant relation of Holmes, and that Holmes found the money for him to make the purchase.

VERNET:
>"The Greek Interpreter"
>>French artist whose sister is Holmes' grandmother.

VERNON LODGE:
>"The Adventure of the Illustrious Client"
>>In Kingston, it is the home of Baron Gruner.

VIBART, JULES:
>"The Disappearance of Lady Frances Carfax"
>>Head waiter at the Hotel National, she becomes engaged to Mary Devine while she is maid to Lady Frances Carfax, who is staying at the Hotel.

VICTORIA:
>"Silver Blaze"
>>A train depot.

"The Valley of Fear"   Part 1: "The Tragedy of Birlstone"
Rail station Holmes, Watson and Inspector MacDonald
leave from to reach Birlstone.

"The Adventure of the Sussex Vampire"
Train station in London.

VICTORIA, AUSTRALIA:
"The Boscombe Valley Mystery"
Where Mr. Turner & Mr. McCarthy met, at the Gold
Mines.

VIGOR:
"The Adventure of the Sussex Vampire"
The Hammersmith wonder. May be an unrecorded case
or simply accumulated information for reference.

VIPERS:
"The Adventure of the Sussex Vampire"
Notation appears in Holmes's index concerning vipers.

VITTORIA:
"The Adventure of the Sussex Vampire"
The circus belle.   May be an unrecorded case or simply
accumulated information for reference.

VIXEN TOR:
"The Hound of the Baskervilles"
A high rocky hill visible from Baskerville Hall.

VON HERDER:
"The Adventure of the Empty House"
Blind German mechanic who constructed an admirable
and unique weapon, a powerful air-gun, on the order of
Professor Moriarty.

VON KRAMM, COUNT:
>"A Scandal in Bohemia"
>>See Bohemia, King of.

VOODOOISM AND THE NEGROID RELIGIONS:
>"The Adventure of Wisteria Lodge"
>aka "A Reminiscence of Mr. Sherlock Holmes"

>>Book authored by Eckermann and studied by Holmes
>>while in the British Museum in an attempt to discover the
>>background for the discovery of "the torn bird, the pail
>>of blood, the charred bones..." in the kitchen at Wisteria
>>Lodge.

CHAPTER W

WAGNER:
"The Adventure of the Red Circle"
> A playwright whose plays appear at Covent Garden. At the conclusion of this adventure, Holmes remarks that tonight is "Wagner night at Covent Garden" and he and Watson can make the second act.

WAINWRIGHT:
"The Adventure of the Illustrious Client"
> An accomplished artist, he was also an accomplished criminal with a complex mind, as most great criminals have.

WALDRON:
"The Adventure of the Three Garridebs"
> He vanished and nothing more has been heard of him for almost five years. He was tall, with a beard and very dark features. Very similar in appearance to Rodger Prescott.

WALKER BROTHERS:
"The Valley of Fear"   Part 2: "The Scowrers"
> Business in Vermissa Valley which pays protection money to the Vermissa Lodge, ('Eminent Order of Freemen,' "The Scowrers,") to be left alone.

WALSALL:
"The Adventure of the Copper Beeches"
> Town where Miss Violet Hunter becomes head of a private school after her ordeal at the Copper Beeches.

WALTER, JAMES:

"The Adventure of the Bruce-Partington Plans"

Sir James is the official guardian of the Bruce-Partington papers. He is a famous government expert whose decorations and sub-titles fill two lines of book reference. He is one of two people with a key to the safe which holds the Bruce-Partington papers. He has grown gray in the service, is a gentleman, a favoured guest in the most exalted houses, and above all, a man whose patriotism is beyond suspicion. Found dead within a few days of the disappearance of the Bruce-Partington papers.

WALTER, VALENTINE:

"The Adventure of the Bruce-Partington Plans"

Colonel Valentine Walter is the brother of Sir James Walter. He has testified that his brother left Woolwich at about three o'clock on the day the Bruce Partington papers were stolen. He is a very tall, handsome, light-bearded man of fifty, the younger brother of Sir James Walter. He had incurred substantial debt in the stock exchange and agreed to sell the Bruce-Partington papers to Hugo Oberstein so as to   pay off his debt. He is captured by Holmes, Watson, Mycroft, and Lestrade and confesses as well as agreeing to write a letter to Hugo Oberstein concerning additional papers so as to trap Hugo and recover the missing papers. He dies during the second year of his imprisonment.

WALTERS:

"The Adventure of Wisteria Lodge"
aka "A Reminiscence of Mr. Sherlock Holmes"

A policeman under Inspector Baynes.

WANDSWORTH COMMON:
>"The Greek Interpreter"
>>About a mile or so from Clapham Junction train depot. Where Mr. Melas is dropped off after his visit with Mr. Latimer, Mr. Melas, having been blindfolded knew not where he was.

COLONEL WARBURTON'S MADNESS:
>"The Adventure of the Engineer's Thumb"
>>An unrecorded case. One of two cases Watson introduced to Holmes.

WARDLAW, COLONEL:
>"Silver Blaze"
>>Owner of the race horse 'Pugilist' which was entered in the Wessex Cup race.

WARNER, JOHN:
>"The Adventure of Wisteria Lodge"
>aka "A Reminiscence of Mr. Sherlock Holmes"
>>Was the gardener at High Gable until fired by Mr. Henderson in a moment of temper.

WARREN, MR.:
>"The Adventure of the Red Circle"
>>Husband of Mrs. Warren, he is a timekeeper at Morton and Waylight's, in Tottenham Court Road. He was kidnapped by strangers on his way to work and dumped at Hampstead Heath from where he returned home by bus shaken and confused.

WARREN, MRS.:
>"The Adventure of the Red Circle"
>>Landlady of boarding house sent to Holmes by an old lodger who had had Holmes's help in the past. Mrs. Warren request Holmes assistance in investigating one of

her lodgers who has failed to leave his room for more than ten days. Her home is located in Great Orme Street, near the corner and it commands a view down Howe Street.

WARRENDER, MINNIE:
"The Adventure of the Mazarin Stone"
Miss Minnie Warrender's complete life history is in Holmes's hand and he asserts   that he can make something of it to Count Sylvius's dismay.

WATERBEACH:
"The Adventure of the Missing Three-quarter"
A sleepy hollow in England.

WATERLOO:
"The Adventure of the Solitary Cyclist"
Rail Station, trains arrive and depart for Farnham.

WATERLOO BRIDGE:
"The Five Orange Pips"
Location of the death of John Openshaw.

WATERLOO STATION:
"The Hound of the Baskervilles"
Train station where Dr. Mortimer meets the young Henry Baskerville after his arrival from Canada.

WATSON, MRS.:
"The Final Problem"
In Holmes final note to Watson, which Watson finds in Holmes' cigarette-case at the Reichenbach falls, Holmes ask Watson to "give my greetings to Mrs. Watson."
See Watson, John, See Marstan, Mary

WATT STREET CHAPEL:

"The Crooked Man"

Roman Catholic Church affiliation, connected with the 'Guild of St. George.'
AKA Watt Street Mission.

WATT STREET MISSION:

"The Crooked Man"

See Watt Street Chapel.

WEALD FOREST:

"The Valley of Fear"   Part 1: "The Tragedy of Birlstone"
Forest surrounding the village of Birlstone.

WEISS & COMPANY:

"Silver Blaze"

London company that makes knives. Its name was stamped upon a knife found by Holmes. The knife was a cataract knife with a very delicate blade devised for very delicate work.

WELBECK STREET:

"The Final Problem"

London, at the corner of Bentinck and Welbeck Street a two-horse van furiously driven, whizzed round and almost ran Holmes down. This incident occurs just prior to a brick falling from a building on Vere Street and almost striking Holmes on the head.

WESSEX CUP:

"Silver Blaze"

Trophy for horse-race in which the famous Silver Blaze is the favorite. The race is for four and five year olds and is a distance of one mile and five furlongs. Held in Winchester.

WEST, ARTHUR CADOGAN:

"The Adventure of the Bruce-Partington Plans"

A young man found dead on the Underground railway. He was twenty-seven years of age, unmarried, and a clerk at Woolwich Arsenal, a government employee. In his pocket was found seven papers on the secret Bruce-Partington submarine, three additional papers were missing. He was a straight and honest man, with a reputation as being hot-headed and impetuous. He had been with the service for ten years and his daily duties brought him into personal contact with the Bruce-Partington plans. He is originally suspected of stealing the plans and arranging to sell them to foreign agents.

WEST COALING COMPANY:

"The Valley of Fear" Part 2: "The Scowrers"

Business in Vermissa Valley which pays protection money to the Vermissa Lodge, ('Eminent Order of Freemen,' "The Scowrers,") to be left alone.

WEST GILMERTON GENERAL MINING COMPANY:

"The Valley of Fear" Part 2: "The Scowrers"

Purchased the ironworks of Mason, and of Shuman, and of Van Deher, and of Atwood when these businesses refused to pay any more monies to the 'Scowrer' to leave them alone.

WESTAWAY'S:

"The Adventure of the Copper Beeches"

A well known agency for governesses in the West End. Westaway being the name of the founder, it is really managed by a Miss Stoper. Miss Violet Hunter applies for work through this agency and is hired by Mr. Rucastle to serve as governess for his young son.

WESTBURY HOUSE:
> "The Adventure of the Noble Bachelor"
>> Furnished house at Lancaster Gate taken by Aloysius Doran, while visiting from America, prior to the marriage of his daughter to Lord St. Simon.

WESTBURY, VIOLET:
> "The Adventure of the Bruce-Partington Plans"
>> Miss Westbury was the fiancee of Arthur Cadogan West, a government employee working on the Bruce-Partington submarine plans. See West, Arthur Cadogan

WESTERN MORNING NEWS:
> "The Hound of the Baskervilles"
>> English newspaper (London), Holmes remarks that he once confused it with the Leeds Mercury due to the similarity of their print.

WESTHOUSE & MARBANK:
> "A Case of Identity"
>> The great claret importers located on Fenchurch Street. Business by which Mr. James Windibank was employed.

WESTMINSTER:
> "The Adventure of the Solitary Cyclist"
>> Location of the famous electricians, Morton & Kennedy.

WESTMINSTER BRIDGE:
> "The Disappearance of Lady Frances Carfax"
>> Holmes and Watson pass over the London bridge as they travel to Poultney Square.

WESTMINSTER ROAD:
> "The Disappearance of Lady Frances Carfax"
>> Street in London, home to Bovington's pawn shop.

WESTMORELAND:
> "The Hound of the Baskervilles"
>> James Desmond, relative of Sir Henry Baskerville, is a
>> clergyman here.

WESTPHAIL, MISS HONORIA:
> "The Adventure of the Speckled Band"
>> Aunt, maiden sister of Mrs. Stoner, lives near Harrow and
>> is visited by Helen and Julia Stoner on occasion.

WESTVILLE ARMS:
> "The Valley of Fear" Part 1: "The Tragedy of Birlstone"
>> Where Holmes and Watson stay while investigating the
>> murder of Mr. John Douglas in Birlstone.

WHITAKER'S ALMANAC:
> "The Valley of Fear" Part 1: "The Tragedy of Birlstone"
>> An almanac in common use in England. Holmes is able
>> to determine that a message from his spy, Fred Porlock,
>> can be deciphered through the use of the almanac.

WHITE, ABEL:
> "The Sign of Four"
>> An indigo-planter in India, he took an interest in
>> Jonathan Small and hired him on as an overseer for his
>> coolies. His plantation was a place called Muttra near the
>> border of the Northwest Provinces. He was killed in the
>> great Indian mutiny in India.

WHITE HART:
> "A Study in Scarlet"
>> A bar near Henrietta Street where a fight took place the
>> night the body of Enoch J. Drebber was discovered. The
>> fight occurred about 11 PM. It is along the beat of
>> Constable John Rance, the individual who discovered the
>> body of Mr. Drebber.

WHITE JASSAMINE:

"The Hound of the Baskervilles"

Holmes detects the odor of white jassamine on the note sent to Sir Henry Baskerville warning him to fear for his life. Holmes notes that there are seventy-five perfumes, which it is very necessary that a criminal expert should be able to distinguish from each other.

WHITEHALL:

"The Naval Treaty"

Connects with Charles Street at the offices of the foreign minister, the main door, from the building housing the foreign minister's offices, opens onto Whitehall.

"The Adventure of the Mazarin Stone"

Area of London from where the Crown Diamond was stolen.

WHITEHALL TERRACE:

"The Adventure of the Second Stain"

Home to Trelawney Hope.

WHITNEY, ELIAS:

"The Man With The Twisted Lip"

See Whitney, Isa.

WHITNEY, ISA:

"The Man With The Twisted Lip"

Brother of the late Elias Whitney, D.D., Principal of the Theological College of St. George's, was much addicted to opium. He was yellow faced, with drooping lids, and pinpoint pupils, a slave to the drug. Husband of Kate Whitney, friend to Dr. & Mrs. Watson.

WHITNEY, KATE:

> "The Man With The Twisted Lip"
>> Wife of Isa Whitney. Old friend and school companion of Dr. Watson's wife. A young timid woman.

WHITTINGTON, LADY ALICIA:

> "The Adventure of the Noble Bachelor"
>> One of the few invited guest at the marriage of Lord St. Simon and Hatty Doran

WIGGINS:

> "A Study in Scarlet"
>> One of the members of the "Baker Street division of the detective police force." As described by Watson: They are "a half a dozen of the dirtiest and most ragged street Arabs" he had ever seen. Holmes states "there's more work to be got out of one of those little beggars than out of a dozen of the force."

> "The Sign of Four"
>> Lieutenant in Holmes' Baker Street Irregulars.

WIGMORE STREET POST-OFFICE:

> "The Sign of Four"
>> Post Office where Watson has visited to send a telegram, his travel to Baker Street results in his picking up some red-clay which Holmes is able to deduce came from the area of the Post Office much to the surprise of Watson.

WILCOX, CHESTER:

> "The Valley of Fear" Part 2: "The Scowrers"
>> An attempt to kill him by the 'Scowrers' resulted in the death of a 'Scowrers's, Jim Carnaway. His position is as chief foreman of the Iron Duke Company. He's a hard man, an old color sergeant, all scars and grizzle. He lives at Marley Creek at the Iron Dike crossroad. John

McMurdo, Manders, and Reilly are sent by Boss McGinty to settle the matter which failed earlier. Unfortunately for McMurdo and gang, Wilcox was tipped-off about the attack and moved himself and family to safer quarters before McMurdo could strike. Nevertheless, it was reported in all the newspapers that Wilcox was shot and it was widely believed that McMurdo was following up on his 'job.'

WILD, JONATHAN:

"The Valley of Fear" Part 1: "The Tragedy of Birlstone"
A master criminal who lived in 1750 or there about, he was the hidden force of the London criminals to whom he sold his brains and his organization for a fifteen percent commission.

WILDER, JAMES:

"The Adventure of the Priory School"
Secretary to the Duke of Holdernesse. He kidnaps Lord Saltire with the help of Reuben Hayes. He is the illegitimate son of the Duke of Holdernesse, his mother has died and he is seeking to eliminate his half-brother so as to inherit his father's fortunes.

WILHELM GOTTSREICH SIGISMOND VON ORMSTEIN:

"A Scandal in Bohemia"
Grand Duke of Cassel-Felstein, and hereditary King of Bohemia. Is about to be married "To Clotilde Lothmon von Saxe-Meningen, second daughter of the King of Scandinavia" "A Case of Identity" Mentioned in passing. "The Adventure of the Copper Beeches" Mentioned in passing. AKA: Count von Kramm, See Von Kramm, Count.

WILLABY:
> "The Valley of Fear"   Part 2: "The Scowrers"
>> The two Willaby brothers join Ted Baldwin, Mansel, Scanlan, Gower and John McMurdo in 'warning' the "Vermissa Herald" editor/owner James Stanger to curb his stories on the 'Scowrers.' One of the brothers, Arthur, stands guard at the door to the newspaper offices with John McMurdo.   He is one of the seven chosen to capture the Pinkerton man, Birdy Edwards. He was arrested by Captain Marvin and Birdy Edwards while waiting with his comrades to capture Edwards and kill him.

WILLABY, ARTHUR:
> "The Valley of Fear" Part 2: "The Scowrers"
>> During the 'warning' provided to James Stanger, owner/editor of the "Vermissa Herald", Arthur Willaby and John McMurdo stood guard at the door to the newspaper office to make sure the road was kept clear for the getaway. He is one of the seven chosen to capture the Pinkerton man, Birdy Edwards.   He was arrested by Captain Marvin and Birdy Edwards while waiting with his comrades to capture Edwards and kill him.

WILLESDEN:
> "The Adventure of the Bruce-Partington Plans"
>> Train service to Aldgate Station, it is an outlying junction from London.

WILLIAMS:
> "The Sign of Four"
>> Drove the carriage with Holmes, Watson, and Mary Marstan to meet Thaddeus Sholto. Was once light-weight champion of England and one of two body-guards to Major Sholto. Became servant to Thaddeus Sholto upon death of Major Sholto.

WILLIAMS, CHARLIE:

"The Valley of Fear" Part 2: "The Scowrers"
Individual killed by Lawler and Andrews in the past.

WILLIAMS, JAMES BAKER:

"The Adventure of Wisteria Lodge"
aka "A Reminiscence of Mr. Sherlock Holmes"
Mr. Williams resides at 'Forton Old Hall' which is located along the road between Wisteria Lodge and Oxshott.

WILLIAMSON:

"The Adventure of the Solitary Cyclist"
A white-bearded man, he lives alone with a small staff of servants at Charlington Hall. His career has been a singularly dark one and he was at one time a clergyman. He rents Charlington Hall as part of the conspiracy with Woodely and Carruthers. Performs marriage ceremony binding Roaring Jack Woodley and Miss Violet Smith. Tried for abduction and assault, he was sentenced to seven years. He calls Holmes: "Mr. Busybody Holmes"

Dr. WILLOWS:

"The Boscombe Valley Mystery"
Mr. John Turner's Doctor.

WILSON:

"The Hound of the Baskervilles"
Manager of the district messenger office. Holmes had assisted him in the past.

WILSON:

"The 'Gloria Scott'"
Disguised as a chaplain, he buys the conspiracy of the crew sailing the 'Gloria Scott', a prisoner transport, to

over-throw the captain and soldiers, with the resulting freedom of the convicts.

WILSON:
"The Adventure of Black Peter"
An unrecorded case. It involved the arrest of the notorious canary-trainer, thereby removing a plague-spot from the East End of London.

WILSON:
"The Valley of Fear" Part 2: "The Scowrers"
A boy in his teens, he is chosen to assist Tiger Cormac in doing 'a job' on Andrew Rae, of Rae & Sturmash, for the Merton County Lodge 249, 'Ancient Order of Freemen.'

WILSON, BARTHOLOMEW:
"The Valley of Fear" Part 2: "The Scowrers"
District ruler whose district includes Lodge 29 of Chicago of the 'Eminent Order of Freemen' of which John McMurdo was a member.

WILSON MATTER:
"The Hound of the Baskervilles"
An unrecorded case.
Mr. Wislon, manager of the district messenger office is helped by Holmes who saves Wilson's good name and perhaps his life. One of the messenger boys, Cartwright, helps Holmes out during his investigation.

WILSON, JABEZ:
"The Red-Headed League"
"... average commonplace British tradesman, obese, pompous, and slow. He wore rather baggy gray shepherd's check trousers, a not over-clean black frock-coat, unbuttoned in the front, and a drab waistcoat with a heavy brassy Albert chain, and a square pierced bit of

metal dangling down as an ornament. A frayed top-hat and a faded brown overcoat with a wrinkled velvet collar lay upon a chair beside him" "there was nothing remarkable about the man save his blazing red head ..." According to Holmes's observations "he has at some time done manual labor, that he takes snuff, that he is a Freemason, that he has been to China, and that he has done a considerable amount of writing lately, ..." Mr. Wilson began as a ships carpenter. He wears the Freemasons arc-and-compass breastpin. He has a tattoo immediately above his right wrist which Holmes points out could "only have been done in China" due to the staining of the fishes' scales of a delicate pink which is peculiar to China. Additionally, Mr. Wilson has a Chinese coin hanging from his watch chain. Mr. Jabez Wilson is a pawnbroker, his business is at Coburg Square, near the City -- not a very large affair, he used to have two assistants but now has only one, a Vincent Spaulding, who works for half wages. Becomes member of "Red-Headed League" and copies. Encyclopedia Britannica for eight weeks when he is informed that the "Red-Headed League" has been dissolved, hence his coming to Holmes.

WILSON, SERGEANT:
"The Valley of Fear" Part 1: "The Tragedy of Birlstone"
Of the Sussex Constabulary, he was in charge of the small local police station in Birlstone.

WILSON, STEVE:
"The Valley of Fear" Part 2: "The Scowrers"
Named being used by Birdy Edwards while he investigates the 'Scowrers' of Vermissa Valley. He is living at Hobson's Patch. He has claimed to be a reporter wanting to know all he could about the 'Scowrers.'
AKA Birdy Edwards,

See Edwards, Birdy

WINCHESTER:
"Silver Blaze"
Location of the famous horse race, the Wessex Cup
(Plate).

WINCHESTER:
"The Valley of Fear"   Part 2: "The Scowrers"
Police with Winchester rifles were requisitioned to guard
the offices of the "Vermissa Herald" after the attack upon
the life of its editor, James Stanger.

WINCHESTER:
"The Problem of Thor Bridge"
Town in the county of Hampshire, location of the
Assizes, an English court.

WINDIBANK, JAMES:
"A Case of Identity"
Perpetrator of the Hoax. Step-father of Miss Mary
Sutherland, he travels for Westhouse & Marbank, claret
importers.   " ... sturdy, middle-sized fellow, some thirty
years of age, clean shaven, and sallow-skinned, with a
bland, insinuating manner, and a pair of wonderfully
sharp and penetrating gray eyes."

WINDIGATE:
"The Adventure of The Blue Carbuncle"
Ruddyfaced, white-aproned landlord of the Alpha Inn.
See Alpha Inn.

WINDLE, J.W.:
"The Valley of Fear"   Part 2: "The Scowrers"
Division Master of Merton County Lodge 249 of the
'Ancient Order of Freemen.' He request a return favor of

Lodge 29 Vermissa for past services. He request 'a job'
be done on Andrew Rae of Rae & Sturmash, coal owners.

WINTER, JAMES:

"The Adventure of the Three Garridebs"
See Evans, Killer

WINTER, KITTY:

"The Adventure of the Illustrious Client"
Miss Winter, a slim, flamelike young woman with a pale,
intense face, which was youthful, and yet so worn with
sin and sorrow. She claims that she is what she is, a
tramp, because of Baron Adelbert Gruner. She assist
Holmes in trying to persuade Miss de Merville against
marrying Baron Gruner. As Holmes is escaping the
Baron's home with the valuable diary, Kitty throws vitriol
upon the face of the Baron just as he reaches the open
window Holmes has jumped from.

WISTERIA LODGE:

"The Adventure of Wisteria Lodge"
aka "A Reminiscence of Mr. Sherlock Holmes"

Located two miles on the south side of Esher on the way
to Oxshott, the rented home of one Mr. Aloysius Garcia.
A fair sized house standing back from the road,   it was
old, falling down and in a crazy state of disrepair.

WOKING:

"The Naval Treaty"
Reached via train from Waterloo. Location of Briarbrae,
home to Percy Phelps and family.

WOMBWELL:

"The Adventure of the Retired Colourman"
A showman and rival of Ronder's wild beast show.

WOOD, DR.:

    "The Valley of Fear" Part 1: "The Tragedy of Birlstone"

        Doctor who accompanied Sergeant Wilson to the Manor
        House to examine the murder scene. He discovers a
        brand on the dead man's right forearm, a triangle
        enclosed in a circle.

WOOD, HENRY:

    "The Crooked Man"

        He had a very dark, fearsome face, and a gleam in his
        yellow-shot, bilious eyes, his hair and whiskers were shot
        with gray, and his face was all crinkled and puckered like
        a withered apple. He was late of India where he was
        Corporal Henry Woods of the One Hundred and
        Seventeenth stationed at Bhurtee. He competed with
        James Barclay for the love of Miss Nancy Devoy, she
        returned his love but married Barclay upon the supposed
        death of Wood. During the Mutiny, his regiment was
        shut up at Bhurtee surrounded by ten thousand rebels.
        With supplies running out he volunteered to attempt to
        reach General Neill's column, which was moving
        up-country. (Colonel) James Barclay provided the map
        for Henry Wood which led him directly into the hands of
        the rebels and Miss Nancy Devoy to James Barclay.
        While in the hands of the rebels, he was tortured,
        captured trying to escape and   tortured again. He was
        taken to Nepal and then Darjeeling where the rebels were
        murdered by the hill-folk who in-turn made Henry Wood
        their slave until his escape north to the Afghans and
        finally back to Punjab. He sees Nancy Barclay as she
        passes Hudson Street in Aldershot, and screams out "My
        God, it's Nancy!" She stops and speak to him,
        discovering his identity. Having followed Nancy home

he enters 'Lachine,' home of Colonel and Mrs. Barclay during an argument where she is accusing the Colonel of being a coward. When the Colonel sees Henry Wood his heart gives out killing him. As Barclay fell he hit his head on the fender.

WOOD, J.G.:
"The Adventure of the Lion's Mane"
Author of "Out of Doors," he was a famous observer and had encountered the "Lion's Mane" while swimming off the coast of Kent. He lived to tell about it and write of its deadly powers.

WOODHOUSE:
"The Adventure of the Bruce-Partington Plans"
One of fifty men Holmes believes have good reason for killing him.

WOODLEY, ROARING JACK:
"The Adventure of the Solitary Cyclist"
A coarse, puffy-faced, red-moustached young man, with his hair plastered down on each side of his forehead. A friend of Ralph Smith of Africa, partner with Mr. Carruthers. He and Carruthers conspire to force Miss Violet Smith to marry Woodley so they can steal her inheritance. He wins the right to marry Miss Smith by besting Carruthers at cards. He was known as the greatest brute and bully in South Africa -- a man whose name is a holy terror from Kimberley to Johannesburg. He is shot by Carruthers just as his marriage ceremony to Miss Violet Smith concludes. He was tried and convicted of abduction and assault, sentenced to ten years.

WOODMAN'S LEE:

> "The Adventure of Black Peter"
>> Home of Peter Carey, it is located near Forest Row in Sussex.

WOOLWICH:

> "The Adventure of the Bruce-Partington Plans"
>> Section of London, a branch of the Capital and Counties Bank is located there and is where Arthur Cadogan West had a checking account.

WOOLWICH ARSENAL:

> "The Adventure of the Bruce-Partington Plans"
>> The government employer of Arthur Cadogan West.

WOOLWICH THEATRE:

> "The Adventure of the Bruce-Partington Plans"
>> Located in Woolwich, Arthur Cadogan West had two dress-circle tickets for the theatre in his pocket when his dead body was found outside Aldgate Station.

WORCESTERSHIRE:

> "The Sign of Four"
>> Area in Worcester where Jonathan Small lived before joining the military.

THE WORTHINGTON BANK GANG:

> "The Resident Patient"
>> Five bank robbers, Cartwright, Biddle, Hayward, Moffat, and Sutton. They were involved in a bank robbery in 1875. Seven thousand pounds were stolen and the caretaker, Tobin, was murdered. All five were arrested, though the evidence against them was slight. One of the gang, Sutton, turned informer and on his evidence, Cartwright was hanged and the others (Biddle, Hayward, and Moffat) were sentenced to fifteen years each. Of

Biddle, Hayward and Moffat, one was an elderly man, thin, demure and commonplace. One of the others was a tall young man, surprisingly handsome, with dark, fierce face, and the limbs and chest of Hercules. They have joined together to find Sutton and kill him for his treachery.

WRIGHT, THERESA:

"The Adventure of the Abbey Grange"

Maid to Lady Brackenstall (Mary Fraser). Came with her to England 18 months earlier from Australia. Has been with Mary Fraser since her birth.

WATSON, JOHN, Dr.:

"A Study in Scarlet"

Took his degree of Doctor of Medicine at the University of London followed by the course prescribed for surgeons at Netley. Thereafter attached to the Fifth Northumberland Fusiliers as assistant surgeon which was stationed in India.

Prior to his joining, the second Afghan war broke out. Met up with his regiment in Candahar, undertaking his new duties. He was removed from his brigade and attached to the Berkshires with whom he served at the fatal battle of Maiwand. It was there that he was struck on the shoulder by a Jezail bullet. He was almost captured by the Ghazis but for the devotion of his orderly, Murray. He was removed to the base hospital at Peshawar, but after marked recovery he was taken with enteric fever. He was returned to England upon the troopship, Orontes, landing at Portsmouth.

Watson lived for some time at a private hotel in the Strand. While standing at the Criterion Bar he meets an old friend, Stamford, who had been a dresser under him at Bart's, St. Bartholomew's Hospital. It is through this friend, Stamford, that Watson meets Holmes sometime around 1880/81 and moves to 221B Baker Street with Sherlock Holmes.

"The Sign of Four"
Case took place in summer of 1888.

Mary Marstan is a client who comes to Holmes for assistance in "The Sign of Four." Watson becomes engaged to her in September 1888 and marries her a few months later. Watson states at end of case: "I get a wife out of it (the case)."

See Mrs. Watson.

Watson's Marriage: Took place within a few months of September 1888. Caused Watson and Holmes to drift away from each other.

See "A Scandal in Bohemia"

"The Crooked Man"
Took place in late 1888, early 1889, a few months after Watson's Marriage.

"The Naval Treaty"
Occurs in the July following Watson's marriage, July 1889.

"The Adventure of the Engineer's Thumb"
This adventure happen not long after Watson's marriage, in the summer of 1889.

"A Scandal in Bohemia"
>Mary Jane: Watson's servant girl. According to Holmes she is "a most clumsy and careless servant girl."
>According to Watson "incorrigible, and my wife has given her notice"
>
>March 20, 1888, Watson visits his friend Holmes at Baker Street (after a journey to see a patient) which results in his becoming involved in "A Scandal in Bohemia."
>
>**Medical Practice:** Prior to "A Scandal in Bohemia" and some time after "A Sign of Four" Watson had "returned to civil practice."
>
>See "A Scandal in Bohemia"
>
>**Boswell:** Holmes refers to Watson, "I am lost without my Boswell."
>
>See A Scandal in Bohemia"

"The Man With The Twisted Lip"
>Watson's wife calls him by the name "James."

"The Adventure of the Speckled Band"
>Eley's No. 2, Watson's revolver.

"The Final Problem"
>After Watson's marriage and subsequent start in private practice, the very intimate relations which had existed between Holmes and Watson became to some extent modified. Holmes still came to Watson from time to time when he desired a companion in his investigations, but those occasions grew more and more seldom, until Watson found that in the year 1890 there were only three cases of which he retained any record.

Watson has written this adventure to set the facts straight regarding Professor Moriarty. Watson travels with Holmes to Switzerland and on May 4, 1891 discovers Holmes has fallen, locked in the arms of Moriarty, to his death at the Reichenback Falls. Holmes left a note for Watson which he copies at the end of the story for the reader.

"The Adventure of the Norwood Builder"
Watson has sold his practice and moved back to Baker Street with Holmes. No mention of Mrs. Watson's whereabouts is forthcoming. The date, Spring/Summer 1894, can be determined from Watson's statement that Holmes had "been back for a few months" and the story follows "The Adventure of the Empty House" however, the reader will note that Holmes dates Watson as still being married in 1903.

"The Adventure of Charles Augustus Milverton"
Watson threatens Holmes, with going to the police, if Holmes refuses to take him along on the planned burglary of Charles Augustus Milverton's safe. Lestrade describes a criminal escaping from Charles Augustus Milverton's home: "He was a middle-sized, strongly-built man -- square jaw, thick neck, and moustache." This description is of Watson, he and Holmes were escaping the home of Milverton after witnessing his murder by a distraught woman he had blackmailed. It is the only description provided of Watson in any of the Adventures.

"The Adventure of the Devil's Foot"
Watson and Holmes test Holmes's theory regarding the poison Holmes has found in Mortimer Tregennis's room after his death. Watson's brain and imagination went completely out of control, the poison worked quickly and

thoroughly but at the last instant Watson "dashed from
his chair, threw [his] arms round Holmes, and together
[they] lurched through the door." Holmes responds:
"Upon my word, Watson!" "I owe you both my thanks
and an apology." Watson answers: "you know that it is
my greatest joy and privilege to help you," realizing that
he has never seen so much of Holmes's heart before.

"The Adventure of the Mazarin Stone"
Watson is not living at the Baker Street lodgings when
this adventure begins.

"The Problem of Thor Bridge"
Watson's bank, Cox and Co., located at Charing Cross, its
vault contains a travel-worn and battered tin dispatch-box
with the name 'John H. Watson, M.D., Late Indian
Army,' painted upon the lid.

It was filled with papers, nearly all of which consisted of
records of the cases which illustrated the curious
problems which Sherlock Holmes had at various times
come to examine.

"The Adventure of the Creeping Man"
He received a message from Holmes on a September
Sunday evening in 1903:
"Come at once if convenient--if inconvenient come all
the same." Watson believes he has become one of
Holmes's habits, their relationship being rather peculiar in
these latter days.

Watson was a whetstone for Holmes's mind. He
stimulated him. Holmes liked to think aloud in Watson's
presence. Watson felt 'if I irritated him by certain
methodical slowness in my mentality, that irritation
served only to make his own flame-like intuitions and

impressions flash up the more vividly and swiftly. Such was my humble role in our alliance.'

"The Adventure of the Sussex Vampire"
Having played rugby for Blackheath in his younger days, Watson remembers Robert Ferguson, Holmes's client, as the best three-quarter for Richmond.

"The Adventure of the Three Garridebs"
When Watson is shot by Killer Evans, Holmes responds, after examining Watson's wound, "By the Lord, it is well for you. If you had killed Watson, you would not have got out of this room alive. Watson believes it to be "the one and only time I caught a glimpse of a great heart as well as of a great brain. All my years of humble but single-minded service culminated in that moment of revelation." "It was worth a wound - it was worth many wounds - to know the depth of loyalty and love which lay behind that cold mask."

"The Adventure of the Illustrious Client"
This case is "the supreme moment of [Holmes's] career." Watson, as did Holmes, had a weakness for the Turkish bath. Watson had his own rooms in Queen Anne Street at the time of this case.

"The Adventure of the Blanched Soldier"
Holmes writes: "The good Watson had at that time [January 1903] deserted me for a wife, the only selfish action which I can recall in our association." Holmes describes Watson as having "some remarkable characteristics of his own which in his modesty he has given small attention amid his exaggerated estimates of my own performances." Holmes continues with: "A confederate who foresees your conclusions and course of action is always dangerous, but one to whom each

development comes as a perpetual surprise, and to whom the future is always a closed book, is indeed an ideal helpmate."

Holmes, having retired to the South Downs, Watson has "passed almost beyond [Holmes's] ken." Except for occasional week-end visits, Watson sees little of Holmes.

"The Adventure of the Retired Colourman"
Holmes sends the good doctor to investigate this case due to other more pressing business. Once again Watson is kept in the dark as to Holmes' real plans. When Watson does report on his findings, he is once again berated for a poor job: "[you] have missed everything of importance." But Holmes tries to placate Watson with: "Don't be hurt, my dear fellow. You know that I am quite impersonal. No one else would have done better. Some possibly not so well."

"The Adventure of the Veiled Lodger"
Holmes has been engaged in private practice for some 23 years, of which Watson has been with him for 17 years.

"The Adventure of Shoscombe Old Place"
Watson's summer quarters were once down in Shoscombe. Holmes asked him to be his 'Handy Guide to the Turf' during the investigation into Sir Robert Norberton, Watson being familiar with the art of horse racing.

CHAPTERS X & Y

X

XX.31:

        "The Illustrious Client"
                Private telephone number of Sir James Damery.

Y

THE YELLOW FACE:

        Published in "The Strand": February 1893
        Published as part of: "The Memoirs of Sherlock Holmes"

                Holmes is consulted by a husband concerned with his wife's recent strange behavior. Watson notes at the beginning of the story that Holmes has failed in the past, but where Holmes failed, it too often happened that everyone else failed as well. Additionally, Watson points out that occasionally Holmes erred, but usually the truth was still discovered. Watson mentions examples of this: the story mentioned here, 'The Yellow Face,' and another, 'The Musgrave Ritual.'

YOUGHAL:

        "The Adventure of the Mazarin Stone"
                Of Scotland Yard and the C.I.D.

YOUNG, BRIGHAM:

        "A Study in Scarlet" Part 2 -- "The Country of the Saints"
                Leader of the Mormons, he takes John and Lucy Ferrier into the fold and provides them with a tract of land and place to live. During a visit with John Ferrier Young points out the "thirtieth code of the sainted John Smith:"

                    "Let every maiden of the true faith marry one of

the elect; for if she wed a Gentile, she commits a grievous sin."

When Lucy has grown of age, Young visits with John Ferrier informing him that the time has come for her to wed. Young points out that two of the 'elect,' Stangerson and Drebber, each have a son that is wealthy and looking for another bride. Young gives John Ferrier a month to discuss it with his daughter, Lucy, before she must make a choice. When John Ferrier hesitates, he is threaten by Brigham Young: "it were better for you John Ferrier that you and she were now lying blanched skeletons upon the Sierra Blanco, than that you should put your weak wills against the orders of the Holy Four!"

YOXLEY OLD PLACE:
"The Adventure of the Golden Pince-Nez"
Located in Kent, seven miles from Chatham. Taken by an elderly old professor by the name of Coram.

YUAN:
"The Adventure of the Illustrious Client"
Watson studies Chinese Pottery in preparation for a disguised meeting with Baron Gruner about the sale of a genuine eggshell pottery saucer of the Ming dynasty. In this quest, he studies the primitive period of the Yuan.

YUNG-LO:
"The Adventure of the Illustrious Client"
Watson studies Chinese Pottery in preparation for a disguised meeting with Baron Gruner about the sale of a genuine eggshell pottery saucer of the Ming dynasty. In this quest he studies the beauties of the Yung-lo.

CHAPTER Z

ZAMBA:
"The Adventure of the Red Circle"
> Partner with Tito Castalotte in the firm of Castalotte and
> Zamba, chief fruit importers of New York, he is an
> invalid.

ZEPPELIN:
"His Last Bow" "An Epilogue of Sherlock Holmes"
> German airship filled with helium.

**BOOK TWO
INDEX BY ADVENTURE**

A STUDY IN SCARLET:
Published November 1887, 'Beeton's Christmas Annual'
The First of the four novels. The first of Watson's stories.

Part 1 - "Being a Reprint from the Reminiscences of John H. Watson, M.D., Late of the Army Medical Department."

Part 2 - "The Country of the Saints"

URRAY
BARRAUD
STAMFORD
GUION STEAMSHIP COMPANY
CRITERION BAR
AMERICAN EXCHANGE, STRAND
STRAND
RANCE, JOHN
BAKER STREET
LAURISTON GARDENS
LESTRADE
WHITE HART
"THE BOOK OF LIFE"
MURCHER, HENRY
DUPIN
DENNIS, SALLY
LECOQ
SAWYER, MRS.
GREGSON, TOBIAS
DENNIS, TOM
DREBBER, ENOCH J.
KESWICK
DREBBER, "ELDER"
BRIXTON MYSTERY
RACHE
STANGERSON, JOSEPH

STANGERSON, "ELDER"
THE GREAT ALKALI PLAIN
DAILY TELEGRAPH
SIERRA BLANCO
THE STANDARD
FERRIER, JOHN
THE DAILY NEWS
FERRIER, LUCY
ECHO
YOUNG, BRIGHAM
WIGGINS
KEMBALL
CHARPENTIER, ARTHUR
JOHNSON
CHARPENTIER, MADAME
DANITE BAND
JOHN UNDERWOOD AND SONS
AVENGING ANGELS
CHARPENTIER, ALICE
EAGLE RAVINE
HALLIDAY'S PRIVATE HOTEL
COWPER
HOPE, JEFFERSON

THE SIGN OF FOUR:
Published October 1890 The Second of the four novels
    AKA 'The Sign of the Four'
    The second story.

WIGMORE STREET POST-OFFICE
FORRESTER, Mrs. CECIL
JONES, ATHELNEY
Mrs. HUDSON
MORSTAN, Captain ARTHUR
MORSTAN, MISS MARY

A SCANDAL IN BOHEMIA:

Published in the 'Strand' July 1891.
Published as part of:
"The Adventures of Sherlock Holmes"

BOSWELL
ADLER, IRENE
MARY JANE
NORTON, IRENE (ADLER)
COUNT VON KRAMM
NORTON, GODFREY
HARE, MR. JOHN
CLOTILDE LOTHMAN VON SAXE-MENINGEN
WILHELM GOTTSREICH SIGISMOND VON ORMSTEIN
TURNER, MRS.

THE RED-HEADED LEAGUE:
Published in the 'Strand' August 1891
Published as part of:
"The Adventures of Sherlock Holmes"

WILSON, JABEZ
ARCHIE
SPAULDING, VINCENT
MORRIS, WILLIAM
CLAY, JOHN
JONES, PETER
HOPKINS, EZEKIAH
MERRYWEATHER, MR.
ROSS, DUNCAN

A CASE OF IDENTITY:
Published in the 'Strand' September 1891
Published as part of:
"The Adventures of Sherlock Holmes"

SUTHERLAND, MISS MARY
HARDY, MR.
WINDIBANK, JAMES
ESTHEREGE, MRS.
THE MORNING CHRONICLE

THE BOSCOMBE VALLEY MYSTERY:

Published in the 'Strand' October 1891
Published as part of:
"The Adventures of Sherlock Holmes"

ANSTRUTHER
TURNER, ALICE
PADDINGTON STATION
VICTORIA, AUSTRALIA
BOSCOMBE VALLEY
Dr. WILLOWS
TURNER, JOHN
HEREFORD
MCCARTHY, CHARLES
BRISTOL
BLACK JACK OF BALLARAT
MEREDITH, GEORGE
BOSCOMBE POOL
HATHERLEY FARM
CROWDER, WILLIAM
COOEE
MCCARTHY, JAMES
BALLARAT
MORAN, PATIENCE
TOBACCO
LESTRADE
REGENT STREET
HEREFORD ARMS

COBB, JOHN
ROSS

THE FIVE ORANGE PIPS:
Published in the 'Strand' November 1891
Published as part of:
"The Adventures of Sherlock Holmes"

RUSSEL, CLARK
COOK, Police-Constable
OPENSHAW, JOHN
CALHOUN, CAPTAIN JAMES"
OPENSHAW, JOSEPH
MARY
OPENSHAW, ELIAS
PONDICHERRY
MAJOR FREEBODY
DUNDEE
KU KLUX KLAN
EAST LONDON
WATERLOO BRIDGE

THE MAN WITH THE TWISTED LIP:
Published in the 'Strand' December 1891
Published as part of:
"The Adventures of Sherlock Holmes"

WHITNEY, ISA
BRADSTREET, INSPECTOR
WHITNEY, ELIAS
PAUL'S WHARF
WHITNEY, KATE
THE CEDARS
BAR OF GOLD

ABERDEEN SHIPPING COMPANY
UPPER SWANDAM LANE
ST. CLAIR, MRS.
LONDON BRIDGE
CAPITAL AND COUNTIES BANK
ST. CLAIR, NEVILLE
THREADNEEDLE STREET
BOONE, HUGH

THE ADVENTURE OF THE BLUE CARBUNCLE:
Published in the 'Strand' January 1892
Published as part of:
"The Adventures of Sherlock Holmes"

PETERSON
ALPHA INN
TOTTENHAM COURT ROAD
WINDIGATE
GOODGE STREET
BRECKINRIDGE
COUNTESS OF MORCAR
COVENT GARDEN MARKET
HOTEL COSMOPOLITAN
MR. COCKSURE
HORNER, JOHN
BILL
RYDER, JAMES
OAKSHOTT, MRS.
CUSACK, CATHERINE
KING OF PROOSIA
THE BLUE CARBUNCLE
MAUDSLEY
BAKER, HENRY

THE ADVENTURE OF THE SPECKLED BAND:

Published in the 'Strand' February 1892
Published as part of:
"The Adventures of Sherlock Holmes"

STONER, HELEN
ARMITAGE,PERCY
STONER, JULIA
CROWN INN
SURRY FAMILY
THE SPECKLED BAND
ROYLOTT, DR. GRIMESBY
ELEY'S NO. 2
STONER, MAJOR-GENERAL
DOCTOR'S COMMONS
WESTPHAIL, MISS HONORIA
STOKE MORAN

THE ADVENTURE OF THE ENGINEER'S THUMB:

Published in the 'Strand' March 1892
Published as part of:
"The Adventures of Sherlock Holmes"

HATHERLEY, VICTOR
FERGUSON
VENNER & MATHESON
ELISE
STARK, COLONEL LYSANDER
HAYLING, JEREMIAH
EYFORD
BECHER, DR.

THE ADVENTURE OF THE NOBLE BACHELOR:

Published in the 'Strand' April 1892

Published as part of:
"The Adventures of Sherlock Holmes"

ST. SIMON, LORD ROBERT
WALSINGHAM DE VERE
DUKE OF BALMORAL
ST. GEORGE'S
DORAN, MISS HATTY
WESTBURY HOUSE
MOULTON, FRANCIS HAY
BLACKWATER, LORD
MCQUIRE
DUCHESS OF BALMORAL
GORDON SQUARE
EUSTACE, LORD
ALICE
ST. SIMON, LADY CLARA
MILLAR, MISS FLORA
WHITTINGTON, LADY ALICIA
MORNING POST

THE ADVENTURE OF THE BERYL CORONET:

Published in the 'Strand' May 1892
Published as part of:
"The Adventures of Sherlock Holmes"

METROPOLITAN STATION
HOLDER, ARTHUR
HOLDER, ALEXANDER
BURNWELL, SIR GEORGE
HOLDER & STEVENSON
HOLDER, MARY
THREADNEEDLE STREET
FAIRBANK
BERYL CORONET

PROSPER, FRANCIS
PARR, LUCY

THE ADVENTURE OF THE COPPER BEECHES:
Published in the 'Strand' June 1892
Published as part of:
"The Adventures of Sherlock Holmes"

STREATHAM
RUCASTLE, ALICE
DAILY TELEGRAPH
BLACK SWAN HOTEL
MONTAGUE PLACE
SOUTHERTON, LORD
HUNTER, VIOLET
RUCASTLE, MRS.
MUNRO, SPENCE (COLONEL)
RUCASTLE, EDWARD
WESTAWAY'S
TOLLER
STOPER, MISS
CARLO
RUCASTLE, JEPHRO
FOWLER. MR.
THE COPPER BEECHES
SOUTHAMPTON

SILVER BLAZE:
Published in the 'Strand' December 1892
Published as part of:
"The Memoirs of Sherlock Holmes"

ROSS, COLONEL
LESURIER, MADAME

STRAKER, JOHN
DAWSON
TRAVISTOCK
PLYMOUTH
WINCHESTER
THE NEGRO
WESSEX CUP
PUGILIST
KING'S PYLAND
IRIS
BAYARD
RASPER
HUNTER, NED
NEWTON, HEATH
BAXTER, EDITH
WARDLAW, COLONEL
DARTMOOR
BALMORAL, DUKE of MAPLETON
SINGLEFORD, LORD
DESBOROUGH
BACKWATER, LORD
SIMPSON, FITZROY
CLAPHAM JUNCTION
WEISS & COMPANY
VICTORIA
DERBYSHIRE, WILLIAM
GREGORY, INSPECTOR

THE YELLOW FACE:
Published in the 'Strand' February 1893
Published as part of:
"The Memoirs of Sherlock Holmes"

GROSVENOR MIXTURE
MIDDLESEX

MUNRO, GRANT
NORBURY
MUNRO, EFFIE
CRYSTAL PALACE
HEBRON, EFFIE (Mrs)
HEBRON, LUCY
PINNER
HEBRON, JOHN

THE STOCK-BROKER'S CLERK:
Published in the 'Strand' March 1893
Published as part of:
"The Memoirs of Sherlock Holmes"

FARQUHAR
NEW STREET
BRITISH MEDICAL JOURNAL
DAY'S MUSIC HALL
BIRMINGHAM
HARRIS, MR.
PYCROFT, HALL
PRICE, MR.
PINNER, ARTHUR
MAWSON & WILLIAM'S
PINNER, HARRY
BEDDINGTON
TUSON, SERGEANT
AYRSHIRES
NEW ZEALAND CONSOLIDATED
POLLOCK, CONSTABLE
BRITISH BROKEN HILLS
FRANCO-MIDLAND HARDWARE COMPANY, LIMITED

THE "GLORIA SCOTT":

Published in the 'Strand' April 1893
Published as part of:
"The Memoirs of Sherlock Holmes"

JUSTICE OF THE PEACE TREVOR
GLORIA SCOTT
DONNITHORPE
PRENDERGAST, JACK
HOLLY, SIR EDWARD
EVANS
HUDSON
MEREER
BEDDOES
MARTIN, LIEUTENANT
FORDINGHAM
WILSON
FORDHAM, DR.
HOTSPUR

THE MUSGRAVE RITUAL:

Published in the 'Strand' May 1893
Published as part of:
"The Memoirs of Sherlock Holmes"

MUSGRAVE, REGINALD
TREGELLIS, JANET
BRUNTON, RICHARD
NORMAN CONQUEST
MANOR HOUSE OF HURLSTONE
CHARLES THE FIRST
SUSSEX
CHARLES THE SECOND
HOWELLS, RACHEL
STUARTS

THE REIGATE PUZZLE:
> AKA The Reigate Squire
> AKA The Reigate Squires
> Published in the 'Strand' June 1893
> Published as part of:
> "The Memoirs of Sherlock Holmes"

HOTEL DULONG
CUNNINGHAM, ALEC
LYON
KIRWAN, WILLIAM
HAYTER, COLONEL
FORRESTER, INSPECTOR
ACTON, OLD
QUEEN ANNE
HOMER
MORRISON, ANNIE
CUNNINGHAM, Mr.

THE CROOKED MAN:
> Published in the 'Strand' July 1893
> Published as part of:
> "The Memoirs of Sherlock Holmes"

ARCADIA
MORRISON, MISS
ALDERSHOT
LACHINE
THE ROYAL MUNSTERS
WATT STREET MISSION
BARCLAY, COLONEL JAMES
HUDSON STREET
JACKSON
WOOD, HENRY

BARCLAY, NANCY MRS.
TEDDY
MURPHY, MAJOR
DAVID
ROMAN CATHOLIC CHURCH
BHURTEE
GUILD OF ST. GEORGE
DEVOY, NANCY
WATT STREET CHAPEL
SIMPSON
STEWART, JANE
NEILL, GENERAL

THE RESIDENT PATIENT:

Published in the 'Strand' August 1893
Published as part of:
"The Memoirs of Sherlock Holmes"

NEW FOREST
BLESSINGTON
SOUTHSEA
LADY DAY
GORDON, GENERAL
THE WORTHINGTON BANK GANG
BEECHER, HENRY WARD
BIDDLE
TREVELYAN, DR. PERCY
HAYWARD
BROOK STREET
MOFFAT
BRUCE PINKERTON
SUTTON
CAVENDISH SQUARE
LANNER
LONDON UNIVERSITY

NORAH CREINA
KING'S COLLEGE HOSPITAL
OPORTO

THE GREEK INTERPRETER:
Published in the 'Strand' September 1893
Published as part of:
"The Memoirs of Sherlock Holmes"

VERNET
KRATIDES, PAUL
HOLMES, MYCROFT
KRATIDES, SOPHY
PALL MALL
KEMP, WILSON
DIOGENES CLUB
DAILY NEWS
ADAMS
WANDSWORTH COMMON
MANOR HOUSE
CLAPHAM JUNCTION
MELAS, MR.
DAVENPORT, J.
LATIMER, HAROLD
LOWER BRIXTON
CHARING CROSS
GREGSON, INSPECTOR
SHAFTESBURY AVENUE
THE MYRTLES
OXFORD STREET
BECKENHAM
REGENT'S CIRCUS
BUDA-PESHT
ST. JAMES
ATHENS

THE NAVAL TREATY:

Published in the 'Strand' October and November 1893
Published as part of:
"The Memoirs of Sherlock Holmes"

PHELPS, PERCY
TANGEY, MRS.
HOLDHURST, LORD
TANGEY, MR.
WOKING
COLDSTREAM GUARDS
BRIARBRAE
FORBES, MR.
HARRISON, JOSEPH
FERRIER, DR.
HARRISON, ANNIE
DOWNING STREET
GOROT, CHARLES
HUDSON, MRS.
THE TREATY
BERTILLON SYSTEM
TRIPLE ALLIANCE
RIPLEY
CHARLES STREET
SURREY
WHITEHALL

THE FINAL PROBLEM:

Published in the 'Strand' December 1893.
Published as part of:
"The Memoirs of Sherlock Holmes"

MORIARTY, JAMES (COLONEL)

THE HOUND OF THE BASKERVILLES

Published in "The Strand Magazine"
August 1901 through April 1902.
The third of four novels.

MORTIMER, JAMES

SWEDISH PATHOLOGICAL SOCIETY
PENANG LAWYER
THORSLEY
CHARING CROSS HOSPITAL
HIGH BARROW
BERTILLON, ALPHONSE
OXFORD STREET
BASKERVILLE, CHARLES, SIR
REGENT STREET
LEGEND OF THE HOUND
No. 2704
DEVON COUNTY CHRONICLE
WILSON
BASKERVILLE, HUGO
CARTWRIGHT
MURPHY DIRECTORY
BASKERVILLE, HENRY, SIR
BOND STREET
STAPLETON, JOHN MR.
JOHNSON, THEOPHILUS
PERKINS
OLDMORE, MRS.
WATERLOO STATION
BARRYMORE, JOHN
BASKERVILLE, ROGER
DESMOND, JAMES
SOUTHAMPTON
WESTMORELAND
GRIMPEN
PADDINGTON
HIGH TOR
OFFICIAL REGISTRY
NORTHUMBERLAND HOTEL
CLAYTON, JOHN
TIMES
BOROUGH

LEEDS MERCURY
TURPEY STREET
WESTERN MORNING NEWS
SHIPLEY'S YARD
TRAFALGAR SQUARE
PRINCETOWN
SELDEN
RODNEY
BARRYMORE, ELIZA
BASKERVILLE, WILLIAM
JAMES
CHAIRMAN OF COMMITTES
THE MOOR
PITT
GRIMPEN MIRE
LESTRADE
BITTERN
VANDELEUR, MR.
CYCLOPIDES
VANDELEUR, MRS.
STAPLETON, MISS BERYL
ST. OLIVER'S PRIVATE SCHOOL
LEPIDOPTERA
GODNO
PLYMOUTH
ANDERSON MURDERS
CLEFT TOR
THE HOUND
COOMBE TRACEY
MEYERS
LYONS, LAURA
ROSS AND MANGLES
LYONS
CRAVEN STREET
REMINGTON
MEXBOROUGH PRIVATE HOTEL

BLACK TOR
ANTHONY
MIDDLETON
WHITE JASSAMINE
MORLAND, JOHN
LES HUGUENOTS
COUNTY CONSTABULARY
FERNWORTHY
BELLIVER TOR
FOLKESTONE COURT
VIXEN TOR
FOULMIRE
BRADLEY
FRANKLAND, MR.
OXFORD STREET
FRANKLAND V. MORLAND
KNELLER
FRANKLAND V. REGINA
REYNOLDS
FRASER
BASKERVILLE, REAR-ADMIRAL
FULHAM ROAD
THE JACKSON PRIZE FOR COMPARATIVE PATHOLOGY
MUSEUM OF THE COLLEGE OF SURGEONS

THE ADVENTURE OF THE EMPTY HOUSE:
> Published in "Collier's" September 26, 1903
> Published in "The Strand" October 1903
> Published as part of:
> "The Return of Sherlock Holmes"

ADAIR, THE HONOURABLE RONALD: EARL OF MAYNOOTH
ADAIR, HILDA
MECCA
MURRAY, MR.

STEWART, MRS
HEAVY GAME OF THE WESTERN HIMALAYAS
THREE MONTHS IN THE JUNGLE

THE ADVENTURE OF THE NORWOOD BUILDER:

Published in "Collier's" October 31, 1903
Published in "The Strand" November 1903
Published as part of:
"The Return of Sherlock Holmes"

MORIARTY, PROFESSOR
LESTRADE
VERNER, DR.
ANERLEY ARMS
MCFARLANE, JOHN HECTOR
HYAMS
OLDACRE, JONAS
LEXINGTON, MRS.
DAILY TELEGRAPH
NORWOOD DISAPPEARANCE CASE
LOWER NORWOOD
STEVENS, BERT
DEEP DENE HOUSE
CORNELIUS, MR.
SYDENHAM

THE ADVENTURE OF THE DANCING MEN:

Published in "The Strand": December 1903
Published as part of:
"The Return of Sherlock Holmes"

CUBITT, HILTON
SAUNDERS
RIDING THORPE MANOR

KING, MRS.
NORFOLK
ELRIGE'S FARM
RUSSELL SQUARE
EAST RUSTON
PARKER
SLANEY, ABE
PATRICK, ELSIE
DANCING MEN
LIVERPOOL STREET
HARGREAVE, WILSON
NORTH WALSHAM
JOINT, THE
MARTIN, INSPECTOR
PATRICK, OLD
EAST ANGLIA

THE ADVENTURE OF THE SOLITARY CYCLIST:
Published in "Collier's": December 26, 1903
Published in "The Strand": January 1904
Published as part of:
"The Return of Sherlock Holmes"

HARDEN, JOHN VINCENT
CHARLINGTON HALL
STAMFORD, ARCHIE
CROOKSBURY HILL
SMITH, VIOLET
MIDLAND ELECTRIC COMPANY
FARNHAM
COVENTRY
SURREY
FARNAHM STATION
SMITH, JAMES
WATERLOO

SMITH, RALPH
PALL MALL
TIMES
WILLIAMSON
CARRUTHERS, BOB
CHARLINGTON WOOD
WOODLEY, ROARING JACK
PETER
MORTON, CYRIL
JOHANNESBURG
IMPERIAL THEATRE
KIMBERLEY
CHILTERN GRANGE
MORTON & KENNEDY
DIXON, MRS.
WESTMINSTER
CHARLINGTON HEATH

THE ADVENTURE OF THE PRIORY SCHOOL:

Published in "Collier's": January 30, 1904
Published in "The Strand": February 1904
Published as part of:
"The Return of Sherlock Holmes"

HUXTABLE, THORNEYCROFT
HOLDERNESSE, DUCHESS
FERRERS DOCUMENTS
EDITH
ABERGAVENNY MURDER
WILDER, JAMES
HOLDERNESSE, DUKE OF
HEIDEGGER
MACKLETON
EUSTON
PRIORY SCHOOL

PEAK COUNTRY
HOLDERNESSE HALL
LOWER GILL MOOR
CARLTON HOUSE TERRACE
HIGH ROAD
CARSTON CASTLE
RED BULL INN
GLOBE
FIGHTING COCK INN
BARON BEVERLEY
RAGGED SHAW
EARL OF CARSTON
DUNLOP
LORD LIEUTENANT OF HALLAMSHIRE
PALMER
APPLEDORE, CHARLES
AVELING
SALTIRE, LORD
HAYES, REUBEN
HUXTABLE'S SIDELIGHTS ON HORACE
CHESTERFIELD
LEVERSTOKE, LORD
THE CAPITAL AND COUNTIES BANK
BLACKWATER, EARL OF
OXFORD STREET
SOAMES, CATHCART

THE ADVENTURE OF BLACK PETER:
Published in "Collier's": February 27, 1904
Published in "The Strand": March 1904
Published as part of:
"The Return of Sherlock Holmes"

TOSCA, CARDINAL
NELIGAN, JOHN HOPLEY

THE ADVENTURE OF CHARLES AUGUSTUS MILVERTON:
Published in "Collier's": March 26, 1904
Published in "The Strand": April 1904
Published as part of:
"The Return of Sherlock Holmes"

THE ADVENTURE OF THE SIX NAPOLEONS:
Published in "Collier's": April 30, 1904
Published in "The Strand": May 1904
Published as part of:
"The Return of Sherlock Holmes"

HARKER, HORACE
LABURNUM VILLA
KENSINGTON
LABURNUM LODGE
HARDING BROTHERS
CHISWICK
HIGH STREET STATION
LOWER GROVE ROAD
CAMPDEN HOUSE ROAD
READING
NIHILIST
BLACK PEARL OF THE BORGIAS
RED REPUBLICANS
COLONNA, PRINCE OF
GELDER & CO.
DACRE
CHURCH STREET
BORGIAS PEARL
STEPNEY
VENUCCI, LUCRETIA
BEPPO
CONK-SINGLETON
KENSINGTON OUTRAGE

THE ADVENTURE OF THE THREE STUDENTS:
Published in "The Strand": June 1904
Published as part of:
"The Return of Sherlock Holmes"

SOAMES, HILTON
FABER, JOHANN
THUCYDIDES
GILCHRIST
COLLEGE OF ST. LUKE'S
GILCHRIST, JABEZ

FORTESCUE SCHOLARSHIP
MCLAREN, MILES
BANNISTER
SOUTH AFRICA
RAS, DAULAT
RHODESIAN POLICE

THE ADVENTURE OF THE GOLDEN PINCE-NEZ:
Published in "The Strand": July 1904
Published as part of:
"The Return of Sherlock Holmes"

CROSBY
CORAM, PROFESSOR
RED LEECH
MORTIMER
ADDLETON TRAGEDY
UPPINGHAM
BRITISH BARROW
CAMBRIDGE
SMITH-MORTIMER
ANDAMAN ISLANDER
HURET
CHUBB'S KEY
ORDER OF THE LEGION OF HONOUR
IONIDES
YOXLEY OLD PLACE
ALEXANDRIA
SMITH, WILLOUGHBY
CHATHAM ROAD
OXFORD STREET
ANNA
HOPKINS, STANLEY
ALEXIS
KENT

SERGIUS
CHARING CROSS
ORDER, THE
CHATHAM
BROTHERHOOD

THE ADVENTURE OF THE MISSING THREE-QUARTER:
Published in "The Strand": August 1904
Published as part of:
"The Return of Sherlock Holmes"

STRAND
THE STRAND
TIMES
MOUNT-JAMES, LORD
OVERTON, CYRIL
BAYSWATER
TRINITY COLLEGE
KING'S CROSS STATION
CAMBRIDGE
GRAY'S INN ROAD
HOPKINS, STANLEY
ARMSTRONG, LESLIE
STAUNTON, GODFREY
JOHN
MOORHOUSE
CHESTERTON
STEVENSON
HISTON
MORTON
WATERBEACH
JOHNSON
OAKINGTON
STAUNTON, ARTHUR H.

DIXON, JEREMY
STAUNTON, HENRY
POMPEY
BLACKHEATH
TRUMPINGTON
BENTLEY'S
LIGHT BLUES

THE ADVENTURE OF THE ABBEY GRANGE:
Published in "The Strand": September 1904
Published as part of:
"The Return of Sherlock Holmes"

CHARING CROSS STATION
BRACKENSTALL, EUSTACE
KENTISH TRAIN
BRACKENSTALL, LADY
HOPKINS, STANLEY
WRIGHT, THERESA
ABBEY GRANGE
FRASER, MARY
MARSHAM
ADELAIDE-SOUTHAMPTON LINE
KENT
ROCK OF GILBRALTAR
CHISELHURST STATION
BASS ROCK
LEWISHAM GANG
CROCKER, JACK
SYDENHAM

THE ADVENTURE OF THE SECOND STAIN:
Published in "The Strand": December 1904
Published as part of:

"The Return of Sherlock Holmes"

BELLINGER, LORD
MARGATE
HOPE, TRELAWNEY
DAILY TELEGRAPH
WHITEHALL TERRACE
FOURNAYE, HENRI
LUCAS, EDUARDO
FOURNAYE, Mme. HENRI
GODOLPHIN STREET
CHARING CROSS STATION
PRINGLE, MRS.
MacPHERSON
MITTON, JOHN
JACOBS
HAMMERSMITH
MERROW, LORD
BARRETT
HARDY, CHARLES
OBERSTEIN
BELGRADE
La ROTHIERE
RUSSIAN-GERMAN GRAIN TAXES
EASTBOURNE
HUDSON, MRS.
MADRID
HOPE, HILDA TRELAWNEY
FLOWERS, LORD

HIS LAST BOW: This compilation of adventures was published as "His Last Bow" which began with a 'preface' stating that the adventures "involved Holmes coming out of retirement to assist the British government in the war against Germany and several previous experiences so as to complete the volume."

THE ADVENTURE OF WISTERIA LODGE aka "A Reminiscence of Mr. Sherlock Holmes"

Published in "Collier's": August 15, 1908
Published in "The Strand":
      September/October 1908
Published as part of: "His Last Bow"
Consists of two sections:
    1. "The Singular Experience of Mr.
      John Scott Eccles"
    2. "The Tiger of San Pedro"

CHARING CROSS
HIGH GABLE
CARRUTHERS, COLONEL
NETHER WALSLING
ECCLES, JOHN SCOTT
BULL
HUDSON, MRS.
WALTERS
GREGSON, INSPECTOR
MARX AND CO.
BAYNES, INSPECTOR
BRITISH MUSEUM
SURREY CONSTABULARY
THE OXSHOTT MYSTERY
POPHAM HOUSE
DOWNING, CONSTABLE
LEE
LUCAS, MR.
MELVILLE
BURNET, MISS
WISTERIA LODGE
WARNER, JOHN
ESHER

THE ADVENTURE OF THE CARDBOARD BOX:
Published in "The Strand": January 1893

Published as part of: "His Last Bow"

POE
BROWNER, JIM
GORDON, GENERAL
MAY DAY
BEECHER, HENRY WARD
CONQUEROR
CUSHING, SUSAN
STRADIVARIUS
A GRUESOME PACKET
TOTTENHAM COURT ROAD
DAILT CHRONICLE
PAGANINI
BELFAST
A STUDY IN SCARLET
LESTRADE, INSPECTOR
THE SIGN OF FOUR
PENGE
NIAGARA
CUSHING, SARAH
ALGAR
CUSHING, MARY
LIVERPOOL
MONTGOMERY, INSPECTOR
THAMES
SHADWELL POLICE STATION
ALBERT DOCK
FAIRBAIRN, ALEC
NEW BRITIAN
ANTHROPOLOGICAL JOURNAL
LIVERPOOL, DUBLIN, AND LONDON STEAM PACKET
COMPANY

THE ADVENTURE OF THE RED CIRCLE:

Published in "The Strand": March & April 1911
Published as part of: "His Last Bow"

WARREN, MRS.
NOTTING HILL
HOBBS, FAIRDALE
CASTALOTTE, TITO
DAILY GAZETTE
ZAMBA
WARREN, MR.
CASTALOTTE AND ZAMBA
GREAT ORME STREET
BOWERY
BRITISH MUSEUM
BROOKLYN
HOWE STREET
POSILIPPO
GREGSON, INSPECTOR
NAPLES
LEVERTON, MR.
BARELLI, AUGUSTO
PINKERTON'S AMERICAN AGENCY
BARI
LONG ISLAND CAVE MYSTERY
RED CIRCLE
GORGIANO, GIUSEPPE
CARBONARI
LUCCA, EMILIA
WAGNER
LUCCA, GENNARO
COVENT GARDEN

THE ADVENTURE OF THE BRUCE-PARTINGTON PLANS:
Published in "The Strand": December 1908
Published as part of: "His Last Bow"

BROOKS
HOLMES, MYCROFT
WOODHOUSE
WEST, ARTHUR CADOGAN
MASON
CHARING CROSS HOTEL
WESTBURY, VIOLET
MEYER, ADOLPH
LONDON BRIDGE
GREAT GEORGE STREET
WOOLWICH ARSENAL
La ROTHIERE, LOUIS
ALDGATE STATION
CAMPDEN MANSIONS
WILLESDEN
NOTTING HILL
WOOLWICH
OBERSTEIN, HUGO
CAPITAL AND COUNTIES BANK
CAULFIELD GARDEMS
WOOLWICH THEATRE
KENSINGTON
LESTRADE, INSPECTOR
GOLDINI'S RESTAURANT
BRUCE-PARTINGTON SUBMARINE
GLOUCESTER ROAD
ESTIMATES
DAILY TELEGRAPH
WALTER, JAMES
POLYPHONIC MOTETS OF LASSUS
SINCLAIR, ADMIRAL
GLOUCESTER ROAD STATION
WALTER, VALENTINE
HOTEL DU LOUVRE
JOHNSON, SIDNEY

ADVENTURE OF THE GREEK INTERPRETER

THE ADVENTURE OF THE DYING DETECTIVE:
Published in "Collier's: November 22, 1913
Published in "The Strand": December 1913
Published as part of: "His Last Bow"

HUDSON, MRS.
MORTON, INSPECTOR
ROTHERHITHE
LOWER BURKE STREET
SUMATRA
NOTTING HILL
MEEK, FASPER
KENSINGTON
FISHER, PENROSE
STAPLES
TAPANULI FEVER
SAVAGE, VICTOR
BLACK FORMOSA CORRUPTION
COOLIES
AINSTREE, DR.
SIMPSON'S
SMITH, CULVERTON

THE DISAPPEARANCE OF LADY FRANCES CARFAX:
Published in "The Strand": December 1911
Published as part of: "His Last Bow"

LATIMER'S
BARBERTON
OXFORD STREET
SOUTH AFRICA
LAUSANNE
LANGHAM HOTEL

MIDIANITES
STIMPSON AND COMPANY
GREEN, PHILIP

THE ADVENTURE OF THE DEVIL'S FOOT:
Published in "The Strand": December 1910
Published as part of: "His Last Bow"

CORNISH HORROR
RICHARDS, DR.
AGAR, MOORE
PORTER, MRS.
POLDHU BAY
TREGENNIS, GEORGE
MOUNTS BAY
REDRUTH
CORNISH LANGUAGE
TREGENNIS, BRENDA
CHALDEAN
STERNDALE, LEON
PHOENICIAN TIN TRADERS
BEAUCHAMP ARRIANCE
CORNWALL
PLYMOUTH HOTEL
TREDANNICK WOLLAS
DEVIL'S ROOT
ROUNDHAY, MR.
UBANGI COUNTRY
TREGENNIS, MORTIMER
BUDA
TREDANNICK WARTHA

HIS LAST BOW
"An Epilogue of Sherlock Holmes":

Published in "The Strand": September 1917
Published as part of: "His Last Bow"

MORAN, SEBASTAIN
SCHOENBRUNN PALACE
ADLER, IRENE
CLARIDGE'S HOTEL
UND ZU GRAFENSTEIN, COUNT VON
CHICAGO
HEINRICH
BUFFALO
BOHEMIA, KING OF
SKIBBAREEN
KLOPMAN
MORIARTY, PROFESSOR
THE DANGLING PRUSSIAN
"PRACTICAL HANDBOOK OF BEE CULTURE
WITH SOME OBSERVATIONS"
UPON THE SEGREGATION OF THE QUEEN

THE VALLEY OF FEAR:

Published in "The Strand":
September 1914 - May 1915
It is written in two parts:
Part 1 - "The Tragedy of Birlstone"
Part 2 - "The Scowrers"

POLLOCK, FRED
GREUZE, JEAN BAPTISTE
MORIARTY
BIRLSTONE MYSTERY
THE DYNAMICS OF AN ASTEROID
VICTORIA
BILLY
WILD, JONATHAN
WHITAKER'S ALMANAC
MORAN. SEBASTIAN
MacDONALD, ALEC

DEUTSCHE BANK
ABERDEEN
CREDIT LYONNAIS
CAMBERWELL
BIRLSTONE
MASON, WHITE
CHANDOS, CHARLES
DOUGLAS, JOHN
RUDGE-WHITWORTH
WEALD FOREST
BENITO CANON
TUNBRIDGE WELLS
CHICAGO
KENT
VALLEY OF FEAR
MANOR HOUSE
EAGLE COMMERCIAL
DOUGLAS, MRS.
HARGRAVE
BARKER, CECIL JAMES
NOTTINGHAM
AMES
RICHMOND
ALLEN, MRS.
DERBY
WILSON, SERGEANT
EAST HAM
SUSSEX CONSTABULARY
SOUTHAMPTON
WOOD, DR.
LEICESTER
WESTVILLE ARMS
LIVERPOOL
BIRLSTONE RIDGE
HYAM, MR.
NEAL

JAMES, BILLY
VERMISSA
MARKET SQUARE
VERMISSA VALLEY
WILSON, BARTHOLOMEW
BALDWIN, TED
PINTO, JONAS
GILMERTON MOUNTAINS
PHILADELPHIA MINT
STAGVILLE
MacNAMARA, WIDOW
BARTONS CROSSING
MARVIN, TEDDY
HELMDALE
ANCIENT ORDER OF FREEMEN
MERTON
WINDLE, J.W.
EMINENT ORDER OF FREEMEN
MERTON COUNTY
SCANLAN, MIKE
RAE, ANDREW
SCOTT, JAMES H.
HIGGINS
McMURDO, JOHN
CORMAC, TIGER
SHAFTER, JACOB
WILSON
HOBSON'S PATCH
BLAKER, FOREMAN
McGINTY, JACK
HARRAWAY
McGINTY, BOSS
CARNAWAY, JIM
McGINTY, BLACK JACK
WILCOX, CHESTER
UNION HOUSE

JENKINS
SCOWRERS
MURDOCH, JAMES
SHAFTER, ETTIE
MAX LINDER & CO.
MURPHY
WALKER BROTHERS
COUNTY MONAGHAN
WEST COALING COMPANY
MILMAN
SWINDON, ARCHIE
VAN SHORST
MORRIS
NICHOLSON FAMILY
MASON
TODMAN
LEE
SHUMAN
STANGER, JAMES
VAN DEHER
LYNCH, JUDGE
ATWOOD
GOWER
MANSEL
MANDERS
WILLABY
REILLY
WILLABY, ARTHUR
IRON DIKE COMPANY
UNION BAR
HUNT
WINCHESTER
EVANS
MILLER HILL
LARBEY, MRS.
MINE CONSTABULARY

STAPHOUSE FAMILY
REILLY
STENDALS
McMURDO THE SCOWRER
EDWARDS, BIRDY
POTT, EVANS
PINKERTON
LAWLER
LANDER
ANDREWS
EGAN
WILLIAMS, CHARLIE
CRABBE
BIRD, SIMMON
STYLESTOWN
KNOX, JACK
CARTER
IRONHILL
CARTER
STRAUSS, HERMAN
WILSON, STEVE
CROW HILL
SMITH & WESSON
DUNN, JOSIAH, H.
QUARTER SESSIONS
MENZIES
PALMYRA
HALES, WILLIAM
CAPE TOWN
SCOWRERS OF GILMERTON
SOCIETY OF FREEMEN
STATE & MERTON COUNTY RAILROAD
COMPANY
WEST GILMERTON GENERAL MINING Co.
I'M SITTING ON THE STILE, MARY
ON THE BANKS OF ALLAN WATER

THE ADVENTURE OF THE MAZARIN STONE:
Published in 'The Strand': October 1921
Published as Part of:
"The Case Book of Sherlock Holmes"

BILLY
WARRENDER, MINNIE
HUDSON, MRS.
CREDIT LYONNAIS
CROWN DIAMOND
WHITEHALL
MAZARIN STONE
SANDERS, IKEY
MERTON, SAM
BARCAROLE
STRAUBENZEE
HOFFMAN
MINORIES
TUSSAUD, MADAME
SYLVIUS, NEGRETTO
AMSTERDAM
YOUGHAL
VAN SEDDAR
TAVERNIER
LIME STREET
DOWSON, BARON
HOLLAND
ALGERIA
DUTCHMAN
HAROLD, MRS.
LIVERPOOL
BLYMER
CANTLEMERE, LORD

THE PROBLEM OF THOR BRIDGE:
Published in 'The Strand':
February/March 1922
Published as part of:
"The Case Book of Sherlock Holmes"

COX AND CO.
CLARIDGE HOTEL
CHARING CROSS
THOR BRIDGE
PHILLIMORE, JAMES
BATES, MARLOW
ALICIA
FERGUSON, MR.
PERSANO, ISADORE
PINTO, MARIA
FAMILY HERALD
DUNBAR, GRACE
GIBSON, J. NEIL
THOR PLACE
HAMPSHIRE
COVENTRY, SERGEANT
WINCHESTER
CUMMINGS, JOYCE
GOLD KING

THE ADVENTURE OF THE CREEPING MAN:
Published in 'The Strand': March 1923
Published as part of:
"The Case Book of Sherlock Holmes"

COPPER BEECHES
CHEQUERS

ROY
BUSY BEE AND EXCELSIOR
PRESBURY, PROFESSOR
DORAK
CAMFORD
COMMERCIAL ROAD
BENNETT, TREVOR
MERCER
MORPHY, PROFESSOR
MACPHAIL
MORPHY, ALICE
LANGUR
PRAGUE
LOWENSTEIN, H.
PRESBURY, EDITH

THE ADVENTURE OF THE SUSSEX VAMPIRE:

Published in 'The Strand': January 1924
Published as part of:
"The Case Book of Sherlock Holmes"

FERGUSON, ROBERT
CHEESEMAN'S
MORRISON, MORRISON, AND DODD
LAMBERLEY
FERGUSON AND MUIRHEAD
SUSSEX
MATILDA BRIGGS
HORSHAM
MINCING LANE
ODLEY'S
OLD JEWRY
HARVEY'S
VOYAGE OF THE GLORIA SCOTT
CARRITON'S

LYNCH, VICTOR
OLD DEER PARK
VENOMOUS LIZARD
DOLORES
VITTORIA
MASON, MRS.
VANDERBILT AND THE YEGGMAN
FERGUSON, JACK
VIPERS
MICHAEL
VIGOR
VICTORIA
VAMPIRISM IN HUNGARY
CHEQUERS
VAMPIRES IN TRANSYLVANIA
CARLO

THE ADVENTURE OF THE THREE GARRIDEBS:
Published in 'Collier's': October 25, 1924
Published in 'The Strand': January 1925
Published as part of:
"The Case Book of Sherlock Holmes"

SOUTH AFRICAN WAR
GARRIDEB, HOWARD
GARRIDEB, JOHN
BIRMINGHAM
GARRIDEB, NATHAN
GROSVENOR BUILDINGS
GARRIDEB, ALEXANDER
ASTON
MOORVILLE
SAUNDERS, MRS.
TOPEKA
HOLLOWAY AND STEELE
HUDSON, MRS.

EVANS, KILLER
STARR, LYSANDER, DR.
WINTER, JAMES
LITTLE RYDER STREET
MORECROFT
EDGWARE ROAD
LESTRADE
TYBURN TREE
NEWGATE CALENDAR
SOTHEBY'S
PRESCOTT, RODGER
CHRISTIE'S
WALDRON
SLOANE, HANS
BANK OF ENGLAND

THE ADVENTURE OF THE ILLUSTRIOUS CLIENT:
Published in 'Collier's': November 8, 1924
Published in 'The Strand':
        February/March 1925
Published as part of:
"The Case Book of Sherlock Holmes"

NORTHUMBERLAND AVENUE
VERNON LODGE
CARLTON CLUB
KINGSTON
DAMERY, JAMES
HURLINGHAM
LEWIS, GEORGE
JOHNSON, SHINWELL
HAMMERFORD WILL CASE
STRAND
QUEEN ANNE STREET
SIMPSON'S

GRUNER, ADELBERT
LE BRUN
SPLUGEN PASS
SHINWELL, PORKY
MORIARTY, PROFESSOR
MONTMARTRE DISTRICT
MORAN, SEBASTIAN
WINTER, KITTY
de MERVILLE, GENERAL
BERKELEY SQUARE
KYBER
GRAND HOTEL
de MERVILLE, VIOLET
CHARING CROSS STATION
PEACE. CHARLIE
REGENT STREET
WAINWRIGHT
CAFE ROYAL
CHARING CROSS HOSPITAL
MING DYNASTY
GLASSHOUSE STREET
CHRISTIE'S
OAKSHOTT, LESLIE
SOTHEBY
MORPHINE
PEKING
LONDON LIBRARY
BARTON, HILL
LOMAX
HALF MOON STREET
ST. JAMES SQUARE
TANG
HUNG-WU
SHOMU, EMPEROR
YUNG-LO
NORTHERN WEI DYNASTY

TANG-YING
SHOSO-IN
SUNG
NARA
YUAN
MORNING POST
MURDEROUS ATTACK UPON SHERLOCK
HOLMES

ADVENTURE OF THE THREE GABLES:
Published in 'Liberty': September 18, 1926
Published in 'The Strand': October 1926
Published as part of:
"The Case Book of Sherlock Holmes"

PERKINS
SUSAN
BLACK STEVE
FERFUSON
BULL RING
RAPHAEL
BIRMINGHAM
SHAKESPEARE
HOLBURN BAR
CROWN DERBY
STOCKDALE, BARNEY
HAINES-JOHNSON
SPENCER JOHN GANG
MILANO
HARROW WEALD
LUCERNE
THE THREE GABLES
PIKE, LANGDALE
MABERLEY, MORTMER
ST JAMES STREET

MABERLEY, MARY
MARY
MABERLEY, DOUGLAS
KLEIN, ISADORA
SUTRO, MR.

THE ADVENTURE OF THE BLANCHED SOLDIER:

Published in 'Liberty': October 16, 1926
Published in 'The Strand': November 1926
Published as part of:
"The Case Book of Sherlock Holmes"

DODD, JAMES M.
ABBEY SCHOOL
MIDDLESEX CORPS
SULTAN OF TURKEY
IMPERIAL YEOMANRY
DUKE OF GREYMINSTER
BOER WAR
BEDFORDSHIRE
EMSWORTH, COLONEL
EUSTON
EMSWORTH, GODFREY
KENT, MR.
TUXBURY OLD HALL
SAUNDERS, JAMES
RALPH
LANCET
SPECTATOR
BRITISH MEDICAL JOURNAL

THE ADVENTURE OF THE LION'S MANE:

Published in 'Liberty': November 27, 1926
Published in 'The Strand': December 1926

Published as part of:
"The Case Book of Sherlock Holmes"

FULWORTH
THE HAVEN
STACKHURST, HAROLD
AIREDALE
THE GABLES
SUDBURY
SUSSEX
BLOUNT
McPHERSON, FITZROY
BARDLE, INSPECTOR
MURDOCH, IAN
CYANEA
ANDERSON
WOOD, J.G.
BELLAMY, MAUD
OUT OF DOORS
BELLAMY, TED
KENT
BELLAMY, WILLIAM

THE ADVENTURE OF THE RETIRED COLOURMAN:
Published in 'Liberty': December 18, 1926
Published in 'The Strand': January 1927
Published as part of:
"The Case Book of Sherlock Holmes"

AMBERLEY, JOSIAH
LITTLE PURLINGTON
LEWISHAM
MOORSMOOR
BRICKFALL AND AMBERLEY

FRINTON
COPTIC PATRIARCHS
ESSEX
ERNEST, RAY
CROCKFORD
HAYMARKET THEATRE
LIVERPOOL STREET
BLACKHEATH STATION
RAILWAY ARMS
LONDON BRIDGE
BARKER, MR.
MASONIC TIE-PIN
MacKINNON, INSPECTOR
BLUE ANCHOR
BROADMOOR
CARINA
NORTH SURREY OBSERVER
ALBERT HALL
THE HAVEN HORROR
ELMAN, J.C.

THE ADVENTURE OF THE VEILED LODGER:

Published in 'Liberty': January 22, 1927
Published in "The Strand": February 1927
Published as part of:
"The Case Book of Sherlock Holmes"

MERRILOW, MRS.
LEONARDO
RONDER
GRIGGS, JIMMY
ABBAS PARVA
EDMUNDS
ABBAS PARVA TRAGEDY
ALLAHABAD

BERKSHIRE
RONDER, EUGENIA
WOMBWELL
MARGATE
SANGER
PRUSSIC ACID
SAHARA KING

THE ADVENTURE OF SHOSCOMBE OLD PLACE:
Published in "Liberty": March 5, 1927
Published in "The Strand": April 1927
Published as part of:
"The Case Book of Sherlock Holmes"

ST. PANCRAS
GREEN DRAGON
MERIVALE
FALDER, BEATRICE
NORBERTON, ROBERT
STEPHENS
BREWER, SAM
EVANS, CARRIE
CURZON STREET
BAIN, SANDY
NEWMARKET HEATH
HARVEY
GRAND NATIONAL
BERKSHIRE
SHOSCOMBE OLD PLACE
SAXON
MASON, JOHN
NORMAN HUGOS
FALDER, JAMES
FALER, DENIS
HARLEY STREET

FALER, WILLIAM
SHOSCOMBE PRINCE
ODOS
DERBY
NORLETT, MR.
BARNES, JOSIAH
NORLETT, MRS.